ACTS OF CONTRITION

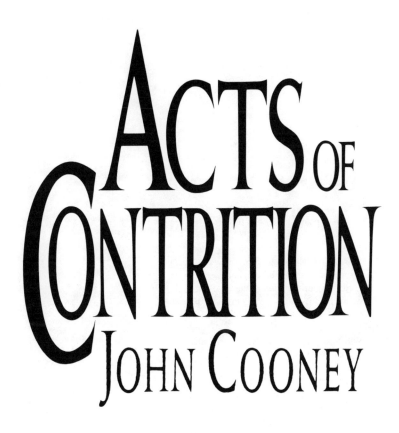

ACTS OF CONTRITION

JOHN COONEY

CROWN PUBLISHERS, INC.

NEW YORK

Published by Crown Publishers, Inc.
201 East 50th Street, New York, New York 10022.
Member of the Crown Publishing Group.

CROWN is a trademark of Crown Publishers, Inc.

Manufactured in the United States of America

Library of Congress Cataloging-in-Publication Data
Cooney, John.
    Acts of contrition / by John Cooney.—1st ed.
        p.   cm.
    I. Title.
PR6053.0529A66   1991
823'.914—dc20   90-27283
                                                CIP

ISBN 0-517-57677-5

Book Design by Shari deMiskey

10 9 8 7 6 5 4 3 2 1

FIRST EDITION

For Glynis and Shamus

COMPARED TO SHAME, DEATH IS NOTHING.

— LEONARDO SCIASCIA

The Day of the Owl

Prologue

SILVER SUNLIGHT PIERCED THE RADIANT STAINED-GLASS WINDOWS AND bathed the altar of New York's St. Patrick's Cathedral in a warm glow. In the sacristy one floor below, Monsignor Francis Maguire surveyed the three young deacons who were about to accept the awesome duties and responsibilities of the priesthood.

Preordination jitters were taking their toll. Usually gregarious, Patrick Hogan was somber. His brilliant green eyes and handsome features were clouded by consternation. Only his red hair, glinting like flames in the flickering light of candles, revealed his spirited disposition.

Tempestuous Damian Carter, who hid his piety beneath irony, was quiet. His lively, round, freckled face and sturdy body were stiff with tension; his soft brown eyes intently stared at the floor, as if the marble tiles held a vision of his future.

Only William Witten, with the powerful physique, dark complexion, and chiseled features of an Indian chieftain, seemed unaf-

1

fected. Maguire, however, detected a crack in the man's stoicism: a nervous tick in his steely gray eyes.

As rector of Gethsemane, a seminary of the Congregation of the Mission of St. Vincent de Paul, Maguire had had them in his charge for more than a half dozen years. Today, he would serve as master of ceremonies during the ritual crowning their years of study and dedication. How old were they now? Twenty-six?

Having watched their spiritual and intellectual development all this time, he once thought he would hate to see them leave his fold. Of the hundreds of seminarians who had passed through Gethsemane during his tenure as rector, Maguire until lately believed these three, though they differed so temperamentally, came closest to approaching the seminary ideals of spirituality, brilliance, and physical prowess. Acknowledging both their similarities and their contrasts, their classmates nicknamed them the Trinity.

Their athletic and academic accomplishments, as Maguire knew from counseling them, tended to obscure a problem they shared. Achieving their level of spirituality was torturous. Hogan struggled with his sensuality, which could destroy any priest unless he was ever vigilant. Carter's impulse to rebel against authority could put him on a dangerous collision course with his superiors. Witten's intensity, his striving for perfection in every area of his life, was potentially self-destructive as well. Their mastery of these particular demons made them stand apart in Maguire's mind more than these extraordinary men's other achievements.

But these last few weeks, they were unlike themselves. They banded together more closely than ever, shutting out everyone else. Moodiness and irritability were their shared characteristics. They wouldn't open up about what was bothering them. For the first time in his life, Maguire seriously thought about postponing ordination for men who verged on it. His reluctance and events overtook any chance he might have had of doing that. Now, they were being ordained two months ahead of their classmates.

Hogan was to act as a temporary adviser to Vatican Radio, the result of a remarkable invitation extended by the head of the station after he visited the seminary three months ago and Hogan outlined to him how to improve the communications center.

Because of his astonishingly perceptive proposal after spending a vacation hiking, riding horseback, and hitchhiking throughout Puerto Rico, was to help design a program for diocesan missionary priests and

2

lay volunteers in Puerto Rico. Witten was to replace an ailing Spanish teacher at the Collegio di Nobili Ecclesiastici, where gifted priests trained for the Vatican diplomatic crops, until the teacher was fit to return; this was the first time anyone still in a seminary was offered a professorial position at the prestigious university.

There was a good deal of cosseting of priests and seminarians these days as a result of the vast number of defections during the last ten years. The rector knew, however, that, in the case of these three, his superiors were responding to their overwhelming potential, not a fear of losing them to the outside world.

Even before these unusual opportunities arose, the three were destined for greatness. Witten, the most brilliant of these intellectually gifted seminarians, was selected to study for a doctorate at Rome's North American College, *the* training ground for American career churchmen. Hogan, less intense than Witten but more personable, was to further his studies at Georgetown University. Carter had turned down a fellowship at Harvard to work in a poor urban parish in New York, a position he would assume at the conclusion of his assignment in Puerto Rico. Maguire believed Carter's vitality and wit would reap great dividends among the urban poor; he could always go back for a higher degree.

They were sure to snap out of whatever made them act so peculiarly of late. Suddenly, the rector felt a sense of awe. For the first time in his life when in the presence of men about to be ordained, Maguire believed these were born leaders for whom there were no limits in the Church. Each had the potential to become a cardinal. It occurred to him that someday one of them might even be a candidate for pope.

Given the Second Vatican Council, which shook the very foundations of the Church a decade ago, Maguire mused, Carter's way of spending his early years as a priest might one day be the best credential of all for becoming pope. Pope John XXIII had elevated helping the downtrodden from a duty to the fashionable. His successor, Pope Paul, while lacking John's warmth, left most of his humanistic policies in place.

What kind of a world were these men inheriting? Sometimes Maguire wondered if both the Church and America became so insular and claustrophobic during the first half of the century that the tumultuous change of recent years was a kind of collective nervous breakdown. Now everything was in a state of upheaval. Like the laity,

3

many members of the clergy were radicalized by the bloody civil rights demonstrations and the assassinations of the Kennedys and Martin Luther King. Priests and nuns stood trial as antiwar activists or were in the forefront of social revolution in Latin America, which set them at loggerheads with members of the hierarchy who blessed the war in Vietnam or backed repressive regimes in Central and South America.

The world was changing so fast the rector felt the country needed an anchor. Nixon's being reelected president dismayed Maguire. He never trusted the man. The bombs still fell and boys still died in Vietnam after all these years; the excuse was still "anticommunism." Yet, in a ridiculous inconsistency, Nixon was hailed for opening up Red China, the biggest communist nation on earth. If he could do that, why couldn't the president end the war and get the legions of demonstrators off the streets? It seemed as if the country would never settle down.

What worried Maguire more were the convulsions in the Church herself. Horrified at the prospect of two thousand years of tradition being razed, inflexible conservatives struggled with passionate progressives who called for the rebirth of the Church. Now priests wanted to marry, nuns wanted to be priests, and demands from the congregation for a more active role in a more democratic Church grew daily. Maguire knew from the confessional and from gossip that priests and nuns were experimenting sexually in unprecedented numbers.

Turning his attention back to the ordination, the rector felt reassured by the traditional snowy-white raiment the deacons wore to receive the sacrament of Holy Orders. White was a symbol not just of purity and joy but of a kind of wedding that was about to take place, the marriage of these men to the Church. The *amice*, or linen cloth worn about the neck and shoulders. The long linen *alb* that almost touched the floor. The *cincture*, or girdle. The *maniple*, or silk cloth that was worn on the left forearm. Last came the silk *chasuble*, which symbolized charity for covering a multitude of sins the way it covered all other vestments. The chasuble was carried over the left arm and would be put on later, but with the back pinned up so that it hung at the shoulder blades until the sacrament was actually conferred. The remaining adornment was the white silk stole, the narrow strip of silk usually worn around a priest's neck when dispensing sacraments.

"I just want to thank you for everything you have done," Hogan said as the rector placed a lighted candle in his right hand.

"We owe you a great deal, Monsignor," Witten said, accepting his candle.

"You are a good teacher," Carter said simply as he took his candle.

Suddenly, the swells of organ music filled the church and flooded the sacristy. "It's time," Maguire said as he started mounting the twenty-six marble steps to the floor of the cathedral.

Momentarily, the Trinity paused as one and gazed at each other. "Let's hope we're doing the right thing," Hogan whispered almost inaudibly as he started after Maguire.

"The moment of reckoning is upon us," Carter said as he followed.

"Perhaps not yet," Witten said softly while bringing up the rear.

The other two heard him. They pretended they had not.

As he pushed open the sacristy door and set foot inside the cathedral, Maguire felt intoxicated by the strong scent of incense that was embedded in the century-old stone walls and woodwork. The choir began signing "Here I Am, O Lord" in English.

Momentary nostalgia for the Church into which he himself had been ordained as a young man swept over the rector. The Church of wondrous mystery and elaborate, colorful ceremonies celebrated in Latin and Gregorian chant. For the most part, that liturgy was brushed aside in the 1960s in favor of today's informality and English. Now, in 1972, ordination was one of the few colorful Roman rites still remaining.

As he made his way to the altar, Maguire noted how few people were here. The twenty-two other members of their class were present, but they were swallowed up in the vastness of the cathedral. For most ordinations, friends and family flocked to see one of their own take his priestly vows. In this instance, the sparse gathering was understandable. Each was an only child; none came from large extended families. In the cases of Hogan and Carter, he was glad anyone was present. Their entering the seminary had caused a great deal of heartache at home.

He recognized Witten's rumpled uncle Geoffrey sitting near the front, staring around the cathedral with great curiosity. An inventor with a dazzling mind, he had given his brilliant nephew a strange education after Bill Witten became his charge at the innocent age of seven. The man had meant well and developed his nephew's mind and body. The young Witten's upbringing was stimulating and challenging and took into account everything from nights in observatories studying the stars to hunting trips in Kenya, everything except the fact that, despite his awesome mind, Bill Witten had been a child.

Two rows behind Geoffrey Witten were Carter's parents, Louise and William Carter III. Maguire wasn't surprised that mentally he put the mother ahead of the father. From his few encounters with her over the years, he found Louise the more driven of the two. A brittle but attractive woman, she wore her wealth with arrogance. The habitual wince on her bald, impeccably-attired husband's face suggested that he was always in pain. They sat more than a comfortable distance apart, which was the way they went through life together. Maguire was saddened because they saw their son's ordination as the final of the affront to them that had begun the day he set foot in the seminary. At least they overcame their resentment enough to attend the ceremony.

Off to the right was Hogan's father, Sean. He sat with Pat's young and pretty cousin, Peggy Sullivan, who had visited Gethsemane more often than Hogan's father. Sean Hogan. A man with a perpetual scowl. Maguire knew the type well and felt sorry for him. A lifetime of bile. Defensive and quick-tempered. An immigrant laborer who worked hard, drank too much, prayed too little, and buried his wife at an early age. During his infrequent visits to Gethsemane, Sean never hid his resentment of his son's being there, seeing Pat's vocation as a betrayal of the world of opportunities that had been denied him but were open to his son.

When notified about the early ordination, Maguire immediately petitioned New York's archbishop, Michael Cardinal McCormick, to assist him on this special day. The cardinal dawdled over his decision for weeks until Maguire reminded him of several past favors, including bending the seminary rules to accommodate one of the McCormicks' nephews whose high school academic achievements were lusterless at best.

As they drew near the sanctuary, Maguire turned solemnly and grasped Hogan's hand to show that the *ordinandi* were being *led* to the altar, not presenting themselves. They stopped before the baldachin, the graceful canopy built over the altar and made of neutral-toned bronze. Supported by four piers providing niches for statuettes and shields symbolizing mankind in his longing for God, the baldachin's delicate details created a rising motion. A moment later, three acolytes, the middle one bearing a long, slender golden cross, appeared at the back of the cathedral. Two priests, who would assist during the ceremony, followed. The dour, ramrod-straight Cardinal McCormick brought up the rear. The choir began singing *Ecce Sacerdos Magnus*, "Behold the High Priest," while the entourage walked slowly to the altar.

During the Mass, the gaunt, dark-eyed cardinal sat on his ornately carved wooden throne with the scarlet cushion. A hush settled over St. Patrick's. Monsignor Maguire called out: "Let those to be ordained priests come forward."

The first name rang out: "Patrick Hogan."

"Present," Hogan replied while advancing to the edge of the sanctuary, just as Carter and Witten did seconds later as their names were called.

"The Most Reverend Father and Lord in Christ, by the grace of God and the Apostolic See Bishop of New York, commands and charges under pains of excommunication, that no one here present for the purpose of taking Orders shall presume to come forward under any pretext if he be irregular, excommunicated in law or by judicial sentence, under interdict or suspension, illegitimate, infamous . . ."

As Maguire read the words, he glanced at each of the *ordinandi* and was startled. The gladness he expected to see on their faces was missing. They appeared strained, ill at ease. Without knowing why, the rector found himself praying that the words of warning had no significance in their lives.

Dismayed, Maguire noticed the same expressions return when the cardinal called upon the gathering to testify to their characters: "If, then, anyone has anything to say against them, in place of God and for the sake of God let him confidently come forth and speak. . . ."

The cardinal cast his stern gaze over the congregation, slowly meeting the eyes of each of those who were in attendance. Maguire believed he must be imagining that the Trinity's discomfort spread to the congregation. When the ceremony resumed, he felt an almost perceptible easing of tension.

Hogan, Carter, and Witten prostrated themselves before the altar like white human crosses, a mark of great devotion and supplication. The prostration was also a symbol of the mystical death they must die, so that when they rose up to receive the priesthood, they rose as if from a tomb in which they had left behind their vices and lust.

One by one, the Trinity knelt before the cardinal. In silence, Cardinal McCormick laid both hands on each head, a validation that

7

he conferred the sacrament of Holy Orders. The agonizing looks they shared drained away any joy Monsignor Maguire felt as he unpinned their chasubles so they rippled down their backs, symbolizing that they now were priests.

New York, 1990

1

"MONSIGNOR HOGAN, IT WAS LIKE I HAD DIED," MARTY COLTRAIN SAID.

Though thinner and more haggard than usual, Coltrain was easily recognizable to the millions of TV viewers tuned to superstation XTV-NY. The red hair pulled into a ponytail, the blue jeans, and the open-neck black shirt with the sleeves rolled up to reveal a small American flag tattooed on each forearm were his trademarks, which had graced the covers of national magazines, a half dozen platinum record albums, and three movie posters. Most recently his photo had made front-page news coast to coast, not for a new record or for a film role, but because of his troubles.

At the moment, his feet were anchored to the floor of the New York TV studio by black lizard-skin boots that glittered like obsidian in the harsh overhead lights. He gripped the neck of his old Gibson guitar as if it were a security blanket, and in many ways it was. His pale blue eyes squeezed shut, Coltrain groped for words to explain why his career verged on being washed-up and how he had almost died of a drug overdose.

"I . . . I," he said.

"Take your time, Marty," Monsignor Patrick Hogan said soothingly.

Resonant and compassionate, the voice made Coltrain feel that it would be unfair to deny the questioner anything. The singer opened his eyes and looked into the concerned gaze of his interrogator and felt his anxiety seep away. The handsome man in the clerical garb had the genial, reassuring smile Bing Crosby wore when playing a priest in the old movies Coltrain enjoyed on TV late at night. He wasn't like the preachers Coltrain knew while growing up in Texas. Those men of God were either coarse, leathery fanatics or soft boy-men with pompadours who looked as if they worked in shoe stores so they could peek up ladies' dresses.

The priest had rugged Irish good looks and the weathered, reddish tan of an outdoorsman. He seemed as if he would be as at home on a horse under an endless Western sky as he was in front of a TV camera. His hair was more coppery than Coltrain's, and his teeth were white and even. His jaw was squared off with a cleft chin. A nose that was a little large kept the face from being too good-looking.

What struck Coltrain most was the man's almost haunting eyes, which seemed to feel his own woes. They were green and didn't smack of the sanctimony he had originally feared he would encounter when he found out the show's host was a man of the cloth.

When his agent suggested that he appear on "Life Has Meaning," Coltrain had been more than dubious. All he knew was that it was some kind of a religious program. His wife watched it all the time, and Lorraine was no dummy. Even so, what good would it do? He was about to beg off when his persistent agent rattled off the program's ratings and the high-powered guest list, including prominent politicians, academics, and business leaders as well as entertainers. The show's gorgeous ratings and religious nature, the agent insisted, were the combination he needed to survive.

"Hell, boy, you're a wounded buck and the wolves are closing in for the kill," the agent finally said.

Persuaded by those comforting words, Coltrain told him to book the show. He was in a fight for his career. He had to get the public back on his side, if overnight he wasn't going to get sucked into the trash can and out of the life in the gold lane he'd clawed his way into ten years ago. After all, it wasn't just the drugs. The press and then the moralizers made more out of the age of the girl who was with him than his overdosing. She looked twenty-five and was as jaded as fifty, but the damned birth certificate insisted she was only sixteen.

"Well?" the monsignor asked patiently.

Marty Coltrain hadn't climbed the slippery pole of success in Nashville and then Hollywood because he was a fool. He came on the show determined to play the most sincere role of his life, but when he looked again into Monsignor Hogan's eyes, he felt deeply ashamed. Before he realized what was happening, tears rolled down his cheeks.

"I had abused myself for so long with drugs and alcohol that I might as well have been dead. I had made a mess of my marriage, my relationships with my two kids, my friends, my work. Believe you me . . ."

For the next ten minutes, he talked nonstop, wanting to unburden himself to his host. He reconstructed a harrowing tale about hitting rock bottom. Twenty million TV viewers were glued to his every word.

"What do you mean when you say that life on the road can lead a man to drink or drugs or sexual escapades?" Hogan interjected, sounding more like a friend or confidant than an interviewer.

"Well, it's that you get so darn lonely or keyed up or bored that . . ."

In the control booth, Ed Murphy groaned when the red warning light flashed, signaling a commercial break that would disrupt the flow of the interview. Raking his fingers through his short, silver hair, Murphy implored, "No, not now! Not now!"

Gratefully, he watched Hogan nix the break with a wave of his hand that couldn't be seen on camera. Murphy smiled and shook his head, wondered again about Hogan's natural instincts for the medium. "A born TV baby," he muttered, without realizing he'd said that at least once every Tuesday night for the past three years.

Edmund Murphy owned station XTV New York and knew he had done two smart things in his life. The first was following in Ted Turner's footsteps. Right after the Atlanta media maverick put his station WTBS on satellite, Murphy did the same thing, thus blasting XTV across the nation as a superstation and making it a national medium. The second was airing "Life Has Meaning."

Shortly before he died in 1987, Cardinal McCormick asked Murphy to air a religious program to compete with the TV evangelists who were luring a lot of viewers, including many Catholics, into their folds. Murphy wasn't crazy about the idea, but being a staunch Catholic,

13

there was no way he could refuse a cardinal. He dismissed "Life" as a do-good, public-service program. A tax write-off that could be thrown together on the cheap. With luck, the show might crank out the kind of ratings generated by a bad wildlife documentary on PBS.

When Murphy met Hogan he started to change his mind. The priest appeared intensely interested in him and the show and gave the impression that everything Murphy said was fascinating. Murphy had found himself flattered by the attention. He believed other people must be too. There was something magnetic about the monsignor; those eyes were riveting.

He got his hopes up when he went over the format Hogan wanted. An interview talk show featuring prominent people who were in the news because of personal problems, such as messy divorces, troubled children, sexual issues, crises of faith. A Donahue or an Oprah with a moral message.

When he saw Hogan on TV, Murphy knew he had hit on something. Hogan came across as a religious knockoff of Ryan O'Neal. The guy was a natural. It wasn't just Hogan's looks and presence; his instincts were on target. Most of all, he projected a warmth on TV, even more so than he did in person. But then Murphy knew that a lot of TV performers projected more pleasant personalities than they actually possessed. The tube even lied. Some of TV's warmest-appearing stars were private bastards.

Hogan's warmth combined with those eyes, which were even more haunting when seen on the screen, was a dynamite combination. No matter how many times he studied the show's early rushes, Murphy had found Hogan sincere, believable, and, he had laughed, sexy. There was no doubt about it. The guy was a very sexy priest.

From the first month on the air, "Life Has Meaning" rated among the top ten TV shows. When the station got the "Life" demographics, something else surprising emerged. Hogan's appeal was universal. Almost 50 percent of the audience was composed of Protestants and Jews as well as the usual assortment of religious show junkies who worshiped everything from snakes to peanut butter. A month after its inception, "Life" moved to prime time. The show was aired in more than a hundred metropolitan areas across country.

Hogan took his hand-held mike and stepped into the audience. Except for the turned collar and the slender silver cross suspended from a chain around his neck, the tall, broad-shouldered cleric could have been an actor who had spent his life being groomed for big-time

14

TV. As he moved among the mostly women in the studio, he kept up a teasing banter.

"Now, I'm sure everyone has something they'd like to ask Marty," he said. Looking at an elderly woman, he added, "Please try to control yourself. He is a married man."

Gales of laughter met the remark. Midway down the center aisle, Hogan placed the microphone before a heavyset, middle-aged woman who stood and beamed at the TV camera while she posed her question.

"Do you believe the bad things that happened to you were a punishment from God for the kind of life you were leading?"

"Maybe, ma'am, maybe," Coltrain replied. "I'd like to think God has better things to do than come after one old sinner like me, but that could have been the way it was."

"Do you go to church?" another woman asked.

"Sometimes, but not on a formal basis."

"Are you back together with your wife?"

"Yes, and for that I'm very thankful."

The questions went on in a similar vein as Hogan wove up and down the aisles, making comments of his own, patiently helping an old lady articulate her question, easing another woman through her self-consciousness, and laughing with yet another.

"How old were you when you lost your virginity?" a teenage girl asked.

Hogan's hand holding the microphone trembled violently. He stared heavenward, his eyes beseeching God for forgiveness while the audience roared with laughter.

The only sour note was struck by the last questioner. "With all the opportunities you've had, why should God or anyone give you any more?" a woman demanded in an accusatory tone.

Hogan withdrew the microphone and gently chastised her as he walked back up the aisle. "Maybe God is a bit more compassionate than the rest of us."

Sitting next to Coltrain again, Hogan turned to his guest and asked, "Do you think it was God who made you change?"

The singer cast his gaze down in a manner that he hoped conveyed true repentance. He thought of an answer the crowd could accept, and hell, maybe it was true.

"I like to think so. I can't be sure, mind you. But I like to think so."

The audience erupted into applause and cheers. Marty Coltrain

15

managed to refrain from shouting "Hot damn!" He made a mental note to send his agent a case of bourbon.

"I was going to ask Marty if he would sing a song for us before he leaves," Hogan said.

Glancing around the audience, he added in a voice that sounded as if he were addressing each person individually, "That is, if it's okay with you."

Cheers and applause thundered from the crowd.

When the show was over, Coltrain was covered with sweat. Hands shaking, he unclipped the minimike from his shirtfront and breathed a sigh of relief. They were with him. If the ratings were as big as usual, a healthy chunk of the whole damned nation was in his hip pocket right now.

He turned to Hogan. "Thanks, Padre. You may have put me over the top again. If I can ever help *you*, I will."

"I didn't do it, Marty," Hogan replied, giving him a serious look. "You did. I hope you stay straight. If you ever get in a jam or just want to talk, please call."

Coltrain looked a little sheepish. "Thanks, Padre. I may just do that."

Monsignor Hogan ducked into Beatrice Inn, a little Italian restaurant in Greenwich Village, annoyed with himself that he was running late. A balding, thickset waiter approached him and smiled.

"How are you, Monsignor Hogan?"

"Good, Mario," Hogan said, flashing a dazzling smile and clasping his shoulder. "How are you?"

"Okay, given the circumstances. Nicky got rejected by the college of his choice, so going home is like attending a wake."

"Tell him I'll say a prayer he gets into a good school."

Mario shrugged. "Thanks, but don't waste your time, Monsignor. With his marks, I doubt if your saying a High Mass for him would do much good." The waiter nodded to the side room. "He's in there. I'll take your order in a minute."

Hogan hung up his coat, delaying a moment without realizing

16

it. Imperceptibly, he stiffened as he entered the side room and forced a smile, even as he cast a worried look at the several empty drink glasses lined up in front of the man waiting for him.

"Well, well. The actor's finally here," a mocking voice declared.

"Sorry I'm late, Dad, but I got tied up for a bit after the show." Smiling, but not feeling like it, he took the chair opposite his father.

"A big shot like you can't be expected to drop everything for his old man."

Hogan gave an exasperated sigh. His father had no idea how hard it was to squeeze him into his tight schedule. The speaking engagements at luncheons, dinners, fund-raisers, spiritual retreats. The articles and books editors wanted him to write. The other TV shows asking him to appear. The bishops around the country wanting him to preach in their archdioceses.

"Right, Dad," he said.

The waiter came over and looked at the priest's father. "My cousin Gina found out your son comes in here. Do you mind if I get his autograph for her and her kids?"

"If you get us a drink, you can have him turn all your water into wine for all I care," Sean Hogan said, tapping a swizzle stick on a near-empty glass.

Hogan kept a smile on his face as he reached into his pocket and pulled out a business card and a pen. "I'd be happy to give them my autograph," he said, signing the card with a flourish. "How many do you need?"

"Three, if it's not too much trouble."

"No trouble at all," Hogan said, withdrawing two more cards from inside his jacket.

"What'll you have to drink, Monsignor?" Mario said.

"Scotch and a little water," Pat Hogan said, patting the waiter on the shoulder.

Turning his attention back to his father, he said, "You're looking terrific!"

"Save the charm for somebody you're trying to get money out of," Sean said.

Hogan smiled ruefully, fervently wishing he could change the pattern he and his father had fallen into over the years. He believed his father wished they could too, but they were stuck in a bad groove. Sean made an effort to come to New York to see him a few times a year, and he went to Philadelphia whenever he could. While making

17

plans to get together over the phone, each felt how badly they wanted to get along. Once they hung up, a sense of futility over what the actual meeting would be like gripped each of them.

Looking at his father, Pat realized how old he was getting. He himself was forty-four. That made his father sixty-seven. Sean didn't look it. His red hair was graying and his good-looking face was weathered. He didn't have an ounce of flab, and he still worked. Even today, Pat felt uncomfortable as he always did when he realized the depth of hurt his entering the seminary had caused his father.

The stricken look on Sean's face the day he told him was a scar on his memory. Pat realized much later that he had been so preoccupied with his vocation that he failed to see part of his father was dying. Pat was his only child. There would be no grandchildren, no bloodline that carried the family. His wife was dead. His son seemed to have turned his back on him. As he later told Pat, Sean felt as if his whole life were a joke.

Not knowing how to phrase the rejection he felt, Sean opened his mouth to warn his son about what he was losing, but he sounded angry, as he often did with Pat. "But this is your goddamn life, boy!" the father roared in pain and frustration. "Are you so afraid to face the future that you want to hide out from what life can hold?"

Those last few weeks before entering Gethsemane, Pat lay awake at night in a cold sweat, wishing to God that he had never agreed to go. He himself was suddenly confused. Maybe his father was right. Was it courage or cowardice that led him to the seminary? Gethsemane. The name reflected his own tortured frame of mind. Gethsemane, the place where the agonized Christ pleaded with His Father to let Him forgo the crucifixion.

The last days at home had the taste of vinegar. Sean barely acknowledged that his son was leaving until the evening before his departure. Then he tensely put down his newspaper, folded until the creases were razor sharp, and confronted Pat one last time. He had practiced over and over what he was going to say. He desperately wanted to understand the boy and his view, but when he looked at his son, bile rose in his throat. "When you want to come back to the real world, let me know," Sean said as his parting blessing.

As though paralyzed, he was unable to reach into his pocket and take out the two hundred dollars he had put in an envelope to give his son. Later, when he wanted to mail the money to the seminary, he was too ashamed to do so. Pride had withered his will. Only at his son's ordination had he been able to tell him what happened, and he self-consciously handed Pat an envelope that now contained a thousand dollars.

At the seminary, Pat, on the surface, readily adapted to his new life. He quickly made friends. The serenity and devotion to scholarship were seductive. He liked the regimentation, having his days planned out, the dedication to God. He also knew he could do well. As in high school, his teachers liked him and so did his classmates, and he took easily to the academic work.

He also quickly realized that he could get pretty much out of this life what he wanted. Most of his classmates tended to see the limitations of the priesthood, dwelling on the restrictions and the hierarchical authority. But Hogan knew that rules were routinely bent for those in favor. The priests who got to study abroad. Those who got plum diplomatic assignments. Others who carved out careers in social services. He didn't see why he shouldn't be among the chosen.

Hogan also befriended Witten and Carter, and the three spent so much time in one another's company that they picked up their nickname. Initially, Hogan sought out Witten because he was obviously so intelligent and Pat thought he could help him with his schoolwork. He struck up a friendship with Carter when he learned who his family was, assuming that wealthy people could help priests as well as anyone else. They became close friends. Hogan found that these two brilliant youths were much more politically sophisticated than he was and they challenged him.

"Why are you here, Pat?" Witten asked him one day when the three of them were first together.

"I admire what Phil and Dan Berrigan are doing," Hogan replied, naming activist priests who made headlines for their antiwar activities. "I hope that one day I might do much the same thing. But I don't know if I'm made of the right stuff for it."

"How are you going to do it?" Witten persisted.

Hogan shrugged. "Oppose the war, help poor people."

"Why wait?" Carter asked.

Before he knew it, they had Hogan writing to pacifist and poverty organizations, asking what he could do for them. He found his vacations spent working in soup kitchens or stuffing fund-soliciting letters for peace groups. And always, he was involved in passionate arguments and conversations with Witten and Carter. It was exhilarating.

The major problem he confronted on a daily basis was his sex-

19

uality. He thought often of the girlfriend he left behind, and how she wept when he told her about his vocation. He channeled his sexual energy into sports and studies, but there were many nights he lay awake in torment, when he saw the faces and bodies of girls he would love to kiss and hold. It was all he could do to will himself to stay a seminarian during those nights when he believed his father had been right.

Turning his attention back to his father, Hogan tried to make up to him the pain and rejection Sean felt as the result of his son's becoming a priest. Leaning toward his father, he asked quietly, "Dad, what can I do for you?"

His father looked up, his eyes steady. When he spoke, the sarcasm was gone. "Nothing, Pat. Even your God couldn't give me what I need."

"What's that?"

"I want your mother back."

Pat reached across the table and clasped his father's hand. Sean pulled his back. "Still playing the good priest?" Sean asked, the derision back in his tone of voice as he held up his glass for a refill.

After dinner, Pat fell into the end-of-the-evening ritual with his father that he would love to change as well. He eased Sean into a cab, took him back to his apartment, and helped him into bed. Long ago, he gave up saying anything to his father about his drinking. After the death of his wife, Sean was inconsolable. Alcohol helped disguise the pain.

When he turned in, Pat lay awake for a long while, his head a little muddled from having drunk too much himself. He made a vow to watch the drinking. He didn't think it was a problem, but everywhere he went someone was shoving a drink in his hand. He should cut back a bit. Suddenly, he flushed and felt the heat of shame on his face in the dark. Don't lie to yourself too, he thought. There are times you need a drink as much as Dad does to keep from thinking about what a fraud you are.

20

2

"WHAT DOES CLARIZIO WANT WITH ME?"

Irritably, Father Kevin Kelly asked himself the question again as the taxi from Washington's National Airport approached an estate in Virginia surrounded by a high, white mortar wall. Kelly checked his watch and stared out the backseat window. The trip had taken a good forty minutes. He also wondered why Archbishop Clarizio wanted to meet here rather than at the massive Romanesque building on Washington's Embassy Row that housed the pronuncio's legation.

"Why me?" Kelly muttered. He just hoped the archbishop hadn't pigeonholed him as somebody to do the Church's dirty jobs.

Tomaso Clarizio. One of the awesome Vatican powers. Priests and bishops dined out on tales of his diplomatic skills and privately wondered at the rumors of his ruthlessness. His nickname in clerical circles was Dagger Tom; he always signed his name with a *T* that resembled a stiletto. The archbishop had recently been named pronuncio, the Church's ambassador to the United States, and would soon be made a cardinal. Previously, he had held the position of Vatican *sostituto segretario di stato* and was a confidant of the pope.

21

Word was out that his appointment was temporary, that he was in America on some secret assignment. Kelly frowned. The gossip was intriguing. But then, the clergy was always a hotbed of rumors.

The cab eased onto a straight driveway lined with towering oak trees, past spring-fed ponds, manicured lawns, and beds of pink petunias, yellow, pink, and orange lilies, and purple iris. To the left was a three-hundred-foot reflecting lake with a fountain spewing water thirty feet in the air.

The paved driveway ended in a circle before a massive stone château with leaded windows, an orange-tiled roof, a dozen chimneys, and a cross on the front of the oak door. The mansion appeared deceptively weighty with age and could easily have been mistaken for a provincial house built in the Middle Ages for Capuchin monks, rather than a Vatican nerve center not far from the political heart of the greatest superpower of the twentieth century.

As he admired the imposing structure, Kelly couldn't help thinking that the medieval impression was fitting. Inside that door, the contemporary world was displaced by an older, feudal order, where everyone had a specific place, assigned duties, and the human drama was played out differently by men who had dedicated themselves to the service of God.

After paying the driver, Kelly walked up three steps to the door and pressed the bell. Melodious chimes were barely audible when the door was opened by a tall, spare Italian whose cassock was trimmed with the red piping of a monsignor although he could not have been more than thirty. Long ago, Kelly had perversely refused to memorize the shades of purple and red that distinguished monsignors or proclaimed grades of bishops and archbishops. The rigid stratification reminded him too much of his years in the military, a period of his life he found these days he was almost able to forget on occasion.

"Welcome to Royal Oaks, Father Kelly," the monsignor said with a slight, gracious bow. "We spoke on the telephone. I am Enrico Perdomo. I hope you have had a pleasant journey."

Kelly wasn't surprised Perdomo opened the door. Clarizio was known for giving his aides humbling tasks. "Monsignor, if fretting about why you asked me here qualifies as pleasant in your book, then it was."

Perdomo remained unruffled. "I am sorry for that," he said soothingly, "but it could not be helped."

Kelly mentally cataloged the monsignor as upper-crust Italian.

22

dual freedom, so much so that Rome always feared
rch might one day declare its independence. He
he bishops who worried that their voices went un-
well as the priests, nuns, and laity demanding the
on birth control, celibacy, female priests, and other

tic level, his job was perhaps even more demanding.
with matters as trivial as arranging audiences with
ressman visiting Rome to as critical as articulating
e role the Church wanted to play in the new political
Europe, and how America and the Vatican could
quell leftist movements in Latin America.

the monsignor's use of the exalted title *eminenza*,
rizio wasn't yet a cardinal, wasn't lost on Kelly. The
ers. Perdomo was a representative of the Vatican, the
the Western World.
he would meet Clarizio any minute, he felt more
han ever, afraid he would be asked to embark on an
ilar to his last one. God, he hoped not. He didn't think
nach for it. For six months, he had practically lived on
spearheaded an investigation into the sordid financial
arge Midwestern archdiocese. Part of his stomach prob-
gover from a life-threatening case of food poisoning that
when he started working on the case. The rest was in-
ed by the information he had uncovered.
s predecessor, Archbishop Paul Pizzaro, had mishandled
siness, making Kelly's job even tougher. "Shivers," as
icknamed for wearing wool trousers and a sweater under
ven in summer, had gently rebuked the guilty cardinal,
uld somehow get the man to change his ways and atone
Not just Kelly but the pope himself had been disgusted.
he had tried mightily, Kelly couldn't repair the damage
barrassment to the Church. To the horror of the Vatican,
mped on the story, laying bare not only the cardinal's
rruption but also his relationship with a woman that went
pastoral care. Kelly himself came across unseemly reve-

His English was excellent and delivered with the British accent taught
in private schools in Italy. More telling was the ease and self-assurance
clinging to him as finely as his hand-tailored cassock. Clarizio had a
reputation for attracting sophisticated secretaries who learned the use
of power at his feet and went on to distinguished careers. Perdomo
obviously fit the mold.

The monsignor crossed the glistening, black marble floor of the
walnut-paneled foyer. The only adornment was a towering, white
marble statue of St. Peter, a crosier in his left hand and a miniature
globe in his right. Opening two massive walnut doors that stretched
the height of the sixteen-foot ceiling, Perdomo bowed slightly again
and stepped aside.

Kelly was always uneasy when entering the regal chambers of the
hierarchy. He felt that if he breathed too hard, he'd break something
irreplaceable. Walnut bookcases climbed the walls on either side of
the room's massive, gray marble fireplace that was large enough to
roast an ox. The furnishings were a curious and enchanting blend of
European and Asian art. Against the opposite wall was a huge eighteenth-century gilded table, intricately carved with masklike faces, that
had been created after the designs of Pierre LePautre, the decorator
to Louis XIV. To the right stood a table that was a large circular
porcelain dish set atop three carved, gilded cranes, a superb example
of a *japonaiserie*. Two eighteenth-century red and gold lacquer ar-
moires graced another wall.

Kelly found the treasures to be museum quality, such as private
collectors only dreamed about. Seventeenth-century ivory statues of
the Madonna, and Saints Paul and John the Baptist, stood atop rose-
wood pedestals. An ornate silver cross hung on the wall at the opposite
end of the room. The Sultanabad rug was a beautifully woven pattern
of small birds in different shades of blue blurring from robin's egg to
navy. The chairs and divans were Chippendale.

"Eminenza loves antiques, and a few of these are part of his
personal collection," Perdomo said, walking to a six-foot-tall bronze
pagoda. "This is his favorite."

"Beautiful," Kelly said. "It bears the crest of the Tokugawa, the
leading shogun family of the Edo period."

Surprised by the knowledgeable response, the monsignor caressed
one of the miniature bells that dangled by slender silk ropes from the
corners of the pagoda, setting off a rippling chime. "I will tell Eminenza
you are here."

Leaving Kelly to wander among the antiques, Perdomo hurried to Archbishop Clarizio. He paused outside the music room, and out of habit, he examined his appearance in a mirror and stroked his hair into place before entering. The rich swells of Bach's Mass in B Minor seeped into the hallway.

As he rounded the doorway, Perdomo found the archbishop seated in a high-backed chair, his eyes closed. The only indication that he was not asleep was the gentle tapping of his right index finger to the tempo of the music.

"What do you think of him, Enrico?"

As always, Perdomo wondered how Clarizio knew, and with the music playing loudly. It was eerie. No matter how quietly anyone entered a room, the archbishop sensed the person's presence, even when his back was turned or his eyes were closed.

"Shrewd and iconoclastic, a man whose intelligence is hidden inside a body like a bear's," the monsignor replied. "He is also apparently an art connoisseur."

"Can he do what is needed?"

For a fraction of a second, Perdomo hesitated as he shaped an appropriate response. "We will not know until he has tried."

"Clever, Enrico," the archbishop said dryly.

"Will you tell him everything, Eminenza?" the secretary asked, knowing he himself knew little of this matter.

Opening his eyes, Clarizio glanced up disdainfully. "From the clever to the absurd."

Perdomo flushed. His mouth tightened as he bit back an angry retort. Of course, Clarizio would never tell until the time was right, if that ever came to pass. Still, he resented the archbishop's barbs. No one had ever addressed him the way Clarizio did. Never in his entire life. But if he must suffer the man's rebukes in order to learn from this mercurial archbishop, he would. Clarizio struck him as an enigma, a man of many faces. Often Perdomo wondered who the real Clarizio was. The icy dictator, the charming host, the devious schemer, the sarcastic wit, the penitent who spent hours on his knees in his chapel, the kingmaker, the obedient servant of the pope?

The archbishop enjoyed Perdomo's agitation. He needed to be toughened, disciplined. His life had been too easy; raised in splendor,

24

he had been cod_
in Italy. Everythi_
he wanted or to b_
presented itself.

Clarizio alway_
been and these brigh_
neled his way over_
wealthy families wh_
izio was a poor, you_
fluential mentors wo_
more than forty year_
was a burning ambiti_
devoted themselves to_
glorious.

Where was the hu_
understand the scorchin_
rise to power and promin_
the manners and bearing_
least of it. He had honed_
Vatican, and performed e_
his abilities. He sought ou_

He had cultivated po_
as mentors and protectors._
between with wealthy patron_
mies. He had fawned over th_
had sharpened his wit in the_
like razors. Above all, he h_
information, by diligent obse_
by extracting it from eavesdro_
of friends, and he doled out l_
gold.

Clarizio vividly remember_
he too was accepted as one of th_
of the Vatican, the Church, and_
world itself.

Now he was pronuncio to th_
was a ceremonial one, a gentle n_
powers, America and the Vatican_
reality, the ambassadorial post wa_
clesiastic power in this nation of_

the concept of indiv_
the American Chu_
must reason with t_
heard in Rome as_
easing of teachings_
controversial issue_

On a diploma_
He was involved_
the pope for cong_
to the President th_
realities in Easter_
work together to_

Downstairs_
even though Cl_
flattery of courti_
last true court i_

Now that_
apprehensive t_
assignment sim_
he had the stor_
Maalox as he_
dealings of a l_
lem was a han_
had hit him_
digestion cau_

Clarizio_
the messy bu_
Pizzaro was_
his cassock e_
as if that wo_
for his sins.

Thoug_
or avoid em_
the press j_
financial c_
well beyon_

26

lations onto which the press never tumbled. Each new bombshell gave him worse indigestion than he had before.

Mercifully, the cardinal under investigation had the grace to die of a heart attack. Suddenly, the pope, overriding the objections of powerful friends Pizzaro had made during his many years in Washington, brought the archbishop back to the Vatican and gave him an ill-defined job. When Kelly asked a friend in Rome who had a sardonic sense of humor about Pizzaro's new responsibilities, he was told, "The bishop's in charge of watering the Vatican lawns."

Trying to push those memories out of his mind, Kelly concentrated on his surroundings. The French doors to the right of the fireplace as well as the room's soaring windows filled the chamber with dying-afternoon golden sunlight and gave a languorous impression of a bygone era. That listlessness was as deceptive as being lulled into believing the Church was simply an aged, worn institution glimmering in the light of past glory. A swift perusal revealed how the room's decor reflected the Church's accommodation of the present with the past. Whereas until recently secret couriers carried the Vatican's messages, today the Holy See kept in touch with the world and her far-flung empire through sophisticated technology. A Reuters financial wire, an Associated Press news wire, a computer console, and a fax machine sat on a table beneath an oil painting depicting the pope's strong, thick-featured visage. The impersonal green light on the computer screen flickered while receiving a message. When he looked, Kelly could not decipher the communication. It was in code.

Kelly caught himself smiling wryly at this blend of antiquity and high tech. From the time of Constantine, Church leaders recognized that adaptation was the key to endurance. Whereas the Church once embraced the festivals of pagans and made them her own, She now embraced technology.

Glancing down, he winced. He'd forgotten to shine his shoes this morning. Sitting on one of the Chippendale chairs in front of an ivory-inlaid desk, he wiped his oxfords with a handkerchief. He was taking a second swipe when a voice stopped him.

"Father Kelly, I am Archbishop Clarizio."

The archbishop addressed him in Italian, knowing that was one of Kelly's languages. "*Parla italiano . . . vero?*"

Turning, Kelly found himself staring at a man wearing the purple, watered-silk garb of the episcopacy. Small and slight, he had thinning gray hair and almost translucent pale, yellowish skin; he looked like a wise old turtle. His most remarkable feature was his eyes. Deep set above a beaklike nose, they were dark and bright, highly intelligent and shrewd.

Getting up awkwardly, Kelly hastily stuffed the hanky into his back pocket. As he walked to the doorway and genuflected to kiss the archbishop's ring, the priest instinctively knew Clarizio to be an astute judge of character. Those piercing eyes looked as if they could x-ray his soul.

Clarizio took his hand away from Kelly's lips, thinking how much this man resembled the beefy, watchful bodyguards the pope used when on foreign trips. Except this priest was disheveled and had that kind of thick, black Irish hair that has an aversion to combs.

"Please, get up, Father Kelly," he said, and moved toward the sitting area.

An expectant look on his handsome face, Perdomo quietly followed, and as the sun was setting, the monsignor blended into the shadows. The pronuncio sat on a sofa and indicated that Kelly should take the chair across from him. Perdomo remained standing.

"You have had a tiring trip, Father. Let me offer you a drink."

Without waiting for a reply, Clarizio imperceptibly nodded to Perdomo, who silently left the room.

"You must be wondering why I have asked you to visit," he continued softly. "As you must realize, I have a great many weighty issues in front of me. One of the foremost is the question of leadership. The political leaders here have far-ranging influence, and I must try to express His Holiness's concerns and desires, but . . ."

He interrupted himself as Perdomo returned and set a silver tray on the table between them. Clarizio took a glass of port and raised it.

"*Salute*, Father Kelly. I am grateful that you were willing to come all this way."

"Thank you, Archbishop."

Kelly sipped his drink and was surprised. It was Wild Turkey, his favorite. Perdomo's serving it was either a minor miracle, or it meant that Clarizio had taken trouble to learn a good bit about him. He steeled himself for the worst.

"As I was saying," the archbishop continued, "the leadership of the Church here is a more vital concern than the leadership of state . . ."

Taking another sip of bourbon, Kelly put on a blank face and started to let what sounded like a canned speech go over his head. Suddenly, a note of apprehension crept into the archbishop's voice as Clarizio spoke of men who climbed the clerical ladder.

"Of course, it is essential that the leadership be free of taint. That their personal lives be beyond reproach. That they do not tarnish the Church by their actions."

Kelly grimaced. Good Lord, was another member of the hierarchy caught with his hand in the till? If so, he wanted no part of it.

Clarizio leaned forward and locked his eyes on Kelly's. "There is a need for us to create new bishops in this country, but we must be very, very careful about the kind of men we choose."

Kelly nodded soberly. For a moment, he had the crazy sort of urge people feel when tempted to step off a platform in front of a speeding train. He almost blurted out, "Sorry, Your Excellency. I'm not interested in being a bishop." Instead, he forced himself to adopt a solemn expression. If it didn't exactly convey wisdom and confidence, he hoped it would at least keep Clarizio from thinking he was a complete ass after catching him shining his shoes.

"We have a list of men we are considering," the archbishop continued. "Men who, throughout their careers, have shown extraordinary leadership and spiritual qualities."

Kelly nodded. Sure, he knew of the list. Hell, every priest did. There was always a good deal of gossip about who was on the list and why. The toadies who curried favor with their superiors. The terrific fund-raisers. Those men who were truly good people and conveyed a spirituality without crossing the line into fanaticism or nuttiness. Then there were the politicians who were always wheeling and dealing. Others were the charmers or the natural leaders. The men others followed without hesitation.

Clarizio rose from his seat and took a few steps toward the center of the room, wondering how Kelly would react to what he was about to propose. No priest would want such an assignment. Priests were trained to look for the good in everyone, not the worst. What worried him more than any priest's natural recoil from an unpleasant assignment was a streak of independence he detected in the man. Too many in the American clergy had it, a dangerous trait in an institution that depended upon a hierarchical chain where ideally everyone knew his place and practiced blind obedience. He sensed that this big man had it more than most.

"Your work for the previous nuncio regarding Cardinal Carruthers

29

was exemplary. Now, I too am turning to you for help. We simply cannot afford to make that kind of mistake again."

He paused uncomfortably. "Father Kelly, as you well know, priests in recent times have much more freedom than ever in the history of the Church. Such freedom has resulted in many men's leaving the priesthood. But for those of us who stay, it can lead to a more rewarding life. A renewal of the commitment we made as very young men."

The archbishop's gracious demeanor cracked slightly, and he appeared agitated. "But it also means that priests have had more opportunities to do things that may not be pleasing to God. Thus, before we admit anyone into the hierarchy, we must be absolutely sure of his character. This is where I need your help."

Kelly's stomach soured. He wasn't sure what Clarizio was driving at, but he knew he wasn't going to like it. Romans, he grumbled silently. Their spirit expresses itself in innuendo.

As if reading his mind, Clarizio suddenly approached him and put a slender hand on Kelly's shoulder. The touch was as delicate as a shadow.

"Forgive me, I forget that Americans find the obliqueness of Italians trying. People here like one to 'get to the point,' as you say."

He sat again. "The point that I have been trying to make, Father Kelly, is that I would like you to investigate the life of a man who is a candidate for bishop. He is valued very highly and may have a glorious career ahead of him. But he may bear a taint that will close the doors of advancement to him forever."

Kelly was stunned, not believing what was being asked of him. The process of approving bishops was much more demanding in recent years. Questionnaires seeking detailed information about a candidate's life were sent to various parties, but he had never heard of anyone's being assigned specifically to dig into a candidate's background. What could have brought this on? What the hell did Clarizio think he was?

Momentarily, curiosity dominated Kelly's anger. The man must be very important, and the reason for the investigation must be very serious.

"Whom are we talking about, Archbishop?"

Clarizio overlooked Kelly's bluntness. "One of your seminary classmates. Patrick Hogan."

Good Lord, Kelly thought angrily. Pat Hogan. Of course, his name was on the bishop list. It was probably placed there the first day he set foot in the seminary, if not the day he was born. The charismatic Pat Hogan, who hosted the spectacularly successful television show "Life Has Meaning." Hogan was a celebrity priest the likes of which the American Church hadn't had since Fulton Sheen's popular TV show was aired in the 1950s. Routinely written about in publications as varied as *The Nation* and *People*, Hogan was on a first-name basis with movie stars and the President. TV executives tried to lure him to their networks with the same huge salaries and golden promises that they offered a top anchorman or a series star.

Clarizio moved to defuse the outrage he saw in Kelly's eyes. "You see, Father," he said calmly, "the pope is especially concerned. With the unification of Eastern and Western Europe under way, the Church wants to have an English-language television program that would be aired throughout the continent. We are considering Monsignor Hogan to head that project. He would be the Church's voice on two continents. Perhaps one day, the entire world."

Kelly stared back belligerently. "I'm sorry, Archbishop. I know the man. I'm not right for the assignment."

Clarizio nodded sympathetically, but his eyes were steely. "That is precisely why you were chosen for this task. You are familiar with him from the days when he was in the seminary with you, when he was part of what was known as the Trinity."

Inadvertently, Kelly whistled softly. He hadn't thought of the Trinity for years. The nickname for the seminary's top guns, the three members of the class who had stood out for their brilliance, athletic prowess, and spirituality. Pat Hogan. Bill Witten. Damian Carter. The extraordinary, inseparable friends once were expected to conquer the Church much the way they had the seminary. But life, Kelly thought, has a way of slipping a banana peel under just about anyone on the run. Hogan was the only member of the Trinity who hadn't stumbled. Now the Archbishop said maybe Pat had too.

Kelly's resentment flared again as his worst fear was borne out. Another dirty job. The archbishop considered him a goddamn bloodhound. Bitterly, he knew there was no way to dodge the assignment. Clarizio would see to it that his life was made miserable until his dying day if he begged off.

Suddenly, he felt conflicted. Men should be weeded out of the Church who weren't fit to be there. Apparently pious churchmen could lead sinful secret lives. If nothing else, his last assignment had taught him that. He could understand the archbishop's concern. Hogan was

31

no ordinary priest proposed for a fat office. If a scandal hit, a lot of people who believed in the persona Hogan portrayed on television would be hurt. The effect on the public perception of the Church would be devastating as people confused the actions of a weak man with the institution.

Still, he gritted his teeth when he replied, "With God's help, I will try."

Clarizio looked at Kelly appreciatively and with surprise. The response was appropriate but not one he expected in those words from this big, rough-looking man. Even priests, he was afraid, discounted relying on God in many of their activities, even when they needed Him the most.

"What makes you believe that Monsignor Hogan has anything to hide?" Kelly demanded.

"This," Clarizio said, extracting a piece of paper from the sleeve of his gown, the document whispering against the silk. "Somehow this came into the hands of His Holiness. I myself do not know how, but now the pope wants every precaution taken against scandal harming Mother Church."

Kelly unfolded the paper. The message was brief:

Patrick Hogan must never be made a bishop. He was part of the Trinity's mortal sin.

Beneath the cryptic message was:

Washington. March 20, 1972.

Kelly's stomach felt queasy. Damn, damn, damn. Suddenly, he realized Clarizio was speaking, but he had difficulty concentrating. "I'm sorry, Your Excellency. Would you repeat that?"

A bit annoyed, Clarizio reiterated, "Your investigation must be most thorough. Spare no expense. Go anywhere, see anyone you think you must. Remove any doubts that may arise."

He stared into the priest's eyes. "Father, we want to know everything about Monsignor Hogan, including what happened in Washington with the Trinity. Everything! Also, don't discuss this note with anyone."

"Does that mean I can't ask Monsignor Hogan about it?"

"Yes. That should only be a last resort."

"You realize, Archbishop, that I will have to tell him about the investigation. Once I start asking questions about him, people will call him to let him know what's going on."

"Yes, of course, you should tell him. There is no way this can be done in secrecy. Certain members of the hierarchy are already aware that there is to be such an investigation."

Clarizio arose, indicating that Kelly was dismissed. "Go with God, my son."

"Thank you, Your Excellency," Kelly said rotely.

As he made his way out, Kelly was troubled. The assignment would be difficult. With dismay, he felt certain that he would uncover things about Hogan he didn't want to know. What bothered him more was what went unspoken. Why hadn't the archbishop simply confronted Hogan with the note? Why the hell had the pope taken the note so seriously? It didn't make sense. Clarizio had to be holding back something crucial. But what?

When Perdomo closed the door behind him, Kelly found himself staring at a priest wearing a cassock and leaning against the rear fender of a Mercedes limousine. Drawing on a cigarette, the priest nodded and held open the back door.

"Thanks," Kelly said before getting in. "I'm Kevin Kelly."

They shook hands and the man indicated with deft movements that he was mute. Climbing in, Kelly was grateful to be able to stretch out in the backseat, but was irritated anyway by the job he had just taken on. What had he gotten himself into?

The priest drove expertly and swiftly. Looking at the driver's profile, Kelly became conscious how truly ugly the man was. His nose was large. Small eyes were buried behind fleshy folds, and his bruised-looking, purplish lips were fleshy as well. His thinning hair was jet black and his skin swarthy. The hands were strong but held the steering wheel delicately.

Kelly knew who he must be. The legendary Paolo Bisleti. He examined the man's neck. Yes, it was there when he raised his chin— the beginning of a thick scar that disappeared beneath his collar. It was Bisleti.

There were dozens of fascinating stories about the man. A Sicilian, he had been involved in a wide variety of dangerous criminal activities until Clarizio somehow persuaded him to change his ways and even pursue Holy Orders. There were people who looked upon Bisleti's being a priest almost as a sign from God that man could be

33

perfected. Some cynics, however, countered that Bisleti had never changed much more than his clothes. That he still had Mafia ties and was a pawn in the elaborate games Clarizio played.

Quickly, Kelly gambled on his instincts, something he did routinely and trusted. "Will you help me if I need you?" he asked.

Surprised, Bisleti stared into the rearview mirror, as though assessing the nature of the man who had asked something of him. Slowly, he nodded his assent. He drove the rest of the way to the airport without looking back.

3

KEVIN KELLY MADE HIS WAY UP THE AISLE AT THE TV STUDIO, SLIPPED
into the next to the last row of seats, and sat uneasily. "Life Has
Meaning" was about to begin. Glancing around at the cameras focused
on the front of the stage, the lights dangling from the ceiling, and the
people scurrying about, he wondered again whether he should have
let Pat Hogan know he was coming.

Hogan was on the stage talking amiably to Sen. Russell Harris,
who was being fussed over by a young woman pinning a microphone
to his lapel. The senator from Alaska had spoken out strongly against
Exxon Corp. for not doing enough to clean up the *Valdez* oil spill.
Kelly imagined the man next to him was an Exxon representative.

A red light went on on the TV camera. Hogan turned and addressed the audience. "Thank you for being with us this evening. The
planet is facing a number of ecological crises, some of which appear
to be threatening the way we live our lives in these closing years of
the twentieth century. The theme of tonight's show is 'Moral Responsibility versus Corporate Responsibility.' We have with us . . ."

Kelly's mind wandered. Hogan's Donahue routine struck him as

35

perhaps not too out of character. When they were seminarians, Kelly thought of Hogan as leading a gilded life. Both his teachers and classmates admired him. Kelly never doubted that Hogan worked for his achievements, but Kelly always thought he charmed his way through those years. Kelly smiled a bit, thinking how he himself had a habit of stepping on toes that were in his way. Noting the way Hogan deftly handled the oil-spill adversaries, he envied Hogan his social skills. He could take lessons from the guy.

Watching Hogan in front of the TV lights made Kelly think of the first time they met. What was it early 1968? Yes. It was only about six weeks after Tet, when the Viet Cong mocked U.S. claims of success in Vietnam on the lunar New Year holiday with a surprise offensive that even penetrated the U.S. embassy compound. A few months later, Martin Luther King was gunned down and then Bobby Kennedy. He remembered feeling so out of touch at the time. Twenty-two years go. It didn't seem possible to Kelly he was in the religious life that long.

Kelly had just been released from the army, intending to become a member of the Vincentian order of priests. Still in his lieutenant's uniform, he headed straight to Gethsemane Seminary in Pennsylvania's Pocono Mountains. His anxiety about entering the priesthood was compounded by the hostility he felt many people directed at him because of his uniform. In the town of East Stroudsburg, Pennsylvania, he waited at the cold, shabby bus depot for someone to drive him to the seminary. Suddenly, he was surrounded by a group of youths who began taunting him.

"Hey, murderer!" one yelled.

"Kill any babies today, man?" shouted another.

Already tense about embarking on a new life path, Kelly grew angry, ready to smash back, but tried to hold himself in check. Back in the States only about a week, he was sick of the way so many people recoiled from his uniform or acted wary of him, as if he were a pariah. Out of perversity, he continued wearing the uniform. Ignoring the youths, he told himself to cool it, that they were just foolish teenagers. But when one came over and sneeringly flipped the bronze star pinned to his tunic, he was about to grab him.

Before he could, a handsome, athletic, young man in his early twenties seized the boy by the shoulder and led him away. Unprepossessing in his jeans, sweatshirt, and sneakers, he stood between the boys and Kelly, speaking quietly to them. By the way the kids stood

36

taller and by the shame on their faces, they obviously respected the guy. The youths left mumbling apologies to Kelly.

"Sorry about that," the man said, turning to Kelly. "They're not bad kids. It's just that they act like jerks sometimes."

"Thanks," Kelly said.

"My name is Pat Hogan. I'm from Gethsemane. You aren't my pickup by any chance are you?"

"I am," Kelly said, introducing himself.

"Welcome home, Kevin," Hogan said as they shook hands.

Startled, Kelly was at a loss for words. In the eight days since he'd returned to the United States, no one had welcomed him back.

Hogan insisted on carrying Kelly's duffel bag to the seminary car parked outside. While driving to Gethsemane, Hogan said, "Several of those guys are on a basketball team I coach for the Catholic Youth Organization league. They should know better. You've been through enough. You don't need that kind of grief."

For a moment, Kelly's eyes narrowed as he glanced at Hogan's profile, wondering how much about his background this guy knew. Then he relaxed. Hogan was just being friendly.

The rock music on the radio station was interrupted by a news bulletin. "Senator Eugene McCarthy, who trailed President Johnson by just seven thousand votes in the New Hampshire primary, predicted he will win the Wisconsin primary," a reporter said. "Is that right, Senator?" "Yes, I think I can get the nomination," McCarthy replied. "I'm ahead now."

"Is McCarthy for real?" Kelly asked.

"Yes," Hogan said, shooting him a questioning look. "You must feel sort of lost coming home, don't you?"

"Lost," Kelly repeated. "I guess I do. I just hope the feeling goes away soon."

"It will," Hogan said. "Gethsemane is a good place to get your head straight. If there's anything I can do, let me know."

"Thanks," Kelly said.

For the first time in he didn't know how long, Kelly found himself at ease with a civilian. Later, he found out Hogan was passionately opposed to the war. As he learned a bit more about Hogan's personality, he found him to be a complicated guy. Very personable, very smart, somewhat egotistical.

At the conclusion of the TV show, a pretty brunette wearing gray slacks and a white sweater and carrying a clipboard rushed up to Monsignor Hogan. "Pat, our guest next week will be Karl Jordan, the hotshot junk bond salesman who was found guilty last week of insider trading."

"Why him?"

"He just found religion. Or he claims to have. He's getting sentenced next month. We can get into the questionable sincerity of sudden religious awakenings of guys like him and Ivan Boesky and the old Watergate crowd."

She turned away and wheeled around again. "Also, he just donated a half mill to the New York archdiocese. We can raise the issue of when the Church should reject ill-gotten money."

"Thanks, Ellen," Hogan said dryly. "With you around, I'm sure to get excommunicated one of these days. Archbishop Murray will tune in to watch one of his big contributors say nice things about him, and he'll see me harpooning the guy. You know Murray's stand on money."

He pursed his lips and upped his voice to the range of the archbishop's reedy voice. "The Church should be blinder than justice when it comes to taking a buck from a saint or a sinner."

In his own voice, he added, "Sounds okay until you see some of the people he hits up on his fund-raising drives."

"Now, now, Pat. You're still mad about the archbishop calling you on the carpet for the show about gays in public office."

"Good Lord, Ellen, why is the Church hierarchy full of guys who only care about sex? They get more upset over gay rights than they do over murder."

"You should know better than me. You're the priest."

"I am? Oh, I am. I am."

Ellen laughed. "You're terrible."

He put his arm around her shoulders and whispered, "Don't tell anyone else."

She laughed again and flushed at the warmth she felt. As she walked away, she thought about how long it had taken her to realize priests were human. For months, she was intimidated by the monsignor's collar and position and walked on eggshells around him, watching everything she did and said. Eventually, she forgot herself and began behaving naturally. Though he never said anything, she could

tell Hogan breathed a big sigh of relief at her change in attitude, and he got chummier. Sometimes she wondered if there was a bit more to his playfulness than he let on. He was a good-looking guy. Priest or not, half the women on the set would go to bed with him. There were times she wondered whether some of them did. Sometimes she wondered whether she would.

Fifteen minutes later, Hogan was in his dressing room taking off his makeup. He looked at his watch. It was almost eight-fifty. He had promised that he would stop by the party marking Cal Robbins's acquisition of the Waldorf. There was no rush. Robbins's parties went on half the night.

He had watched the growth of Robbins's fortune with a sense of dismay over the past few years. Ten years ago, even five, Robbins was still making a name for himself as a real estate wheeler-dealer. Now that he was immensely rich and powerful, he was driven to keep himself in the news with his ridiculous jumbo yachts, planes, and mansions and by leaking private talk of running for the presidency. Whenever Cal and Connie gave anything to the Church or even wined and dined the monsignors and bishops who loved being in the company of the prominent, he turned it into a circus of publicity.

What concerned Hogan was that while Robbins's fortune grew, so did Cal's bleak view of the world. He saw rottenness and corruption everywhere, chronically complaining about "pollution" in the Church. At the same time, he carped that his hard work and money had not brought him happiness.

"Pat, why do I have everything a man could want and half the time I'm bored out of my goddamn skull?" he asked recently.

"You've got too much money and you don't do enough for other people with it," Hogan recalled telling him.

"That's what I thought you'd say," Robbins replied, and laughed.

Hogan had noted that the laughter was uneasy. He wondered about Robbins's erratic behavior, his desperation to buy the kind of fulfillment he so feverishly sought. He sometimes worried that the man might be a potential suicide. Some grand gesture to make the world sit up and take notice of him one last time.

A knock on the door broke his train of thought. "Just a minute," he called out, wiping the remaining beige gunk from his face.

He hoped it wasn't Ed Murphy. The station owner usually hung around to watch the show and frequently stopped by the dressing room for a drink. Drink led Murphy to complain about his marital problems, which had been going on for thirty-five years. There was no escape for him. Death is Catholic divorce.

Opening the door, Hogan saw someone he had least expected to show up here. "Hello, Kevin!"

Kevin Kelly stuck out his hand, amazed as always how Hogan made him feel as if they were best friends. In truth, they had had a good relationship at the seminary, but on the odd occasions when they'd run into one another since their ordination, Hogan always seemed absolutely delighted to see him. Other members of the class said the same thing. It was part of Hogan's charm.

"The show was terrific, Pat."

"Stop this flattery. It will get you everywhere."

Hogan stepped back and seemed to drink Kelly in. "Judging by that ominous look on your face, you've got something serious on your mind."

"Actually, I do. I have to talk to you for a few minutes."

Hogan put his hand on the big man's shoulder. "You're not in trouble are you, Kevin?"

"No, but thanks for asking. This is more about you than me."

"You've hooked me." Hogan turned to the mirror and wiped a few stubborn smudges of makeup from his face with a tissue that he tossed into a wastepaper basket.

"Done. Now, if you don't mind, let's go somewhere else. Sometimes the studio starts to feel like a prison. I always have to be on my best behavior because millions of jailers out there are keeping tabs on me."

Hogan put on his suit jacket as they headed down a cement corridor. A moment later, his right hand shot out and grasped Kelly's arm as the priest stumbled.

"I should have warned you, Kevin. I always forget these wires are here and almost kill myself on them."

This was the first time Kelly had visited a TV production studio, and he was amazed at how much really was illusion versus reality. Cavernous as a hangar, the studio's floors were bare, and there were enough wires snaking about to qualify as an electrician's convention. The makeshift sets for shows were small and tacky compared with the way they came across on the screen.

They were almost to the exit when a woman's husky voice stopped them. "The place is turning into a retreat house for wayward priests."

Hogan gave a strained laugh. "Hello, Lane." He turned to Kelly. "Kevin, this is Lane Woods."

40

The beautiful blonde wore an outsize gray silk sports jacket over a blue silk blouse and a short black skirt that set off a spectacular pair of legs. Yet, her outfit wasn't sexy. It struck Kelly almost as a uniform.

"Miss Woods doesn't need to be introduced," he said, holding out his hand. "I'm Father Kelly."

Kelly considered himself pretty much an illiterate when it came to contemporary culture, but even he knew something about Lane Woods. Alluring posters of her promoting XTV's evening news were on the back of every city bus and on the walls of every subway station. Kelly recalled reading somewhere that she had just signed a contract making her the highest-paid reporter in the cable TV news industry. He decided she was even better looking in person than on TV.

"Father Kelly is a gallant priest." She shot Hogan an antagonistic look. "I didn't think the two went together."

Hogan's jaw tightened imperceptibly, but he tried to shrug off the comment with a forced smile. "We've got to be going."

"Your friend is very rude to run away just as we were getting acquainted," she said, pressing Kelly's hand.

"Good-bye, Miss Woods," Kelly managed to say, wondering why she was needling Hogan.

As they entered the corridor to catch the elevator, Kelly's throat was dry and he felt as dumb as a schoolboy. Once in a while the presence of a beautiful woman still did that to him. He wasn't sure whether to be glad or annoyed.

The elevator came almost immediately to take them to the lobby. On the way down, Hogan looked at Kelly and rolled his eyes.

"Prepare for the most ridiculous aspect of this job," he said.

"What are you talking about?"

"You'll see in a minute."

It was just about sixty seconds later that they went through the revolving brass-and-glass front door. Immediately, they were met by calls of "Monsignor Hogan!" and even a few squeals as a group of bright-eyed women besieged them.

"He's here!" several women yelled simultaneously.

"Autograph!" others screamed.

Suddenly, both priests were engulfed in a swarm of bodies as arms thrust autograph books at Pat Hogan. Kelly extricated himself with ease since no one paid the least bit of attention to him as they lunged for Hogan.

"Please, ladies." Hogan's rich baritone rose above the shrieks. "Please. Can we just have a bit of order."

The cries subsided while Hogan signed one autograph after another. The beaming smile on his face belied his halfhearted complaint of a few minutes ago. Hogan obviously enjoyed the limelight.

"Thank you, Father," most said.

"Thanks, Pat," one pretty teenager said cheekily while Hogan arched an eyebrow at her in mock indignation.

Just then a man shoved through the crowd, pushed Hogan, and punched him in the face. Hogan reeled back and the man punched him again, sending the priest sprawling. The attacker jumped on him, screaming, "Bastard! You dirty bastard!"

Kelly seized the man and yanked him to his feet. As the attacker lashed out at Kelly, the big priest bashed him in the chest with his elbow and kneed him in the groin. As the man doubled over, Kelly karate-chopped him in the neck. The assailant fell to the ground unconscious just as a patrol car screeched to a halt at the pavement and two policemen jumped out.

"What's going on here?" demanded one officer.

Hogan, Kelly, and the women all started talking at once.

"Whoa," the policeman said. "One at a time."

Then the officer recognized Hogan. "Oh, God. Monsignor Hogan."

Kelly could see what was going on in the cop's mind as he sized up the situation. A TV celebrity was mugged. The police would be blamed for not being able to keep the muggers away from even the city's stars.

Still startled and breathing deeply, Hogan explained what had happened. The police turned the assailant on his side and handcuffed his arms behind his back. Groaning, he was just coming around. Kelly was surprised when he saw the man's face clearly. A nice-looking guy. He was in his early twenties and well dressed. Some poor crazy, Kelly thought as the guy was dragged to a patrol car and shoved in the backseat.

Fifteen minutes later, the police had taken statements from Kelly and Hogan and the witnesses. "We'll get back to you on the charges, Monsignor." He gave both Hogan and Kelly his name and phone number.

"Thanks, Officer Williams," Hogan said.

A few minutes later, the priests were walking down Sixth Avenue. Hogan turned up his collar as if to ward off any more assailants.

"You okay?" Kelly asked.

"Yes. A little scared though. Fortunately, he didn't get a good shot at me." He smiled ruefully. "Thanks for the help."

"Part of the price of being a celebrity?" Kelly asked uneasily.

"God, I hope not. If it is, it's the first time my career brought anything like this on."

Actually, the more he thought about it the stranger Kelly found Hogan's career. How did he wind up doing this? Maybe it did help people, but it seemed more like tabloid sensationalism than reaching out to humanity. Funny, he thought, how many people wind up later in life doing what would have seemed preposterous at one point in time.

"Maybe you should get a bodyguard, Pat," Kelly said, thinking it was a hell of a price to pay for success.

"The day I do that is the day I quit," Hogan said quietly. "But there *are* times I'd just like to disappear into a crowd and I can't."

Hogan shrugged as if to shake off impending gloom, and it seemed to work. "Do you care where we go?" he asked lightly.

"No," Kelly replied.

Hogan stepped into the street and hailed a passing cab. As they climbed in, he gave an address Kelly didn't catch.

"Hey, you're that TV priest," the driver said. "I watched the show a couple of times, but I usually drive on Tuesday nights. I picked up some of your guests though. Lemme see, there was . . ."

Fortunately, his monologue was brief because the cab stopped in front of the Four Seasons. Before Kelly could dig into his pocket, Hogan had paid the fare.

"I hope you can catch the show next week," Hogan said.

"I'll try, Father," the cabby called out as he pulled away.

Kelly thought this celebrity stuff could be a curse. You always had to be on.

"Hello, Monsignor Hogan," the doorman said, smartly opening the door.

"Hello, Steve."

Once they were inside, the maître d' rushed forward. He beamed at Hogan and nodded at Kelly as though trying to ascertain whether he should know him, or whether he was worth knowing. A tiny polite smile showed he decided no on both scores.

"Are you here for dinner, Monsignor?"

"No, Marco. Just drinks."

"The Pool Room?"

"That will be fine," Hogan replied.

The maître d' led them into a large dining area and gave them one of the tables that radiated from the small pool that gave the room its name. Once they were seated, he snapped his fingers for a waiter. "Enjoy," he said, turning on his heel like a Prussian army officer.

"What will it be, Kevin?" Hogan asked.

"Wild Turkey on the rocks."

While Hogan placed the drink order, Kelly looked around the enormous room. Along a glass wall in the rear, a massive curtain made of copper gently rustled as it was brushed by air currents. With the towering ceiling and cold, modern decor, he found the place as comfortable and inviting as an international airport.

Kelly had not been in an expensive restaurant for years, never finding it a deprivation, but he found himself curious about this one. The restaurant was one of the city's magnets for heavyweights in TV, publishing, politics, and business. A "power watering hole," he thought *New York* magazine had referred to the Four Seasons as in a recent issue. And it was. The rich and famous were on display everywhere. A former secretary of state sat across the room with a Rockefeller. An NBC network correspondent was at another table. The chairman of one of the Big Three auto makers was at another. Half the people around them were familiar. Many of them looked over, nodding and smiling at Hogan, who flashed a smile back.

Kelly smiled to himself, thinking how weird all this was. So many of these guys put on airs when a lot of them were just like Hogan, the son of a bricklayer. The American Revolution got rid of the monarchy; now everybody wanted to be king.

A moment after their drinks were set down, a procession of important people started drifting by the table with studied nonchalance, saying hello to Hogan and shaking hands with Kelly as they were introduced. City officials. TV and movie personalities. Business leaders. Their parting remarks were similar. "We must do lunch"—or "dinner"—"soon."

Kelly was amused by the dog and pony show these prominent people put on for one another. He also wondered how sincere Hogan was about missing anonymity when he chose a place where his celebrity status was the rule rather than the exception. Maybe he was being too hard on Hogan and his pals. Who knows? Maybe for the famous, being around others who were just as well-known was the closest they came to being ordinary.

The last of the table hoppers was Charles Edwards, the head of the huge Edwards Mines and a prominent Catholic. "How are you, Bishop?" he asked Hogan with a wink.

Hogan looked a little uncomfortable but parried the comment with laughter. "Surely you jest."

"The word is out, Pat. You are number one on the bishop list."

"They need better men than me," Hogan said, and introduced Kelly.

During their banter, Kelly studied the mining magnate. He was slight, wore glasses, had thinning gray hair and a patrician air. He had inherited a huge asbestos mining company and turned it into a powerful conglomerate with diverse interests worldwide. Besides being rich, Edwards was influential in conservative national political circles and was a powerhouse in the Church. Kelly thought the man came down on the wrong side of most social issues, but churchmen catered to him for the same reason politicians did. His donations were huge. The Church, Kelly groused silently, readily accommodated too many fools because of their money.

Edwards patted Hogan on the shoulder. "You're okay, Pat, even if you do have a few foolish liberal notions."

"I wish I could say the same about you, Charlie."

Edwards laughed and waved good-bye. "Good luck, Your Excellency. See you at Cal's party?"

"In a while," Hogan replied.

Turning to Kelly, he said, "Sorry for the interruptions, Kevin. I didn't mean to come on like one of the hot-shot celebrities around this town."

"Hey, that's what you are."

Kelly was trying to keep things light, but as the words came out of his mouth, he wished he could learn to be a bit more diplomatic. Who the hell was he to talk? Yet, he couldn't help wondering again how one of the glorious Trinity wound up a TV host, granted a spectacularly successful one. What kind of a life was that for a priest? He guessed that was at the core of the questions he must answer. At the moment, though, he didn't have the heart to ask.

Hogan lowered his eyes. "You're right. I try to think of myself as something more, but essentially you're right. Pathetic, isn't it?"

Now Kelly was embarrassed. "Stop the tears. From what I've heard, most of your lucrative salary goes to Catholic Charities, and a lot of people are taking a renewed interest in their religion because of your show."

"So they say. It's a sad commentary on our civilization that people get religion from TV," Hogan said.

"Hell, they get everything else from the tube. Why not salvation?"

Hogan laughed and ordered another round. Uneasily, he noticed his glass was empty while Kelly's was still half full. He decided it was time to find out why Kelly had materialized in his life after eons and looking as if he'd been sentenced to thirty days' hard labor. Kelly was one of the classmates he could never figure out. The body of a stevedore and the brain of a poet. A man apparently totally without ambition, which made him an anomaly in the clergy as well as everywhere else. A little older than most of the seminarians, he seemed to have lived a lot more than the rest of them, although he never talked about his background. In fact, he had kept pretty much to himself. It probably had something to do with Vietnam.

Hogan always had the impression something horrendous had happened to Kelly. He seemed like a man who had suffered a terrible injury after which he had had to learn how to walk and talk again. There was a distance about him that he couldn't quite describe, as if he were always holding a part of himself away from everyone, so it couldn't be hurt. Probably his heart. At the seminary, Kelly seemed not so much drawn to God as in retreat from the world. Hogan remembered him also as smart and having an odd mélange of artistic and linguistic interests. At the same time, he would be at home with cops or longshoremen. He had a directness, a bluntness, often found in such men.

"How can I help you, Kevin?"

Unconsciously Kelly hunched his shoulders, which he did whenever he had to discuss something he found unpleasant. "Edwards's congratulations can't be the first you've heard. They want to make you a bishop, Pat."

"So I've heard," Hogan said slowly as he looked curiously at Kelly. "What does it have to do with you?"

Almost as suddenly as he asked the question, the answer occurred to him. His eyes clouded over and the corner of his mouth twisted. "Did my name crop up in that Carruthers flap?"

"No."

Perplexed, Hogan stared at Kelly. "Then what are you doing here, Kevin?"

46

Kelly hunched again but kept his gaze steady. "I've been asked to check out your background."

Hogan stared at him, his eyes widening in amazement. When he spoke, it was slowly, incredulously. *"You have been asked to check out my background.* God, I never heard of such a thing!"

"I know it's unusual."

"Unusual, hell. It's outrageous!" he said angrily. Hogan's voice became grim. "If Murray thinks he can get away with this, he's mistaken."

"It isn't Archbishop Murray, Pat."

"Then who?"

"Clarizio."

Hogan sat back stunned; his mouth fell open as if he had been hit again by a crazed stranger. "Clarizio! This is rich. What have *you* got to do with Dagger Tom?"

"He called me down to Washington and asked me to check you out. I want you to know what's going on when word starts coming back that I'm asking questions about you."

"May I ask why, in God's name," Hogan demanded furiously, "I'm being investigated like some thief in the night?"

Kelly hunched uncomfortably under the sarcasm, feeling even sleazier than he thought he would. For at least the seven hundredth time, he resented the rotten position in which he found himself. He'd given Clarizio his word that he wouldn't say anything about the note that had come into the pope's possession, but he didn't want to mislead Hogan. He sure as hell wasn't going to lie to the man. Fortunately, Hogan himself provided an escape.

"I know. I know. Because Carruthers turned out to be a crook, anybody put up for bishop is now suspect. Damn it, Kevin, the Carrutherses are going to slip by any kind of a screening process that's set up."

Though Hogan stared at him with an accusatory gaze, Kelly didn't flinch. "You and I know that, Pat. The brass has other ideas."

Hogan finally averted his eyes. "It's just that I feel . . . I don't know . . . as if the rug were pulled out from under me. I've spent my life in the Church and now I feel . . . Damn it, I feel betrayed!"

"Come on, Pat, it's just a couple of guys who need a bit of reassurance," Kelly said, thinking poor Hogan would croak if he knew one of the guys was the pope. "I want to be straight with you and hope there are no hard feelings."

Hogan shook his head angrily. "Oh, I don't blame you, Kevin. It's the lousy system."

"Don't worry about it, Pat. You were born to be a priest. Probably a bishop too."

Hogan tightened up again as he thought how far off the mark Kelly's words were. Entering the seminary was the most difficult decision of his life and on the surface, hadn't made sense to family or friends.

Ruefully, he recalled what led him to the seminary. There were two turning points in his life while growing up in Germantown, a tough, working-class section of Philadelphia. The first was in his freshman year at Cardinal Dougherty High School. His mother was dying of cancer. Nightly, he knelt beside her bed, begging God to spare her, willing to barter anything for her life. He spent hours with her every day before and after school, doing what he could to cool her feverish, wasted body, holding her hand, wiping her brow, combing her hair. Her death devastated both him and his father.

Sean Hogan never snapped out of his depression and largely ignored his son. Dead tried from working all day, Sean sat in a bar in the evening with other construction workers or came home with a six-pack and watched TV until he tumbled into bed. When addressing his son, his remarks were usually sarcastic. "Going out again with those juvenile delinquents?" when friends dropped by. "Who's the unlucky girl tonight?" when Pat had a date.

Unsupervised, Pat ran wild, drinking, fighting, staying out all night. His schoolwork, which always came easily, slipped. He verged on being thrown off the basketball team, only months after showing signs of becoming a star.

Finally, his coach, Father Tom McBride, took him aside. The even-tempered priest drew the best out of players through treating them with fairness and expecting excellence. His boys played fiercely, so as not to let him down. McBride knew there was something very wrong. Hogan had struck him as a natural leader and playmaker. Yet the boy bothered the priest a little. There was a bit of the con about Hogan. It was obvious that he wanted to be captain of the junior varsity team, but he tried to charm his coach, relying on his good looks and quick tongue rather than trusting in his considerable athletic abilities. Lately,

48

however, Hogan was moody and listless, disturbing signs in a usually very vibrant youth.

"What's wrong, Pat?" McBride asked. "You're wrecking your life."

At first, Hogan was too proud to answer. Then all the anger he felt burst forth. "There is no God! A God would never have killed my mother."

McBride empathized with the boy's anguish and put his hand on his shoulder. "I can't justify your mother's death. Terrible things happen and we don't know why. But there's no sense hating God for what goes on in life. That just leaves you alone, feeling life is useless. You have a chance to do something good with your life. But it's up to you whether you want to throw away your talents and shame your mother's memory."

The words jolted Hogan. Somehow he hadn't thought of how his mother would view his behavior. Even in all her pain, she had never rejected God. Shortly before her death, she even spoke to him about her desire that one day he would become a priest. "I'm not exacting a promise," she said, smiling. "I'd just like you to consider it."

His mother's request didn't surprise him. Like a lot of his friends' mothers, she was very religious. A joke in the neighborhood was that the way out lay in the "four Ps," politics, the police force, prison, and the priesthood. "I'll think about it," he replied, knowing that entering the priesthood was the last thing in the world he wanted to do.

He got his life back on track. It wasn't just his mother's memory that motivated him but the knowledge that he didn't want to wound his father more than he already was. With determination, he set about making something out of himself, studying hard, running for school offices, excelling at sports, and cultivating teachers who could help him. By his senior year, he was one of the few boys trusted by both the school administration and his classmates.

The second turning point came in 1965, during his senior year. He was a delegate at a United Nations session for high school students. After the meeting, he crossed the cement expanse in front of the UN headquarters in New York. The March day was crisp and sunny. Graduation was only months away. Preying on Pat's mind was whether to accept an academic scholarship to Georgetown or a basketball scholarship to Boston College and how his girlfriend Mary Beth would feel about his leaving.

Just beyond the UN entrance, he paused out of curiosity to listen to a man speaking to a large crowd. The onlookers were tense and restless. Sometimes people cheered the speaker. Often, he was booed or hissed at. Occasional yells of "Communist!" rang out.

Pressing closer, Hogan was startled to see the tall, dynamic speaker was a priest. Amazed, Hogan listened intently.

"Do you honestly expect that we could so abuse our black citizens for three hundred and forty years, so resist their moral and democratic rights, so mistreat, exploit, starve, terrorize, rape, and murder them without all this showing itself in our foreign policy?" the priest demanded.

"Is it possible," the speaker continued, "for us to be vicious, brutal, immoral, and violent at home and be fair, judicious, beneficent, and idealistic abroad?"

Hogan was mesmerized. The strapping priest, who looked like an Irish warrior-chieftain, linked the plight of the nation's Negroes to the war that was going on in Vietnam. Hogan hadn't heard anyone do that before, and somehow it made sense. How could a country that cared so little for so many people of color at home claim it waged war to help people of color on the other side of the world?

Just last month, President Johnson ordered "retaliatory strikes"; round-the-clock bombing of North Vietnam began. Hogan and several his friends wanted the faculty at Cardinal Dougherty to discuss whether the bombing was the right thing to do, but their homeroom priest warned them they'd be viewed as "troublemakers" if they tried. Most priest at high school were suspicious of the motives of civil right activists or pacifists. Like the detractors in the crowd, many of them accused civil rights workers and anyone opposed to war of being "troublemakers" and "Communists." Yet, he hadn't pushed the issue at the time. He was class president and stood an excellent chance of winning a scholarship. He needed good recommendations from his teachers.

Hogan felt himself swayed by this impassioned priest with the piercing blue eyes. He had to do something against the war. "Who is he?" Hogan asked a woman next to him.

"Father Philip Berrigan," she replied.

Hogan knew the name. He had followed the civil rights movement closely, marveling at the courage of the demonstrators who placed their lives on the line. Berrigan was the first Catholic priest arrested for civil rights activities in the South. He and his brother, Daniel, a Jesuit and a poet, were the only Catholic priests to have signed the first "declaration of conscience" against the Vietnam War.

He couldn't tear his eyes from the priest. Suddenly, Phil Berrigan

50

pointed a finger at Hogan. "Boy," he thundered, "you too can make a difference!"

Returning on the train to Philadelphia that evening, Hogan was in a daze. He had never heard so powerful a speaker or seen such a committed man. Suddenly, he scared himself. He saw himself as a priest, embracing social causes and changing people's lives for the better. He saw himself heady with the power to sway crowds, fighting for the rights of the poor and downtrodden. He also remembered his mother's ambition for him.

The idea didn't pass. Week after week, he tried to reject it, but when he closed his eyes at night, the image of Father Berrigan pointing at him was more vivid than ever, and he heard his thundering words. Pat ate and slept badly, and friends started asking him what was wrong.

Shortly before graduating, he confided in Father McBride that he wanted to become a priest. McBride listened carefully to the youth's reasons. The priest was surprised. Hogan struck him as ambitious for what the world at large offered, and he knew how popular he was with girls. These sentiments about helping people were ones he hadn't heard from him before. He felt an uneasiness.

"Also, I admire you a great deal, Father McBride, and hope that I can become like you. You helped me at a time I really needed it, and I know you help a lot of other boys as well."

McBride flushed with pleasure. "You don't think that you might be momentarily deceiving yourself as a result of being overwhelmed by *Father* Berrigan?" he asked.

"No," Hogan replied, gazing directly at McBride with his haunting eyes.

McBride's doubts dissolved. The boy sounded so sincere. Well, he thought, the seminary was the place to test his dedication.

Hogan chose Gethsemane, a Vincentian seminary, because his parish priests were Vincentians and he liked their flexibility of being able to do both domestic as well as foreign mission work, which diocesan priests did not have.

When he revealed his plans to his father, he steeled himself. Sean never had any use for the Church, believing one of Ireland's problems was that his native land was priest ridden, that the clergy perpetuated the people's troubles by telling them to roll over and play dead; their reward for a miserable life was in the afterlife.

"Goddamn brainwashing in Catholic schools," Sean Hogan roared upon hearing of his son's vocation.

Pat tried to explain how he felt singled out, special. His choice had nothing to do with proselytizing for priests in the classroom. Nor had he gone to the weekend retreats organized by the legions of good-looking recruiters from religious orders around the country who swept through Catholic parishes and high schools in the 1960s, extolling the advantages of a vocation with the zealotry of Green Berets. But his father refused to listen.

Coming out of his reverie, Hogan glanced around the Four Seasons. Sometimes the years since the seminary seemed to have passed in a flash. What happened to that youthful idealism? Looking back, he felt a familiar burning shame. He knew what it was. After his ordination, he didn't have the stomach or the heart for it. There were times such as now when he thought of his cowardice, his lack of moral honesty, the sham of a life he lived. Mostly, he avoided introspection. The path he followed had made that relatively easy. The fame, the glamour, the power. How easy it was almost to forget what troubled him the most. He took a deep pull on his drink. Maybe he'd always kidded himself about wanting to help anybody but Pat Hogan.

Inflamed now with the old disappointment in himself, his anger exploded again. "What do they expect to find out about me that they don't already know, Kevin?" he demanded bitterly.

Without answering, Kelly nursed his drink while Hogan ranted awhile longer. He couldn't help thinking, what did anybody know about Cardinal Carruthers before somebody blew the whistle? Finally, Hogan called for the check.

"Sorry, but I have to leave, Kevin. I promised to drop by a party Cal Robbins is throwing."

"No problem."

Hogan looked at Kelly. "Why not come along? You should get a glimpse of some of the worlds I live in."

Kelly's instincts told him not to accept, but he saw that Hogan was serious. Feeling as if he owed the man, he nodded okay. "If anybody asks, just say I'm an old classmate and leave it at that."

When Hogan made a grab for the check, Kelly put his hand over it first. He tried to bring some levity back to the evening.

"Pat, it's on Clarizio. Or maybe even the pope. Neither of us feel great about this. The least they can do is pick up the tab."

4

WHILE THE TWO PRIESTS GRAPPLED FOR THE CHECK AT THE FOUR SEA-
sons, a strong night wind propelled father damian carter as he hurried
toward Rome's Via dei Fori Imperiali, the broad boulevard separating
him from the Colosseum. He thought again of the caller who had
brought him out tonight. Tense and secretive, the bishop had named
the Roman ruin as the meeting ground.

"Alone! Be alone!" he insisted.

The stocky Carter rocked from side to side when walking, as if
he had spent his life on ships. A black raincoat covered his cassock.
A navy beret was jammed over his long, curly hair. Caught in a brief
downpour only minutes ago, he was damp, chilled, and tired.

Carter was accustomed to strange calls in the middle of the night,
but his antennae told him that something was out of kilter. Was he
wise to have come? Should he go back? Not many people knew he
was in Rome for the Antiapartheid Conference. How did the caller?

Even though one of the conference organizers, he almost hadn't
been able to attend for lack of airfare. At the last minute, a wealthy

Italian socialist friend ho learned of his plight booked his passage and paid for a hotel.

As the Colosseum loomed in fronted of him, Carter brushed aside trepidations. As always, curiosity overcame caution. Even so, he wasn't heedless. Pausing before crossing the boulevard glistening in the new-fallen rain, Carter slipped warily into a darkened doorway. Despite the cold, he was covered with sweat from hurrying and nervousness. He listened for footsteps and searched vainly for cars that would slowly drive by, eyes searching shadows, perhaps looking for him.

At this time of night there was little traffic. Suddenly, a police car tore by, its whining siren menacing anyone who had anything to fear. Scanning the intersection carefully once more, Carter forced himself to maintain a leisurely pace as he crossed, conscious of the had leather heels of his shoes clicking eerily like a metronome on an empty stage. I must get rubber heels, he thought, and laughed silently at the mundane consideration at such a time.

The Colosseum rose before him like a huge, broken crown. The meeting point of the Palatine, Caelian, and Oppian hills, the four-story oval struck Carter as being much like his Church. An ancient ruin that was barely still standing.

The hopes that he once cherished for the Church were crushed over the years. In his youth, he had embraced the heady changes that happened so rapidly. The move toward social justice for everyone in the world was very apparent to him during his stay in Puerto Rico right after his ordination. When he went to New York as an assistant pastor, he had felt that at any moment the Church was going to flower into God's true instrument for transforming the planet. The nations of Central America, South America, the Caribbean, Africa, Asia, would take their place in the world alongside the Western countries, not subservient but equal. Priests and nuns would elevate the people, show them how to get what they needed, help them overthrow their dictators and lead them to God at the same time.

Bitterly, he remembered the encounter he had had years ago with Cardinal McCormick when the prelate banished him from New York, the moment when he realized he had to participate actively in the Liberation Theology movement sweeping the third world. The cardinal summoned him to the chancery and told him to stop politically organizing the Puerto Ricans who were his parishioners.

"The Church's job is these people's spiritual welfare, not their politics," McCormick told him.

54

Carter had expected the crackdown. McCormick had long been suspicious of what he was doing, thinking it smacked of communism. "But one of the reasons these people are so poor is because the Church supported the rich oligarchies that kept them down for so long," Carter replied.

"Don't argue with me, Father," McCormick said icily. "The Church does not engage in politics."

Carter almost laughed out loud. Hypocrite, he thought. McCormick's priests lobbied congressmen, the state legislature, and the city council for and against bills. The cardinal himself indirectly endorsed political candidates by condemning their opponents' positions on birth control or abortion. McCormick had publicly backed Lyndon Johnson's Vietnam War efforts and had himself photographed with foreign dictators during his frequent trips to foreign lands. At least, Carter thought at the time, the McCormicks in the Church were anachronisms, a dying breed.

Before meeting the cardinal, carter contacted a classmate who was working in Nicaragua with a group of rebels who intended to overthrow the repressive Somoza regime. The priest had repeatedly asked him to come down and help the cause. Carter finally accepted the offer. "No, Your Eminence, I'm sorry, but I cannot willingly abandon the work I have started," he replied, aware how McCormick would react to what he said.

"For your insolence and the harm you have already caused, you are banished from New York," McCormick said.

Sitting in the Colosseum, Carter thought how shortsighted he had been in expecting the McCormicks to dry up and blow away. Now, the Church was changing once again. Retrenchment. Reversing the policies that were intended to remake societies. The pope talked of the gross inequities of wealth and of pulling the have-not countries into the present. Yet, the pope penalized the priests and nuns who chose that as their mission. The Church, he believed, was abandoning the poor and the needy.

On previous visits to Rome, Carter had met other night callers here. The Flavian amphitheater was popular among radical political groups. The Colosseum's accessibility, ease of keeping under surveillance, and its many hidden recesses combined to make it an attractive meeting ground for people who dealt in secrecy. Most of all, there was the romanticism. The scene of brutal contests between gladiators lent an aura of high drama to "the struggle" in which he and those like him were engaged. The romanticism provided a welcome relief from much of the tedium that was their day-to-day reality.

The night was cloudy and the moon strained futilely to light the sky. The cool wind whispered of more rain to come. From the arena's main gate, Carter stole swiftly northward, passing thirteen looming black archways, before ducking into the fourteenth and being swallowed up in darkness. Moving stealthily, he slid his hands and feet along the cold ruins as he crept along the first level of the ancient arena, the tier where patricians long ago were amused by macabre games. He silently charted northward, once again passing thirteen arches.

At the precise location where he had been asked to come, Carter sat. The air seemed colder here. He shivered inside his raincoat. There was always the waiting. The waiting and the paranoia. Few people could sit still, wondering if they were being hunted. Over the years, Carter had trained himself to be vigilant and still.

The time-rotted walls of the oval were barely visible against the dark sky. Rome seemed very far away. Night noises scratched the quiet. Unseen animals scurried about. The wind breathed through cracks, moaning lowly. From his stone seat, Carter imagined himself inside a volcano and smiled at such childish nonsense.

He blew on his fingers, much the way he had done as a boy when he went riding to hounds and bitter cold claimed his hands and feet. Thinking of his boyhood in Connecticut, he was detached, as though contemplating someone else's life, that of a stranger.

He smiled wryly at what his parents would think if they could see him at this moment. Probably have a heart attack. This was such a far cry from his running the family business, which was their expectation when he was growing up. His great-grandfather William Carter had opened paper mills throughout New England. Damian's grandfather enlarged the family fortune by buying tobacco farms in Georgia and South Carolina. Thirty years ago, the business was turned over to Damian's father, who increased the holdings by investing in plastic packaging.

Vividly, Damian remembered approaching his parents to tell them he wanted to enter a seminary. It was a snowy night and he asked them to meet him in the library of their huge Tudor manor in Greenwich. They both happened to be home that Thanksgiving, which was a rarity. His harried father, who Damian was convinced felt inadequate to be running the company, was usually shuttling between business operations around the country. His blond mother spent much of her time in Europe and the Caribbean, engaged in not-very-discreet liaisons.

To date, he had done pretty much as they wanted. He attended Exeter and was now in his freshman year at Princeton. While at prep school, he had deliberately indulged in every vice imaginable in hopes of finding some insight into life. All he had managed to do was feel empty. Then he read Thomas Merton and felt a sense of relief. Having similarly experimented senselessly before becoming a Trappist monk, Merton wrote that there was much more to life than a feeling of hollowness.

Carter's family was nominally Catholic. Suddenly, inspired by Merton's selflessness, he became intensely religious but avoided Catholicism, fearing it was too hierarchical. On weekends, he worked in soup kitchens in Trenton where he was exposed to men and women who were part of Dorothy Day's pacifist Catholic Worker Movement, which for thirty years focused on societal problems such as racism and poverty. Many of the young men he met were conscientious objectors who dedicated their lives to helping others.

In New York with friends one weekend, he visited Emmaus House, a self-described "experiment in Christian living" and "center for radical social change" in East Harlem. There was a cheerful shabbiness about the brownstone. Photos of Pope John, Gandhi, Malcolm X, Martin Luther King, Dorothy Day, and Daniel Berrigan covered the walls. The ballads of Joan Baez filled the air.

"Put this on the bulletin board," a girl said to Damian as soon as he entered.

He looked at the leaflet she shoved in his hand. It stated, "Send a Christmas Card to Jail," encouraging people to write to conscientious objectors serving time. Glancing about, he saw a bulletin board and pinned the leaflet next to a list of names of COs and where they were imprisoned.

The people at Emmaus House were mostly young and vital and dedicated to being the Church's loyal opposition. Masses were celebrated by bearded young priests wearing blue jeans and sweaters. Guitars were played during the ceremony, and readings during the service were as varied as excerpts from Henry Miller's *Tropic of Capricorn* to Dylan Thomas's poetry.

Damian found himself heading to Emmaus House most weekends, involving himself with discussions on the war and the right of protest within the Church. He constantly probed priests about why they stayed in the Church when so many priests were leaving. "I might not like much what she's become, but she's my mother," a priest answered simply. "Why don't you give the life a try?"

Though the question was half in jest, Damian considered it seriously. He admitted he was drawn to the self-sacrificing nature of the priesthood, and he desperately wanted his life to mean something. He decided to try a seminary. One of the priests at Emmaus House suggested Gethsemane. The priest, a Vincentian, stressed his order's not just identifying social problems but seeking solutions for them as well.

On the day he was to tell his parents he believed he had a vocation, Damian stood in the library in the awkward silence in which he and his father found themselves when alone together. His mother rushed in, looking at her watch.

"Now, Damian, what's this little meeting all about?" she demanded.

"I want to become a priest," he told them.

"Be serious," Louise said, groaning.

"I think he is," his father said.

"Good Lord, what brought this on?" his mother asked accusingly, as if he were being spiteful and trying to embarrass her.

"We Carters have managed not just to exploit workers in our mills but promote cancer with a product that's killing the whole planet," Carter deadpanned. "I decided to stay out of the family business for the sake of humanity. With a track record like the Carters, Lord knows what terrible things I would have taken the company into."

"Damian," his father said sharply. "Don't be flippant. Now what's this all about?"

"I want to follow in the footsteps of St. Francis," he told them.

His mother stormed out without speaking. His father tried to convince him to see a psychiatrist.

Remembering how he renounced his parents' wealth and set off to the seminary in search of God after his freshman year at Princeton, Carter laughed mirthlessly. How naive he had been, expecting to find

God in stone churches with stained-glass windows. In that sense, his parents had been right when they objected to his wanting to be a priest.

"My Church doesn't have walls or the usual cast of saints and sinners," he often told friends and acquaintances for more years now than he liked.

Peering around the arena, he wondered how, in the same pursuit, he had evolved into a night creature helping people others feared. He thought about the priestly vows he had broken, the shattered ideals, how he believed the Church had to be dramatically changed if She were to be redeemed. "If I am to be redeemed," he muttered as he shifted a bit on the cold stone. The incongruity of life was something he readily understood and accepted. In his wildest imagination, however, he had never expected to be summoned here or anywhere by the bishop who had called.

Behind him, a shoe scraped rock. The waiting was over. He stared in the direction of the sound but saw no one for a moment. Then a man came near. He too was dressed all in black; the shadows hid his face. Carter had never met him, but he had recognized his name immediately. One of the Vatican strongmen. The questions Carter had asked himself right after the man phoned still buzzed in his mind. Why does he want to meet me? A priest who criticizes what the man stands for, the Church's social failings, its vast financial holdings, its conservatism? Why here? Why now? The answer, Carter concluded, was that the bishop thought he had found some way to stop him.

"You must forgive me, but I never expected such an honor," Carter said sarcastically.

"Nor I," the other replied.

As he stood, Carter said, "I don't think you are here to expurgate my treatises on how much the Church has to learn from socialism and Christian humility."

The bishop exhaled in exasperation. He had expected this priest to be trying. He didn't have much time, so he decided to be direct. "No, but I have information that in the end will probably advance your cause."

Carter became warier, wondering what sort of game he was playing. "What is it?"

"You will know soon enough. But there are two conditions that I must insist upon."

Carter was confused. He discerned notes of desperation and fear

59

in what the bishop said, not the arrogance he expected. "What are they?" Carter asked suspiciously.

"You must never reveal where this originated."

Tensely, Carter leaned forward, as if getting a little closer to the prelate would give him some understanding of what he meant. He had always assumed the bishop ardently opposed what he himself represented. The assumption was based on the bishop's wealth, prestige, and power.

"Why give me a bombshell?"

"You might help avert a catastrophe in the Church."

"What's the other condition?"

"You publicize this material when I tell you the time is right. Not before."

The force behind the man's words impressed Carter. Again that strong note of fear clanged like a warning bell, but there was dignity in the way the prelate spoke as well. Carter's mind worked feverishly, trying to imagine what was so valuable that the bishop would possibly endanger himself by placing it the hands of someone who was ostensibly an enemy.

"What if something happens to you?"

"You may then do as you believe is right."

"Agreed."

"Here," the man said, thrusting out a shadowy hand that found Carter's.

From the feel of the metal and the size of the canister, Carter realized the object was film. He immediately began searching his mind. Who could develop it at this time of night?

"Please! Please! Keep your word."

"I will," Carter said.

"Be extremely careful. If . . ." The bishop didn't finish the thought. He turned abruptly. "There is nothing more for us to say to one another. Don't contact me. I will not acknowledge you if you do. Please give me five minutes before you leave too."

Carter peered into the darkness, still unable to see the man's face clearly. From the touch of his hand, he knew that the prelate wore gloves. There would be no fingerprints on the canister, and there would be no other way of having it traced back.

"If what you have given me is that valuable, thank you for trusting me."

"I rarely like what you say or write, but I believe your are as

60

concerned in your way about the Church as I am in mine." The prelate sighed. "There are times I even think that the path you want the Church to lead is the right one. Good night."

Suddenly, there was a break in the clouds and moonlight momentarily bathed his face. Bishop Eugenio Falconi was as pale as a ghost. He managed a small smile as he nodded before walking away.

Carter sat again and pocketed the film. Unable to see the dial of his watch in the dark, he had to estimate the time. Squirming in his seat, excitement and skepticism dueled for his attention. Doubt won out. The man was not to be trusted. Most likely the film contained disinformation that Falconi hoped Carter would leak to the press in order to discredit the cause when it turned out to be false. Why the power play? Where did this fit into the Vatican game?

"Is he someone's pawn?" he muttered. "Am I?"

Breaking from his preoccupation, he listened intently. It started again. He heard the soft sound of someone running on padded feet. Carter froze. Quietly, he called out, "Who's there?"

Silence greeted him. Then, once again, he picked up the faint padding, which was getting closer. Was it from his left or right? "Who is there?" he whispered hoarsely.

Warily, Carter turned 360 degrees. In the dark, no one was visible. No one answered. The footsteps drew nearer. A stone skittered about fifteen yards away. Carter felt chilled as sweat suddenly covered his body. His heart pounding, he dared not call again. Think clearly, he ordered himself.

Crouching, he backed to fencing barring entrance to the arena itself and climbed over. Edging backward, he lowered himself over the wall. He hung to drop into the arena. At the last moment his hands slipped and he fell, cracking his left knee on the ground. He let out a soft groan. The footsteps padded toward him. Carter looked up. A huge black figure was barely silhouetted against the dark gray sky like an avenging angel.

Getting up, Carter paused to get his bearings. In front of him were the lanes that were all that remained of the field once bloodied and littered with limbs and entrails of martyrs and gladiators. The hidden tunnels were once used to bring lions into the arena; others were footways for gladiators. Together with the aqueducts they were all exposed to the night like the core of a decayed molar.

Carter almost stumbled as he precariously bolted down a path. Since his legs were broken by South African police when he was

61

arrested in an antiapartheid demonstration five years ago, he had difficulty running. The heels of his shoes sounded to him like brass knockers pounding on a door. He thought of taking off his shoes, but was afraid to stop. Suddenly, he tripped and sprawled over the rocks and stones. Pain seared his hands and face as they scraped the rubble. Getting up again, he hobbled forward.

The steady, rhythmic padding behind him drew closer and closer. As he ducked into a tunnel, Carter heard a laugh, a harsh sound like a clap of thunder that echoed throughout the darkness. His breath rasping and shivering with cold and fear, he picked up a rock and pressed against a wall.

Suddenly, an arm snaked around his face, covering his mouth and muffling his cry. He tried to jerk forward, but he was held fast as a noose was wrapped around his throat. Wildly smashing the rock over his head and toward his assailant's face, Carter heaved his body backward. He heard a scream as they both toppled over just as total blackness enveloped him.

When he came to a few minutes later, Carter coughed and gasped for air. Terror welled up again. Frantically, he looked around. His hysteria ebbed slightly as he realized he was alone. Only then did he tug at the noose wrapped around his neck. Later, beneath a streetlight, he saw what it was. A purple and gold stole, the long strip of embroidered silk that priests wear when giving the last rites to the dying.

Sitting at her vanity, Connie Robbins raised her voice so Cal could hear her through the open door joining her bedroom to her husband's. "Will anyone I like be there or are they all your boring business friends?"

Robbins came through the doorway snapping a gold cuff link and looked up. From fifteen feet away, Connie was still incredibly beautiful. A willowy, icy brunette, she appeared to be so self-possessed that she struck many people as unapproachable. Cal liked to think she had the look of breeding, attributing her high cheekbones and fine bone structure to the Huguenots on her mother's side, and her height and bearing to the Puritan stock on her father's side.

Cal still embarrassed his wife by managing to work her Mayflower lineage into the conversation when he wanted to impress someone. She found the practice dreadful, as if she were one of his racehorses with bloodstock from "Man o' War." His boasting reminded her of the way certain dreary little men mentioned within five minutes of your meeting them that they had gone to Harvard or Yale.

Connie would have been the most desirable debutante of 1970 if her family fortune hadn't been almost as dissipated as her father, who had more pedigree than bank balance. Her mother, humiliated by her ne'er-do-well husband, had raised Connie to esteem money and admire greatly men who made it in vast quantities. Connie had recognized his instinct for acquiring money as Cal Robbins's most charming trait when she first met him a dozen years ago, even though he was not yet fabulously wealthy.

"You'll know half the people there," he muttered absentmindedly as he examined his thinning brown hair, certain that less of it was there today than yesterday.

"That's not what I asked," she replied. "I said will there be anyone there I *like*."

"I guess so."

"How about Pat Hogan?"

"I invited him."

"Good."

"And Monsignor Beck?"

"Same thing. He was invited."

Connie smiled charmingly and was about to say something witty but decided not to. Cal might take offense. Her husband's professed sensibilities amused her. He made much of his generosity to Catholic charities, but was offended by nuns doing social work. He resented that the Mass was no longer said in Latin, but couldn't order from a menu in a French restaurant. Though he had the morals of an alley cat, he was one of those Catholics who thought priests were superhuman. She kept the juicy rumors concerning the monsignor and Roberta Lang to herself.

Out of habit, she checked the mirror again. Age was starting to be a trifle unkind to her. Her breasts were small but firm, but after decades of sunbathing, her skin was beginning to coarsen. When they had married, she was lithe and supple as a ballet dancer. Now, she wondered if she was too thin from too much dieting; her long neck was still elegant, but the clavicle was a bit knobby and stood out in high relief. Her gray eyes glittered from the diet pills, and at times she chattered nonstop, which her husband put down to the diet pills as well.

While adjusting the tie of his tuxedo, Robbins leaned over so that

63

both their heads were framed in the vanity mirror. He stretched his neck so that his double chin was less pronounced and refused to look at his hairline. The plaid cummerbund camouflaged much of his pudginess. He raised his chin a little higher. Not too bad though, he thought.

"Do you still want to go to the spa with me?"

His wife shattered his illusion and he resented her for it. He patted his double chin with the outside of his fingers as if that would make it disappear. "I guess I should," he said grimly.

Connie stood and raised the skirt of her mauve silk Adolfo to straighten her stockings, showing a bit of garter belt and smooth thigh. She always had good legs. In defiance of her mother's insistence upon "ladylike" behavior, Connie stopped wearing panties when she was sixteen, which, over the years, certain men were as shocked and delighted to find out as Cal had once been.

"Sorry to be such a pest," she said. "After all, I didn't even have to do anything for this party. The hotel staff did it all, so I guess buying the Waldorf wasn't a bad thing to do."

Robbins laughed. "We just show up by walking downstairs. Everybody should be here. Let's make our grand entrance, Mother."

Connie winced at the pet name. "One more thing, Cal."

She held out the emerald necklace he'd given her for her last birthday. As he draped it around her throat, she recalled how annoyed she was when he told one of the gossip columnists that he paid over a million dollars for the gift. Cartier's told her the price was only $487,000. Why did he have to put a price tag on everything? And a higher one? And why did he have to tell gossip columnists anything, always cheapening the moment?

Exaggeration was one of Cal's vulgar faults, a result, she supposed, of his insecurities. When she became really unhappy at something he did or said, she reminded herself that few men could afford to be as generous as Cal.

Five minutes later, they were circulating through the crowded ballroom of their Park Avenue penthouse. Connie preferred their small dinner parties for a dozen people, where her talents as a hostess were appreciated, but she had grown used to the extravaganzas that Cal increasingly insisted upon. It was a way he could see legions of powerful people as well as all the people who might one day be important to his business.

While she chatted with the wife of an investment banker, her

64

practiced eye swept the room, keeping tabs on the waiters, the bartenders, the people who needed help at socializing, what other women were wearing. The gathering was like so many others in New York, full of the crude vitality peculiar to the city. Just about everyone she saw was in the process of recreating themselves, dramatically altering their pasts and buying respectability for the present. She found it quite delightful. The offspring of Bronx tailors and Brooklyn dockworkers were intent on becoming country squires. The size of one's portfolio was the only pedigree that mattered.

Out of the corner of her eye, she saw Cal talking intently to a vivacious young blonde and her husband, who was something or other in state government. She had always found power a more potent aphrodisiac than money, but obviously the little wife was intoxicated by the reverse. Connie smiled. Conversation with Cal was less art than rustic craft. Yet, the young woman fiercely made Cal the focus of her attention, her eyes glittering as she hung on every banal word tumbling from his mouth.

Those perky cheerleader types were Cal's weakness, as she well knew. When the ignored husband went off to get a drink, Cal led the young woman out to the garden on the terrace. He delighted in showing these young lovelies the spectacular view of the city, promising them who knows what if they would go to bed with him. Connie supposed he felt like Satan tempting Christ with all He could see if He would only honor him.

As she made her rounds, Connie found herself in a conversation with a small cluster of Italians. Two were bankers and a third owned a major shoe-manufacturing company. The other two were clerics. She knew the businessmen as well as the bishop, who shuttled back and forth between Rome and New York on mysterious business with the regularity of a transatlantic pilot. She had never met the other clergyman, a monsignor whose English was the best of the lot and who had a glint of mischief in his eyes.

"Will you be returning to your villa in Rome for the investiture of the cardinals?" he asked.

He was small and in his midforties with sharp features, a lively face beneath dark, curly hair. He had introduced himself as Monsignor Vincenzo Ruggieri. The appraising look he gave her was distinctly worldly.

"Wouldn't miss it for anything," she said. "I'm waiting with bated breath for more cardinals."

65

"How we have managed to get by without them is amazing, isn't it?"

She laughed, appreciating his impudence and glad that he wasn't like so many of the Italian clergy who took themselves too damn seriously. Few people knew how to make her laugh, and she looked at him as if seeing him in a slightly different light. She knew the type, having met them occasionally in Rome. "Rogue priests," she called them. They attached themselves to wealthy women, often widows, with whom they managed to live like well-fed house cats while performing unmentioned services for their patronesses. Usually, Connie dismissed them as ciphers. Yet, she found herself intrigued by this handsome little man. He did not quite fit the mold. He had more self-assurance, and he was more amusing than most.

"You can get in trouble for saying things like that, even in jest," she said.

"I have a habit of getting into trouble," he said, giving her that mischievous look again.

"I'm sure you do."

"Perhaps we will meet again in Rome."

"Perhaps," she said.

Connie excused herself as Pat Hogan came in the front door. As she walked away, she was startled that she actually blushed slightly, feeling as though handsome little Monsignor Ruggieri could tell that beneath her dress she was nude from the tops of her stockings to her emeralds.

"Pat, dear, you look wonderful, and the show simply gets better and better," she said, proffering her right cheek to receive a light kiss.

"Thanks for asking me, Connie," Hogan said.

She put her arm around his waist familiarly.

"Connie is known for her engaging irreverence," Hogan said to Kelly as he carefully removed the hostess's arm, wishing she didn't also engage in public displays of affection. "On more than one occasion she has deflated the pomposity of certain high-ranking churchmen as well as celebrities. To my great relief, she doesn't show me off like a prized weimaraner, the way many hostesses do."

Connie gave him a bemused look. "Pat, without you this would have been simply dreadful. And whom have you brought us?"

"Connie, meet Kevin Kelly. He's here on a very important mission."

"Oh, oh. Sounds mysterious and juicy."

Hogan leaned toward her and said in a stage whisper. "Kevin has the awesome responsibility of determining whether I am fit material to go places in the Church."

"Stop joking this moment," she said, turning to Kelly. "Pat can be a terrible tease. Now to what do we owe this honor?"

Amazed that Hogan had told her the nature of his assignment, Kelly realized just how angry the monsignor was. Nonetheless, he resented being put on the spot like this and vented his indignation without thinking. "Pat's telling the truth, Mrs. Robbins. They want to make him a bishop, and he's ticked off because I'm doing a bit of a background check on him."

Hogan flushed as Connie looked at him with concern. "What's this all about? Everyone knows you are going to be a bishop. We just all wondered why it hasn't happened before this."

Turning back to Kelly, she looked at him oddly. "Why in the world would anybody want to check up on Pat? I could make your ears burn with some of the things I hear about some of the clergy, but not Pat."

"Terrific," Kelly said sourly. "If he needs a character witness, I'll put you on the stand."

Connie laughed. She found it amazing that two priests had made her do so within almost as many minutes if for very different reasons.

"I'm sure you would, Father Kelly, and I enjoy your frankness. Too many people, including the clergy, tiptoe around me because I'm a rich bitch."

Kelly looked at her appreciatively. "Then maybe you can get Pat to stop feeling sorry for himself."

"Look, I'm sorry I brought the whole thing up, Kevin," Hogan said. "It was a dumb thing to do, okay?"

"You're calling the shots here, Pat," Kelly said.

Connie put her hands on each man's arm. "Let's all have a drink and start over on a better footing. We don't want this to turn into a holy war."

"The first ones didn't do anybody much good," Hogan said.

"Perhaps they didn't go far enough," Connie said.

"What do you mean?" Kelly asked.

"What was it Jean Rostand said? 'Kill a man, and you are a murderer. Kill millions of men, and you are a conqueror. Kill everyone, and you are God.'"

Hogan gave Kelly a questioning look. He was never sure whether

Connie's irreverence came from a lack of belief or was a cynical pose, hiding how much she believed.

Kelly, however, smiled, recognizing her attempt to shock them as a ploy to bond him and Hogan together against her blasphemy. "That's one test for the existence of God none of us needs," he said.

Connie smiled. "Touché, Father Kelly."

With the priests no longer sniping at one another, she moved off to a knot of people nearby. She couldn't blame Pat for being upset. From her knowledge of Church politics, she knew it was very odd that this priest should go snooping around about him. Very odd.

Accepting a drink from a waiter, Kelly moved to the edge of the gathering, while Hogan circulated easily through the crowd, accepting attention as his due. Most guests seemed to know the TV priest. People who didn't pointed to him or edged nearer until they introduced themselves. Kelly couldn't help thinking that being constantly on display was a hell of a life. He often wondered for just that reason why anyone would want to be pope.

Seeing Hogan in this milieu didn't really surprise him. Hogan had always been adaptable, moving easily among social classes. When they were seminarians, he remembered, the Trinity were involved with a lot of pacifist groups and radical social-welfare organizations. Of the three, only Carter had the passion necessary for total commitment. Witten was too introspective, forever weighing the moral consequences of not just his own actions but those of any organization with which he was affiliated.

Hogan was too ambitious, Kelly remembered, to be a full-fledged radical. He put his self-interest above his politics, realistically accepting foibles in people that both Carter and Witten tended to see more harshly as character deficiencies. He remembered how, on one occasion, a well-known conservative was scheduled to visit the seminary. The man was widely known for his hawkish views and tightfistedness when it came to social programs. A delegation of seminarians chose Hogan as their champion to tell the man the wrongness of his ways. After an hour together behind closed doors, the industrialist and Hogan emerged smiling and chatting amiably. The man wound up giving a large donation to the seminary.

"How could you stand to butter the guy up like that?" Carter disgustedly asked Hogan.

"He's not bad once you get to know him," Hogan had said with a slight laugh. "Besides, Gethsemane needs his money."

68

If Kelly remembered correctly, the man put in a good word about Hogan with Cardinal McCormick, which later bore fruit when the cardinal actually spoke on the seminarian's behalf when Hogan was up for the plum Vatican Radio assignment when he was ordained.

Suddenly, Kelly became conscious that wherever Connie Robbins went a man or a woman would glance at him with a perplexed expression. He realized she was telling everyone who he was and what he was doing with Hogan. Wryly, he congratulated himself for taking Hogan up on the offer to come along. He checked his watch, deciding to give the party another few minutes before ducking out. Besides the awkwardness he felt over the Hogan business, he always found functions such as this about as pleasant as a hangnail.

His concentration was broken by a familiar husky voice. "You look about as bored as I am."

Turning to his right, Kelly found himself staring into Lane Woods's hazel eyes. He hadn't realized how tall she was. She stood a good five ten and in spiked heels she was over six feet, or about two inches shorter than Kelly.

"It shows that much?"

"Uh-huh. What are you doing here?"

"Pat Hogan shanghaied me. What's your excuse?"

"I'm always keyed up after the program and I don't like going home right away."

Her reply reminded him a little of what the singer Marty Coltrain had said on Pat's program last week about why people get in trouble on the road.

"Why not curl up with a good book?"

"Sometimes I get on to a story at these things. Cal and Connie get a lot of the power crowd out. A lot of them know intriguing stories, and sometimes they want them publicized. When that happens, I suddenly become their favorite person."

"Do I detect a note of petulance over being used?"

"My, my, aren't we candid tonight." She shot him a rueful smile. "But you're right. Perhaps a little petulance goes with the territory. Using people and being used. Sounds nice, doesn't it?"

Kelly shook his head. "Not the life for me."

"What about Pat Hogan?"

"He seems suited for what he does."

"Are you?" she asked, looking at him directly for the first time.

"On good days."

69

She laughed. "At least you're honest."

Thoughtfully, she swirled the drink in her hand and then looked at Kelly again. "Is the rumor about you buzzing around the room true?"

"About my being pope? Pure hearsay."

She didn't crack a smile. "About Hogan being up for a big job and you doing some background investigation of him."

"I have to do a little probing. That's all."

She frowned and her gaze wandered over the crowd again. "When you have some free time, I'd like to tell you about Monsignor Hogan, something that perhaps no one else will tell you."

Her voice was laced with anger and sexual innuendo. The combination made Kelly's stomach muscles tighten. Damn, he muttered to himself. This was exactly the kind of crap he was afraid of. The gossipmongers' parade. Gloomily, he figured he might as well hear whatever was bugging her and get it over with as quickly as possible. Noticing again how beautiful she was, he hoped it wasn't what it sounded like.

"How about tomorrow?"

She took a final pull on her glass and set it down on a tray as a waiter walked by. Taking a pen and notepad from her purse, she jotted something down and handed it to Kelly "Okay. About an hour after the late news show. This is my address. Now, I'm getting out of here."

Without looking back, she made her way across the room to Connie Robbins to say good-night. Kelly admired her deftness as he prepared to head out as well. She graciously took her leave of at least thirty people and was out the door while he was still trying to find Hogan to tell him he was going.

His search was broken off by the voice of someone else he had met briefly and only this evening.

"We meet again, Father."

Kelly nodded. "How are you, Mr. Edwards?"

"Actually not so well," Edwards said, a tight smile on his thin lips. "Look around and tell me what you see. Go ahead."

To humor him, Kelly glanced around the room and then turned back to the tycoon. For some reason, an overwhelming dislike for this man came over him. He wasn't sure why. Maybe it was Edwards's prissy little mouth.

"I see a room full of people, many apparently having a pretty good time."

70

"Well, I see a bunch of people who, with few exceptions, are letting the world go to hell. All this drug business, AIDS, women having abortions right and left. People without the self-control to practice natural birth control. Let me tell you, Father, it makes me ill. Then we have these weak presidents who won't stand up for America anymore, let the Japs or anybody else with half a brain and two cents in the pockets take business from us."

Kelly wondered what he had done to get cornered with the man. Edwards was a walking headache.

"There are plenty of people in the Church who are just as bad," the tycoon continued. "Have been ever since Pope John XXIII. Liberals who don't have any idea of what morality means anymore. John XXIII almost wrecked the Church. Catholics were little more than Protestants and Jews when he was pope. And this pope's not much better. We've got to get back on track."

Kelly wished someone would put Edwards back in his cage. He wondered what went haywire in guys such as him. John XXIII had not only been a breath of fresh air in the Church but probably the only pope since Peter who'd ever truly been a saint. But what good would it do to argue with a maniac? Instead, he remained quiet, letting Edwards rant on a bit longer, hoping that the man would soon race after somebody more important. With relief, he heard Edwards bid good-bye a minute later.

"Well, it's been good talking to you, Father Kelly," Edwards said. He dropped his voice several octaves. "We should have lunch one of these days. There are a few things about Monsignor Hogan that you will want to know. I'll call you and we can set up something."

Kelly winced, wondering if Edwards was going to tell him Hogan was a pinko because his father had been in a union. Then he remembered that Edwards was a bosom buddy of Archbishop Murray. The rumor mill had Murray being down on Hogan. Maybe the archbishop was using Edwards to convey some dirt about Pat.

"I'm at Saint Mary's. I'll expect your call," he replied perfunctorily.

"Good boy," Edwards said. He was about to pat Kelly's arm, but looked up at the priest's face and thought better of it.

Glancing around, Kelly finally saw Hogan regaling a group of men and women about twenty feet away. He made his way through the crowd until he caught Hogan's eye and gave him a little wave. Hogan excused himself and came over.

"Pat, I didn't mean to break that up. It's just that I've got to be going."

"Okay, Kevin. I just want to say again I'm sorry about earlier. I shouldn't have done that. I hope it didn't embarrass you that Connie spread the word that you were the Church's KGB. I asked her to stop when I found out what she was doing."

"Don't worry about it."

"Anything you need or want me to explain, please don't hesitate to get hold of me." Hogan gave him a guarded look. "Some people color events and situations with . . . well, you know what I mean."

Kelly didn't, but he saw a flicker of worry in those famous green eyes. For the first time tonight, he thought that maybe Hogan had something serious to hide.

At a phone booth a five-minute half-run, half-walk from the Colosseum, Damian Carter fingered his worn address book. His hands were shaking so badly he dropped the book. When he picked it up, he could barely see what he was doing. His fingers fumbled. Pages stuck together.

"Damn!" he muttered. Hurriedly, he rubbed his blurry eyes. He wondered whether it was the poor light or fear or whether his eyes were going as middle age made another claim on his body. At last he came to S and found the name Carla Sarfina.

She was a free-lance photographer, one of the violence junkies who were of all nationalities and poured into international hot spots, such as Beirut, El Salvador, Panama, Nicaragua, and South Africa. Her name and phone number had been in his address book since he met her in Nicaragua three years ago. She had a darkroom in her apartment.

Tentatively, he dialed the number. Shrill rings burst from the earpiece so that he momentarily pulled the receiver away from his head. All the while, he kept fearfully turning and looking up and down the street.

A woman's sleepy voice finally answered. "Who is calling?" she asked warily.

"*Pace e fraternità*," he whispered. Peace and brotherhood.

Suddenly, she sounded awake. "Identify yourself."

"Romero," Carter said, using the name of the archbishop of El

Salvador whose murder by right-wing death squads made him a martyr to the Church's political left.

"The phone is safe," she said. "Go on."

"It's . . . it's Damian. I would like to see you. To . . . to make use of your darkroom."

"When?" She sounded startled.

"Tonight. Right now if possible. It is very important!"

Her silence telegraphed her reluctance. Sitting up in bed, Carla pushed her long, chestnut hair from her eyes. Actually she was glad to be awakened, but she was troubled by the caller. She had had the dream again, the one in which she was tortured with electrodes the way Sandra Segovia, the labor organizer in Chile, had been. God, would she ever forget the harrowing look on the woman's face? Ever forget her shrieks? The police forced her to watch as a warning after some of her candid pictures about their brutal activities appeared in the international edition of *Newsweek*. She left Santiago the next morning, but could not shake the horror. That was a month ago.

Since then the radicals in her own country seemed anemic. How serious were they? Their counterparts in underdeveloped lands fought for their beliefs, suffered for them, died for them. How serious was she herself? So much in Italy was posturing. The left dramatized too much. Everything hung in the balance. Life or death, the fate of the world, the fate of the Church. Now, here was Damian in the game again.

Why had he called? What was it this time?

About to hang up, she hesitated. There was always the outside chance he was telling the truth. That he had something truly important. That he wasn't trying to pick up where they'd left off.

Through his fear, Carter had an inkling of how she must feel, getting a call in the middle of the night after all this time. What was it, two years?

He too was acutely aware of how they'd parted the last time. Maybe she thought his request was simply a ruse to see her. He wanted to say something to convince her of his sincerity but could think of nothing. He forced his eyes from frantically searching the street to glance at his watch: four-thirty A.M. Getting a call from him at this time of night, it was a wonder she didn't slam down the phone.

"All right," she finally said. "Are you alone?"

"Yes." The word sounded like a sigh as he exhaled, not realizing how tense he was.

"I have a new apartment," she said, swiftly giving him the address. "Where are you?"

"Near the Colosseum. How long will it take me to get there?"

"A twenty-minute cab ride."

Five minutes later, Carter was in the back of a cab, grateful that the vehicle had appeared from nowhere. He looked out the rear window. They weren't followed.

When he stopped his taxi, the big, gregarious driver saw how frightened the priest was. The scraped face. The trembling. How he bunched himself together in his arms when he took the backseat. What had happened? A robbery? A beating? A fight with a whore? He was tempted to pull away without the fare. He didn't need trouble. But the night was slow.

"What's the matter, Father? You get jumped?"

Carter breathed deeply. "In a way, yes."

"These damn gypsies get worse every day. Where can I take you?"

When Carter gave him the address, the driver turned and rolled his eyes. "They don't respect the cloth around there, Father."

The cabby began chuckling but caught himself. The priest had already run into somebody tonight who didn't think much of the clergy. "We'll go by Via . . ." he said as he started telling the route he would take.

Carter barely listened. The last thing he cared about was the kind of neighborhood the photographer lived in or how the hell they would get there. He hugged his raincoat around him. His heart still pounding, he forced himself to look behind them repeatedly to make sure that the cab wasn't followed. Over and over he asked himself, who sent an assassin? Who sent an assassin? Then he asked, why me?

Suddenly, he became conscious of the canister clenched in his fist and knew.

The information must be as valuable as the prelate suggested. Still, he probed at suspicion like a tongue returning over and over to a sore tooth. Suppose it was all an elaborate charade to discredit him? Suppose the assault was part of a setup so that he would believe unconditionally what appeared on the film?

With no traffic around, the taxi sped through the twisting rain-slick streets. Fifteen minutes later, the driver announced almost proudly, "This is one tough neighborhood."

The cab pulled to a stop on a street without any lights. "Watch yourself around here," the driver said. "If you want me to wait, I will."

Carter hurriedly paid him. "No thanks. I'll be a while. Where's a likely place to get a cab going back?"

"Not around here. Nobody in his right mind comes here looking for fares. Walk four blocks north and hope you see someone rolling back to better parts of the city."

In the dark, Carter had trouble finding the doorway marked No. 49. The wooden door of the aged building was ajar, the locks broken. He merely touched the door and it swung open all the way, unleashing the stench of old cooking odors, mildew, and age. The stairwell was darker than the street. Slowly, Carter climbed a narrow flight of wooden stairs, each step creaking as he put his weight on it. He stopped and listened after each step. At the second floor, he turned down a narrow, unlit corridor, moving as quietly as he could.

Suddenly, he froze, his heart pounding fiercely. Above him came an almost imperceptible squeak in the floorboards as if someone heavy shifted his weight. Cold, oily sweat covered his back as he thought again of the black figure silhouetted against the sky. The booming laughter still echoed in his head. Unconsciously, his hand edged to his neck where the noose had twisted. His breath came in gasps. His legs wouldn't move. He could go no higher.

There was the faint jiggle of a key in a lock, and a door opened as someone entered one of the apartments. Carter collapsed against the wall in relief and wiped the sweat from his forehead. An act of will forced him to climb the steps again.

As he continued up the next three flights, the stairwell narrowed with each level, making him feel more vulnerable, easy prey to anyone in the black shadows. Finally, he was at the top and once again mopped the sweat beaded on his face. Moonlight came through a small, grimy window and illuminated the landing. Two doorways were on the fifth-floor landing. The name on the first was Caeserelli. None was on the second.

When he rapped on the nameless apartment door, the woman's voice asked quietly, "Who is there?" She must have been listening to his footsteps.

"*Pace e fraternità*," Carter replied.

Three locks were undone. A silver of a woman's face appeared as the door opened a crack. She acknowledged Carter's presence with a suspicious look. "Still alone?"

"Yes."

A chain lock was hastily removed and the door swung open. "Thanks, Carla," he said, ducking inside.

She bolted the door again, carefully securing each lock, thinking how, whenever she left Rome for an assignment lasting a few weeks or a few months, she expected the apartment to be broken into.

"I had no trouble finding the place. . . ."

Alarmed, she stared at him. He tried to sound as if nothing were wrong. Yet, his face was swollen and scraped. His complexion was stark white, making the droplets of blood in the facial cuts appear brilliant. He stank of fear and trembled like a trapped rabbit. What was the matter?

The answer came to her. The police were after him! God, she wondered, what have I done? Why did I say he could come? Closing her eyes, she leaned back against the wall, knowing she had made a terrible mistake. He had led others here. The Red Squad had followed him since he came to the city. In a moment, they would crash through the front door. He must go. Now!

Fatalistically, she opened her eyes, realizing it was too late. Whatever was going to happen would happen. Maybe she'd be lucky. To date, luck ran with her, but she knew that was all it was. Chile taught her that. One day the knock on the door would come. Tonight. Another night. It would come.

Carter averted his eyes from her accusing look and struggled to pull himself together. He too suddenly realized the danger in which he had placed her. He remembered being told about the police assault on the family he had stayed with in Soweto two days after he left. One of his failings was that in his efforts to save humanity he was capable of harming the people around him.

"Forgive me. I shouldn't have come. I am sorry to awaken you, but as I said over the phone, what I have may be vital. I . . . I didn't want to wait."

Dejected, he turned to leave but was unable to move. The terror hadn't left him. He started shaking again. He was light-headed and afraid his legs might buckle any second. The woman took him by the shoulders and led him to a chair.

"Sorry," he muttered, holding his arms tightly across his chest as an icy chill seized him.

She went to a cabinet and brought back a bottle of cognac and a glass. The glass was a third full when she handed it to him. "Obviously, something terrible has happened to you."

"*Grazie*," he said, taking a large swallow and then another. Immediately, he started coughing as the warm alcohol rushed through him, displacing the ice that had filled the marrow of his bones. He trembled so violently he almost dropped the glass.

Compassionately, Carla knelt and grabbed the glass before it fell. She gently took his shaking hand and guided the glass to his mouth. He gulped the rest and started coughing again, but the heat in the room and the fire in the cognac began bringing him back to life.

As his eyes focused on her for the first time since entering, Carter realized once again what a handsome woman she was. Her strong, intelligent face was surrounded by her only vanity, a mane of luxuriant chestnut hair that tumbled around her shoulders. Her lips were full and sensual, her cheekbones prominent. Wide, expressive eyes contained a scratch of fear like a hairline crack in a diamond. Remorse swept over him for having put it there.

When she stood, she was nearly his height and full figured. She wore a man's old paisley silk bathrobe with a sash knotted at the waist.

The living room in which he found himself was small. Newspapers, books, and photo prints were scattered about. A doorway to the right revealed a tiny kitchen. Another doorway led to a small bedroom. Off the bedroom was a smaller room that served as a darkroom. Being on the top floor, the apartment was extremely warm, but no windows were open. The shades were raised, revealing a row of dark apartment windows across the street.

"Well," she said with a note of exasperation. "Are you going to tell me what happened?"

He nodded and debated momentarily about what to say, finally deciding to tell her the truth. "I'm in danger because of what I have brought here tonight. I . . . I don't think you are in any danger. I double-checked to make sure I wasn't followed. No one was on the street when I came into the building."

Relief in the form of hope momentarily flickered across her eyes, but fled just as quickly as her alarm mounted.

"Someone tried to kill me a little while ago," he said almost apologetically. "If you want me to leave right now, I'll understand."

Her eyes widened fearfully. "Just tell me what happened."

He started speaking, but she held up her hand to silence him and rushed to the window overlooking the street and peered outside. Satisfied, she pulled the shade down and peeked out again. When she seemed certain that he hadn't been followed, she came back and poured herself a drink as well as another for Carter.

"Begin," she said.

Briefly, he told her about the phone call, his going to the Colosseum, and the rendezvous. He told her the name of the man he met as well as his reservations about getting anything from him. This time he drank slowly, savoring the warmth. Taking a deep breath, he related what happened with the assailant after Falconi left. While he told the story, the color slowly returned to his face.

Monitoring him carefully, Carla realized that he wasn't making up any of it. The night's events had terrified him. As she stared at him, she finally recognized the expression he'd worn since he first came in. She had seen the look on the faces of soldiers who returned from battle and once, on the face of a politician who had eluded an assassin's bullet. Carter had escaped death by the narrowest of margins.

Remembering the pain when their affair ended, she didn't want to feel anything for Carter again. Even so, a wave of sympathy welled up in her. She wished she could do something for him, hold him against her until the pain and fear drained from him. At the same time, she fervently hoped he didn't spell her ruin. Until now, she had been safe here.

After finishing his story about what had happened at the Colosseum, Carter looked at her pleadingly and held out the canister containing the film. "I won't know until this is developed whether I was sent on a fool's errand. You don't have to do it. I can still leave right now."

Gingerly, she accepted the canister he placed in the palm of her hand. If anyone broke in on them while she was developing the film, she would be killed too. Yet, he came to her because they shared the same beliefs.

She announced her decision by clenching her hand into a fist that locked around the film. "You can wait here," she said, and started toward the darkroom.

"No!" Carter said, rising from the chair.

Anxiously, he reached out and clamped his hand over hers. "I'm sorry, but I want to remain with this during the entire process. Just behave as if I weren't there."

She smiled bitterly. How typical. Even now, he didn't fully trust her. That had been the cancer in their relationship. That and his god-awful guilt. Guilt about his affairs. Guilt about not doing more for people, for the movement, for the Church. Guilt over everything! She was torn between wanting to lash out at him and to help him. What good would berating him do? He wouldn't understand what she was talking about.

Breathing deeply, she sucked back her anger. "Sure. Okay. Come with me."

They entered the darkroom through the bedroom. The work space was stifling and barely large enough for both of them. The only light was a single amber bulb. The terror drained from Carter now that he was thawing out. Soon, he would know what the prelate had given him. Then he could decide what course of action to follow.

Carla took three graduated measures from a shelf and lined them up on a countertop. Into the first, she poured alkaline-based negative developer to make the image on the negative visible to the naked eye. Stop bath, which stops the alkaline solution at the appropriate time, went into the second, and fixer, which makes the developed image permanent, into the last. She flicked off the amber light, plunging the room into total darkness. With a can opener, she pried open the film canister, extracted the film, and rolled it onto a reel. She cut the film and placed it into the tank, clamping a lid on the tank as a safeguard against light's accidentally hitting it.

"How can you work in the dark?" Carter asked.

"When you know what you are doing, it comes out right," she replied.

Getting a grip on himself, Carter's senses became more alert. He was especially conscious of her presence. Her damp sweat mingled with the trace of her rosewater perfume, making him think of when they first met that summer in Managua. Her slow, steady breathing was soothing. Though they didn't touch, he felt her nearness, her body heat as she moved about.

She turned on the light and poured the developer into the light-proof hole in the tank. Less than ten minutes later, she poured in the stop bath. A short while later, she added the fixer. Finally, the film was ready to be washed.

Carter watched her work with efficiency and incredible concentration. Once, she brushed against him. He felt the touch of her breast and gasped. She rolled up the sleeves of her robe, and sweat trickled down her arms. Strands of hair were pasted by sweat to her brow where she pushed her hair back by using her forearm as she poured Hypo-clean, which makes the washing easier, into the tank.

Glancing at him, she saw fear still burned into his eyes. Something else was there now as he looked at her. An intense longing, that hunger. She turned away and sighed, debating how far she should let this go. She had vowed never to see him again. As a child, she had always taken in dogs and cats and birds that were sick or maimed, trying to nurse them back to health. Sometimes she succeeded. As an adult, she was drawn to men who were damaged, who needed momentary comfort. Such men confused love, need, and affection.

Finishing up, she smiled tensely as she decided what to do about him. Rivulets of sweat trailed between her breasts, which were half revealed as she leaned forward. Finally, she removed the film and standing on tiptoe, hung it from a wire strung across the room.

"How long will that take to dry?"

"About two hours," she replied. "Come."

She led him to her bedroom. With a half-angry motion, she yanked at the belt on her robe and let the garment fall to the floor. In the moonlight streaming through the window, he saw again that she was built like a woman who had once complained to him years ago that she had been put together from the parts of two babies when she was born. Her torso was slender, graceful, and her breasts like a young girl's. Her legs and hips were muscular, strong like a peasant's.

Resigned, she helped him remove his clothes while he gently ran his hands over her face and down her breasts. He sank to his knees and pressed his face against the curve of her belly. As always, he felt a sense of betrayal, of going against what he was supposed to do. Without a word, they moved onto the bed. In the darkness, he whimpered in anguish as he held her against him. Desperately, he pulled her down toward him, kissed her, and buried his face in her breasts.

She raised his face and kissed him. Startled, she tasted droplets of salt. As she licked them away, she realized they were tears, knowing how the salt in the tears must hurt the bruises on his face. She found herself crying as well and knew they were crying for different reasons. Their communion was in their bodies and their sense of loss.

Long ago, Carter had told himself that it didn't matter, that when he was a seminarian he had committed a sin far more grievous than anything he had ever done since. One for which he could never be forgiven. Holding Carla, he kissed her hungrily, despairingly. He entered her in a frenzy that for a moment drove away the horror of the night. The second time was slower, gentler, the tuning of bodies and souls that achingly come together at the moment because they fear there may not be a tomorrow. Damnation was placed on hold once again.

At eight A.M., Carter felt himself being shaken. Carla hovered over him and memories of the night flooded in. He reached out and touched her face as though he could smooth away her worried look.

"I was going to check the film, but I wanted you with me."

Forcing himself into wakefulness, he nodded and got out of bed. A few minutes later, he stood in the doorway as he once again watched her efficient movements. She took down the negatives and placed them on a light table.

Carter picked up a magnifying glass and wiped his bleary eyes before studying them. He found himself looking at a manuscript and rubbed his eyes again because the document appeared illegible. Looking closely, he realized that it was written in Latin. For the first time in his life, he wished that Latin had not been dropped as the official Church language so that he would have studied it more intensively while at the seminary. He hadn't a clue to what the document contained. Who could translate it? Whom could he trust? Momentarily, anger welled up. Another delay! Or was it all part of an elaborate joke?

Ten minutes later, he was dressed, his raincoat draped across his arm. Carla stood by the front door, acting as though nothing had happened between them, and thinking of the mindless litany of rationalizations common in the movement for such moments. For them both, the night had been another lifetime. There was no room for emotionalism in their lives; sentimentality was a luxury. She tried to believe that as she thought it, but as always, she failed.

"Good luck," she said, keeping her voice steady. "Call me if you need me for anything else."

"Thank you." He wrote down a name and phone number. "If you have to reach me, he will know where I am."

Carla shut the door quickly behind him, hoping he didn't see the tears in her eyes as he stepped out of her life once again. Furious, she tried to brush them away, but finally let them come. A moment later, she curled up on her bed and wept. Hugging herself and rocking back and forth, she wondered why she did not have more to hold on to. Why didn't he put an end to his charade and leave the priesthood and come to her?

81

At a kiosk near Carla's apartment, Carter bought a newspaper and asked directions. His face burned when he thought of Carla. He didn't deserve her. How many times had he vowed never to see her again? How could he touch any woman after what he had once done?

Three blocks away, he caught a bus. When he settled into a seat, he opened the early edition of the paper and stared at a picture of a familiar face. The story said that Bishop Eugenio Falconi had been killed last night. His body was found in the Colosseum. He had been strangled. Around his neck was a priest's stole.

5

IN WASHINGTON SO SOON AGAIN AFTER NOT HAVING BEEN IN THE CITY for more than a year, Kelly had the cabdriver drop him at the main entrance to Catholic University. A few minutes later, he was at Curley Hall, the priests' residence where Bishop John Gibbons lived. He climbed to the second floor and rapped on the door to his left, regretting he hadn't been able to reach him after he'd left Clarizio. The bishop might have a handle on what was happening.

When Kelly had called Gibbons this morning, the bishop had asked him to come in the late afternoon, saying he would squeeze him into his teaching schedule. Today was his heavy course day. Kelly was grateful that Gibbons always accommodated him. As much as any man in the Church, Kelly considered Gibbons his mentor. The bishop was the first person in whom he had confided in Vietnam that he wanted to be a priest. To Kelly's eternal gratitude, Gibbons had concealed his shock well and listened to Kelly's reasons. Kelly still appreciated his not having passed judgment on him.

There was no answer, so Kelly turned the knob and entered the three-room apartment. The door was never locked. Gibbons's lack of pretension was reflected by the spareness of his furnishings. A sofa, table, and several chairs, all in the severe Spanish Mission style. Like most priests' rooms, there were shelves filled with books. In Gibbons's case, reading was almost an obsession. Besides the overflowing bookcases, there were piles beside chairs and against walls. The little study was even more cluttered. Smiling, Kelly wondered how Gibbons even got in there to work.

A classics teacher and Church historian, the bishop wrote more on contemporary social and political issues for publications as varied as the Jesuit magazine *America* and *The Atlantic*. He especially delighted in writing about controversial topics in a way that raised the hackles of some of the more conservative members of the hierarchy.

In the 1960s, Gibbons's writings had come to the attention of Pope John XXIII, who found them honest and courageous. Overriding the objections of certain powerful American ecclesiastics, Pope John, shortly before his death, told Gibbons he was making him a bishop. At first, Gibbons refused, saying he had never wanted to be admitted to royalty, but the pope had cautioned him not to be foolhardy.

"The way you write," Pope John told him in Rome, "you will need the protection of a bishop's miter. Sometimes the miter is mightier than the pen."

Whenever recounting the story, Gibbons laughed. He came to realize the truth contained in the pope's quip. His writings rankled enough members of the hierarchy with prickly egos who would like nothing better than to pack him off to one of the Church's Siberias, the way they did priests who got on their wrong side.

Kelly went into the kitchen, took a beer out of the refrigerator, and settled into an easy chair. He reviewed his assignment, replaying different scenes with Clarizio over and over. Twenty minutes later, the door opened.

"Kevin, how are you?" Gibbons boomed.

The bishop strode across the room and yanked Kelly to his feet. "Let's get a good look at you. Good. Good. You're still fit."

"You look as if you're ready to go to war," Kelly said, noting that the bishop, who wore a priest's simple black cassock, was holding his weight down by jogging and playing handball four or five days a week.

A big-boned man nearly as tall as Kelly, Gibbons had been a linebacker at Notre Dame before entering the seminary. He had the bulk of an athlete past his prime but still in good shape. The long horse face, prominent nose, and fierce gray brows over stern blue eyes gave Gibbons the slight cast of a zealot, earning him the nickname St. Paul.

The bishop's hair was a tad grayer than the last time Kelly had seen him, but his handshake was strong and his manner vigorous. Gibbons had never looked young, even when they first met in 1967. Now, at age sixty-three, his years and appearance had finally reached an accord.

Gibbons headed into the kitchen and took a beer too. He spoke as he moved about.

"I just had a little run-in with Archbishop Dinsmore over an article of mine that just appeared in *America*. It's about racism in the Church." He looked at Kelly with the hint of a smile. "Dinsmore got upset."

"As usual, your timing was perfect," Kelly said dryly.

Archbishop Robert Dinsmore had his hands full at the moment as head of the Washington archdiocese. A black priest, Jonathan Simmons, had decried racism within the Church and started an African American Catholic Church. The act received a great deal of publicity and put Dinsmore in the middle of a prickly mess. The potential for a full-blown schism horrified Rome and embarrassed Dinsmore, who initially ranted and raved about Simmons and now glumly waited for Rome or the pronuncio to try to find a solution. Meanwhile, the more media attention Simmons received, the more elusive the possibility for reconciliation.

"Dinsmore thought I timed the article to support Johnny Simmons. I explained to him that the piece was commissioned months before Simmons went public. But I said I'd write it again today anyway."

Gibbons's eyes flickered with dismay. "There is racism in the Church as there is in every institution in the country, if not the world. But we are trying to deal with it, and that is the message the Church should be giving instead of denying it."

Frustrated, Gibbons shook his head. "Hell, they should've made Johnny a bishop and let him head up a commission on racism and find solutions. This African American Catholic Church business never had to get off the ground."

Kelly laughed, believing Gibbons was probably right. He thought of the mess Rome had created by the way it mishandled Seattle's Hunthausen when the Vatican clamped down on the archbishop for being too liberal. Too often, members of the hierarchy actually in-

85

flamed issues in their diligence to suppress them, rather than looking for sensible solutions.

"I ran into Joe Devine a couple of weeks ago," Gibbons said. "He was asking about you."

"What's he doing now?" Kelly asked. He remembered Devine, a tall, thin, nervous man who, like Gibbons, had been an army chaplain in Vietnam.

"He's teaching not all that far from you. At Fatima College in Westchester."

While he talked, Gibbons thought, as he always did in Kelly's presence, about what an oddity Kelly was in the religious life. He remembered the first time he saw him in Vietnam. It was at a medical detachment in the mountains west of Chu Lai, where the wounded were ferried in by helicopters, given emergency and trauma care, and flown out to hospitals in Da Nang or Chu Lai. A lonely spot on a river, the facility was encircled by mountains and dense wilderness. Most of the work was amputations.

It was nightfall. After hearing confessions, Gibbons had celebrated Mass. He was talking to a group of men when a hush fell over them. A squad of Vietnamese materialized from the forest led by a big American. Though they passed quite near, they moved soundlessly, like ghosts. There was a separateness about them, severing them from the rest of the men in the camp. When Gibbons looked at their eyes, he shivered. They had the cold watchfulness of snakes.

"Who are they?" Gibbons asked the captain he was talking with.

"No ID," the captain said.

"What do you mean?" Gibbons asked.

"They don't belong to regular army. They get the dirtiest jobs, the kinds nobody else wants or wants to know about."

"Who's the American?"

"Kevin Kelly, one of those dangerous, shadowy CIA types," the captain said.

Gibbons didn't like the rumors he heard about the group over the next day or so. There were stories about village leaders, suspected of being Viet Cong, disappearing, brutal interrogations, and even strange cannibalistic rites on the part of the "hunters" as the cadre was known. The tales made the chaplain pray harder for the dreadful, dehumanizing war to end.

About four months later, Gibbons met Kelly at a hospital in Da

Nang, where the lieutenant was recovering from a shoulder wound. When they played chess, Gibbons was constantly dismayed that this kind of soldier was a Catholic. He ran into Kelly several times over the next month, and they started up a friendship. Still, he was shocked when a haggard Kelly came to him one night and told him he wanted to become a priest.

"Why?" Gibbons asked, truly curious.

Kelly told him that his wife and child had been killed in a plane crash two months earlier. Unsolicited, Kelly gave a few details about what he had done in the service, activities about which he never told another soul. "I want to try to atone for some of the wrong I've done," Kelly said matter-of-factly. "Maybe I can do that as a priest."

When he stared hard and long at the soldier, Gibbons didn't see any signs of wavering. Kelly had put much deliberation into what he now sought, probably a lot more reflection than he put into the terrible work he did in the military.

"Let me pray on it, Kevin."

"That's all I ask," Kelly said when he left Gibbons's bunker.

As the soldier walked away, he had a timeless weariness about him. For a moment, Gibbons felt that, of the two of them, it was Kelly who, even though he was only half Gibbons's age, was the older. He had seen more evil in his years. What have we done to these men? the chaplain wondered. What have we done?

Before giving Kelly an answer, Gibbons discreetly talked to certain military officers about Kelly's classified activities, including the stark truths about his so-called "intelligence" work. Coupled with the bits and pieces that Kelly had volunteered and that weren't related to him by others, Gibbons gained a grip on Kelly's military career. Gibbons didn't consider himself squeamish, but some of the information made him feel that way. What a terrible life for a young man. Terrible for anyone. Together with the dreadful business with his family, Kelly had a heavy cross to bear.

Gibbons had not been certain that a man with such a violent past would make it through the seminary, let alone remain in the priesthood. Yet, he detected something deep in this man who knew so much about tragedy at such an early age. What was Kelly at the time? All of twenty-four or perhaps twenty-five? When he had looked at the young officer, he saw more than what the compilation of facts suggested. He had prayed mightily before he encouraged Kelly to enter the Vincentian seminary he himself had attended. So far, the gamble had paid off. Still, he was never sure whether Kelly would always remain content with his lot in the Church.

"So, Kev, what's this business about Clarizio?"

Briefly, Kelly filled in the bishop on what had transpired. "They want to know everything about the Trinity. I'll have to get hold of Damian Carter. Hell, I may even have to get to the bottom of what happened to Bill Witten."

Straining forward, Gibbons listened intently. When Kelly finished, the bishop sat back and took a pull on the beer bottle in his hand. He stared thoughtfully at the ceiling.

"Well, what do you think?" Kelly asked.

"Something's not quite kosher," the bishop replied.

"What?"

"To begin with, having you check out Hogan. Clarizio could have had just about anyone do that. Yet, he clearly wanted you. The Carruthers business probably had something to do with it, but for some reason, I don't think it had all that much bearing on your selection."

Gibbons fell into thought, and Kelly didn't disturb him. Gibbons had good contacts at the Vatican. He heard a great deal of what was happening there before it hit the clerical grapevine. Moreover, he was a shrewd analyst of the information that came his way.

"It sounds to me if this wasn't Clarizio's idea," he said finally. "Probably the pope's. I'll bet Clarizio's largely acting as the pope's errand boy on this matter."

Not bad, Kelly silently congratulated Gibbons. He hadn't told him about the note that had come into the pope's hands.

"No, there must be some international angle to this or Clarizio probably wouldn't want you."

"Why not?"

Gibbons laughed. "Your probe of Carruthers was perhaps a little too diligent. You lifted stones that some of Carruthers's friends felt would have been better left unturned."

"I got that feeling myself," Kelly admitted. He paused and added, "I also thought about the international possibility, but there's nothing to indicate that's the case."

"He told you to go anywhere. Obviously, that means at some point you will have to go outside the country, at least to Rome."

Gibbons raised one of his bushy eyebrows as he looked at Kelly. "Whatever someone has on Pat Hogan, it must be big-time."

Monsignor Hogan slid into the backseat of the limousine next to the corpulent figure of Henry Cardinal Turner, archbishop of Los Angeles. He patted the back of the elderly cardinal's hand, grateful that he would be able to catch the red-eye back to New York.

"Thank you for inviting me to Los Angeles, Your Eminence," he said.

Cardinal Turner, known among the clergy as the Buddha because of his inscrutable look, broke into an uncharacteristic warm smile. "They told me you had the persuasive powers of a Daniel Webster," the cardinal's deep voice rumbled. "But judging by some of the checks turned in today for the renovation of our cathedral, your talents were underestimated."

The words made Hogan feel a tug of guilt. He had turned down another request by Archbishop Dinsmore to speak at his cathedral in Washington. He had rejected Dinsmore so often that the archbishop was beginning to think Hogan didn't like him. Nothing could be further from the truth, he thought dismally. But how could he explain? How could he tell the archbishop that he could *never* speak at his cathedral and that he could never tell him why?

"So what about Tom Brokaw?" the cardinal asked.

Hogan couldn't help smiling, even though the long day was catching up to him. He flew in this morning and spent the few hours before the fund-raising dinner with the cardinal, telling him amusing stories about New York television personalities, stories to which Turned listened raptly. The cardinal was a celebrity junkie. Turner knew quite a few movie stars and TV personalities in Los Angeles, but he didn't know the New York–based talk show hosts or the newscasters. A lot of people would be shocked to find out the formidable-looking cardinal was as knowledgeable about entertainment trivia as an editor for *People* magazine.

"Yes, that is who first media-trained him," Hogan replied to one of the cardinal's queries, knowing this rapport should help his own cause.

Now he had to catch the exhausting overnight flight that would get him into New York about six-thirty A.M., which wouldn't give him much time other than to change his clothes and celebrate mass before he had to rush to another TV show where he was appearing on a panel about whether rap music should be banned as obscene. In the afternoon, he was giving a lecture at St. John's University as a favor to a friend, and in the evening he was meeting an editor from *the New York Times Magazine* to discuss an article the editor wanted him to write.

"Good luck on this bishop business," the cardinal said as the limousine came to a stop to drop Hogan off. "I'll see if I can't put in a good word for you."

Hogan lowered his lips to the cardinal's ring. "If you'd like me to come back, just let me know."

"Not if but when," the cardinal said, smiling again and patting Hogan affectionately on the shoulder as the monsignor left the limousine.

As he hurried to the check-in counter, Hogan felt a wave of exhilaration. The grind today was worth it just to hear Turner say that. The cardinal had extraordinary influence on the hierarchy both in America and Rome. A kind word from him would mean a great deal toward helping him become a bishop.

Kelly caught a late Trump shuttle back to New York and spent the flight thinking about Hogan. What had the guy done?

He remembered walking across the quad at Gethsemane with him one afternoon in 1968, about nine months after Kelly entered the seminary. During that period, Kelly came to resent the government for continuing to send hundreds of thousands of young men to fight in Vietnam. Kelly knew that Hogan was opposed to the war and corresponded with peace organizations. Maybe he had an idea of what Kelly himself could do.

"Pat, a lot of men I served with have joined the Vietnam Veterans Against the War. I feel that I should do something too, but I don't know what."

"I'm taking some personal time and going to Baltimore next week," Hogan replied. "Why not join me?"

"What's happening down there?"

"The trial of the Catonsville Nine starts," Hogan said.

The previous May, seven men and two women entered the Selective Service Office in Catonsville, a white, middle-class, suburban town eight miles west of Baltimore, and shocked the nation. They

90

seized draft records, took them into the parking lot, doused them with blood and napalm, and set them on fire. Waiting for the police, they sang and prayed while the records burned. They were all Catholics. Two of them were priests, Philip and Daniel Berrigan.

"What can we do there?" Kelly asked.

"Bear witness to brave people," Hogan replied.

The following week they were among thousands of protesters who descended on Baltimore. Kelly was stunned when they entered St. Ignatius Church, which served as the headquarters for the demonstrators. Halls, rooms, and the basement were jammed with well-known antiwar protesters as well as legions of priests and seminarians wearing the peace sign, the upside-down enclosed in a circle. Many also wore black armbands for the Americans killed in Vietnam and white headbands to honor the Vietnamese dead. Nuns, some of whom wore their traditional habits while others wore skirts, high heels, and had teased hair, mingled with ex-servicemen wearing field jackets and bandannas on their heads.

The two days the seminarians spent there were a whirlwind of petitions, rallies, marches to the courthouse. Rumors were rife about impending actions against Selective Service Offices elsewhere. Kelly was enthralled by the sight of squads of priests marching in protest down the street in their clerical collars and black suits bedecked with peace symbols. And he felt an emotional surge as it became clear that the Catholic clergy assumed leadership roles in every facet of the antiwar activities.

Likewise, Kelly was swept up in the impassioned speeches given by Rabbi Abraham Heschel, Episcopalian bishop James Pike, and radical journalist I. F. Stone. He was surprised by the ease with which Hogan insinuated himself among even the most important of such people.

He found some of Hogan's behavior disturbing as well. On the way to Baltimore, he and Hogan had agreed not to do anything to call attention to themselves while here. Because they hadn't told Monsignor Maguire they were coming, they didn't want to do anything that might potentially embarrass the rector. Yet, as Kelly once made his way to the command center in the basement of St. Ignatius, he passed Hogan in a hallway being interviewed by a TV crew. The reporter obviously felt getting a handsome, dedicated seminarian on the tube was a great visual, and, Kelly thought wryly, Hogan probably charmed the newsman into choosing him for the spot.

91

"We've been working long and hard to bring an end to the war," Hogan said as Kelly was passing by.

Kelly shot Hogan a glance, wondering whether this was a bit of self-promotion or if his fellow seminarian was being sincere. Probably a bit of both. He knew Hogan had long opposed the war, but here was Hogan taking a public stand after they'd agreed not to do so. Another factor bothered him as well. Hogan did little in the way of antiwar activity other than keeping in touch with peace groups and doing occasional drudge work for them during vacation time. He always said he wanted to do more, but he never risked going to jail or being hurt for his beliefs. It struck Kelly that Hogan believed he was truly doing something because he empathized while watching a lot of TV coverage of what the dedicated activists were doing.

Later, Hogan sheepishly came up to him. "I guess I shouldn't have spoken to that news crew, but I just got caught up in everything."

Kelly could accept that. The longer they were exposed to the emotionalism around them, the more Kelly began to question what it meant. Just about anyone could be swept up by impassioned rhetoric and symbolism, no matter what the political cause. Finally, Kelly came away with a troubled feeling that people, including himself, were too easily stirred by the heat of the moment. The sight of priests protesting was exhilarating; he was sure they would certainly sway people's attitudes against the war. But he thought that the sight of bishops blessing the military also swayed people. He concluded that the clergy should stay away from politics and the military.

Climbing into a cab at LaGuardia Airport, Kelly's stomach churned. All anybody had ever accused Hogan of was being ambitious. Since when is ambition a crime? Then he started berating himself for trying to dodge the real issue. Hogan must have done something pretty awful, offended someone pretty powerful. He and the other two members of the Trinity. He gave the cabdriver a Manhattan address.

On the ride into the city, he turned over and over what Gibbons said. What did someone have on Hogan that was big-time? What had he done in tandem with Carter and Witten? He remembered the Trinity's spending a great deal of time together, but was there anything devious about their behavior? He racked his brains but couldn't remember anything. Besides being very bright, all three were at the center of Gethsemane's peace movement. Could that have a bearing on this? Had they gone off the lunatic end for a while the way some radicals did? A chill went through him as he remembered some of the crazy bombings radicals were responsible for in the early 1970s out of frustration over the war. They hadn't gotten mixed up in that kind of insanity, had they?

As the taxi pulled in front of an apartment building on Central Park West, he pushed such thoughts from his mind. Still, he felt more frustrated than he had in ages.

While the doorman phoned apartment 18C, Kelly absolutely despised the situation in which he found himself. What did this woman have on Hogan? What did Edwards have? What did it matter? When he was in the military, he came to loathe spying on anyone, probing people's lives and preying on their weaknesses.

That was one of the reasons he decided on the priesthood, he thought ruefully. He had wanted a sanctuary from the harsh secular world of corruption and betrayal. To a certain extent, the priesthood had offered that. What he hadn't fully counted on was that men were men no matter where they played out their humanity. There were degrees of difference between this life and the old one. Usually for the better but not always.

The doorman hung up. "Go right up," he said with an indifferent glance.

The detached look told Kelly that Lane Woods had a lot of callers at all times of the day or night and that they were from all walks of life. He crossed the lobby's marble floor and said "Eighteen-C" to the elevator operator, thinking an apartment in such a building cost a fortune.

On the way up, he thought about what an odd business journalism was. Rummaging around in people's lives, but often never seeing the subjects again. Always gnawing at issues and ideas, sifting through information, trying to get as close to the truth as possible, and believing that, with a lot of work and a certain amount of luck, journalists could get a healthy percentage of the truth into their stories. What percentage? Fifty percent? Seventy? Ten?

When did they decide they had a story? When were they convinced they had the truth? How often did they have time to get the truth, not just surface facts but the real "why" behind whatever happened? The thoughts made him uneasy. That was the unnerving role Kelly found himself in now. Judgments would be made on what he turned up. He wondered, as he did years ago, how some journalists developed the arrogance to believe they were always right. He guessed the alternative was too threatening.

Lane half stood in the hallway at her open apartment door. "Hello, Father," she said, extending her hand.

She had changed from her work armor to a floor-length, white, silk kimono embroidered with tiny red chrysanthemums. The robe softened her looks, bringing a delicacy to her features that he hadn't noticed before. When she spoke, her voice had softened too, as if in her own sanctuary she didn't have to be guarded.

"Greetings," he said, shaking her hand. "Very posh place you have here."

"Keep it up and you'll make me feel more guilty about my outlandish salary."

"No offense meant."

"To be on the safe side, I'll give everything to the poor in the morning. In the meanwhile, come on in."

She shut the door and took his topcoat. "Is there something less formal I can call you?"

"My friends call me Kevin."

"Okay, Kevin. Make yourself at home."

Crossing the entryway's mauve Aubusson carpet, Kelly stepped into the huge, modernistic, sunken living room. The room was airy and decorated in soft pastels and natural woods. End tables and coffee tables were carved from oak, the artist following the wood's natural contours. Ficus trees and cactus plants seemed to be everywhere. An entire wall of glass had a view of Central Park and the night sky, which was like a giant motion picture screen with twinkling stars, lights of commercial aircraft, and shadowy clouds crossing the moon. A grand piano filled one corner formed by the glass wall.

The room was dominated, however, by a large, almost life-size oil portrait of Lane Woods that hung over the fireplace mantel. She was nude and standing in profile by a large vase of wild flowers that only allowed an outline of her figure. She looked graceful; her expression was wistful, yet strong and independent. She had wildflowers in her hair and was holding a daisy cupped in her hands, as if she were afraid it might break.

The artist had captured her beauty and a certain indefinable quality that Kelly had recognized in her when he met her but couldn't quite name. He knew it now as his gaze locked on the painting.

94

"That doesn't bother you, does it?" she asked tentatively. "I didn't think when I asked you up here." She sounded a little flustered. "I had forgotten that a priest might find it . . . objectionable."

Kelly smiled. There was nothing lascivious about the work and he recognized the artist. "No, not at all. How did you get Adele Cummings to paint you? She rarely does portraits."

"She's my mother. And she'd be very pleased that you recognized her work."

"I was just thinking how, well, unworldly you appear in the painting. Rather like Atalanta."

She looked at him curiously. "That's funny. My mother always says she should have named me Atalanta because of the way I turned out. A woman who runs with the male hunters and outdistances them."

"Remember how she was finally caught?"

"Through trickery."

Kelly smiled again, recalling the myth of how Atalanta lost a foot race and was forced to marry the winner. A goddess gave him magical golden balls to use during the race. Whenever Atalanta forged ahead, he tossed one of the balls to the ground. Atalanta was so enraptured, she paused to pick them up and eventually lost.

"Some people called it cunning."

"That's a male interpretation, Kevin," Lane said wryly.

She motioned for him to take a seat on one of the two tan leather sofas that faced one another near the fireplace. "I'm fixing myself a drink. Can I get you one?"

"Coffee if you have it. Black."

"No problem. I put some on before you came."

As she went to the kitchen, Kelly noticed how gracefully she moved. She returned with a steaming cup, which she placed in front of him on the free-form, oak coffee table between the sofas. Going to an opposite wall, she pressed a button and a hidden panel opened, revealing a large, well-stocked bar. Pouring herself a short gin, she loaded the glass with ice and tonic. Her motions were exact but elegant. She took a taste, added a bit more tonic, and recrossed the room.

As she sat, she started laughing, more to herself than anything.

"What's so funny?"

"I'm thinking of all the people who imagine that I lead an intensely glamorous life. I'm thirty-four years old, make more money than God, am too bushed to go anywhere but my own apartment, and the man I'm with is a priest."

Kelly laughed as well. "You're as much one of TV's victims as its victors."

"What do you mean?"

"I've always thought TV makes people less content. Life on the tube is a lot more wonderful and exciting than people's lives actually are."

She shrugged. "It's what people want."

"How do you know?"

"Because they watch that stuff. If they wanted something else, they'd get it."

Watching his eyebrow rise skeptically, she laughed again. "God knows, all TV executives want is to make money. They don't care what people watch as long as it sells commercial time. Look at the low ratings PBS draws with the arts. Advertisers want the big numbers they get with commercial TV."

Kelly nodded. "A journalist friend says much the same thing about the quality of newspapers. 'Kevin,' he says, 'publishers would give people very good newspapers if people wanted them.' Maybe I'm just being optimistic in believing people want something more."

"You're paid to be optimistic. Journalists aren't."

"Then why do we get paid so little and you get so much?"

"Maybe God likes us better."

"Most days I'm sure of it," Kelly said.

They both laughed, and Kelly found he was enjoying himself. He couldn't remember the last time he sat talking to a young woman who wasn't in some kind of trouble. He found himself surprised that Lane didn't seem more self-centered, although exhibiting that painting carried a heavy hint of narcissism. She was different from the way she came across on the TV screen, or maybe he'd just been braced for a prima donna.

"What does your father do?" he asked.

"He died several years ago. He had been a scriptwriter in Hollywood and was caught up in the McCarthy blacklisting. As a very young man, he was committed to a lot of causes designed to make the world a better place. For a while, he flirted with communism, but dropped it. Years later, it came back to haunt him. With the paranoia in the country then, it didn't take much to lose your livelihood."

"What happened to him?"

Lane paused for a moment, thinking of what her mother told her about the depression her father fell into when doors were suddenly

96

slammed in his face. Then came the bitterness and cynicism at the hypocrisy that had worked against him. Men who wouldn't hire him because of the blacklist would knowingly use his material anyway but at cut-rate fees. "He wrote for magazines and TV under different names and never got paid what he should have. Even so, he did what he could to work for causes that would improve the lot of the poor and underprivileged."

Though he could tell she was trying to be dispassionate, Kelly discerned the trace of hurt in her voice and imagined that growing up under such stress had left its mark on her. He changed the topic. "You must get asked this all the time, so don't answer if you don't feel like it. How did you wind up in TV?"

"I don't mind," she said. "I went to Bennington and wanted to be a dancer. I actually did a few off-Broadway shows, but I wasn't terrific."

Pausing, she took a sip of her drink. "I went from one extreme to the other. I joined the Peace Corps and spent two years in the Marshall Islands, which are those little dots hundreds of miles southwest of Hawaii. I wasn't much good as a teacher either."

Her expression turned more thoughtful. "While down there, I wrote about some of the difficulties in the islands, and a couple of magazines picked up my articles. The Marshalls are a U.S. territory, and there were a lot of problems with the U.S. agencies dealing with the people. After my articles appeared, some federal faces got red and they paid a bit more attention to what they were doing.

"When I came back, I landed a newspaper job. Six months later, I joined a local TV station in St. Petersburg and got lucky. I worked my way up, winding up in Miami. Actually, my first big story concerned the pope when he came through the United States. Some good old boys from Miami Beach tried to sabotage his trip. I broke the story."

"Good for you."

"Funny, the Church has been very good for my career. I got to know a lot of activist clergy, and I did in-depth pieces on the FBI's illegally monitoring religious groups, such as Sanctuary, and other hot stuff. I guess I'm drawn to these kinds of stories because I was into leftist politics when I was in college. My dad's influence, I guess."

On a hunch, Kelly asked, "Is Damian Carter one of the priests you came to know?"

"Of course. Damian is one of the most involved priests in the

97

nation. He still puts me onto stories. Anyway, someone at XTV saw my work and liked it. That led to this job."

"Sounds too simple. There must have been a lot more to it."

"There was," she admitted. "A lot of hard work. I was on the go around the clock, trying to do my job as well as possible. Unlike my earlier career disasters, I found that I'm pretty good at this and want to get better all the time."

She looked at him curiously. "Two can play this game. What about you?"

Kelly stared at his hands. "I was raised in the Bronx where my father had a used-furniture store and yearned to be an art and antique dealer. He knew his stuff and taught me a lot, but he never had the money to make his dream come true. I had a scholarship to Fordham. After I graduated, I was drafted and sent to Vietnam. I was married right after I went into the army and had a daughter."

He paused, squinting. "They . . . they died in a plane crash while coming to visit me in Thailand. I was pretty much of a basket case and tried to figure out what to do with the rest of my life. I wanted to find some meaning to being here, and I wanted do something for someone else. The priesthood came to mind one day and didn't leave."

She looked at him compassionately. "I'm very sorry about your family."

"Thanks," Kelly replied, wondering why he had told her. He hadn't talked about Helen and Janie for ages. He began to feel sad. To change the topic, he turned to the reason why he'd come here.

"So what's this about Pat Hogan?"

She picked up the reluctance in his voice. "You don't like what you're doing right now, do you?"

"That obvious?"

"Definitely."

"It's not something I volunteered for."

"A lousy job but somebody's got to do it, huh?"

Ruefully rubbing his fingers through his hair, he felt like kicking himself for being so open. "That's about it. But please don't let my indiscretion go beyond these walls."

She heard his concern. "I won't."

He kept his eyes down to avoid looking at her. Suddenly, he felt a bit edgy as he realized how very beautiful she was and just how much he enjoyed talking to her. She reminded him a little of Helen. Some priests developed free and easy relationships with women, but

98

he wasn't one of them. In fact, he had always felt awkward around most girls and women when he was young, and since Helen's death he had reverted to his former behavior. What surprised him when he had first met Helen was how easy it was being with her. He always knew that was what led to his falling in love with her and marrying her. That ease was what he felt now, and it was disconcerting.

Lane sensed the change in his mood and guessed why. She was enjoying herself and wondered what was wrong with her. Was she falling into a pattern of liking the unattainable? Several months ago, she almost started up something with a guy who was married. He didn't tell her he was until their third date, and she dismayed herself by actually wavering about seeing him again because he seemed like a nice guy and she hadn't met a nice guy in ages. Most men saw her only as some kind of damned trophy they could boast about. Now the first guy in a long time she'd enjoyed talking to other than people she worked with or interviewed was a priest. Oh, what am I doing? She asked herself, and shoved such thoughts aside as she answered his question.

"I'll make this as painless as I can, Kevin. I don't particularly care for Pat Hogan, apparently being one of the few women in America who feels this way. You should factor that into what I'm about to tell you. I'm not religious, so that doesn't have anything to do with it either. Whatever shtick people use on TV is okay with me. Jimmy Swaggart or Pat Hogan, as far as I'm concerned, all the TV preachers are pretty much the same. They've found a hook that appeals to a lot of people. So be it."

Kelly sat back. "Then what about Pat makes you feel so strongly?"

"There was a young woman who worked in the news division as a production assistant, and then she moved over to 'Life Has Meaning.' She's a nice kid and it looked as if she had a big future in front of her. At least until Hogan forced her out."

Kelly set his coffee cup on the table, preparing for the worst. "Why did he do that?"

"The age-old story. She had a crush on the guy, he took advantage of her. When he tired of her, he got rid of her."

Kelly felt as if she had kicked him in the stomach. "How do you know?"

"The girl came to me."

"And you believed her?"

"Kevin, in this business that kind of thing happens every day.

99

Look, I'm no moralist, but I don't like to see people exploited. Especially someone very young."

"Why didn't she bring a sexual harassment suit against him?"

"I guess for two reasons. First, she went along with his advances. Second, he said something to her that she believed."

"What was that?"

"She told him she was going to tell what had happened. His response was, 'Who would believe it?' He also told her that her name would be mud all over this business if she did, and she'd never get another TV job."

"I find it hard to believe," Kelly said slowly.

"Sorry to burst your bubble," Lane said.

When she saw him wince, she felt bad. "Look, Kevin, television changes people and usually not for the better. I try to keep on guard against it all the time, but I find myself falling into the trap too."

"What do you mean?"

"Being on the tube makes you a celebrity," she said. "That's powerful stuff in our culture. People think it imbues you with all sorts of qualities. All of a sudden, very ordinary human beings become transformed because they are on the screen. People think you're beautiful or handsome, smart, wonderful. It's almost like you're some kind of a god, or magical or something. People are awed by you. They want to be near you, touch you. It's very exhilarating . . . and very seductive."

Absorbing what she said, Kelly stared out the massive window. Maybe it was inevitable, he thought. Hogan always had a large ego. Though he didn't like it, he could see Hogan falling into the trap she spoke about. He remembered the star-dazzled women seeking autographs. Putting Pat or anyone in that kind of position was probably presenting them with too much temptation. The fame, the money, the prestige, the power. How many people could avoid succumbing? Still, if the guy exploited a young woman for the sake of his vanity, it was a terrible business. If true, it would cost him a miter.

"Can you add anything else?"

"I went to Hogan, but he refused even to discuss it. I guess I got a little abusive. It's funny, until then I thought he was different. He seemed pretty much a straight arrow, and I used to like talking to him. But I guess all these celebrity preachers are pretty much the same, aren't they? Saying one thing and behaving by a different code."

100

Kelly didn't reply. He still felt as if the wind were knocked out of him.

Lane got up and walked through the door to her study, where she flipped through her Rolodex. When she returned, she held out a piece of paper.

"Here's the girl's name, address, and phone number. I don't expect you to believe me. I wouldn't. Always go to the source."

With a sinking sensation, Kelly accepted the slip of paper. The name written on it was Frances Cook. The address was on West Tenth Street in Greenwich Village. Of course, he had to get hold of the girl, and of course, he didn't want to. He folded the paper and put it in his wallet, thinking this was the death sentence for Hogan's ambitions.

This was the part of the assignment he had dreaded from the very beginning. Sifting through a life for what had gone wrong, not for what was right. This was the same process the Church used when investigating the lives of men and women being considered for sainthood. Hell, he thought, all they wanted to do was make Pat a bishop, and sanctity had never been one of the chief qualifications for the job.

6

EVEN AFTER ALL THESE YEARS, THE TWISTS AND TURNS IN THE ROAD were still as familiar to kelly as if he drove them yesterday. Gethsemane Seminary sprawled over the slope of one of the Pocono Mountains, about thirty-five minutes from the town of East Stroudsburg, Pennsylvania. He hadn't been back since his ordination and was surprised at the edge of anxiety he felt, reminding him of his apprehension when he first came here more than twenty years ago.

The large cedar sign, weathered to a silver shade and with the iron Gothic lettering forming CONGREGATION OF THE MISSION OF ST. VINCENT DE PAUL as well as the seminary's name, came into view. A moment later, he turned right into the long, narrow driveway that snaked through a grove of dense pine trees leading to the campus. After a quarter of a mile, the woods opened to grassy fields.

The day was crisp and clear. The spires of the Gothic buildings soared into a soft blue sky, making Gethsemane appear as picturesque as Kelly remembered. His heart felt a little lighter. When he first visited the campus, he fell in love with Gethsemane's physical beauty. That and the aura of serenity had calmed him at a time when his life was filled with confusion, turmoil, and despair. The rules and regimentation, the intensive studies, and the expectations of seminarians to excel on the part of teachers as well as the seminarians themselves gave him an orderliness and a sense of purpose he needed at the time.

The tarmac road circled the ivy-covered, fieldstone buildings that bordered a grassy quad almost as big as a football field. Several young men in black cassocks hurried across the flagstone pathways that crisscrossed the quad. In the center was a twenty-foot-high wooden cross that was supposed to be a replica of the one upon which Christ had died.

During his years here, Kelly had spent many hours contemplating the cross, wondering what that slow, agonizing death must have been like. He had surprised himself by actually finding crucifixion somewhat humane compared to the mechanized methods of torture and death he had witnessed. He had other thoughts that may have verged on blasphemy. If Christ came today, how would He be killed? Electricity? Cyanide? An injection? An assassin's bullet? Would Mary be mutilated in order to make Him confess? Would Judas be given a new identity and a house in the suburbs?

As he closed in on the administration building, Kelly was struck by how much smaller the place was than he remembered. Ruefully, he shook his head. How real are our mental images of anything?

He pulled into the parking area. Muscles cramped, he climbed out of the car and stretched before crossing to the marble steps leading to the arched front door. If the seminary was altered in his perception, he wondered if his image of Monsignor Maguire would hold up. Maguire had been a formidable figure who could silence a room with a glare. "Tough but fair." That was the description seminarians had most often applied to the rector. Kelly had thought you could ask for nothing more.

When Kelly first entered the seminary, the rector had been a big help. A military man only days ago, Kelly felt like an old man in a garden of children even though the other seminarians weren't that much younger than him. Since he already had a university degree and a ton of questionable experience for becoming a priest, he only had to spend four years here before being ordained. Maguire had made certain allowances for him, but he also let Kelly know he would have to extend himself as much as he could to get the most out of the institution. He liked Maguire because he played it straight.

"Hey, Kevin. What brings you up here?"

Kelly turned and saw an old classmate, Tommy Heron, his cassock billowing in the cool breeze. Once again, he realized how many years had passed and that time, that relentless sculptor, continually molds man. The once skinny young seminarian was now a portly, moon-faced priest whose gray temples telegraphed that he passed his fortieth birthday a few years ago.

Heron was back at Gethsemane teaching after having gone through an agonizing period of reappraisal recently. At one point, he had petitioned Rome to let him leave the priesthood because he wanted to marry. Eventually, he changed his mind and decided to stay. The agony the man went through while coming to grips with the kind of life he wanted, the wrenching choices he had to make, were painful to watch even from afar. A lot of the turmoil had to do with the onset of middle age, a panicky feeling that he had to change his life dramatically if he were ever to change at all.

Kelly had felt sorry for him and even sorrier for the woman involved. In most cases, taking on a priest was more trouble than taking on a married man. Kelly was always amazed at women's capacity for suffering as well as their belief that they can change any man. Often they went hand in hand.

"I'm here to see Maguire."

"Not coming back here for a long stay like me, are you?"

"No, just a talk with him."

"I have to run for a class. Do you have time to stop over at the residence for a drink before you leave?"

"Sorry, Tommy, next time. I have to get back to New York tonight."

Kelly entered the front door of St. Bartholomew's Hall. Automatically, he took the mahogany stairwell to the right and trudged to the second floor. He rapped on the opaque glass pane of the third door on the left.

"Come in!" the rector's familiar voice called out. "Come in!"

Entering the office, Kelly looked around. "Maguire's lair," as seminarians used to refer to the place, while never large in his memory, had shrunk too. Yet, it was reassuringly familiar. The walls lined with bookshelves, the huge window that overlooked the mountains, and the large picture of Christ on his knees in the Garden of Gethsemane, the excruciating agony on his face as he tried to duck the impending crucifixion. Most of all there was Maguire himself, reeking of the stogies that the rector spent a major portion of his waking life reducing to ashes.

Maguire came around his desk and pumped Kelly's hand like an old friend. "Kelly, how are you? Sit down. God, it's good to see you."

The pugnacious, challenging stare habitually on Maguire's square face gave him the look of a bulldog. Kelly thought how much like prisms people are, presenting different sides to the world as new circumstances arise. Fifteen years ago, he ran into Maguire in Rome. The rector had been most cordial to him. They had a pleasant dinner together and reminisced about the school, the changing character of the Church, and what the future might hold. Maguire considered all men who were priests as his brothers, and that included the legions of his former students. It was then that Kelly realized how much Maguire loved Gethsemane and understood the depth of the commitment he had made to bringing along young men who were dedicated to the Church.

"I'm fine, Frank. Just fine. And you?"

After finding Heron looking like a pudgy little insurance salesman, he was glad to see that Maguire appeared much the same as ever. His hair was still the same iron gray it was when Kelly was a seminarian, and, except for a few lines that were more deeply etched in his face, Maguire physically at least was the same man Kelly remembered.

The rector got back behind his desk and exhaled loudly. "Ah, we're on our last legs. Even though three of our seminaries closed down and their operations were consolidated here, we're not getting enough seminarians to stay open. Besides, I'm afraid I'm getting too old for this anyway, Kevin. The job's not as rewarding as it used to be. The quality of the seminarians we do get is generally nothing to brag about. I know I sound like an old windbag when I say that, but it's true. So few boys have a calling these days that we grab just about anybody."

"It can't be that bad," Kelly said, trying to make light of what he heard. He realized, however, the problem must be endemic because he often heard the same regret these days from other priests who taught at seminaries.

Beneath dark brows, Maguire's eyes stared back steadily. "It is, Kevin. It is. You know we've been losing priests like crazy ever since Vatican II unleashed a hurricane in the Church. Many left saying

106

they couldn't deal with the authoritarianism or politics, but I think more of it had to do with living without the solace of a wife and children. A lot of men can't handle that."

Kelly didn't have to be reminded. Out of the twenty-two who were ordained in his class, only nine were still priests. "What does that have to do with the quality of seminarians today?"

"Everything!" Maguire replied emphatically. He issued a short, barking laugh when Kelly gave him a mock look of bewilderment.

"We used to get guys who, if they weren't going to be priests, would've been top doctors, lawyers, corporate executives. Some truly brilliant men came through this institution, men who were worthy of sitting on the Supreme Court bench. Some still are, but like the Supreme Court appointments today, we're grateful to settle for mediocrity."

Maguire scowled. "A lot of them see becoming a priest as a way of always having a roof over their heads and three square meals a day and a way to pick up some respect at the same time."

Kelly laughed. "They have a lot to learn."

Maguire laughed too, but as he did, he looked at Kelly shrewdly, wondering what brought his former student back here after all these years. The priest still seemed solid as a rock. When first meeting Kelly, he had wondered if the guy could become a priest after what he'd been through. The clandestine jobs he'd done for the government. The death and violence to which he'd been exposed, including the terrible deaths of his wife and child.

Maguire knew that no one type of man was called to the priesthood. Hell, the twelve apostles had proved that. What convinced the rector to take Kelly was Bishop Gibbons's vouching for him. Gibbons wrote Maguire that, with effort, Kelly could adopt the Vincentian characteristics of humility, meekness, simplicity, zeal for souls, and mortification. "Meekness will be the toughest for him," Gibbons stated. As far as Maguire was concerned, a nod from Gibbons was worth more than a blessing from the pope. He knew Gibbons well, having gone through the seminary with him forty years ago. He didn't know the pope.

Once he had observed Kelly, Maguire had liked what he saw. The man had a lot of psychic wounds that obviously needed tending, but he was convinced they would heal and they had Kelly had proved to be smart and compassionate, if something of a loner. Maguire had found that understandable, especially in light of his being a bit older than most of the other students and the fact that he'd already packed more into his life than any half dozen of them combined ever would.

But why was he back here?

Kelly's phoning the other day saying he wanted to drop around for a chat meant something was up. He wasn't one of those priests who keep running back to their seminary like children afraid to cut the umbilical cord. That meant he was here on business. But what business?

Maguire was well aware of the work Kelly had done on the Carruthers mess. He had been asked by the pronuncio's office if he thought Kelly was up to the job, and Maguire had assured Pizzaro that he was. Maybe there was more of the kind, but how did it tie into Gethsemane? That was the question Maguire had asked himself repeatedly since Kelly called.

"So, what brings you here, Kevin?"

"Pat Hogan."

"You mean Bishop Hogan, don't you? The grapevine has it that they're finally getting around to turning him into royalty. They would have done it before this, but Murray has always been able to block the move." He leaned back and lit a cigar. "What does this have to do with you?"

Kelly gave Maguire an exasperated look. "I've been asked to check out his background, see if Hogan is really bishop material."

Maguire continued to eye him steadily. He managed to keep his face impassive, but he was shocked. With so much having changed in the Church during the past thirty years, he sometimes wondered if anything would ever surprise him again. Then along came another zinger. His mind scrambled over possibilities. Maybe something came out against Hogan during the Carruthers scandal. Unlikely. Maybe it was Hogan's links to Damian Carter. If certain mindless officials didn't think Hogan kept enough of a distance from his friend, they were apt to think he was tainted. A possibility.

Maybe Hogan had offended some power in Rome. Another possibility and a good one. Some of the prima donnas at the Vatican were known for destroying promising careers if they didn't feel they received the proper obeisance from the men. Hogan, for all his charm, wasn't one to kowtow or put up with slights. He remembered how Hogan once corrected a visiting bishop's French when the churchman made

108

a somewhat disparaging reference to a project the Vincentians had in Haiti.

Maguire wasn't a Vatican watcher. He left that to prelates such as Bishop Gibbons who tried to divine the politics of Rome and drank in the gossip about Vatican personalities as if it were lifeblood. When he thought of Rome at all, Maguire was wary. He loved to visit the place but tried to keep at arm's length from the politics. The Vatican was a factional minefield, as far as he was concerned. One where a man could still get a foot blown off unless he was extremely careful, even if he knew the political terrain inside out.

Looking at Kelly, Maguire felt a pang of sympathy. What a terrible task to have to undertake. He knew Kelly wouldn't have wanted the job, that some Church power had forced it on him.

"How can I help, Kevin?"

"They want to know about his relationship with Bill Witten and Damian Carter."

"Ah, the Trinity," Maguire said. He uttered the word with a combination of pride, pain, and regret, summarizing the emotional wringer Hogan, Carter, and Witten put him through over the years. Of all his seminarians, Maguire had expected the most from those three when they left and often felt that they gave back the least. "What about them, Kevin?"

"Some of our churchmen are worried about the particular friendship they had while here."

"What do you mean?" Maguire asked hotly. "They weren't that way, damn it."

Immediately, Kelly realized he had inadvertently used the seminary euphemism for homosexuality. He spoke up to defuse Maguire's outrage.

"Look, nobody's accusing them of being gay, but the Vatican is worried that they did something in tandem here that was seriously wrong."

"What are they driving at?" Maguire asked belligerently.

"I don't think they know, which is what makes this frustrating. All I know is that I'm supposed to find out if there are any skeletons in Pat's past or current closets. Anything you can tell me will be helpful."

Breathing deeply, the rector made an effort to calm himself. When he looked at Kelly again, his expression was grave. "I'll do that because you have to understand what they were like when they were here, Kevin. They were . . . They weren't perfect, but they were the very best young men *ever* to go through Gethsemane."

Maguire exhaled stale breath. "But before I go on, can you tell me if Murray's behind this? I warned Pat the last time I saw him that the archbishop wanted his head."

"No, Murray's not in the wings. At least not directly that I can tell."

"Good."

Kelly had heard tales about the archbishop's having it in for Hogan. "Why is he down on Pat?"

Maguire grimaced. "Jealousy, as far as I can determine. Murray likes stars in his orbit but only if he can control them. He'd like to haul out his pet celebrity TV priest whenever it suits him, but Pat won't let him do it. You know how Pat is if he gets on his high horse. As a result, Murray's out to wreck him."

"Where did you pick that up?"

"Bishop Regan, who runs the New York archdiocese on a day-to-day basis, is an old classmate of mine. He says Murray's hatchet man, Bishop Lawler, is building a dossier on Pat that's pretty rough."

Maguire looked at Kelly. "You'll want to see that dossier won't you?"

"Yes."

"Make sure you double-check everything in there when you do. Lawler could shade a case against Christ so He couldn't get into heaven."

Maguire drew thoughtfully on his cigar. "Kevin, a man such as Pat can set up resentment in others. He always went after what he wanted. Some people think that's a bit unseemly for someone in the religious life. But he worked for what he wanted too.

"Like the way he got that stint over at Vatican Radio when he was ordained. For several months before the head of Vatican Radio came here, Pat read everything he could about the operation. He wrote to department heads of communications schools and executives at radio stations asking them what could be done to improve Vatican Radio. He took all their responses and synthesized them. . . . He didn't leave anything to chance."

The rector frowned. "I'm not trying to imply that Pat was devious or anything. Just smart, very goal oriented."

The rector looked concerned. "But don't sell Hogan short. That

110

personal striving was offset by a genuine concern for people, including his classmates. He has some sort of emotional barometer in him that tells when people are out of whack, which I think is why his TV show is so successful."

"What do you mean?" Kelly asked.

The rector looked back thoughtfully. "I'll give you an example. When you were coming here, John Gibbons sent me a letter about you. He didn't go into much detail, just said you had been through a great deal and wanted me to look after you a bit. I sent Pat down to get you at the bus terminal. After he brought you back, I asked him what he thought."

Maguire paused. "He said you struck him as a man who had been in hell. That you had experienced a great loss and had done some terrible things. That he thought you had probably even contemplated suicide at one point, but came to grips with yourself and with God."

Amazed, Kelly flushed at the knowledge that Hogan had read him so accurately in such a short space of time. Hogan was more complicated than he realized. "That was a pretty fair summary of my life at the time."

"Pat helped me put my finger on what was bothering a lot of seminarians. I can tell you, I missed that knack when he was gone."

"Frank, do you know what significance, if any, the date March twentieth, 1972, and Washington might have for the Trinity?"

Maguire went to a bookcase where he kept his calendar books from each of the thirty years he'd spent as Gethsemane's rector. He pulled 1972 off the shelf and leafed through to the date Kelly mentioned. When he saw it, he almost blanched.

Unconsciously, Maguire turned his back on Kelly and stared out the window at the mountains in the distance. His face and his head throbbed as he once again thought of the trip the Trinity took to the nation's capital. Long ago, he had concluded that the seeds of their destruction were sown on that visit. He knew something was wrong, terribly wrong, when Hogan, Carter, and Witten returned. They were changed men.

"You don't remember, Kevin," Maguire said slowly. "That was when I gave permission to three of our seminarians to go to an antiwar demonstration in Washington."

"I recall it now," Kelly said, trying not to show his intense interest and excitement now that Maguire had connected the Trinity to Wash-

111

ington. He remembered his own indecisiveness about whether anyone should represent Gethsemane there. He also thought again about what passed through his mind when he was going to see Lane Woods. Had the Trinity gotten mixed up in some crazy radical crime? He made a mental note to check newspaper files to see if the date of the demonstration was the same as the one on the note the pope had received. "The first demonstration any seminarians from here were ever officially allowed to attend. You sent the Trinity."

"That's right. When they came back, I knew something had happened down there. They were unlike themselves. Their work here went to hell. They were indifferent. Withdrawn. Moody. Edgy. Sharp-tempered. They barely spoke to anyone else. At first I put it down to their impending ordination. Some seminarians get very uptight as the reality sets in that very soon they will be priests."

"How did you know it wasn't that?"

"From the vantage point of being rector, I'm able to see the people here more clearly than anyone else. The seminarians are preoccupied with their studies, the faculty with their jobs and careers. I'm the only one who gets to see the patterns of their lives. When those patterns change markedly for the worse, I step in and see if I can be of help."

"You did that in the case of the Trinity?"

Maguire paused, exasperated. "I tried. You see, they were barely being civil to anyone, including me."

"You got nowhere?"

"Nowhere. Ever since then I've felt guilty about them, especially Carter and Witten. Pat has done well, of course. Not what one expected, but still and all no one can take his accomplishments away from him, and he is up for bishop today."

The rector leaned back and reminisced. "When they first came here, they stood out. It wasn't just their brains and ability. They all had an air of authority that was unusual for youths their age. Pat was a kid off the streets, but he had the bearing of someone used to giving orders, not taking them. Bill had a strength about him too, but it was different. It was the flintiness of a boy who is truly confident in his choices in life."

"How about Carter?"

Maguire laughed, thinking of the dynamic little seminarian, the only one ever to have arrived in a Rolls-Royce. "Oh, he was the oddest. A regular princeling when he showed up, but one who sounded like Karl Marx wanting to get rid of the aristocracy. He had a bearing too

112

as he expounded on socialist theories and his readiness to save the world. His family had a lot of money, everything from tobacco to plastics. They almost dropped dead when he came here.

"Witten was undoubtedly the most unique though," the rector said.

Maguire still remembered being greatly impressed when he interviewed Witten, more impressed than he ever was by any boy applying for admission. From the youth's scholastic record and staggering IQ, he had expected someone remarkable. A straight-A student who was head of his class at a large public high school in Philadelphia and lettered in three sports in each year of school. The young man was offered scholarships by nearly twenty colleges, including Yale and Notre Dame. What Maguire found intriguing was that half the scholarships were academic and half athletic.

The rector had Witten's records on his desk when the prospective seminarian entered, a towering, muscular youth whose dark, serious eyes were old for his years. He stared intensely at Maguire, who asked him to be seated.

"Bill, it says here that you went through private schools in your early years and then public high school."

"Yes, Monsignor Maguire. My parents were killed in a car crash when I was seven. My uncle Geoffrey was named my guardian. He wanted me to be roundly educated. The private schools were so that I could learn languages while young. He sent me to a public high school so I could appreciate how most people in the country are educated."

Noticing the quizzical look on Maguire's face, Witten continued, "My upbringing was a little offbeat. My uncle's patents have made him rich and give him a great deal of free time to pursue varied interests, including my education."

As Witten continued talking, Maguire thought *offbeat* wasn't the word for Geoffrey Witten's use of his nephew to test his educational theories. Fortunately, the uncle's curious notions fed the boy's thirst for knowledge. From the outset of their relationship, Maguire gathered, the uncle had talked to his nephew as an adult. He ruminated on the world and its complexities, but never tried to impose his own beliefs on the boy. He enjoyed his nephew's brilliance and seriousness, liking to show him off to a circle of friends who included politicians, entertainers, and businessmen. Over dinner, he questioned Bill on a range of topics: astronomy, history, mathematics, physics, religion. At the

113

end of the meal, the uncle announced what the next evening's topic would be, so that young Bill would have a chance to bone up.

"I notice you are a convert," Maguire said. "We don't have many boys who are converts. What made you decide upon Catholicism?"

"I'm afraid that has to do with my uncle again. He's a freethinker. It's fairly involved, but he let me choose a religion. One evening at dinner, Uncle Geoffrey asked if I believed in God. I told him yes, but I couldn't say why."

Maguire could still picture the scene Witten re-created for him. The intense boy and his strange uncle seated opposite one another at a long dining table at the uncle's Gothic manor on Philadelphia's Main Line. The uncle raising a glass of wine with a flourish as he responds to his nephew's lacking a reason for his belief in God.

"Then damn it, boy, find out!" Geoffrey roared. His beefy face was flushed with excitement as if he verged on a great truth. "The worst thing in the world is people believing in something and not knowing why. It leads to all kinds of idiocy."

"Such as?" young Witten asked.

"Such as religious wars and burning people at the stake and forcing Galileo to recant the truth. Too many people believe something simply because they were raised with a belief. That's just another form of ignorance. Nothing is worth believing in unless you struggle to come to grips with the truth."

Over the next year, Bill Witten systematically examined the religions of the world. He tried to work out a rational belief for the existence of God but failed. When he turned to such philosophers and theologians as Socrates, Thomas Aquinas, Spinoza, and Kant, he determined that they could not prove his existence.

"I accepted Blaise Pascal's 'Why not believe?'—the final necessity of mystic faith for true understanding of the universe and its meaning to man. I came to accept the totality of the Catholic Church's insistence on blind faith, so I converted.

"When my uncle asked me why, I told him, 'There is no other way to know God. At least none that I can see.'"

Maguire had never heard a boy give such an articulate and analytical explanation for his belief in God, yet one that rested on the mystery of belief. "Why do you want to be a priest?" the rector asked.

"So I can become closer to God," Witten replied simply.

Maguire looked at the young man and felt a rush of wonder. The boy led with his heart as well as his head.

114

As Maguire thought of Witten, he remembered the seminarian's burning desire to know God. He clearly recalled entering the chapel one morning at the special moment when night shadows silver with the encroaching dawn light. It was Witten's last year in the seminary, and he was kneeling before the altar. As Maguire approached, he saw a look of anguish on the young man's face.

"What's the matter, Bill?" he asked gently.

Witten rubbed his dark eyes with both hands, as though trying to dispel a terrible vision. "It's this war, Monsignor. Last night, I dreamed about all the death and destruction."

The young man glanced up. "In my dream someone kept asking over and over, 'For what purpose? For what purpose?'"

Maguire hadn't known how to console him. He patted his shoulder and left him kneeling there. The rector had an uneasy feeling about the intensity Witten projected at times. Where would it lead him?

Because of what Witten said, however, Maguire also came away with a feeling that perhaps the seminary should play a role in winding down the war in Vietnam. President Nixon had just bombed Cambodia, setting off a new wave of despair and demonstrations across the nation. Priests and nuns were protesting in the streets and going to jail for their antiwar activities. At Gethsemane, Hogan, Carter, and Witten were in the forefront of seminarians petitioning Maguire that the seminary be shut down so they could go to a massive antiwar demonstration in Washington.

That morning Maguire posted a notice saying the issue of whether seminarians should go to the antiwar demonstration would be debated after dinner. He prayed that he was doing the right thing.

That evening, Pat Hogan, eyes flashing, stood at the lectern, facing the seminarians and faculty members seated at the rows of long wooden tables in the seminary dining hall. In the severity of his black cassock, the erectness of his posture, and his clean-shavenness, he was severely handsome and conveyed the militancy that he himself once found so awesome in Father Philip Berrigan.

"Even seminaries can no longer remain silent!"

Pausing dramatically, he gripped the lectern and leaned toward his audience. "In conclusion, I would like to quote Dorothy Day. 'I came here to express my sympathy for this act of peaceful sabotage, which is not only a revolution against the state but against the alliance of Church and state, an alliance which has gone on much too long

. . . only actions such as these will force the Church to speak out when the state has become a murderer!'"

Foot stomping and whistles spontaneously erupted from the seminarians. "Right, Pat," a seminarian yelled out.

"Right on, Pat!" yelled another.

Several faculty members, however, pointedly got up and walked out.

Maguire himself sat stony faced at the head table. Hogan was the last speaker. As Maguire had expected, he found Hogan's argument moving and convincing, but he heard something else in Hogan's voice that he hadn't expected to be there. Almost a yearning that he could speak out like this more often. That edge of the charmer who always wanted a bit more wasn't there.

Speaking in opposition to closing Gethsemane was a thoughtful student who argued that the act would be a presumptuous declaration of support for the antiwar movement when the American hierarchy had not voiced a clear-cut position on the issue.

Until now, Maguire had not realized how divisive the war was within his own institution, especially among the faculty. He grimaced. The faculty had embarrassed him. Two teachers had spoken on the issue as well. Their arguments had degenerated to the simplistic. The conservative faction, led by Father Joseph Donahue, carped that allowing seminarians to go to the nation's capital would be, in his estimation, a "disgrace." The liberal staff members' spokesman, Father Dirk Creedy, carped that it would be a "blow against freedom" if the school did not let all the seminarians go.

Maguire glanced over at Donahue, a smug, inflexible priest who sat as stiff-necked and sanctimonious as some self-righteous judge in Salem three hundred years ago. A fresh idea would fracture his skull. When he looked at Creedy, he felt a similar distaste. With his long, wavy hair, fashionable sideburns, and large cross hanging around his neck, the priest looked like a religious parody of Johnny Cash. To Maguire's dismay, a lot of seminarians admired Creedy, seeing him as a hip priest among an otherwise stale, stodgy faculty.

Prepared to announce his decision, Maguire pondered his own inflexibility. He had already made up his mind. After trying to believe that the White House knew what it was doing, Maguire was plagued with doubts for the past few years. A Marine Corps chaplain in Korea, he knew and liked military men. But the military was just an expression

116

of politics, and too often, political thinking was badly muddled, which struck him as the case now.

Last week, he had received word that one of his former students serving as a chaplain had been killed in action. A tough little "Southie" from Boston, the man was an all-around priest with the potential to do much good. For the past six months, the chaplain had written to Maguire, telling him what he witnessed. The word confirmed Maguire's own suspicions. The young priest concluded just before his death that Vietnam was a ghastly mistake on the part of the U.S.

Pushing back his chair to stand, Maguire hated this role of a latter-day Solomon, even if it was self-imposed. All eyes in the room stared at him, taking mental bets on which camp he would favor. The tension in the atmosphere was so thick, he wished he had a cigar, but smoking wasn't permitted in the refectory. When he thought of hell, it was a good Havana just out of reach. Shoving his fingers through his gray hair, he told himself to get on with it. He leaned aggressively on the table in front of him, palms pressed flat.

"Like all of you, I have listened to what was said here this evening. It is unfortunate that the troubles of the nation have spilled into our house."

He looked around the room, meeting each man's eyes. "I don't think it's a wise precedent to shut down the seminary so that all the students can go to a demonstration for something that is essentially a secular issue."

Murmurs swept through the hall. Donahue and his faction gave one another triumphant looks. Creedy stared around at seminarians and dramatically shook his head in despair.

"However, I am willing to send to Washington three delegates— official delegates—from the student body and one from the faculty. I want a vote now for whom to send."

Pieces of paper were handed to each student and faculty member; their votes were collected in a box. Fifteen minutes later, Maguire rose to his feet. "Your choice is made. The faculty member will be Father Dirk Creedy. The seminarians are Patrick Hogan, Damian Carter, and William Witten."

That time seemed so long ago as Maguire stared again at Kevin Kelly. "Pat's speech was strong stuff, but he was no militant. Anyway,

I expected the Trinity to be chosen. After all, who else would be chosen but the trio who were going to conquer the world?"

The rector paused. "Funny how life is. When they left here, they did all start off fantastically, just the way everyone thought they would.

"After his stint at Vatican Radio, Pat took a master's in communications at Catholic U. Before he even had the degree, he was making fund-raising films for Catholic Charities and the Propagation of the Faith. No ordinary propaganda films either. Not by a long shot. They were emotionally moving, uplifting, and made people want to dig deeper into their pockets to help others. He won a bunch of awards for them. Did you know that several producers in Hollywood wanted him to make feature films?"

"No, I think I was oblivious to everything but getting my own feet wet as a priest."

Kelly's first job had been as an assistant pastor in Brooklyn, where he came to think a measure of a priest was how many bingo games he could hold and how many keys he could carry. Keys to the church, the rectory, the elementary school, the parish hall, the locked closets and file cabinets. Keys seemed to give birth overnight to new ones, to the cars, the kitchen, the gym, the toolshed. At times he thought he packed every key but the one to the kingdom of heaven. Even today, he disliked carrying keys.

"Pat wouldn't do it," Maguire said, "because they wouldn't let him make the kind of film he wanted."

"What was that?"

"I'm not certain, but I remember it was some involved plot of retribution and atonement. He was teaching at Catholic U by then, and his name was all over the place because of his writing on film and television for national publications."

Maguire laughed. "Pat always knew how to play the angles. He was even a judge at some international film festivals. When the Vatican wanted to make a film on the pope, they turned to Pat. You remember how spectacularly successful that was."

The older priest stared thoughtfully out the window again. "Then along came this TV show. I could never figure that one. Have you asked him why he did it?"

"Not yet," Kelly replied, "I'm waiting for a tactful way to raise it."

"Carter started off with a bang too," Maguire recalled. "He was placed in a parish in Spanish Harlem where he found a home and a cause."

Maguire's voice was animated again. "God, was he good with those people. You know, until Carter came along, the New York archdiocese wasn't sure what to do with the Puerto Ricans who were coming into the city in droves. The old Irish gang at the chancery found the Hispanics noisy and immoral and moaned about their displacing the traditional Irish parishioners.

"Damian not only entered the Latin community but seemed to take it over. He visited them in prisons and hospitals and soon had job placement centers for them as well as Sunday camps where they could take their kids. He organized festivals similar to those the people left behind in Puerto Rico and started a training program for young priests who were going to Puerto Rico to learn Spanish.

"What first got him into hot water was the politics he preached along with his community activism. He told the people they had a right to take what they needed because political power had been denied them for too long. He started picketing and demonstrating everywhere, getting his parishioners all whipped up over their rights."

Stretching his arms, Maguire smiled ruefully. "That kind of thing never sat well with the chancery in New York. Then a couple of young hotheads who were in one of Damian's youth groups shot a cop during a bank robbery. When they were caught, there was a scandal. One quoted Damian on why such action was necessary for their political cause."

The rector shook his head with dismay. "Damian had an opportunity to put a lid on things by saying that the young men misunderstood his message. Instead, he made his situation worse by giving inflammatory statements to the press, and then he took on Cardinal McCormick himself. He was reprimanded by the cardinal and exiled from New York."

Maguire looked over at Kelly. "That's when he started showing up in hot spots around the world—Central America, Northern Ireland, the Middle East, South Africa, South America—espousing radical politics, encouraging revolution. There's talk that he's involved with a lot of groups that do terrible things in the name of trying to make a better world."

Frowning, Maguire continued, "He keeps challenging the Church, but I've always believed there's a basic sincerity in what he does and says. It's strange, but he acts almost as if he wants the Church to throw him out. I remember seeing him in New York just after his exile from the archdiocese was announced. He was pleased. Not in a smug way, mind you. But as if he were balancing the scales of justice and found that the punishment fit the crime."

Kelly remembered admiring a lot of the work Carter had done. The priest's praises were still sung in New York's Spanish community. But he too had wondered about Carter's penchant for taking his work and ideas too far. Why? At the seminary, Carter had been a very concerned young man who flirted with ideas on the political left, but he could have pushed for change from within the Church. What tipped him into the zealot camp?

"Then there was Witten," Maguire said finally. He looked at Kelly curiously. "I don't know how much seminarians realize about one another. Did you know that Witten was a certified genius? We try to keep such things from the students so that no one will be treated differently."

"No," Kelly said, but what Maguire said made sense in light of his own limited dealings with Witten during their seminarian days. Kelly fancied himself a good chess player, but whenever he had played with Witten, he felt like a novice. What amazed him was Witten's ability to talk about a very complex subject and get up to find references to support his thesis, then come back to the chessboard and nonchalantly make a devastating move.

"Everyone knew he was brilliant, so the genius business doesn't surprise me."

"The Romans had his records and wanted to get their hands on him. You know how they are always looking for shining young men whom they can mold into future leaders. Well, he got there and knocked their socks off. Went through the curriculum like a hot knife through butter."

Maguire sighed, once again feeling like a failure. If he had only done or said something to get through to them. How could he have let them just walk away?

"After the North American College, Bill studied at Oxford, and then a special honor was awarded him. He was given the opportunity to take another degree, an *agrégé en philosophie*. He was one of the few scholars since the Second World War to receive such an offer. He studied for it in London and Paris and went through the ritual

120

examination before some three hundred of the most learned men in Europe."

Smiling, Maguire savored the moment that had been related to him by one of the professors who had been one of Witten's judges. "After being put through a grueling oral examination, the candidates were sent to their rooms. The student knows he passed if he's invited to dinner. And he knows how well he did by the beverage that's served during the meal, starting with water."

"Do you know what they served Bill?" Maguire asked excitedly.

Without waiting for a reply, he rushed ahead. "Champagne, Kevin! They served champagne! The only one to get that since Fulton Sheen back in the twenties.

"When I told them in Rome that he was absolutely brilliant, I met some skepticism. Even after he was there and they saw what Bill was like, there were still some Italians at the Vatican who didn't like to credit him with his due because he was an American. But after that there could be no detractors."

Suddenly, Maguire rubbed his eyes as if he were very tired, and indeed he was. He also didn't like to think of the rest of it.

"The Vatican offered him all kinds of things after that. A career in the Secretariat of State, a professorship at the North American, a lot of things. Bill took a holiday to think things over. The last thing anyone knew, the car he took was found near Lake Como. His cassock and cincture were neatly folded on the front seat with his breviary and collar sitting on top. His body was never found."

Kelly knew this part all too well. Word of Witten's disappearance had spread through the clergy like wildfire. There was a great deal of talk about his acting strangely shortly before he went away. *Breakdown* was one of the two words most often whispered. *Suicide* was the other. Stories circulated that he had cracked under the intense intellectual strain of his final months in Rome, that the years of feeling he always had to be perfect were simply too much for him to bear.

There were rumors that the police, out of deference to the Vatican, never dredged the lake. Suicide was a mortal sin. A priest who was a suicide was a pariah. It was as if the Church wanted to avoid the issue altogether, so as not to say that the soul of Monsignor William Witten, one of the most brilliant churchmen of his day, was to suffer eternal damnation.

As Maguire spoke, Kelly thought of when they were all in their

121

last year here. How self-absorbed he had been that he hadn't noticed any change in the Trinity or any of his other classmates. How many problems in the world are compounded by our failure to see others, he wondered, because we are so wrapped up in ourselves?

"How much of what happened to them do you relate back to that trip to Washington?"

The rector turned and again stared out the window behind his desk. His voice was hushed when he answered. "On good days? A little of it. On bad days? All of it."

Maguire rose from his desk and kneaded his brow, trying to get rid of the tension pain that had hit his head. The ache settled in when the Trinity came to mind.

"Now, if you don't mind, Kevin, I'd like to stop talking about the past. Besides, I don't have any more to add. I have to think about the students who are in my care today."

Suddenly, Kelly remembered that Dirk Creedy had gone with the Trinity to Washington. Creedy had cut a dashing figure when teaching here. He celebrated Mass on weekends in homes in the ghettos of New York, Newark, and Philadelphia and married young couples in fields, streams, and forests. An army field jacket over his cassock, he spoke out in the strong accent of his home state of Texas against the war and called for some kind of humanistic socialism. There was always a group of students around Creedy who hung on every word the priest said, but Kelly was never sure why. He had listened to the teacher's orations several times, but always came away with the impression that Creedy's pronouncements were not only incoherent but not as extreme as the man pretended. Despite his radical appearance, the teacher took care not to do or say anything that his superiors might find offensive.

"One more question, if I may," Kelly said.

"Shoot," Maguire said, "but I'm warning you that my head is splitting from what I've already told you, so I don't know if I can be of any more help."

"Dirk Creedy went to Washington too, didn't he?"

"Yes."

"You must've talked to him about it."

"Of course," Maguire said disgustedly. "But once they got down there, Creedy went off with a group of his radical friends and didn't really spend much time with the Trinity. That didn't surprise me. Creedy always had his own agenda, and helping seminarians was not very high on it unless there was something in it for him. I remember he told me one time how coming here had stalled his career." Maguire looked at Kelly. "You should talk to him. I always got the feeling he was holding something back. I don't know why. Maybe now that he's a bishop he'll talk."

"Funny how he turned out," Kelly said. "Once he was considered a radical outsider and now he's a paragon of conservatism serving the Vatican."

"A very able politician," Maguire said dryly. "He picks up scents in the wind before anyone else and makes his career moves based on them."

Maguire stood and came around his desk to shake hands as they parted. "I don't know whether what I've told you is useful. I hope it is. And I hope for all our sakes that Pat holds up under your investigation. I'd hate to see the last of the Trinity lose his brightness."

7

THE NEXT DAY, KELLY CROSSED FIFTH AVENUE AT FIFTIETH STREET AND glanced at St. Patrick's Cathedral nestled in the midst of soaring Manhattan skyscrapers. The church was starting to look as if it belonged in a village in the Swiss Alps. As nearby buildings loomed ever larger, the cathedral diminished in size.

Kelly fought his way through the wall of pedestrians. Rush hour seemed to be a permanent condition in this part of the city. Traffic clogged the streets. People bulldozed over one another as if their lives depended on reaching their next appointment in eight seconds flat. He darted across Fifth Avenue and walked along Fiftieth Street on his way to the archbishop's residence on Madison Avenue, just behind the cathedral.

When he'd returned from Gethsemane yesterday, several messages were waiting for him at St. Mary's, the rectory in Harlem where he was staying. One of the notes was from the tycoon Edwards, wanting Kelly to have lunch with him today. The other was from Bishop Lawler, ordering him around to the archbishop's residence at ten A.M. this morning. Not knowing how long Lawler would take, Kelly had called Edwards's office to see if lunch at one o'clock would be all right. It was. Kelly wondered if the two wanting to see him the same day was a coincidence.

Expecting the time with Lawler to be unpleasant, Kelly rang the bell at the archbishop's residence. Bishop Lawler was a scrawny little man in his sixties with an outsize head for his frail body. He wore horned-rimmed glasses and his glistening black hair was slicked across his head with Vaseline, giving him the look of a wizened child. Long ago, Kelly determined the bishop suffered from "littlemanitis," one of the symptoms being bullying priests under the guise of what was good for them. The bishop often got personal. Kelly particularly disliked Lawler's rude remarks about his size. The last time he saw him, the bishop pointedly made a reference to "big dumb oxen." Kelly had been tempted to pick him up and spank him.

The door was opened by a maid wearing a black uniform with white collar, cuffs, and apron. "Can I help you, Father?"

"My name is Father Kelly. I have an appointment with Bishop Lawler."

"Right this way, Father," she said, speaking with a brogue, a reminder that the practice here of hiring Irish help dated back to the nineteenth century when the cathedral was built on the pennies and dimes of the city's largely immigrant Irish population.

"Bishop Lawler is expecting you," she said. She took his coat and led him up the stairs to an office, ushered him inside, and left immediately.

Sitting at his desk, Lawler was reading a letter. He didn't look up, ask Kelly to sit, or otherwise acknowledge the priest's presence.

The cramped office had a large picture of the pope and a larger one of Archbishop Murray. Smaller pictures depicted Lawler with Murray celebrating Mass, dedicating a building, and standing in St. Peter's Square with Cardinals Canali and Tichi, two Vatican power-houses, a demonstration of how well connected the bishop was.

As the minutes ticked by, Kelly wondered how the man could spend so much time staring at one sheet of paper. Glancing around, Kelly thought of the maneuver as a stupid example of one-upmanship that had to be more tiresome for Lawler than for himself.

"Mind if I sit down, Bishop?" he finally asked while taking the seat in front of the desk.

The little man looked up and slapped the paper down on his

desk. "Go ahead," he snapped. "I guess mighty oaks don't always stand tall."

Kelly wondered at the strange metaphor. The time promised to pass even more slowly than he'd imagined.

Lawler shot him a wintry smile and hefted a manila envelope. "So, Archbishop Clarizio has you checking out Hogan. A good thing they didn't just put a miter on that one's head without first seeing what kind of a man he is."

Still holding the envelope, Lawler left his chair and came around so that he sat on the front right corner of his desk, one leg dangling in the air, the toe of his other shoe not quite touching the floor.

"Kelly, I'm going to make your job easy. What I'm holding here is all you need to know. It's all Archbishop Clarizio needs to know."

He held the folder teasingly toward Kelly, as if tempting him to grab it. "You know that your assignment is highly unusual? Of course, you do."

The smile became a grin. "This procedure was deemed necessary because Hogan is *not* bishop material. As far as I'm concerned, he's not fit to be a priest. Now I've been keeping tabs for quite some time on our TV celebrity. Our hotshot TV star. It's all here, Kelly, and you'll be very glad I am willing to share it with you. But first, we have to get some ground rules straight."

For the next fifteen minutes, Lawler strutted around his office, dictating how Kelly wasn't allowed to cite either Archbishop Murray or himself as a source for any of the information. He went to great lengths contending that the archbishop had no knowledge whatsoever of the report, so therefore his name could not be attached to it in any event. He also assured Kelly that the information had been checked and double-checked.

The bit about Murray's not knowing anything amused Kelly. The archbishop was a hands-on administrator and a stickler for detail. Requisitions for everything from altar linens to toilet paper required his approval. To pretend he knew nothing about a special report being quietly concocted on the most prominent priest not only in his archdiocese but in the nation was absurd.

"Now, are we clear?" Lawler asked, finally sitting behind his desk again.

Kelly paused, long enough for Lawler to frown. "Very clear."

"Will you accept the report under these conditions?"

All the while Lawler was talking, Kelly knew he had no choice in the matter. Word of the report would certainly get back to Clarizio. He had to take it. If he didn't, he could be accused of not being diligent. Besides, he had a professional curiosity. Before entering the priesthood, he had seen experts prepare disinformation. He wondered how Lawler's work compared to that of the pros. What made him uneasy, however, was that the report might actually contain damning evidence that was true.

"Yes."

"Good. Good."

The bishop picked up his phone and dialed. Swiveling in his chair, he turned his back on Kelly and spoke so quietly the priest could not hear what was being said.

Hanging up, Lawler stood and said brightly, "Come with me. You're very fortunate. The archbishop would like to give you his blessing."

Inwardly, Kelly groaned. He had hoped to escape without seeing Murray.

A minute later, they made their way downstairs, and Lawler led the way into a small sitting room. Suddenly, Archbishop Murray appeared in the doorway. He too was short, only slightly taller than Lawler. His face was round and his eyes shrewd as he sized up Kelly in a glance. He wore a black cassock with purple embroidery and a purple silk cape. A gold pectoral cross hung around his neck.

The Church is democratic in the breadth of backgrounds from which Her royalty is drawn. The American hierarchy especially showed that pedigree accounts for little in terms of advancement. Murray's father had been a butcher in New Hampshire, and there was still an air of the small-town shopkeeper about him. Despite his unprepossessing appearance, he instinctively knew how to acquire power and how to use it to his best advantage, except in moments when he let his ego override his intellect. Kelly wondered if that wasn't the case in the conflict between him and Hogan. Unless, of course, the archbishop knew something about Pat that others didn't. The document Lawler gave him suddenly felt heavier.

Kelly walked across the room, knelt, and kissed the ring the archbishop proffered. Murray nonchalantly waved him to his feet.

"I know something of your mission, Father Kelly. A sad business, but a necessary one I'm afraid. I hope everything turns out well for

128

Monsignor Hogan. No matter what the outcome, I'm sure everything will still turn out well for the Church."

He smiled benignly at Kelly. "After all, that is where your loyalty lies, doesn't it? That's really where all our loyalties lie. Not to family. Not to friends. But to the Church! Remember that, Father Kelly. Now, go with the grace of God."

As quickly as he had materialized, Murray disappeared. Kelly found himself being propelled by Lawler toward the doorway like a cruise liner being pushed from port by a tugboat.

"For God's sake don't lose that report," Lawler said. "If you have any problems or need any explanations, get back to me. Or if there's anything else I can get, don't hesitate to ask. The Church does not need bums in the hierarchy."

Since he had time to kill before his lunch with Edwards, Kelly went to the main public library at Fifth Avenue and Forty-second Street, making directly for the vaulted reading room on the third floor. The report was burning a hole under his arm and his stomach was in turmoil. What was Lawler so gleeful about?

Kelly sat at one of the long, oak library tables and gingerly extracted the material from the envelope. The dossier consisted of five typewritten pages. Hogan was never referred to by name or title, simply as "The Subject." As he scanned the report, Kelly realized that it was a professional job.

The report contained a signed statement confirming what Lane Woods had told him. The girl's name and the circumstances were the same. A young woman, who had worked on "Life Has Meaning," accused the Monsignor of having seduced her and claimed he had her thrown off his show when he tired of her. There were hints that such behavior had happened before with other women with whom he had worked, but no other examples were spelled out.

The young woman's statement was initialed at key places and signed, dated, and witnessed by Lawler. The statement was clinical but quite specific and left little doubt that Pat Hogan had broken his vow of celibacy. The signature at the end of the report was "Frances Cook."

There was also information about Hogan's having a rendezvous with a woman in Soho. The address was on Mercer Street. Hogan met the woman almost weekly. Her name was Connie Robbins.

In addition, there was a list of lunches and dinners that Hogan had had with an unidentified woman, including names of restaurants and dates. Notations under some of the lunches emphasized that the restaurants were part of hotels.

When he finished the damning reading, Kelly felt drained. He remembered what Maguire had said about Lawler's ability to slant. He would not only have to double-check the information but confront Hogan on much of it point by grubby point.

The true nature of this rotten job suddenly dawned on him. It was the difference between the Napoleonic Code and the English judicial system. In France, a man is guilty until proven innocent. In the eyes of the Church, Pat Hogan was guilty until Kelly could prove otherwise. If he could.

The Edwards Tower was a new, slender skyscraper that soared into the Manhattan sky. The walls were mirrored, allowing those inside to see out; people outside the building only saw what was around them reflected back. The pleasant vaulted lobby contained an atrium with a distinctive international flavor. A huge map of the world on the rear wall showed the locations of the Edwards Corp. holdings like troop movements on a battlefield. On every continent, red flags fluttered in the gentle air currents. Beneath the map were huge pots containing flowers indigenous to each country where there was an Edwards operation.

Kelly approached the gray-uniformed guard behind the reception desk that formed an oval in front of the bank of elevators. The guard was staring at a row of TV monitors.

"I have an appointment with Mr. Edwards. My name is Father Kelly."

Scrutinizing the priest carefully, the guard picked up a phone and spoke so he couldn't be heard, implying that terrorists dressed as priests routinely tried to sneak past him. "Okay, Father," he said, cradling the receiver and handing Kelly a laminated pass. "Take that far elevator. It goes directly to Mr. Edwards's offices."

Kelly entered the brass elevator and pressed the lone button. A moment later, he was being whisked to the thirty-eighth floor. As soon as he stepped into the large reception area, a young woman rushed up. She was tall and her dark hair was pulled into a severe bun. Her long, nondescript, baggy, gray wool dress reminded Kelly of the habits worn by nuns when he was a boy.

"Let me show you into the dining room, Father."

He followed her into an airy chamber with views overlooking the Manhattan skyline from midtown south to the World Trade Center towers. A table, replete with white linen, crystal goblets, silverware, and fresh roses, was set for two.

"Mr. Edwards wishes to apologize. He is on a long-distance call and will be a few more minutes. You can ask Julio for whatever you need."

At the mention of his name, a stocky, middle-aged Colombian waiter entered and smiled as he set a silver ice bucket next to the table. "Is there anything I can get for you from the bar, Father?"

Kelly seldom drank during the day and was about to say no, but changed his mind. After going through Lawler's file, he wanted a drink. Now he wondered what garbage Edwards was going to heap on him.

"Yes, thanks. Wild Turkey on the rocks."

Several minutes later, he took a sip of his drink as Edwards entered. The tycoon bade him remain seated and warmly shook his hand.

"Very good to see you again, Father Kelly. Very good of you to come."

Once again, Kelly was amazed at how much he disliked this man. Edwards's cordiality struck him as being coated in a false unctuousness. He was sure the millionaire was much more accustomed to making demands on people than attempting to be gracious. Giving Edwards the benefit of the doubt, he made an effort to be pleasant.

"Quite a spectacular headquarters you have."

"Yes, we like it."

Kelly found the use of *we* irritating too. Why did Edwards bother him so much? He put it down to the fact that the man was going to say things about Pat Hogan that he didn't want to hear. Lunch promised to be as much of a pain in the ass as his visit with Lawler.

Momentarily taking his eyes off Kelly, Edwards turned to the waiter. "The chardonnay should be chilled by now."

He turned back to the priest. "I had a case of it flown in from France last week. We have our own wine cellar as well as our own

131

cordon bleu chef, so our kitchen can make just about anything you may want. I'm having veal *française*, but please, order anything you like."

Kelly felt like ordering a hamburger with a lot of ketchup, but why push? "That's okay with me too."

"Good," Edwards said as the waiter returned with a bottle of white wine and poured a taste into his employer's goblet. Edwards swirled the wine and sipped it. His lips pursed and his eyes momentarily looked toward the ceiling. He set the glass down with unnecessary exactness and glared at the waiter.

"I told you to chill this wine," he said threateningly. "Now do it."

"But it was chilled," the waiter protested.

"Don't you *dare* argue with me!" Edwards said icily.

Muttering apologies, the waiter took the bottle and left. Kelly shifted uncomfortably, wondering if there was a special ring of hell for people who humiliated those who had to take it.

"I'm really glad you could make it, Father," Edwards said as though nothing had happened. "This Hogan business has us all going these days."

Kelly looked askance. "What do you mean, Mr. Edwards?"

Edwards adjusted his napkin on his knees. When he looked up, his eyes were steely. "There are those of us who care very deeply about the Church, Father Kelly. Very deeply. We don't want to see the wrong men get what they aren't entitled to in the Church."

"I'm not sure what you're driving at. Most Catholics care about the Church and the kinds of men who govern Her."

Edwards's expression became grimmer. "A lot of Catholics *say* they care, but there are those of us who mean it. We actively work for the Church and try to make sure that the men who lead Her are on sure footing."

He carefully aligned his utensils on each side of his plate though they didn't need straightening. When he spoke again, it was slowly, deliberately, as if trying to control himself.

"That isn't an easy task today, Father. You know how much rot there is in the Church. Priests helping the Sandinistas. The Dutch bishops espousing worse heresy than Luther. The Filipino bishops who let their priests openly live with whores. The pope himself preaches against capitalism!"

Edwards made a chopping motion with his right hand. "We have

132

to cut that rot right out, not let more of it in. For every priest and bishop working for Solidarity, there are ten who are trying to undermine the Church in Africa or Latin America."

Kelly cocked an eyebrow at the tycoon, a closet cardinal who thought he should be pope. Laymen who got too wrapped up in Church matters gave him the creeps.

"Which, I assume, brings us around to Pat Hogan, doesn't it?"

The priest's sharp tone made Edwards look up abruptly. "Yes, yes, it does," Edwards said. "Now, I know about the report Bishop Lawler gave you. He's a friend of mine, and believe me, he wouldn't have shown it to me unless he had implicit trust in my discretion. I hope you have come to see me in that light as well, because what I have to tell you is between us. I am trusting you because you have been entrusted with a very serious job. It is as simple as that."

The waiter brought their food while Edwards was talking. The tycoon began eating, pausing between bites to speak.

"Don't get me wrong. I've always liked Hogan on a personal level. But he represents a danger to the Church, and that I can't abide. A very terrible danger."

"How?" asked Kelly, who couldn't bring himself to eat a mouthful now.

Edwards looked at him shrewdly, as if the tycoon were about to make a brilliant observation. "You know who his best friend was at the seminary? Damian Carter. Damian Carter has spent his lifetime trying to destroy the Church! You probably don't know that Carter uses Hogan to further his causes and to try to discredit good men within the Church."

The waiter returned with the wine, and Edwards took the glass into which Julio poured a measure and swallowed it without going through the connoisseur's pantomime. Unconsciously, he lifted the glass for a refill, and Kelly realized the man wasn't a wine aficionado at all.

The tycoon firmly set down the glass as added emphasis for what he was to say next. "Fortunately, no one in a position of responsibility listens to the kind of rubbish he concocts. Still, it is dangerous, very dangerous, because one can never tell where such things may lead. For that reason, I will give you information that will help you. There is a Monsignor Ruggieri in Rome who will talk to you about it too. A brilliant man, absolutely brilliant. He will tell you what Hogan does for Carter. The undermining. The deceit."

133

Edwards angrily dusted his lips with his napkin and then threw it on his plate. "Hogan must be stopped. What he does with women is terrible enough, but there he is only damning his own soul. By being Carter's devious instrument, he harms the Church Herself. If Hogan is allowed to become a bishop, the prominence of the office will increase his potential to cause harm."

Edwards leaned forward, his expression one of alarm. "He could use that TV program more and more as a way to promote Carter's causes! He does that already! The dregs of society appear there. Perverts. Homosexuals. Drug addicts."

Kelly wondered at the man's message of fear and bigotry. A Torquemada chomping at the bit. Where had Edwards gotten it? Why had his religion failed him? Why were too many people unable to learn charity and tolerance? Kelly moved his chair back, indicating he wanted to leave.

"Do you have anything concrete, Mr. Edwards?"

"Of course. I know what's at stake here."

Abruptly, Edwards stood and said, "I'll be back momentarily." He rushed from the room.

Returning a few minutes later, he carried a sealed white envelope and handed it to Kelly. "You will find what I'm talking about in here."

Kelly wasn't about to give Edwards the satisfaction of reading whatever it was in front of him, knowing by the expectant look on the man's face that he would have liked nothing better. Instead, Kelly tapped the envelope nonchalantly on the table before putting it inside his suit jacket, thinking how well prepared these men were with their damaging information. How anxious they were to make his job easier. How lucky he was they lubricated the machinery to damn Pat Hogan out of a position of power and responsibility in the Church. What great guys.

Lawler was easy to figure. He was doing Murray's bidding. But Kelly still wasn't sure what Edwards held against Hogan. There had to be more to it than a conservative's wild-eyed fear of someone he damned as a liberal. Maybe for Edwards that was all it was. He sighed as he gave him the same benefit of the doubt he gave Lawler. Maybe the guy was right about Hogan.

"Just be grateful that I was able to give you this," Edwards said. His curt tone was such that he might have used to dismiss an employee.

Kelly eyed him coolly, wondering if Edwards had a need to be disliked. He stood and loomed over the tycoon. "If what you have is valuable, I will be," he said. "But I guess we won't know that until *I* decide whether it is. Isn't that right, Mr. Edwards?"

Edwards appeared taken aback. His eyes flashed angrily and his answer somehow sounded like a threat. "Yes. Yes, it is, Father Kelly."

Kelly took the No. 1 subway, exiting at 137th Street. There was an eight-block stretch through one of the grimmer sections of Harlem to the old brick rectory next to St. Mary's Church. The contrast between the glitter and glamour of midtown Manhattan and the grime and grinding poverty in this neighborhood was disheartening.

By the time Kelly reached the rectory, he had almost adjusted to the desolation when he became depressed, as always, be by the sight of the iron bars on the rectory windows. Once in the vestibule, he had to unlock a gate in the huge metal web that stretched from floor to ceiling. It was now necessary to go through this prisonlike gate to gain access to the rest of the rectory. The grating was put there the last time junkies broke into the building.

When he returned from the Carruthers mess, Kelly chose to live at St. Mary's while waiting to be assigned to a parish. The pastor, Tim Brady, had been a year ahead of him at Gethsemane and now desperately needed help at this godforsaken parish. The chronic shortage of priests in the U.S. meant they were needed everywhere. St. Mary's wasn't a high-priority assignment.

In his small room, Kelly stretched out on his bed and opened Edwards's envelope. He extracted the neatly typed sheets of paper, thinking once again how easy everything was being made for him. It was a wonder Edwards didn't hand him a leather-covered loose-leaf binder embossed with "The Destruction of Patrick Hogan" in gilt lettering in which to store his and Lawler's material.

The report contained the names of Bishop Falconi and the Monsignor Vincenzo Ruggieri whom Edwards had mentioned. The document stated that Hogan spoke with Falconi on a visit to Rome three months earlier about alleged irregularities regarding Propagation of the Faith funds earmarked for missions in Latin America.

"Monsignor Hogan implied that someone or some people within the Vatican were abusing their offices and misdirecting funding. He demanded an investigation," the report stated. "The allegations were investigated and determined to be false.

135

"The same charge was later made by Father Damian Carter at an Inter-American Catholic Conference in Costa Rica, which resulted in a great deal of embarrassment to the Church and the men in charge of the mission funding. In certain quarters, the unsubstantiated claims are still used to harm the Church.

"Monsignor Hogan later admitted that the only source for this false charge was Damian Carter. This willingness to be a dupe of Damian Carter raises strong questions about Monsignor Hogan's judgment."

Kelly breathed a little easier. While not inconsequential, the issue was one that could have happened to anyone. Hogan had risked a great deal by taking such a matter to the Vatican. That one act would have made him certain enemies. He would also have lost a great deal of credibility since the charges hadn't help up. Quite obviously, there was not enough damage in the wake to jeopardize Hogan's being nominated for bishop. Still, it must have cast a large shadow over whatever he said and did.

Kelly determined to get hold of Ruggieri and try to find anyone else at the Vatican who knew what the hell had happened. He could bounce what they said off Hogan. Who knows? Maybe Edwards was trying to make a mountain out of a mole hill. Or maybe out of Damian Carter. After listening to Edwards today, Kelly could imagine what the man thought of anyone who had anything to do with Carter. To him, Carter must be Satan.

Tossing the Edwards memo on his bureau, he closed his eyes to try to get a little sleep before going downtown. He needed a nap after being dragged out of bed early this morning to give the last rites to an elderly woman who hadn't been able to escape an apartment fire. While he hadn't looked forward to the visit with Edwards, he dreaded the one he had to make this evening.

136

8

SOUTH OF THE HARLEM SLUM PARISH WHERE KELLY EASED INTO SLEEP,
Damian Carter paced back and forth in Pat Hogan's large living room
at the Mayfair Hotel in the pleasant enclave of Manhattan's Gramercy
Park. White winter sunlight streamed through the three large windows
overlooking the park and gave a warm, bright feel to the airy apartment.
The furnishings were a comfortable and graceful blend of traditional
and antiques.

Since coming back to New York after the Antiapartheid Conference broke up yesterday, Carter was tenser than ever. Achy and dizzy,
he was running a temperature. He traced his sickness back to his being
caught in a downpour the night he met Bishop Falconi at the Colosseum. On top of how lousy he felt, he was upset and frightened by
Falconi's murder.

Irrationally, his fear turned to outrage at Hogan for not sharing
his political and social aspirations. Restlessly moving about, Carter
wondered at how his friend had become such a paragon of the pam-
pered clerical elite. In the seminary, Hogan talked about the Berrigans
as if they were gods and how one day he'd follow in their footsteps.

137

Carter shook his head hopelessly. Hell, Hogan was a clerical yuppie. The disparity between this apartment and the hovels called home by many of the conference delegates made him angrier. Pat was even better off than the pastors at rich suburban parishes who lolled their lives away playing golf at country clubs and buttering up little old ladies who would leave a fortune to the Church, not to say a healthy chunk of stock and cash for the good pastor who greased their entrance to heaven.

Hogan sat on a Chippendale chair drinking a cup of Darjeeling tea and with dismay, watched Carter's agitation. Damian was too wound up. He looked as if he wasn't sleeping. His color was high and he was sweating, as if he was ill. He'd been talking and pacing nonstop since he arrived. If Hogan didn't know better, he would think Damian was on drugs.

"For all I know, the Vatican killed Falconi for coming to me," Carter said.

Momentarily, Carter stopped pacing, oblivious to the flash of anger in Hogan's eyes. He started pacing again. "That would be one of the ultimate ironies, wouldn't it? One of the Church's money machines. He lived like a medieval monarch off the backs of the poor, and he called me! Then he was murdered. Nothing makes sense anymore, Pat. Nothing!"

While Carter ranted, Hogan tried to stay calm, but his patience was running thin. He knew part of Damian's gibes were veiled references to his own affluence, but not all. Distraught over what had happened to Bishop Falconi, he was about to tell Carter to shut up.

"Lay off, Damian," he said wearily. "True, the archbishop was aristocratic, but he was also deeply compassionate. Why despise the man so? For God's sake, poor Falconi's dead and you're still picking him apart. Examine some of your own attitudes. You still rant about anyone rich as if you're lashing out at your parents."

For Hogan, Falconi's loss was especially painful. The monsignor came to know the bishop well when he was in Rome shooting his documentary about the pope. Falconi was most helpful. Going far beyond the dictates of protocol, the bishop gave Pat insights into the pope's personality and character that Hogan tried to elicit on film. The reserved bishop and the gregarious American took to one another immediately, and their friendship continued after the film was finished. He also knew that it was as much thanks to Falconi's speaking up for him in Rome as the success of the film that he had been made a monsignor, and that Falconi had also been in the vanguard of the hierarchy who promoted his case for bishop.

"Uh-huh," Carter said sarcastically, thinking how Hogan had buttered up Falconi, just the way he buttered up a lot of the hierarchy. Well, it was paying off. Bishop Hogan.

Hogan shook his head. Carter would have been surprised at some of the socially liberal positions the bishop had privately held. There were numerous unpublicized incidents of Falconi's kindnesses, of his quietly helping the needy, materially and spiritually, whether poor or rich. Hogan was about to give one such example but decided against doing so. It would be wasted on Damian, who had long ago made up his mind about Vatican officialdom. Some of Damian's notions about the hierarchy were as crude as old Marxist cartoons depicting capitalists as bloated, cigar-chomping plutocrats. Damian's harangues at times reminded him of his own father's anticlericalism.

"You seem to be jumping to conclusions," Hogan said.

Carter glared and shook his head in frustration. How could such a smart guy be so damned dense at times? He had just told Hogan about his strange encounter at the Colosseum. He also told him he now possessed information that could be damaging to the Vatican. Information Falconi gave him! All the while, Hogan passively stirred milk into his tea like some English spinster and said he didn't understand what he was being told. Was he still smarting from the mission-fund business?

"Look, Pat. I appreciated your going to bat for me on that money-laundering scam and Propagation of the Faith funds not showing up in Central America and Paraguay. I know you got a little egg on your face because the charges weren't proven. Whoever did it has to have a pipeline right into the Vatican."

"A little egg? Right," Hogan said disgustedly. "Damn it, Damie, you know I looked like an ass in Rome. Apparently, it was just a matter of bookkeeping errors. If Falconi didn't finesse it for me, a lot more people would have known that I acted like a fool."

"Believe me, Pat," Carter said with a dismissive wave of his hand, "you'll prove right on that one yet."

Hogan felt like picking up Carter and shaking him, shaking a lot of the nonsense out of him. For years now, Damian saw conspiracies everywhere. There were times when Hogan wondered if his friend wasn't a full-blown paranoid. He came back from trips with hair-curling tales of intrigue, but when push came to shove, there seemed to be nothing there but smoke. This last wild tale about almost being murdered by an assassin was too much. What a gruesome way to try to capitalize on Bishop Falconi's murder.

Wearily, Hogan rubbed his eyes. Not only that, but Damian was asking him to believe that Bishop Falconi met with him at the Colosseum the night he was killed and that he gave Damian vital information to help his cause. The whole idea was preposterous. Why on earth would the bishop ever meet with Damian of all people? That the elegant bishop would be skulking around on some radical mission was absurd. He found it easier to believe that Falconi, rather than wanting to help Damian's causes, would have wanted to excommunicate his friend. Oh, he was sure they met, but that it was some chance encounter Damian aggrandized for some left-wing purpose that he wasn't revealing.

"Let's try one more time," Carter said sarcastically, stopping directly in front of Hogan. "I'm bringing this to you because you're a powerful guy who has the ear of a lot of the Church's brass. Now, if I give you a copy of the material Falconi gave me, will you place it in the right hands? This will even help make you a bishop."

Hogan laughed ironically. "How do you think anything you do would be helpful with regard to the bishop business?"

Carter flushed but held back his angry reply. Chastened, he spoke again. "Will you help me?"

Hogan wasn't about to make this kind of promise, not with what was at stake at the moment. How would it look to Rome right now if he committed himself to more potential Carter lunacy? Damn it, he went over and over whether he should bow out of the running after Kevin Kelly told him about the investigation he was conducting. He admitted to himself that, yes, he did want to be a bishop, even though . . . He pushed the dark thought from his mind. It was time to stop brokering Damian's harebrained schemes and charges, making them sound plausible to people in the Church. He couldn't protect him forever.

"I don't know," he finally replied.

"What the hell do you mean you don't know?" Furious with himself for being in the position where he might have to beg, Carter turned on Hogan. He looked at this sleek, handsome man sitting in this luxury apartment, thinking again what a coddled creature he'd become. Instead of acting like some celebrity-joke priest, he should be trying to help the people who couldn't afford the goods that were huckstered on his TV show.

Carter yanked at his clerical collar to loosen it, feeling the burning heat of sickness mingle with frustration at not being able to think clearly or to argue his case effectively. Suddenly, he was tired of Hogan and the games he played. "I could blow your whole little world wide open and you know it," he said scornfully. "I never cared about me, and God knows whether Bill was right or wrong in the way he took his leave. But you have a lot to lose, if I ever tell what happened."

Hogan's eyes became noncommittal. Long ago he realized that one day they would have this conversation, and he had dreaded it. Now that it was a reality, he found it almost comforting to touch on something that had never been mentioned in all these years, even though it brought back the most haunting memories of his life.

"So, it has come down to blackmail. Is that it, Damian?"

Suddenly, the anger drained out of Carter as he looked at the tired and fearful expression on Hogan's face. How low could he stoop? He had betrayed his friend and himself as well. He who espoused loving humanity had thought nothing of wounding a friend, the one man in the Church he truly counted on over the years for unconditional trust. He was sick to death of himself. He was losing it. He had to get some sleep. Since Falconi's death, he had been tense and edgy. Whenever he shut his eyes, he had nightmares about the phantom killer that blurred into the nightmares he still had from when he was one of the Trinity. God, he ordered himself, pull yourself together.

"Sorry, Pat," he muttered. "Forget it. Forget everything. I'll never say anything. You know that."

"Maybe it would be better if one of us did," Hogan said. "For all our sakes."

"I said forget it!" Carter shouted tensely as he walked toward the door.

Hogan stood up, not knowing what to do or say. He was truly worried about Carter's emotional state. This wasn't like him. Maybe Damian seriously needed psychiatric help. Or, he thought, giving his friend the benefit of the doubt one more time, maybe he had really encountered something that was terribly upsetting. Maybe even the bit about the meeting with Falconi was true. Who was he to call anyone a liar?

"Wait a minute, Damian. Suppose you let me evaluate the material before I say one way or the other what I'll do with it. Does that sound reasonable?"

"More than reasonable in light of what a bastard I've been. I'll drop it by as soon as I can."

"I thought you had it with you."

"No, it's in Latin, perhaps in code too. I'm giving it to someone to translate it."

Hogan sighed. Of course. What else? More games. More juvenile intrigue. He found himself growing truly alarmed. How could he get Damian to see someone who could help him? He would never go to one of the Church's psychiatric centers. Maybe there was a psychiatrist radicals trusted.

Gathering up his briefcase as he prepared to let himself out, Carter moved more slowly than usual, trying to mend a part of his spirit that he had just badly damaged. He knew he was too tense, too over-wrought, but he sensed that what he had in his possession warranted it. But was it worth it? Nothing merited hurting Pat that way. He felt as if a wire had broken in him and the ends were curling away from one another. He and Pat both knew he had just irrevocably altered their relationship, which may have snapped in two as well.

"Keep the faith, Pat," Damian said, calling out his exit line. Today it lacked the usual edge of bravado and sounded as hollow as he felt at the moment.

Hogan looked after him. He had always admired what Carter tried to do with his life. The dedication. The self-sacrifice. Damian had the guts to do what he himself once wanted to do. There were many times he thought his friend was wrong, but he appreciated the fact that Carter did what so few others, including himself, were capable of sustaining. He was trying to make a better world. He put the poor and downtrodden above all else. He acted selflessly.

As he looked after Damian now, he suddenly saw his friend in a different light. Here was a shabby little man in black who desperately wanted to be a saint but did not know how. Something had gotten twisted in him. Just as it had gotten twisted in Witten and himself. After what they had done, none of their lives could ever be what they wanted them to be. The dark memories clouded his mind again. The time he wished he could forget. The time when they were all afraid of the dark.

Seeing Carter's stricken expression, Hogan felt a wave of remorse. He wanted to gather Carter to him, embrace him, and tell him that everything would be all right. That the world wasn't collapsing around him. He supposed it was cowardice that prevented him from doing that. Or perhaps the silver of a chance that Carter was right in what he was trying to tell him.

"Damian," he called out instead.

"Yes," Carter said, turning.

"Call me when you are ready. I'll come to you."

Looking back curiously, Carter nodded brusquely as he disappeared through the doorway. He wasn't sure whether Pat meant the Falconi document or something personal between them.

Carter walked over to Fifth Avenue and headed north, thinking what he could do for Pat to try to patch things up between them. Maybe whatever Falconi gave him would do the trick. He would let Pat take it public. Twice, he glanced over his shoulder and saw nothing unusual. He could have sworn for the past several days that he was being followed.

Fifteen minutes later, he entered St. Patrick's. The cathedral's beauty and serenity, the scent of incense and the sight of people devoutly praying had once intoxicated him, and he wished it would again. He knelt in one of the pews toward the rear and tried to pray. For what may have been the millionth time in his life, he begged for a forgiveness that he knew wasn't coming.

Kevin Kelly chewed another Tums as he rechecked the address on West Tenth. He glanced up and down the street as if debating in which direction to run before resignedly walking up the stoop of the old brownstone. Evening was closing in on eight o'clock, and the limbs of the sycamore trees lining the block shivered in a sudden gust of wind. In the vestibule, he found Frances Cook's name on the wall directory. After another moment's hesitation, he pressed her bell.

"Who is it?" came scratchily through the intercom.

The voice surprised him. Young, light, and musical. So much for preconceived ideas. Despite Lane Woods's telling him she was just a girl, he supposed he had hoped that she'd at least be older and hopefully somewhat jaded. Someone not as young as this girl sounded might not have been too badly damaged by what had happened. In his heart, he knew he was kidding himself. Hurts between men and women were deep and wounding and knew no age barriers.

"Father Kelly."

"Third floor," she sang out as a buzzer signaling the opening of the lock on the downstairs door sounded.

Kelly pushed through the door and climbed the steps. On the third-floor landing, he saw a young woman wearing a baggy, plaid skirt and a bulky peach-colored sweater, socks but no shoes. She was very pretty and in her early twenties, with a fair complexion and large blue eyes. Her long, dark hair was shiny with strands fetchingly framing a heart-shaped face while the remainder was pulled into a topknot.

"Franny Cook," she said, holding out her hand when he reached the top step.

He grasped her hand and felt the cool smoothness of her skin. "Father Kelly."

She looked at him a little warily, turned, and walked down the hallway. "Follow me," she called over her shoulder.

He trailed after her into a large studio apartment where she motioned for him to sit in one of two stuffed chairs covered in a rose pattern. The only other furnishings were a bed, a small wooden table with two chairs, a nightstand, a TV, a stereo system, and several lamps. A closet-sized kitchen was to the right of the two large windows facing the street. Two other doors were to the left, a closet and a bathroom.

"Not the Ritz," she said, smiling, "but it's what a girl can afford."

The room was dim, lit by a shaded lamp. Kelly took the chair she indicated, while she sat in the other. An open bottle of white wine was at her feet along with a plate of cheese and crackers, a half-full wineglass, and another glass that was empty. She filled the empty glass nearly to the brim and handed it to him along with the plate.

"Help yourself," she said. "I just got home a little while ago and I'm starved."

He took a sip of wine, catching himself this time wishing she looked different. She was so wholesome that he found himself even more embarrassed to be here than he had thought he would. His gaze was returned by eyes that he decided were more gray than blue and contained a big dose of suspicion.

"Where are you from, Franny?" Kelly asked, trying to get her to relax a little.

"Boston . . . well, Newton Center really, Sacred Heart parish," she said, curling a leg up on her chair as she sipped her wine. "I moved to New York about sixteen months ago after working for a TV station in Boston for a year."

144

"New York must be quite a change."

"In some ways, because it's so big and vital, but in other ways not."

"What do you find similar?"

"Oh," she said, shyly glancing up at the ceiling with the look of someone thinking a pleasant thought. "There are a lot of churches around and Mass is always the same no matter where you go, isn't it?"

Her look was open and innocent, so Kelly decided that she wasn't being ironic. In fact, she seemed like a very straightforward girl, but he found her a bit unusual. Very few young people embraced the Church so intimately these days. At least very few were so open about it. Fewer still slept with priests. He scowled, not at the girl or what she said, but at what he had just thought and what he still had to confront. He plunged ahead, just wanting to get it over. "I didn't go into much detail over the phone, but I guess you know why I'm here."

She looked down at her hands and nodded. "Lane called too. She explained something about this investigation you're doing and said it would be a good thing if I talked to you."

Kelly took out his miniature tape recorder. "Mind if I use this?"

Again, she looked wary, but shook her head no. "I guess it's okay."

"Look, I realize this is very difficult for you," Kelly said. "Frankly, I'm not sure where to start. . . . Suppose you begin."

Unconsciously wringing her hands, she nodded again so that strands of hair in her topknot came loose, making her look about twelve years old.

"I met Pat about a year ago when I started working for XTV. I was a production assistant for the news department, which in the TV business means pretty much a slave who fetches coffee and runs errands. Then I was promoted to associate producer, where I contacted guests for shows, was able to offer ideas on themes for shows, and just do a lot more."

Leaning over, she picked up the bottle and topped off more wine into Kelly's glass. "So, I saw Pat up close. I had watched him on TV at home and was really impressed. He seemed so great, and some of the troubled people who came on the show seemed to have gained some inner peace when they left. . . ."

Her voice became almost inaudible. "I thought he was very good-looking, and after a while, he noticed me. I could see the way he looked at me." She blushed.

Raising her voice, she continued, as though determined to persist and air everything, "Anyway, I guess I had a crush on him, and when he asked me to come and work for his show, I jumped at the chance. I mean, not just because of him, but it was a good way for me to move up too."

She looked at Kelly and turned her eyes away. "I mean, the job wasn't because I, uh, went to bed with him. You must understand that." Her voice trailed off again. "I mean, I wasn't sleeping with him yet."

Kelly exhaled in exasperation. "I understand."

"Well, we were both putting out these signals. I mean, this was my fault too. But I guess I was thrilled that here was this big personality who started asking my advice on different things and putting his arm around me as if we'd known one another all our lives."

She laughed ironically. "My crush was getting bigger and bigger, and he kept telling me how well I was doing, how pretty I was, how much I added to the show. Then one night he asked me to dinner after the show. I tried to tell myself that he was a priest, and that we were just colleagues who were going to discuss the show. But that was fooling myself. I was walking on air. We went to a little Italian place not far from here. Everything was very romantic."

The girl had a dreamy look on her face. "I must have told him where I lived because afterward we came back in this direction. I . . . I invited him up for some coffee."

She glanced hesitantly at Kelly. "Once up here, he ordered me to take off my clothes."

"Ordered you?"

"Yes," she whispered. "He reached out and undid the top button of my blouse. Then he ordered me to take everything off."

She got up from the chair and made motions with her hands that Kelly could barely discern in the dim light. "I started taking off my clothes while he stared at me. When I was nude, he made me undress him as well."

Her hands covered her face and she started crying quietly. "It was as if I didn't have any willpower. I had always been trained to do whatever a priest said. I . . . I did as he said. Then he told me to get onto the bed." She pointed to the large bed a few feet from Kelly.

146

"He began caressing my body and whispering to me that it was all right. That it was all right for us to make love."

Kelly sighed again to himself. Ah, Pat. Pat. He knew all the arguments priests used to rationalize active sexuality. That it wasn't until the fourth century that priests were no longer allowed to marry, that celibacy merely meant not being married, not refraining from making love. That celibacy was unnatural. That until a man experienced the physical love of a woman he was unable to counsel people about matters of the heart. He sympathized with the celibacy problem that, by definition, all priest shared, but that was all he could do. He knew how hard it was to repress his own sexuality. He also knew that he had taken a vow to do just that and so had every other priest. That was part of the price one paid for entering the priesthood.

"We made love there," she continued, her finger pointing at the bed again. "Pat and I . . . the priest and I . . ."

She seemed disoriented and her eyes glittered with tears. She began trembling. "Deep down I guess I knew it wasn't right, but at the same time I didn't know what else to do. I . . . I could never look at my boyfriend Jimmy after that. . . ."

Sobs suddenly racked her body and filled the apartment. Feeling sick and ashamed from what she said, Kelly got up and tentatively patted her shoulders and tried to soothe her spirit.

"It's all right now, Franny. It's okay now."

When she looked up at him, her tear-filled eyes were pleading. "What did I do? How did I ever do that? I was all confused. He said it was right."

She stopped crying and calmed down as she sat in the chair again. Her eyes were bloodshot and her face blotchy, making her look incredibly young and vulnerable. Staring down at her clasped hands, she continued.

"He began coming over several times a week. He told me he liked me because I was young and fresh and innocent. But then . . ."

Her voice became almost a moan, and she started sobbing softly. "He . . . he started telling me I was a whore . . . that I was wicked. That only a whore would do what I did with a priest. I . . . I wanted to stop seeing him but I couldn't. I felt as if I were drugged or something."

She turned to Kelly, a look of confusion on her face. "All of a sudden, he stopped calling. He wouldn't look at me at the show. When I tried to ask him what was wrong, he had the station get rid of me."

Brushing away the tears, she stared at Kelly as if still trying to determine how it had all happened. "I believed him. I trusted him. He's a priest."

Outside the apartment, Kelly was furious. This was one issue that Clarizio hadn't told him to be circumspect about. Hogan had some accounting to do. He hailed a cab. "Mayfair Hotel," he told the driver.

The taxi was a half block away from Hogan's apartment building when Kelly saw Pat Hogan emerge from the complex and hail a taxi.

The cab Kelly was in slowed to stop in front of Hogan's place just as Hogan's taxi sped away. Kelly acted again on instinct. "Follow that cab," he told the driver.

"You're kidding, right?" the young Hispanic driver asked.

"No. Just follow it."

The cab rolled over to Broadway and headed south into Soho. At Spring Street, the taxi turned right, turned right again, and dropped Hogan off on the corner of Prince and Mercer.

Kelly had his cabdriver drop him a block beyond. A few moments later, as he headed down the sidewalk, Kelly tensed and felt slimy. Why the hell was he following? Why the zealousness all of a sudden? But he knew what it was. Franny Cook's story was boring a hole in his stomach.

Halfway up the block, Hogan stopped as though waiting for someone. Kelly ducked into the doorway of an art gallery. Another taxi pulled up and a woman wearing a fur with a collar that obscured her face emerged. She approached Hogan and slipped her arm through his. Kelly watched as they paused before the large metal door of what appeared to be a large commercial building. They both glanced suspiciously up and down the block. Just before they disappeared inside, the woman lowered her collar. It was Connie Robbins.

As he got closer, Kelly could tell the structure had been turned into loft apartments. What was going on? Disgustedly, he thought he knew.

When he reached the building, Kelly scanned the names by the doorbells. Even as he did so, he realized it would be useless. Kelly's name wouldn't be there. Neither would Connie Robbins's. The address was the same as that given in Lawler's report.

148

9

ENTERING ST. PATRICK'S CATHEDRAL, LANE WOODS PULLED A SCARF
around her head and face and smiled. Whenever meeting Damian
Carter, life became melodramatic. She walked to the far left-hand
aisle, counted fourteen rows, and sat in the second pew from the aisle.
He insisted on this particular seat, Lord knows why. Sometimes, she
thought Damian, with his love of intrigue, would have made a wonderful TV producer.

A few minutes later, a voice behind her said, "Don't turn around."

"Hello, Damian. I hope this is a hot story."

"It is," he replied. "Listen carefully."

In the next few minutes, as Lane's face looked increasingly troubled, he told her what had happened in the Colosseum. "I received
something from Bishop Falconi that promises to be extremely news-
worthy," he concluded.

"What is it?" she asked, half turning.

"Keep facing the front!" he hissed. "I believe I'm being followed.
I don't want there to be a chance of you being recognized."

Slowly, she faced the front of the cathedral.

149

"I'm not sure what it is yet. But Falconi was a very powerful Vatican official. He said it was very volatile. Very important. I believe it. Especially in light of what happened to him."

"You'll give me an exclusive on the story?"

Momentarily, Carter hesitated. He had intended to give the story to Pat Hogan, but after thinking it through, he decided that a story potentially embarrassing Church figures would do Hogan more harm than good. "Yes."

"What can I do in the meanwhile?"

"I saw the promos saying you are going to Rome to cover the investiture of Murray and the other American archbishops who will be made cardinals. While there, investigate Falconi's death. That in itself should be a story that will make headlines around the world."

"Why?"

"Come on, Lane. He was assassinated! What was a powerful Vatican figure playing around with that warranted his being set up for assassination."

"You tell me."

"No, Lane. I want you to find out and tell the world."

"Sergeant Williams, please," Kevin Kelly said into the receiver.

"I'll try to locate him," the operator said.

Something was gnawing at Kelly. The police hadn't gotten back to him about the guy who attacked Hogan the other night. Why? For some reason, he found himself wondering about the assailant. Was he simply a nut? Did he have some grudge against Hogan? The whole business had disturbed him and he wasn't sure why.

A few moments later, a voice said, "Williams here. Who's calling?"

"This is Father Kelly. Kevin Kelly. I was with Monsignor Hogan the other night when he was assaulted."

Williams's voice became a little flatter. "Oh, sure. I remember you. Don't worry about that, Father. Monsignor Hogan dropped the charges."

"He has?"

"Yeah. He wanted us to let the guy go after he found out who he was."

"Who was he?"

150

There was a long pause. "Uh, obviously you don't know," the sergeant said more to himself than to Kelly. "Look, Father, uh, can I say something confidential to you?"

"Yes."

"The guy said that, ah, that, ah, Monsignor Hogan was, ah, having an affair with his girlfriend. When I told Hogan what the guy said, the monsignor dropped the charges."

Kelly felt more disgusted than ever. An ever-rippling pool of hurt people were surrounding Hogan. "Can you give me his name and address?"

Williams paused again. "I guess it's okay. His name is James Shields and he lives at . . ."

While taking down the information, Kelly remembered that Franny Cook said her boyfriend's name was Jimmy. The connection became very clear. The Hogan case looked as if it would be wrapped up quickly. Kelly found himself furious again. The quicker the better.

Monsignor Enrico Perdomo sat at an Italian Renaissance desk in his small office adjacent Archbishop Clarizio's at the Vatican's chancery in Washington. Although it was evening, he was still answering correspondence. Effortlessly, he aped the pronuncio's ornate, Victorian prose style and felt unappreciated. He was on call eighteen hours a day, but his work was mostly drudgery. Arranging appointments and meetings. Answering the phone. Responding to letters. Sending messages to the Vatican, deciphering those that came back.

The archbishop had Bisleti drive him to the Virginia retreat Royal Oaks, but as usual, he hadn't told Perdomo the exact nature of his business or with whom he was meeting. Something was terribly wrong. Clarizio was more preoccupied than usual, and so far he hadn't revealed to his secretary what was weighing on him. Perdomo doubted that he ever would. The man lived in shadows. *Furtivo* was Perdomo's private nickname for Clarizio.

Perdomo knew only that tonight's meeting had something to do with the pope's impending visit to this country. He had an inkling of what might be involved. Instead of mentioning it, he bided his time to see if he was right, hoping that one day soon Clarizio would trust him enough to take him into his confidence. He smiled ruefully for even harboring such a thought. The archbishop never trusted anyone.

The phone rang, shattering the room's sullen silence. Perdomo reluctantly picked up the receiver. He expected yet another peevish bishop somewhere in this incredibly large country to have a dilemma. There were the routine problems Rome hadn't acted on yet, such as marital annulments, priests wanting to be released from their vows, audiences with the pope for wealthy parishioners. Then there were the dreaded special problems. The Carmelite nuns in New Jersey who barricaded themselves in their convent rather than accept change. The priest in Baton Rouge who was being sued for having seduced young boys. The financial and sexual scandal at Covenant House. The nuns in Madison who signed a pro-choice petition. The litany of woes went on and on. The bishops all expected Clarizio to find solutions. Perdomo's life was spent mollifying them when Clarizio wasn't around.

"Yes," he answered, "Archbishop Clarizio's office."

"*Buona sera,* this is Monsignor Vincenzo Ruggieri. With whom am I speaking?"

Perdomo paused before giving his name. He knew of Ruggieri only by reputation, and that left much to be desired. An oddity in Rome, Ruggieri always verged on being defrocked. The sophisticated son of one of Italy's vineyard owners, he had once had a promising career in Washington too. Ruggieri had been sent home for some questionable activity that was rumored to have something to do with a woman. Today, he lived flamboyantly, going to nightclubs, racetracks, and trendy art galleries, and always, so the tales went, in the company of beautiful women. He was even rumored to have sired a bastard son who was being raised by an aunt in Tuscany. Yet, he was known for doing favors for important people and appeared to have high friends at the Vatican who protected him, especially the former pronuncio Pizzaro. His nickname was *Gatto*, the Cat. He always landed on his feet.

"Enrico Perdomo, how wonderful," Ruggieri said when the secretary gave his name. "What a coup that you became the archbishop's right hand. The Vatican is buzzing that great things are expected of you. Not only the Vatican! I was talking to your cousin Antonio Grimaldi just last week, and he said your family is..."

Ruggieri gushed on about family and friends they knew in common. Perdomo found himself enjoying the man's enthusiasm and his gossip about home.

"Say," Ruggieri said. "I'm only in Washington for several days and I am by myself. You aren't tied up for dinner are you? I hate to eat alone. Besides, you may know that I understand completely what frustrations and nonsense your job entails."

Perdomo laughed, but he still hesitated. He shouldn't, but his work was almost done and the archbishop wouldn't be back until late. He too hated eating alone, and dining with the archbishop these days was like being by oneself because the man was always so lost in thought.

"All right."

"Wonderful," Ruggieri repeated. "Meet me at the Jockey Club. How is nine o'clock with you?"

"That will be fine," Perdomo replied, appreciating the late dinner hour. Americans dined too early.

As he hung up, he found himself looking forward to the meal. It had been so long since he had spoken with anyone from Rome that he felt almost giddy. Suddenly, he realized how lonely he was. Seven months in this country without getting home. It seemed like forever since he had seen a friend, and he missed Rome terribly. Curiosity, however, tinged his melancholy as he wondered what kind of rascal this Ruggieri was. He who had always lived his life so cautiously had a grudging admiration for the rule breaker who knew how to make a system work for him.

At the end of the XTV Evening News show, Edmund Murphy walked over to Lane Woods. Though he had spent most of his life in television and around TV personalities, he was a little uneasy around her. An extremely capable reporter as well as having the face and figure of a movie star, she could be very exacting, very demanding when going after a story. He hated to admit it, but she intimidated him sometimes.

"Say, Lane, can we speak for a minute?" he asked, despising the note of adolescent hesitation that crept into his voice. Hell, he grumbled silently, with what I'm paying her, she'd better have a minute.

"Sure, Ed, what is it?" She had a pretty good idea what he wanted. Like most station owners, Murphy was always niggling over expenses. This must have to do with her extending her stay in Rome.

"The investiture of the cardinals should only take two days, right?" Murphy asked.

"Right."

"So what's this other story that's going to add on to your time over there?"

"Ed, you've read about the bishop who was murdered at the Colosseum. I have a tip that it's a very big and a very hot story if we can find out why he was killed. I'm going to give it a try."

Murphy was well aware of Bishop Falconi's murder. He viewed the killing of a member of the hierarchy as a despicable act. "Okay, Lane, but don't waste a lot of time if it doesn't look like you'll get the story," he said.

"Sure, Ed," she said, letting the somewhat patronizing remark go by.

Murphy walked away, feeling uneasy. Suppose Falconi was involved in something that would embarrass the Church. He fervently hoped not.

Two and a half hours after accepting the dinner date, Monsignor Perdomo was laughing so hard that he thought he might choke. Among his talents, the curly-haired Monsignor Ruggieri was an accomplished mimic. At the moment, his sharp, expressive features were transformed into a steely-eyed impression of Archbishop Clarizio.

"Everyone in the Church will suffer, because I have suffered," Ruggieri said in an eerie duplication of Clarizio's soft voice. "I suffer because I am a Sicilian and that is all that Sicilians are good for."

"Stop! Please, Vincenzo! Let me get my breath."

Ruggieri gave him that look again. "You laugh when Sicilians weep!"

Perdomo barely wiped the tears of laughter from his eyes when they were replaced by more. From his working all day and not being accustomed to being out late, the wine had gone right to his head, but he didn't care.

"Please, no more. Otherwise, every time I look at the archbishop I will think of this and laugh like a fool. Clarizio will have me thrown out on my ear by tomorrow night."

"No, we can't have that, Enrico," Ruggieri said in his natural voice as he poured more wine into Perdomo's glass and signaled to the waiter to bring them another bottle of Banfi's *Brunello di Montalcino*. "And tomorrow you must be my guest again."

Perdomo thought for a second. Yes, it would be all right. The archbishop had to come back tonight, but tomorrow he was spending the night at Royal Oaks and had already told Perdomo that he would not need him.

"*Buono*," he said, "but tomorrow it is my treat. We will try to find a restaurant with Italian food that is edible."

"As you wish, Enrico," Ruggieri replied in that uncanny mimic of Clarizio. He looked appraisingly at the monsignor, doubting that he was wrong. Tomorrow he would bring along a friend he was sure Perdomo would like.

"That is what I wish, Eminenza," Perdomo said, once again choking back his laughter.

"So you mentioned that this priest, ah, what did you say his name was? Ah, Kelly, is that correct? That he is investigating Monsignor Hogan's background? What a terrible thing."

"Why do you say it is terrible?" Perdomo asked, knowing as he did so that he was falling into the role of straight man for the monsignor.

"What happens when they ask me to be pope?" Ruggieri asked indignantly. "Some fool will suggest that my background be investigated. Do you know what they will find?"

He paused dramatically while Perdomo shook his head and took another sip of wine.

"Well, I will tell you," Ruggieri said. "They will find I have lived like some of the popes!"

A burst of loud laughter escaped Perdomo. In embarrassment, he glanced around to see if other diners were watching them.

"Vincenzo, aren't you ever serious?" he whispered. "Here I must go through day after day with a sour face, and you go around with a smile and making jokes. Somehow life doesn't seem fair at the moment."

"Ah, but you obviously don't know how to live," Ruggieri said in a commiserating tone. "So, has your Father Kelly found anything of interest? Any tidbits that can be tossed to the Vatican rumor mongers?"

"I truthfully don't know," Perdomo replied. "I don't believe he has reported back to the archbishop yet."

Later, as Ruggieri helped him into a taxi and paid the fare, the archbishop's secretary was torn by two emotions. One was great affection. He did not want to say good-night to his newfound, very charming friend. The other was fear. It was almost one o'clock. Clarizio was

155

bound to be home by now. What punishment would he exact for Perdomo's violation of protocol?

Ten minutes later, he left the cab and walked unsteadily up the driveway to the chancery. The limousine was not there and hope kindled in his breast. He entered quietly and shut his eyes, weaving slightly as he climbed the stairs and went to the music room. The archbishop was an insomniac who listened to music until the early hours of the morning. Holding his breath and willing himself to speak correctly if called upon to say something, he looked in. Clarizio wasn't there. He breathed a great sigh of relief. They weren't home yet.

Feeling as if a yoke were lifted from his shoulders, Perdomo climbed the stairs to his third-floor bedroom, thinking tonight was the most fun he had had in a very long time. What a great fellow Vincenzo was, a bit naughty perhaps, but a great fellow nonetheless. Suddenly, he started laughing. He remembered when he was a boy and his mother would call him Pinocchio because of the trouble he got into as a result of some of the friends with whom he played. "You, Pinocchio," she said. "You would follow the devil if he promised you fun."

"Pinocchio. Pinocchio," he sang to himself as he struggled out of his clothes. He sank onto the soft bed and pulled up the silk sheets his mother had sent him. "Show me some fun."

Archbishop Clarizio's limousine glided down the pitch-black highway, slipping past distant homes that were mostly dark. Here and there light shone out of an isolated window, making the hour seem that much more lonely. Except for the occasional car whipping by or truck rumbling past, the interior of the Mercedes was as dark and silent as the landscape. Once in a while headlights of oncoming traffic illuminated the backseat.

At one such moment, Bisleti glanced in the rearview mirror at the archbishop and wished he had not. Momentarily frozen in the light, Clarizio's worn face looked like a skull. Bisleti shuddered. The priest was worried. He'd never seen Clarizio so haggard, his expression so forlorn.

"Well, Paolo, what do you think? Did it go as badly as I thought it did?"

He nodded his head. If he could use his vocal chords, he would tell the archbishop that he was still a voice crying in the wilderness.

No one believed him. No one could see. Clarizio had told him enough, not everything, he knew, but enough to realize the depth of worry his superior felt, the kind of anxiety that made men desperate.

Bisleti himself feared that the archbishop was in that vulnerable state when men do something unwise. He had never seen Clarizio this way, and he had thought he never would. The man was always a bedrock. Never in his life had he seen anyone size up a situation and take action with such decisiveness. He was always impressed by the aptness of the archbishop's responses to any situation. Now, he was no longer sure.

They were returning from Royal Oaks, where Clarizio had met with Cardinals Turner of Los Angels, Clay of Atlanta, and Donleavy of Chicago, as well as Archbishops Murray of New York, Moore of Boston, Dinsmore of Washington, and Winkler of Dallas. The pope's visit to the United States naturally was of concern to all of them, and His Holiness would visit each of their cities.

Clarizio wanted to let these powerful men have a hand in devising the pontiff's schedule, so that none of them would later have cause for complaint. If only a few of them were involved, they would monopolize His Holiness for themselves. The process was time-consuming and had to be done in great secrecy. Whenever the pope left the Vatican he was in danger. The attempts on his life had made that extremely clear.

There had been a degree of bickering tonight, but Clarizio expected that. Harmony was rarely characteristic of meetings involving the Church's royalty. Whenever a conclave elected a new pope, Clarizio put it down to a major miracle wrought by God's intervention; otherwise the factionalism would go on forever.

What worried him was that he had not been able to get across his concern about the extremely conservative lay movement Milites Christi, Soldiers of Christ. These men and other church leaders around the world, but primarily these seven, were getting ready to petition the pope to have *Milites Christi* elevated to the canonical status of a religious order, putting it on an equal footing with the Jesuits, Franciscans, and other orders. The pope had privately declared that he would never do that. These men would be most unhappy when their petition fell on deaf ears.

Tonight, Clarizio had tried to tell them they were moving too quickly, that there were concerns, doubts about Milites Christi. When they pressed him about what he meant, he said that he was looking into the organization. How could he explain the fear he shared with the pope? That Milites Christi was becoming ever more powerful. That there was the danger the organization was emerging as a church within the Church. Clarizio dreaded even thinking of that. After years of watching the organization, he was convinced that the goal of certain members of Milites Christi was to dominate Holy Mother Church.

But it was too early to tell them that. They would have demanded proof, but what did he have? Since the organization was so secretive, there was no easy way of even finding out the size of its funding, which members of the hierarchy were sympathetic to its goals, what exactly those goals were. How could he explain what his instincts told him as a result of a lifetime of being vigilant to protect the Church?

Even the document that recently came into his hands was not the ironclad proof needed to convince these men. How could he prove that it was real? When he thought of the document and the evil it had already reaped, Clarizio felt great remorse. Was there an alternative to what he had done? To what he had asked Falconi to do?

He turned his attention back to what transpired tonight. Should he have tried a different tack? But to be more direct might sound worse. He fervently wished he had more time. These American churchmen worried him. When they wanted something, they bulldozed others, sometimes even the pope. The United States contributed so much money to the Vatican that there were times when His Holiness had little will or inclination to fight them, especially being sick as he was.

Clarizio didn't believe the pope should even be contemplating his trip here, but perhaps he was wrong. Travel always lifted the pontiff's spirits. On Milites Christi, though, he knew the pope would fight. Clarizio had no doubt of that, but the pope was pragmatic as well. To fight, he needed ammunition. He had entrusted Clarizio with getting concrete evidence for their concern.

No, the Milites Christi people were very careful to date, especially with the Americans. Unfortunately, their spiritual fervor seemed as genuine as their funds. They recruited laymen of prominence, but because of the organization's code of secrecy, one was never sure who were members. More to the point, Milites Christi was a major contributor to the cardinals' and archbishops' fund-raising projects, and that generosity was not kept secret. To most members of the hierarchy, huge donations could paper over many sins. But what about those of the group known as the Apostles?

Clarizio sighed. The hierarchy was too concerned with money.

Powerful cardinals, archbishops, and bishops spent so many of their waking hours worrying about where to get money that they didn't always question its sources. Staggering amounts of money were needed to sustain the Church these days, and the funding was increasingly difficult to come by. There were salaries for priests and nuns, the soaring costs of parishes, hospitals, universities, old-age homes, and thousands of other necessities as minor as altar flowers and as major as hospices for AIDS sufferers.

When he implied to those prominent prelates tonight that perhaps Milites Christi could pose a danger to the Church, they barely veiled their skepticism. How could any organization that generous to the Church be a threat? Was he a fool? The question was written on their faces even though they were diplomatic enough not to express what they thought.

It was almost two o'clock in the morning when Bisleti opened the rear door of the limousine. The archbishop looked around in surprise. No Enrico. His secretary wasn't holding the front door open with a respectful greeting on his lips. Clarizio smiled. Perdomo must have catnapped and tumbled into a deep sleep.

The archbishop thought momentarily about awakening him and reprimanding him. Then he caught himself. His secretary was making strides. He saw how seriously Enrico took it when he stressed the secrecy of the Pope's itinerary in America. He was adapting to the tedium with good grace, even if it was mostly donkey work, and his arrogance was receding almost by the day. Clarizio's mood lifted a bit. Beneath his finery, the boy had the makings of a strong churchman. Life hadn't been easy for his secretary of late. Cut off from family and friends, he tended to the needs of an old man who had so much work and so many cares that half the time he barely knew his secretary existed and the other half usually pretended he did not. But that was the Roman training, the way of tempering a man's body, mind, and soul so that he only considered what was good for the Church.

To move in the highest reaches of the Church, the wants and demands of family and friends and especially oneself must always come a distant second if they are to be part of one's priorities at all. Ideally, churchmen lost themselves in God's work. Clarizio was always surprised more priests did not know that, including some who had reached some of the Church's highest offices.

Tomorrow, he would tell Perdomo that they must return to Rome almost immediately. The news would lift Enrico's spirits. In that sense, he worried. Enrico was a hothouse flower, the way too many church-men at the Vatican were. They were so inbred that life away from Rome seemed like a punishment.

Several days later, Kelly trudged through the front door of St. Mary's, gave a depressed sigh while opening the metal gate, and threw his coat across a chair by the stairwell. The day had been long and frustrating. As he passed the office, Tim Brady called out, "Just the man I was looking for."

Kelly looked in and saw Brady sitting at his desk, a pained expres-sion on his freckled face, a pile of bills in front of him. Kelly laughed but felt guilty for being tired after what he had done all day. It was nothing compared to running St. Mary's. "You look the way I feel."

"Come in and take a load off your feet, Kevin."

Kelly recognized Brady's need for companionship, which was one reason he stayed here when in the city. Until ten years ago, three priests had lived at the rectory and in years gone by a lot more. Then it was two. For the past year, it was just Tim. His former assistant pastor now had his own inner-city parish, where he struggled alone to make ends meet and tend to his flock just the way Brady did. It was a lonely life.

Kelly always pitched in where he could. He often said two Masses on Sunday, heard confessions, visited the dying in the hospital, and went out at all hours of the night to the scenes of accidents, fires, shootings, and stabbings to give the last rites. But he was a mere Band-Aid for these people; Brady was a spiritual emergency ward.

"Any luck in reaching Damian Carter?" Brady asked as Kelly took one of the wooden seats in front of the pastor's desk.

"For a man who pops up with the predictability of a slug in a poor box when he wants to tick off churchmen, Carter is very elusive," Kelly said. "I've tried his friends and legions of acquaintances and no dice. Even Pat Hogan doesn't know where he is."

False leads were everywhere. Yet, though he didn't say so now, Kelly started to see a pattern emerging that reminded him of some of the people he had tracked down years ago who had gone underground. Sooner or later, he'd latch onto Carter. Meanwhile, he put his failure down as a lesson in humility.

160

At one point, he was tempted to call Lane Woods to see if she knew how to reach him, but had thought better of it. He admitted to himself that he was looking for an excuse to call her again. That was a complication he didn't need. He had found himself thinking about her off and on during the past few days and forced his mind to other matters.

"How about Bill Witten?"

"I haven't even started asking about him."

"A real shame," Brady said. "A brilliant guy like that. Terrible to think he committed suicide."

"Want a drink before turning in?" Kelly asked with a yawn.

Brady started to get up, but Kelly waved him back into his seat. "I'll get it."

He went into the kitchen, got two glasses and a bottle of Wild Turkey from a cabinet and ice from the refrigerator, and returned to the office. Pouring their drinks, he handed one to Brady and sat down again, raising his glass in a salute before tasting it.

"Say, remember when a bunch of us . . ."

Brady paused in midsentence and reached for the ringing telephone. "Father Brady here. . . . Hello, Mrs. Rodriguez. . . . Yes. . . . Certainly. . . . I'll be right there."

He put down the phone, drained his glass in one gulp, and got up. "Sorry, Kevin, I've got to go. That was Carmela Rodriguez. Her boy Juan was just shot when a couple of drug dealers fired on a group of people in front of her building. She's afraid the boy's dying."

Kelly nodded. "Be careful."

Crossing the room, Brady grabbed his coat hanging on the back of the office door. He always carried a stole, crucifix, holy water, and oils for the last rites in an emergency kit in the trunk of his car. There were blankets, dried food, and a little cash for people forced from their homes due to fire or other disasters. He also kept a billy club. Crack heads would kill a priest as soon as breathe if they thought he had money or anything they could sell to support their habits.

"Don't worry," Brady grunted. "Archbishop Murray will protect me. Nobody else could keep St. Mary's running and he knows it."

Kelly laughed, glad to see that Brady still kept up his spirits. He wondered how much more time Brady had left in the job. Priests working ghetto parishes tended to burn out early from all the responsibilities: pastor and confessor, social worker, psychiatrist, fund-raiser,

161

bail bondsman, administrator, and a lot of other roles. Few people could keep going like that. Tim had already been at it longer than most.

About five minutes after Brady left, the phone rang again. Kelly tensed as he picked up, fully expecting to have to go off on a similar mission. Instead, he recognized the voice and felt a different kind of anxiety.

"How are you, Archbishop Clarizio?"

"Fine, fine. Thank you for asking, Father Kelly."

The archbishop sounded tired, a deep, bone-weary tiredness that had little to do with the time of night. "I am leaving for Rome tomorrow for the investiture. I would like you to come to Rome too. There are people you must speak to there regarding the assignment I gave you." Clarizio paused. "Please come to see me when you arrive. There is . . . there is something that I must tell you."

"All right, Your Excellency."

"When do you think you might leave?"

Kelly considered what was on his agenda for the next few days. There was nothing that couldn't be postponed. "I'll try to get on a flight as soon as I can tomorrow. I'll tell your secretary when my plans are firmed up."

"Excellent. Thank you for putting yourself out, Father Kelly. I will make a reservation for you at the Hotel Navarro, which is just off the Piazza Navona."

The phone clicked as Clarizio hung up. Kelly listened to the dial tone as he thought how weird this whole business was. Whatever the archbishop wanted must be crucial. Dagger Tom didn't act on whim.

Kelly was glad for the chance to be in Rome for the investiture. The ceremony was held irregularly, only when a pope decided to replenish the College of Cardinals when its ranks were thinned by death. At the same time, he was uneasy. Once again, Clarizio was playing it close to the vest, not saying over the phone what concerned him. Instinctively, Kelly dialed Bishop Gibbons. After two short rings, the Bishop's sleepy voice was on the line.

"Sorry, John, I didn't mean to wake you. It's Kevin Kelly."

Gibbons's voice was suddenly clear, as if he had snapped the sleep out of it like flipping sand off a blanket. "I was just closing my eyes for a minute. What's wrong, Kevin?"

"I'm not sure."

He hesitated, suddenly feeling foolish for having alarmed the bishop at this time of night. "Clarizio just called. He's heading to Rome tomorrow and wants me over there too."

"I heard he was going back on some urgent matter. I wouldn't be surprised if the pope summoned him."

"Do you have any inkling as to what's going on?"

There was a slight hesitation. "Kevin, certain people at the Vatican are spooked as a result of Falconi's death."

"Is there a possibility he was linked to Hogan?"

"I should have thought of that," Gibbons said more to himself than Kelly. "There is a possibility, at least indirectly. Falconi and Hogan were friends, but I'd look for something else linking them. There are rumors going around that Damian Carter had something to do with Bishop Falconi's death."

Kelly tensed. "What do you mean?"

"That's one of the odd stories floating around. All some sources are saying is that Carter's mixed up in Falconi's death."

"Dear Lord," Kelly muttered.

Suddenly, he remembered the tycoon Edwards's report. He would have to try to check it out while he was in Rome. "Say, John, do you know a Monsignor Vincenzo Ruggieri?"

Gibbons gave a dry laugh. "You're getting the full treatment, aren't you?"

"What do you mean?"

"You'll see. In his infinite bounty, God created the Ruggieris of the world to make the rest of us look like saints."

Before turning in, Kelly flipped on the TV set and turned to the news. Suddenly, Lane Woods's face filled the screen. The background was Capitol Hill.

"President Reagan's taped testimony may have harmed Admiral Poindexter's case rather than helped. Today, the admiral enmeshed in the Iran-contra arms scandal was found guilty of . . ."

Hastily, uneasily, Kelly turned off the set. Since meeting her, he watched her news program whenever he could. He trudged upstairs to bed, feeling lonelier than he had in a long time.

10

THE REVEREND KEVIN ALOYSIUS KELLY STRODE THROUGH LEONARDO DA Vinci Airport, his old leather overnight bag in his right hand and an airline bag over his opposite shoulder. The flight arrived at eight forty-five A.M. Rome time, which gave him time to check into his hotel and catch a few hours of sleep before meeting with Clarizio at three o'clock. He needed some rest, having slept fitfully after what Gibbons told him and never being comfortable enough on a plane to doze off.

As he exited the terminal, he skirted a puddle from the night rain and headed for the taxi line. Suddenly, he stopped when a wheezy voice called out his name.

"Kelly. Kevin Kelly."

Turning, he faced a man looking at him expectantly. He had a leonine head and long, gray hair that gave him a vague resemblance to Einstein. His beige linen suit was shapeless and his shoes badly needed shining. He was handing the last of his luggage to a cabdriver to put into the trunk of a taxi as he stared at the American, a look of amused surprise on his face.

"How are you, *Father* Kelly?" There was a faint ironic emphasis

on the word *father*. "I'd heard that you'd taken up a different calling."
He peered more closely at the priest. "Except for the uniform, you
haven't changed that much after all these years."

"How are you, Gracey?"

Andrew Gracey was a British journalist and a former correspondent in Vietnam for Associated Press. Like certain other old Asia hands
in Indochina, he had been more interested in the human drama of
the war than the politics. He hadn't cared which side won, which had
irritated Kelly when he first met the man. Later, that struck him as
probably the only sane response from someone whose country wasn't
involved.

"Well, thank you. Old Gracey is still able to get these brittle bones
around."

"I read your Vatican dispatches," Kelly said. "Good stuff."

"Nice of you to say. After Vietnam I did a sojourn in Indonesia
and another in Germany. I've been here for the past ten years. Let
me give you a lift into town."

Kelly hesitated. "Gracey, you never did favors, no matter how
small, without expecting one in return, and I doubt if you've changed
over the years. But I'm so damned tired at the moment that I'd ride
in with the devil. Besides, I have nothing to trade."

Gracey laughed. "But one day, you will. Where are you staying?"

"The Navarro."

"Quite nice. With the crowd in the city for the investiture, you
were either very lucky or someone of prominence pulled strings to get
you in there."

"The latter."

As they rode away from the airport, Gracey began questioning
Kelly. "So what are you doing in town?"

"Visiting."

"Who?"

The questions kept coming. Within a short time, Kelly found
himself resenting the probing. Reporters never quit. They pick at life's
scabs, some more gently than others, but they all want to see the blood
beneath the wound.

"Does Dagger Tom have something for you over here too?" Gracey asked, glancing out of the corner of his eyes to see what effect his
words had.

Kelly looked at him sharply, but did not respond.

"I assume this concerns your work for him. How is 'Bishop'

166

Hogan?" An even stronger note of irony clung to *bishop* than that to *father*.

"Gracey, I'd forgotten what a nosy S.O.B. you are. How did you know?"

The correspondent gave the asthmatic rattle that substituted for laughter. "My good Father Kelly, there are few secrets in Rome from old Gracey."

For the duration of the trip, the reporter gossiped with great relish about the soaring, stagnating, or faltering careers of various Vatican figures. Kelly never had anything to do with the men, so he only half listened until one name struck a chord. Soon after they entered Rome, he placed his hand on Gracey's arm.

"What was that about Dirk Creedy?"

"Oh, just that he is rumored to be in line for Falconi's job as second-in-command of the Propagation of the Faith. Would be quite a coup for Creedy. Quite a coup."

Kelly thought how right Maguire was. Creedy's politicking was paying off in spades. He'd have to reach him while he was here. Creedy and that Monsignor Ruggieri. For a moment, he was tempted to ask Gracey what he knew about the Falconi affair to see if he mentioned Carter. He decided to wait until he had something to trade.

A short while later, the cab pulled to a stop in front of the ivy-walled Hotel Navarro. As Kelly climbed out, the journalist handed him his business card.

"Here is where you can reach me. Give a call and we will get together before you leave, Kevin. Old Gracey knows some pretty fair restaurants that are easy on the purse. Who knows? We might be able to help one another."

"Okay. And thanks for the lift." He tucked the card into his coat pocket, wondering what Gracey wanted.

Ten minutes later, he was fast asleep.

When the phone rang, Kelly groggily groped for it. He felt a jet-lag hangover.

"Hello," he muttered.

"*Buon giorno*, Father Kelly," Perdomo's cultured voice said.

"*Buon giorno*, Monsignor."

"Am I disturbing you?"

167

The question was pure etiquette. Some priests moaned that their superiors treated them as if, like doctors, they were always on call, even though the emergencies for which they had to drop everything rarely had anything to do with life or death. Kelly found it more like the military, where the brass considered it as much a duty as a right to make life harder for those of inferior rank. Everybody's agenda was more important than a lowly priest's. Kelly always found that one of the more irritating aspects of the life.

"Sure you are," he replied.

There was a pause and Kelly could imagine the scowl on Perdomo's face. *"The time has been changed for your meeting.* The archbishop would like to see you at one fifteen *sharply."*

Hanging up, Kelly looked at his watch. It was twelve-ten. He stumbled out of bed and headed for the shower.

Fifty minutes later, he walked through twisting, narrow streets leading from the hotel to Vatican City. The day was bright, crisp, and clear. The sky was a brilliant blue, indicating an end to the rain that had plagued Rome for the past ten days. A breeze kicked up, but it lacked a sharp edge and made walking that much more comfortable.

Kelly groused to himself that he was here on business. He had been to Rome several times over the years, but he had never had time to explore the city. He had never even been to the Vatican. The hotel that Clarizio chose for him was within an easy walk of such wonders as the Pantheon, the Trevi Fountain, and the Colosseum, as well as the Vatican. He would have traded another six months at St. Mary's for a few days to explore the city's cultural treasures. Crossing one of the stone bridges spanning the Tiber, he turned left on Via della Conciliazione.

In the distance, the dome of St. Peter's Basilica, the largest cathedral in the world, loomed majestically, projecting a solidity that Kelly wished he shared at the moment. Before he realized it, he was walking directly into St. Peter's Square. The shops along the way displayed bins full of rosaries and scapulars. Storekeepers hawked holy cards, statues of the pope, and napkins with the triple-crown Vatican flag. The glory of the Church was present in the architecture ahead of him if not in the cash registers of the shopkeepers.

Entering the Piazza San Pietro, he walked past the Egyptian Obelisk in the center of the square. The Obelisk was taken from Nero's circus and Christianized by being crowned with a cross. Kelly felt the weight of history as he took in the vast colonnade in the form of an weight of history as he took in the vast colonnade in the form of an ellipse embracing the square. In the midst of such splendor it was easy to imagine what the Church was like when She was the deciding factor in all matters both temporal and spiritual. What power and majesty were contained within the Church's past. When popes spoke, kings trembled and armies moved across oceans.

Kelly went up the great flight of steps in front of the Basilica. He entered the vestibule, or the ancient "endonarthex" of the early Christian basilicas, which was decorated with stuccos and mosaics. Directly, he went to the Arch of the Bells, as the visitors' entrance was known. A towering Swiss guard, wearing the traditional red-, yellow-, and blue-striped breeches and slashed doublet, looked at the American suspiciously when Kelly gave his name. The guard found his name listed on the guest roster, but he carefully examined Kelly's passport before admitting him and giving him directions to Archbishop Clarizio's apartment. Recent assassination attempts on the pope had made the guards vigilant almost to the point of paranoia.

As he strode along the pathways in the Vatican gardens, Kelly wondered at the picturesque hundred-acre estate fanning out on the lower slopes of the Vatican Hill. This was all that remained of the once vast Papal States. From a magnificent kingdom, the Church's geographic core had shrunk to the tiny, almost totally self-sufficient cocoon called the Vatican. The compound had its own firemen, lawyers, carpenters, bakers, gardeners, bricklayers, and other craftsmen. The Do Good Brothers ran the pharmacy. The Sons of St. John Bosco printed confidential documents. Friars of the Little Work of Divine Providence delivered mail. The Vatican had its own flag, police force, postage stamps, and radio station.

Kelly took in the graceful parks and splendid ornate palaces with a sense of awe. The continuity of the very Church itself was contained within these walls. The pope lived here, the place where the Apostle Peter, the first bishop of Rome, had been crucified and buried. Here was the rock upon which the Church was built.

Several minutes later, Perdomo ushered Kelly into Clarizio's Vatican apartment. "*Buon giorno*, Father Kelly. *Buon giorno*. You could not have wished for a finer day in my city. Please sit. The archbishop is expecting you. I will get him."

Kelly found the secretary's enthusiasm surprising after their little phone skirmish. He put it down to the man's being back home after an extended time away.

trappings of nobility were everywhere. A Titian hung over a large white marble fireplace inlaid with what appeared to be fine threads of gold. A triptych by Giotto and paintings by Perugino and Pinturicchio were displayed on other walls in the sitting room, while an enormous tapestry of the Last Supper adorned yet another. The chairs were graceful Italian Renaissance, the seats covered in crimson velvet. Huge, ornate, gilt-framed mirrors reflected the blue skies visible through two large windows overlooking the gardens. A harpsichord stood between the windows.

"*Buon giorno*, Father Kelly."

The American turned as the archbishop stepped into the room. Clarizio wore a black cassock with the purple piping and cape of his office. A pectoral cross, which he had received from Pope Paul VI, hung around his neck. Kelly became concerned. Clarizio appeared frailer than when they last met. Deep circles rimmed his eyes.

Wondering what was wrong, Kelly hurried to him, genuflected, and kissed his ring.

"Please rise, Father. There is much we must discuss."

The archbishop glanced around the living room and gave Kelly a look that implied that *even here walls sometimes have ears.* "Let me show you the Basilica, Father."

Taking their time, the priest and the archbishop strolled through the Vatican grounds, Clarizio lost in thought as he debated how much he should now reveal. There was always the possibility that he was wrong. If he was, he could offend a good many powerful people, perhaps even embarrass the pope. He had to know for sure.

They walked beneath the Arch of the Bells, leaving the private Vatican grounds. Two huge Swiss guards in their operatic-looking uniforms stared at them suspiciously, their automatic weapons a re-minder of contemporary dangers.

Clarizio took note of the concerned look on Kelly's face. "They are trained to distrust everyone. Sometimes I think that is something that more of us should learn."

The sun was bright but not warm. Wisps of dark cloud smudged the sky, belying earlier signs that the rain was over for a while. Puddles from the night rain still shimmered on St. Peter's Square. Stormy weather, however, had little bearing on the volume of visitors to the Vatican. In the short time since Kelly had crossed the square, tour buses had arrived and were parked everywhere. The plaza was filled with tourists, many of them clergy and other religious.

170

Kelly and Clarizio walked up the steps of the Basilica and entered the sculpted left-hand or "Bronze Door," which was part of the original St. Peter's Church. The door to the right was closed. The "Holy Door," it was only open during Holy Years.

"Do you know much of the history of the Basilica?" Clarizio asked, his eyes taking on some of the glow Kelly recalled from when they first met.

"Very little."

"Work on the current church started in the early sixteenth century on a site previously occupied by a church erected in the fourth century by the Roman emperor Constantine."

The archbishop's voice warmed to the topic. He exulted in the Church's past, having devoured Her history with the hunger of a lover. He believed that the Church's true strength and glory rested on each generation of churchmen building on the two-thousand-year-old base that was continually strengthened by men such as himself. Through an intimate knowledge of the Church's history, mistakes could be avoided, and dangers from outside and within the Church's walls could be dealt with properly. If churchmen studied the past, they could recognize and treat heresies, schisms, corruptions, before they became cancers. That was an unshaken belief the archbishop had always held.

"No matter how many times I come here, the sense of majesty and closeness to God still overwhelms me," Clarizio said, his voice tinged with the wonder of the simple villager he was long ago. "I am reminded over and over how, without God, we are nothing."

Kelly was a little surprised to hear the archbishop speak this way. A complex man. With Clarizio's exalted position and his gracious lifestyle, the priest had thought of him as one of the sophisticated churchmen for whom God was little more than an abstraction.

The Basilica was an ideal place for them to go unnoticed. Clergy who were white, black, and yellow and dressed in the garb of religious communities from all over the world streamed through the aisles. In the midst of monks wearing coarse robes, nuns in "civvies" or modified habits of varying shades of blue and black, occasional bishops in scarlet, Kelly and Clarizio blended into the ranks of Christ's legions. They walked through the vestibule decorated with mosaics, including Giotto's *La Novicella* high above the main entrance. Taking Kelly's elbow, Clarizio steered the priest to the right.

"*Scusata! Scusata!*" the archbishop said softly as he pressed through the crowd gathered before the Chapel of the Pietà.

171

The aisle in front of Michelangelo's famed marble statue of Mary holding the body of her crucified son was a solid wall of tourists, but somehow Clarizio's low-key insistence worked. People reflexively formed a pathway when they heard him and saw their clerical garb. The crowds thinned as the priest and archbishop made their way past the Chapel of Relics, the Chapel of St. Sebastiano, the Tomb of Countess Matilda of Canossa, the Chapel of the Blessed Sacrament, and the Chapel of Gregory XIII, which contained the beautiful fresco *Our Lady of the Succor*.

Clarizio paused as they entered the apse of the cathedral. "Look," he commanded.

Directly in front of them was the largest altar Kelly had ever seen. Suspended above the altar was Bernini's magnificent sculpted Chair of St. Peter surmounted by a golden sunburst.

Clarizio began speaking as though mesmerized. "The treasures in this glorious basilica . . . the frescoes by Michelangelo . . . the baroque pillars around the altar by Bramante . . . the art of Bernini. It all pales next to the glory of God."

The archbishop turned in a circle as he appreciated the beauty. "Lovely as this is, mere mortals only make feeble attempts, no matter how magnificent they seem, at paying homage to God. The Church is close to a perfect instrument of the Lord but not flawless. That quality belongs only to God. The Church is composed of imperfect men."

They went through the altar railing and up two steps leading to the vast expanse of green carpet stretching to the altar. On either side of the aisle were the rows of canopied, ornate, wooden thrones with scarlet cushions. This was where the College of Cardinals sat during special ceremonies, the most solemn being the coronation of a pope.

Scaffolding arose at the ends of the thrones at the right. For days, workmen had searched relentlessly before finally locating a leak that had allowed rain to trickle down the soaring walls from the dome above the altar. Finally, they were able to repair the leak, removing a blemish on the perfection of God's house and the glory of the impending investiture.

The archbishop sat on a throne near the altar and beckoned for Kelly to take the seat next to him. "This is presumptuous of me to sit here until the investiture, but His Holiness said this chair is mine."

Kelly laughed. "Did he say one was for me?"

Clarizio smiled for the first time this afternoon. "Perhaps one

172

day, Father Kelly. Perhaps. Stranger things have happened. But I do not wish to disappoint you. That is not why I asked you to come."

"I'm crushed," Kelly said.

Clarizio was glad to see the American's mood lighten. He realized what a toll recent events had taken on himself. What Kelly was doing was extremely difficult and in its own way, even worse than his own task. He sighed and closed his eyes momentarily. Now, he had to ask the priest to resurrect a part of him he so obviously tried to escape. Would this psychologically damage him? Make him reconsider his vocation? Clarizio steeled himself against such concerns. There was no choice. Mother Church came above men. All men!

"How is your investigation of Monsignor Hogan progressing?"

Kelly's smile faded. "It's coming, Your Excellency. If you don't object, I'd rather not tell you anything just yet, other than that I've received some controversial information. You told me to verify everything. That's what I intend to do."

"That is what we wish." Clarizio sighed with resignation before speaking again. "Father Kelly, there is no one else like you in the Church."

Kelly looked up sharply. So it finally came. As much as he tried not to think about it over the years, a dark corner of his mind always knew the day would come when he could not deny his past. But how, he wondered bitterly, could his history claim him in God's house?

"What do you want?" he asked angrily.

Empathizing with Kelly's anguish, Clarizio for once did not mind the man's audacity. Kelly was what the Church now needed. Clarizio feared he saw a cancer in the Church. He hoped and prayed that his conjecture was wrong, but if he was right, swift action must be taken at the appropriate time. This man might be his weapon.

"Once again, what I am going to say to you is of the strictest confidence. You are aware of the murder of Bishop Falconi. What you don't know is that, at the time of his death, Bishop Falconi was conducting a secret investigation for the pope, much the way you are for me."

"What was the object of his investigation?"

"Milites Christi."

Kelly frowned and his stomach curdled. "Why?"

Clarizio spoke even more softly. "The pope is very worried about Milites Christi's mounting influence and power. He feels that there are men within the organization whose goals are dangerous."

173

Kelly believed he now had at least a partial answer to what he and Gibbons had wondered about since Clarizio first approached him. Milites Christi. He knew little about the organization, other than that it was extremely conservative and the global membership included many of the very rich.

"Could they have had a hand in Bishop Falconi's death?"

"We don't know," the archbishop answered simply.

"How does Monsignor Hogan play a part in this, if he does?"

"That we don't know either. The note the pontiff received came to him anonymously. Yet, he has reason to believe the source was someone in Milites Christi who wishes to discredit the monsignor."

"Why would anyone in Milites Christi care whether Pat Hogan becomes a bishop?"

Clarizio looked at his hands folded tensely on his lap. "We have been over that many times. He holds certain views that are incompatible with those of Milites Christi, but then so do a great many people within the Church. But there must be more. Perhaps they fear his association with Damian Carter more than they actually fear him."

"Look, Archbishop. Milites Christi is not alone when it comes to Damian Carter. You and I know most of the hierarchy would be tempted to look the other way if Carter should fall down a mine shaft. So what could it be?"

Resenting Kelly's tone, Clarizio looked intently at the American. Was he the right person for this task after all? His lack of tact could hinder him. But who else was there?

"We cannot take the chance that Milites Christi knows something about Monsignor Hogan and Father Carter that will make us appear foolish if we elevate the monsignor."

"I'll find out whatever I can. But this doesn't make sense, Archbishop. You'd think Milites Christi would *want* to embarrass Hogan and Carter if they could."

Clarizio looked sharply at Kelly, his eyes icy and his words controlled. "I know, Father. *That* is why what I am asking of you is so delicate. *That* is a point of confusion we hope you will be able to clarify."

Kelly wondered at the mess he was handed. There were so many apparent contradictions and loose threads. "Archbishop, before I go any further, I want something cleared up right away. Was Carter mixed up in Bishop Falconi's murder?"

"Damian Carter had nothing to do with his death. The bishop

174

had arranged to meet Father Carter to give him something. He was supposed to call me after seeing Father Carter and tell me what transpired between them."

Trying to consider all the angles, Kelly suddenly began to understand how pivotal Clarizio was to all of this. He backed off from pressing the archbishop to explain why Falconi would call him. He realized it wouldn't do any good. Instead, he asked, "Does Monsignor Ruggieri figure into this?"

As he began to appreciate how intuitively Kelly's mind worked, the archbishop's reservations about him began to subside. "Vincenzo Ruggieri came to me after the bishop's death and recounted something that he claimed Falconi had told him. He said that Monsignor Hogan had been to see the bishop. That the monsignor passed along information about certain problems within the Secretariat for the Propagation of the Faith. An investigation was held, but the charges were not substantiated."

Kelly nodded. That jibed with the Edwards report. Hogan had gone out on a limb for Carter by suggesting there was malfeasance within Propagation of the Faith and its disbursements to missionary work around the world.

"According to Monsignor Ruggieri," Clarizio continued, "Bishop Falconi was angry at Monsignor Hogan, even though he and the American were quite good friends. No one had ever before accused Bishop Falconi's secretariat of not behaving correctly. When questioned about where he received the information, Monsignor Hogan told the bishop that he was relaying it for Father Damian Carter. At that Bishop Falconi apparently became extremely angry and sent Hogan away."

"What do you make of that?"

"The significance of the story is that Monsignor Ruggieri is not being truthful. Rather than being angry, Bishop Falconi was very worried that something was wrong within his secretariat. The matter did not seem to be exactly as Monsignor Hogan had outlined it. Funding was being directed to organizations that were of dubious character. I have been wondering what Monsignor Ruggieri was trying to do."

So Edwards's report on Carter was distorted, Kelly thought. But why? More to himself than to Clarizio, Kelly said, "So you want me to broaden my investigation to cover Milites Christi and Bishop Falconi's death."

Catching the bitterness that flashed across Kelly's eyes, the archbishop felt as if he were plunging a knife into the American's heart. So much to ask of this man. So much. But there was no alternative, he told himself again. Among the more than one hundred and eleven thousand priests around the world, there was only this man who had the kind of background to undertake such a task.

"Yes, Father. The cross has fallen to you. I hope you have the strength to bear it. Father Kelly, I would not ask this of you unless there was the potential for grave danger to the Church. I care about the Church more than myself, more than you, more than anyone."

For a moment, Kelly didn't reply as he considered what was being asked of him. He wanted to go back to the hotel, pack his bags, and walk away, leaving the whole damned mess to someone else, anyone else. But he couldn't pull out now. He remembered the times when the Jesuits, the guardians of the pope, would carry out a papal order with as much ego or emotion as a corpse. That was the attitude he must will himself to adopt. He also remembered how Bisleti said he would help. He figured it was time to reach out to Bisleti and hope at least some of the rumors about him were true. He also decided that he would not tell Clarizio that he was turning to his chauffeur for support. He wasn't sure how the archbishop would react. Besides, he thought wryly, Clarizio could understand not tipping one's hand about everything.

"Okay, Archbishop," he said quietly. "Okay."

"Thank you, Father," Clarizio said simply, and pressed on. "Do you still have any of your old contacts? I should imagine they could be quite helpful. I am certain they monitor Milites Christi with a greater sophistication than we are capable of."

Kelly leaned toward the archbishop, about to reply. From the corner of his eye, he glimpsed a figure in black who slipped off one of the nearby scaffolds, as if he had just climbed down. The priest's face was obscured by shadows, but Kelly found something vaguely familiar about his physique. What the hell was he doing there?

Suddenly, Kelly dived to the floor, yanking Clarizio from his chair. The archbishop gave a startled yell. Kelly rolled on top of him as a huge piece of marble plunged from the scaffold and smashed across Clarizio's throne, setting up a roar that rumbled through the Basilica like a volcano erupting.

A moment later, Kelly helped the archbishop to his feet. He glanced toward the scaffold. The priest was gone. Fled. Why else hadn't he come to help them? Uneasily, Kelly realized the priest had something to do with what had just happened. That he may have tried to kill them.

"Are you hurt?" he asked.

Clarizio was ashen and he trembled, but otherwise he displayed no emotion. Brushing his cassock, he looked down at the shattered wood and velvet ruins.

"I am unharmed. Please, let us leave here now."

Just as the first of the mass of people rushing from everywhere in the cathedral arrived at the altar rail, he led Kelly off the altar and over to the doorway to the sacristy. Inside the sacristy, Clarizio put one hand to his head and momentarily steadied himself by grasping Kelly's forearm with the other until the dizziness that suddenly overcame him left.

"Your Excellency, I saw a priest coming off the scaffold right before that marble fell, and he disappeared right afterward," Kelly said.

Clarizio looked momentarily faint again, but his face hardened. "You think a priest almost caused our deaths?"

"It looks that way."

The archbishop's steely gaze bore into Kelly. "Go with God, my son. I will contact you soon. Be very careful!"

11

THE NEXT MORNING, LANE WOODS TIGHTENED THE BELT OF HER TRENCH coat as a piercing wind bore down. The day was getting colder and colder and the rain had let up only an hour ago. She was one of the few people who braved such weather to visit the Colosseum. Her stop at police headquarters this morning was useless. The young officer who dealt with her spent more time trying to invite her to dinner than being informative. She learned little that she didn't already know from Damian Carter or from the press clippings on the Falconi murder that she had had translated into English.

Walking through the amphitheater, she shuddered, not from the cold, but from thinking of the brutality that once brought people here. The Colosseum was smaller than she had imagined, but in a way, the very intimacy between the audience and the victims made her feel that much more squeamish. Despite the amphitheater's ruined state, it was easy enough to imagine the grisly contests that sated the lust of crowds clamoring for blood.

She wondered if the bishop was stalked in the manner of some of the elaborate hunts once staged here. The ancient Romans had been connoisseurs of violent death. Imaginatively, they often used the arena as a stage that looked like a hill, a forest, or a pastoral setting for their bloody amusement. Sometimes the floor was flooded, creating an artificial lake where miniature naval battles were fought to the death.

Scanning the arena floor, she determined approximately where Falconi's body was found. The police used the word *flung* when saying that his body was apparently thrown into the pit from the spectators gallery. Only a very powerful person could do that. Unless there was more than one killer.

She felt a wave of sympathy for the murder victim. As always, she tried to bring her imagination to bear on the story. Carter, as usual, had been secretive when he talked to her. She hoped he was right when he told her that Falconi put him onto something very important, an exposé, the story of the year.

Though she heeded Carter because he'd proved to be an invaluable source in the past, she felt something was off this time. He hadn't told her everything he knew, but that was par for the course. The way he acted bothered her much more than what he didn't say. He was more guarded. And more strung out. Much more. Damian Carter was very frightened.

She hoped she got a lead on the Falconi business quickly. The investiture was only several days away. The making of American cardinals was a big and highly colorful story, one made for TV. But Murphy would start getting itchy if something didn't crop up on the Falconi story and start petitioning for her return to New York.

Strolling around the arena, Lane wondered what Falconi's thoughts were right before he died. A strange idea gripped her. What if he had been sentenced to death, much like the early martyrs? Had he held beliefs that were considered heretical? Would anyone be killed for such a reason in this day and age?

She smiled at how she let her imagination run away, but she valued that ability. Often, like a lightning flash illuminating a dark room, she experienced a sudden, intuitive understanding of a situation. In the highly competitive world of journalism, all reporters wanted an edge. Intuition was hers. Often, her mental leaps proved to be on target, letting her see things clearly and go after offbeat sources of information that more prosaic reporters never considered.

Damian said the bishop was assassinated, but Damian often believed what he wanted to believe. And he had no facts to buttress his supposition. What, she wondered, was Falconi doing here at such a time of night?

She ticked off possibilities. Was the Colosseum a spot for rendezvous with prostitutes? Gay cruising? Was Falconi a romantic who often visited such places when he couldn't sleep? Again, she thought that it was Carter who put her onto the story. Was the bishop involved in some underground intrigue?

Acutely aware of the disadvantage she was under by being a foreigner and not speaking the language, Lane wanted a cram course in her new environment, the kind that foreign correspondents generally take from one of their own. Each country, each major city, has a journalist whom visiting newspeople rely upon as a source. They know the lay of the land. The local politics. The influence peddlers. The personalities.

Time is the enemy of reporters, and they do anything to keep from wasting it. Such resources tell them who is approachable and who is not. Who does favors and the reasons why they are helpful. What records might be useful, and available, and how to get them. They put into perspective the people who are willing to be quoted, the axes they have to grind, the positions they are promoting. For a drink, a meal, a little flattery, and shared journalistic gossip, such people impart their knowledge. Most of all, they do it because it represents a role reversal. They enjoy being sought out the way they themselves are always cultivating others.

A producer had suggested that Lane look up an old Vatican correspondent. "He's eccentric as hell," he warned when rattling off the man's name and telephone number, "but he knows more about what's going on over there than the pope does."

Ten minutes after leaving the Colosseum, she dialed the reporter's number. There were a half dozen short, shrill rings before the receiver was finally picked up.

"Gracey at your service," a wheezy voice said.

Lane forced a brightness in her voice that she didn't feel. The producer said that Gracey was in his sixties, and long ago, she found that most men of that age preferred women who sounded chipper rather than smart. Over the years, she became accustomed to tailoring her personality to fit the person from whom she wanted information. She no longer thought about it.

"Mr. Gracey, my name is Lane Woods. I'm with station XTV

in New York, and I've heard that you are a friend of a journalist in need."

"How may I help you, Miss Woods—or is it Mrs. or Ms.? One can never tell anymore what women want to be called."

"Mr. Gracey, you can call me Lane," she said, straining to keep that cheerful note in her voice because he sounded like a potential pain in the ass.

Briefly she explained about her ignorance of the city and said that she was assigned to cover the investiture. "I would rather go over particulars of the story with you in person."

"Very well. Let me see. How is tomorrow at three in the afternoon at my apartment."

"That's fine. Thank you very much."

"The elevating of cardinals," he muttered before hanging up. "The last of the world's true princes."

At that point, his voice had such an unnerving effect on her that she was tempted not to see him at all. She brushed aside the feeling. She always said she would deal with a demon if he would help with a story.

Hanging up, she wished he could have seen her right away. Maybe she should have mentioned the Falconi story as well. Not sure what her next step should be, Lane became anxious. She felt a nervous gnawing in her stomach, the "rats-in-my-belly syndrome," as she called the feeling that came over her on major assignments. She couldn't help herself. She started lining up a litany of unsavory possibilities that always concluded with her not getting the story. Suppose she didn't get enough information? Suppose she couldn't get to the right people? Suppose Damian was wrong?

"Suppose, suppose, suppose," she muttered, and then caught herself. Fretting over potential problems was a useless habit that she had fruitlessly tried to change over the years. The rats came with the territory.

Not far from the phone Lane had just used, Paolo Bisleti entered the ZOPPA FURNITURE REFINISHING ESTABLISHMENT on Via Moserrato. He came because the American priest stopped him in the Vatican gardens after he left the archbishop and asked for his help. From what

182

Kelly wanted, Bisleti knew he would be helping Archbishop Clarizio as well.

The word *establishment* on the sign was perhaps misleading. The shop was barely larger than a four-car garage but was so cluttered it seemed to hold half the furniture in Rome. Tables and chairs of various sizes and periods hung from the walls and the ceiling. Huge picture frames, desks, love seats, and pedestals filled the rest of the room. Thick dust blanketed the furnishings, indicating that the proprietor, Vittorio Zoppa, did not work overly hard at the craft that the weathered sign above the front window proclaimed was the way he earned his living.

Zoppa was comfortably ensconced in a chair, reading a newspaper, his Gucci loafers propped up on a desk. He was in his early forties and far more elegant than his surroundings. With graying temples, neatly trimmed mustache, and a profile that belonged to the emperors, he looked like an aristocrat who was slumming. He wore a three-piece, pearl-gray suit. A thick gold chain adorned one wrist, a Rolex watch the other. He also wore a sleepy look that, Bisleti knew, was as deceptive as his storefront.

Halfway across the room, Bisleti caught Zoppa's eye. He smiled and raised his right hand in a loose fist. With the index finger up, he brought his middle finger and thumb together, with his other two fingers arcing behind, to form a *d*. Simultaneously, he swiftly brought his hand to his shoulder, then toward his hip, while bowing slightly. The greeting signified "Duke," which was Zoppa's nickname because of his noble looks.

"*Buon giorno*, Paolo," Zoppa said delightedly as he rose to his feet.

The men embraced warmly.

"How long has it been, Paolo? At least six months. Too long, my friend. Too long."

Smiling affectionately, Bisleti hefted himself up on one side of the desk. He motioned for Zoppa to sit where he had been.

"How are you?" the priest motioned with his hands. As always, he was grateful that Zoppa knew how to sign since his youngest brother, Georgio, was deaf. The inability to express himself to people he knew his entire life was the hardest aspect of losing his voice.

"Not too many complaints," Zoppa said, looking lazily around the shop. "Business could be better."

"A pity you don't have more customers. A real pity."

One of the games Bisleti always played with Zoppa was acting as straight man to the charade that his friend wished the furniture restoration business would pick up. Ever since Zoppa acquired the shop eleven years ago, everything had remained exactly where it was the first time he set foot in here. Occasionally, Zoppa did ply his craft, and he was a true artist when working with wood. He enjoyed himself on such occasions as well, but he seemed ashamed for taking pleasure in the labor that he did with his hands.

"You did such beautiful work on the archbishop's refectory table, you would be the restorers' Michelangelo if you devoted your services to the Vatican," Bisleti's hands said. "But I know you have no interest in becoming a papal slave, so perhaps there is something else I can ask of you. . . ."

Zoppa shrugged. "Paolo, when times are lean, a man must do what he can to survive."

Suddenly, he rose to this feet and shook his body like a horse rising from a bed of hay. The shuddering movement was unexpected, indicating the man's extraordinarily quick reflexes.

"Let us go to the café around the corner," Zoppa said. "A little cognac is good on such a day and gives a man a reason to think before he speaks."

Accustomed to his friend's circuitous approach to business, Bisleti followed him out of the store. Zoppa shielded his eyes from the sun's silvery glare and looked in the grimy front door while determining whether to lock up. With a shrug, he decided against it and walked down the cobblestone street with his right arm resting on the priest's shoulder. A block away, they rounded the corner and entered a small café. The walls were white stucco, the red floor tiles worn, and the tables covered with black-and-white-checkered cloths. A working man's haunt.

A dark-haired young waiter wearing a white shirt, black pants and vest, and a white napkin draped over his left arm hurried over and bowed. His obsequious manner and the fawning expression on his thin, sallow face showed that he only wanted to please Vittorio Zoppa.

"Tonio, give the good father and me two cognacs."

The waiter bowed again, now adopting an almost craven attitude. "Ma certo, Signore Zoppa."

Zoppa sat back and looked at his friend with pleasure. "Paolo, it is good to see you."

184

"You are looking well, Duke," Bisleti said.

The waiter set down their drinks as well as a plate of cheese and olives before them and said, *"Buon appetito."*

The men raised their glasses and with a slight nod to one another, drained them. The ritual over, the priest knew he could now come to the point with this complicated man. He hoped the archbishop would not be too mad at him for seeking Zoppa's help, but he was willing to take the consequences. There were times when all men could help in a good cause.

Making sure that no one else in the café could see the motions of his hands and the expressiveness of his face, Bisleti started explaining his mission. "As you must know, Bishop Falconi was murdered in the Colosseum. If you recall from the newspaper stories, he was strangled with a priest's stole."

"A terrible death," Zoppa said sympathetically.

He still found it strange, as always, when seeing Paolo dressed as a priest. They had known one another all their lives, having been born and raised near Palermo in the northwest of Sicily in a small fertile region known as Conca d'Oro. One day when Vittorio was eight and Paolo was seven and they were not known to each other, they were caught stealing oranges from an orchard. The farmer held a shot gun on them, but Paolo set his dog on the man. The man ran from the dog and the boys became best friends. They grew up sleeping at one another's house, sharing their food, their few toys, their dreams. When they were teenagers, Vittorio, out of pity for his ugly friend, made girls share themselves with Paolo, who was so like a brother but more trustworthy. They had committed many crimes together, watched over one another. There were many days when he missed simply talking to his friend for hours and hours as they had done as boys and young men.

Now, there were moments, albeit not too many, when he thought Paolo may have done the right thing in leaving the life. But at such times he was being selfish. He wanted it to be Paolo who said the prayers over his grave when he died peacefully in his sleep as a very old man.

Zoppa was at home visiting his dying mother when Paolo embarked on the road to the priesthood, but he knew the story well. He and Paolo had planned an armored car robbery, but one of their group was arrested on another charge before the robbery In exchange for having the charge dropped, the arrested man became an informant.

185

Police were waiting at the site of the intended crime. Paolo was shot three times but managed to escape. Somehow, Archbishop Clarizio found him, had a doctor treat him, and brought him back to life. The archbishop had smoothed over the matter with the police, and Paolo was never charged. His friend remained a part of the archbishop's household and then trained for the priesthood.

"Yes, a terrible death, most certainly," Zoppa repeated.

Being with Bisleti, he found it a tragedy that the expression of a mind of such wonderful quickness and imagination was blunted by being limited by such clumsy appendages as hands. It was like watching an opera singer trying to tell what was on his soul through boxing. How strange life is, he thought. He knew the story of Paolo's throat as well. Two men seized Paolo one night shortly after his ordination. They slit his throat and left him for dead as vengeance for something they believed he had done to them many years before. Zoppa's revenge had been both swifter and more lethal than that of the intended assassins.

"What you do not know is that someone tried to kill Archbishop Clarizio yesterday at the Basilica. He was there with an American priest, and they were almost crushed to death by a falling slab of marble."

Zoppa sat still, watching the priest's hands work intently. He nodded again, only to let Bisleti know that he understood.

"Just before the attempt was made on their lives, the American saw a priest acting strangely by the scaffolding from which the marble fell."

"You believe what happened to Clarizio is related to what happened to Falconi?"

Bisleti shrugged and signed that he didn't know but wanted to find out. He had known Vittorio so long that he didn't consider it bizarre that a priest who was an aide to a powerful ecclesiastic was with a man of Zoppa's reputation. There were many strange alliances at the Vatican. Nor, for the same reason, did he think it peculiar what he was about to ask of him. The archbishop would object, of course, but he would tell him only if pressed. After all, information often came through mysterious channels. Information came to Vittorio Zoppa.

On his mother's side, Zoppa was a member of one of the most powerful underworld families in Rome. Two of his uncles were in

Parliament, a distant cousin was one of the nation's leading attorneys. Two other cousins were in the Church hierarchy, and another was mother superior of a convent. As for Zoppa, he now held an influential if ill-defined position in the family. It was rumored that one day soon, he would become head of the family.

The last time Zoppa aided Bisleti, he got him copies of confidential government files and police reports when the archbishop needed such information. When handed the reports, Clarizio had looked at Bisleti noncommittally. He never questioned his aide's very large expense account that month. For a price, Zoppa could get just about any kind of document or verify or disprove just about any rumor. He could also get a lot of other things done that Bisleti no longer cared to consider.

"Would you see what you can learn about these incidents?" Bisleti signed.

"Paolo, of course, but from the look in your eyes there must be something else you want."

The priest smiled. Zoppa knew him so well. Even when he had a voice, Zoppa could always read his eyes. Once again, he checked to make certain they couldn't be seen before he motioned, "See if there is any link to Milites Christi."

Zoppa raised an eyebrow but otherwise showed no emotion. Nothing his friend the priest requested shocked him. "As you wish, Paolo. As you wish."

In Sicily and now in Rome, Vittorio Zoppa looked on the Church as yet another institution inhabited by men. Some good. Some bad. Some actually believed they found God and led others in that direction. So much the better. The world certainly needed good men. Still, he wondered how his friend had chosen such a life, wasted his talents. He had been so good at planning everything from money laundering to major robberies. Paolo always made him think of lost chances.

"There is one more thing," Bisleti indicated.

"Yes?"

"Please keep an eye on a priest, an American. Here is where you can find him." He handed Zoppa a piece of paper with Kelly's name and hotel written on it. "He may be in grave danger. He was the one at the Basilica with Archbishop Clarizio."

Zoppa nonchalantly put the paper in the pocket of his white silk shirt. They both knew it was as good as done.

"Life goes on, Paolo. Our paths were linked for a long time and then separated, but they always come together again. We will always be in the river of life together."

Bisleti smiled. Vittorio grew a little melancholy, a little philosophical, when he put his mind to a task. The price would be more than fair and the undertaking very discreet. As always, Zoppa instinctively knew it would be better if the archbishop remained in the dark about the arrangements. Zoppa took friendship seriously.

The waiter returned with two more cognacs.

"*Salute*, Paolo."

The priest raised his glass. They drank simultaneously.

"Do you know how much money I lost betting on the last papal election?" Zoppa said. "Why, I . . ."

Bisleti smiled again at his friend. Whenever they got together, Zoppa felt obliged to say something about the Church. Bisleti knew his friend was uncomfortable about the lot he had chosen and worried about him. He loved him for it. What Vittorio never comprehended and what Bisleti could never adequately express through sign language was that he was truly happy. The archbishop had shown him that he was a man, a man of God, not an ugly creature to be pitied. He had been surprised, then overwhelmed, when the realization rushed over him one day.

That was all he ever wanted.

The office building near the Rome airport was a nondescript glass tower that could have been in New York, Hong Kong, Sydney, or any other world metropolis. The blandness was appropriate for the Gruson, Dilling Corp., which occupied part of the twelfth floor. Kelly had never heard of the company until David Martin told him the name this morning.

Martin was fiddling with a videocassette recorder when Kelly entered his offices. Exasperation was stamped on his round, pudgy face. His horn-rimmed glasses slid down his nose. He had the frantic look of an accountant whose calculator had broken. His short arms flapped like a seal's flippers as he pushed buttons, turned switches, and tried forcing a tape into the mouth of the recalcitrant machine.

Watching the awkward exercise, Kelly recalled that Martin had the electronic aptitude of a chimpanzee. Who had been foolish enough to let him assault a VCR?

"Try plugging it in," he suggested.

Perplexed, Martin stared down at the plug lying on the floor near his feet. He stopped sheepishly, picked it up, and put it in the wall socket. When he turned, his expression changed from chagrin to delight.

"Kevin!" he cried happily, and hurried to his visitor. He pumped Kelly's hand while eyeing his clerical garb with a look not too dissimilar to when he saw the plug on the floor. "God, I'm one of those people who has to see it to believe it's really true. You went over to the other side."

Nobody had put his career change to Kelly that way before. "I hope so."

Martin clapped him on the back and did a little dance as he completely circled Kelly. "What are you doing over here? Just passing through, or are they going to make you a cardinal this week too?"

Kelly laughed at the unbridled enthusiasm that Martin brought to everything he did, including making someone from the past feel welcome. Kelly had never figured out Martin. The charm rarely ever slipped. How did he keep up the act? When he entered the seminary, he hadn't remained in contact with anyone from the past. He was surprised that Martin made several efforts to keep in touch, but Kelly never responded.

"Thanks for the letters I never answered, Dave. At the time, I wanted to put everything behind me. And everybody too."

"I figured it was something like that," Martin said, his face still wreathed with a welcoming smile even as he wondered why Kelly had surfaced.

Kelly glanced around at the nondescript decor. Planned blandness. Off-white paint on the walls. Some ficus and rubber trees and framed posters. No personal touches on the desks, such as photos of family. Like the building that housed the office, this space could have been anywhere, inhabited by anyone.

"What business are you in now?"

"Packaging. We work with packagers in Italy, Greece, and the Middle East. We match the regional packaging companies with big U.S. consumer-goods companies penetrating their markets. Suppose P and G wants to market a new soap or cereal in Saudi Arabia? We go to the local packager, work on the design concept, and navigate national laws pertaining to disclosure on boxes, et cetera, et cetera. Besides bringing the locals the business, we advise them on technological changes happening in other countries, which often is pretty sophisticated stuff."

"Dave, I have a few things I'd like to put to you. For old times' sake."

Martin's expression didn't change, but he was intrigued. There was the remote chance that Kelly was here on his own, but if the bit of gossip he had picked up was true, the odds were ten to one Kelly was doing a job for the Vatican.

"Sure. Oh, by the way, you're having dinner with us tonight. Gloria insisted. She's dying to see you. You know, when she found out that you actually became a priest, she wept. She was always hoping you'd come out of the seminary because she has three unmarried cousins for you to meet."

"Did she want me to marry all of them?"

"Only two. Suppose I pick you up outside your hotel at seven? Where are you staying?"

"The Navarro," Kelly replied, sure that Martin already knew. When he called this morning, he foresaw dinner on the agenda. He was fairly certain Martin knew he was in town and if contacted, would ask that they get together. Agency people always tried to find out about what former agents were up to, whether they were back in the business for any reason, and if so, for whom. Martin went by the book.

A few minutes to seven o'clock, Kelly stood in the lobby of the hotel. A light rain fell and the din of traffic drifted through the front door. While keeping an eye out for Martin, he talked to a white-haired porter who claimed to have grown up with the last pope.

"He liked the girls so much before he wanted to be a priest," the man said, "I was surprised that he became the Holy Father."

A horn tooted out front. Through the door, Kelly saw Martin seated behind the wheel of a bright orange Volkswagen. Taking leave of the porter, he ducked outside and was barely wet as he crammed himself into the passenger's seat.

"Hitler's people's car," he muttered as he shifted in a desperate

190

attempt to get comfortable. "Hitler's ideal people were all under five feet eight and a hundred and forty pounds."

"*Avanti, avanti,*" Martin bellowed above the roar of the rain that suddenly thundered down.

He pulled out in front of another car, missing it by a hair. The Volkswagen darted in and out of openings that Kelly would have found daunting if they were on a skateboard. Martin honked the horn incessantly. When he wasn't yelling at other drivers, he made insulting motions with his fingers and arms.

"Italy's great, just great," he said. "The Italians are so alive! They enjoy everything! I'm learning so many curses I'll be admitted to the Cosa Nostra."

"You also learned to drive like a maniac. Will you slow down, please?"

"Are you nuts?" Martin replied in a thick, mocking Italian accent. "To drive slow is not to be a man!" Martin laughed his infectious laughter.

Kelly was as amazed now as he was years ago by how congenial this man appeared to be. He didn't seem to have a mean bone in his body, and he wound up as a cheerleader for whatever country in which they told him to serve. His current assignment in Italy was the Vatican. What an enigma he was.

Kelly remembered the last time he saw Martin. There was nothing happy-go-lucky about that encounter. It was about a "target" Martin had given him. The intended victim turned out to be a well-known Buddhist monk. By then Kelly was having serious doubts about what he was doing, whether the Agency had long ago in its zealotry crossed the line from dealing with true enemies to dealing with anyone who was perceived to be unfriendly or inconvenient.

Kelly started asking questions about the monk. The answers were disturbing. The man wasn't a friend of the Viet Cong and he wasn't a friend of the Americans. As far as Kelly could gather, the monk was a Vietnamese patriot who was trying to do what was best for his countrymen.

Trying to disregard his findings, Kelly stalked the monk one evening. He found him in a garden praying. The Vietnamese was a slight figure, his shaven head bowed. He projected a stateliness and serenity that were at odds with the corruption and chaos of the war-bedraggled country. Kelly knew that he couldn't kill him. This wasn't war. It was murder.

191

Kelly confronted Martin. "Damn it, Dave. He's not doing anything against us."

"What do you mean?" Martin asked. "He's leading people in the streets, disrupting order. Telling us we don't belong here." He paused and stared at Kelly. "Suppose I make it an order?"

"Then it will be your last one, buddy," Kelly said. "I'll take you out before I take him."

The sound of Martin's voice brought Kelly back to the moment. "Don't take offense, Kevin, and I'm pleased you looked me up. But what kind of business are you on? I happen to know you've been in Rome on several occasions, and I got nary a phone call. Why flaunt your holiness this time?"

"I guess I wouldn't see you now either, if I didn't have to. For a long time, old friends made me think of Helen and Janie, so I avoided them. Avoidance became a pattern."

"So it's pretty important."

"There are some strange doings going on with the Church and I've been pulled into it," Kelly replied sarcastically.

"Why, Father Kelly," Martin said in his raspy Italian accent, "there have been strange doings in the Church for two thousand years. What the hell you talkin' about?"

Kelly laughed, thinking how bizarre it all was. "I'm not sure myself yet."

"Why not give it a shot?"

"Okay. Give me a realistic scenario why Bishop Falconi was murdered."

Unconsciously, Martin slowed down as he considered the question. It was logical that the Vatican would sic somebody on him. The last person he expected was Kelly. The irony struck him. What do they say when the Agency hires you? You can never put it behind you? *Never* is a very unequivocal word. Kelly was the one guy he had thought had broken the mold. Now here he was, one foot in the old quicksand.

"The rules still apply, Kevin. You go by process of elimination. From our profile of him, we know Falconi had no sex life, so that ruled out a jealous lover or a dangerous liaison. It wasn't a robbery. He still had his watch and wallet with the lira equivalent of one hundred and seven dollars U.S., and all his credit cards were still there. There's the possibility of a plain crazy, especially in light of the unique item used to strangle him. But we don't think so. The hit had a professional quality. The killer was efficient. There was no sign of struggle. He surprised the bishop and dispatched him in seconds. We believe it was an assassination."

"What do you make of the stole?"

"Some kind of warning to other clerics is all we can figure."

"How does Damian Carter figure into this?"

"You know about that, huh?"

"Vatican rumors have him at the scene of the crime. And implications of worse."

"He was there. But ignore the gossip that he did in the bishop."

"You had Falconi under surveillance?"

"No, Carter. From the moment he hit town. Met Falconi in the Colosseum right before the bishop was killed. The killer almost got Carter too."

"Did the watcher see the bishop's murder?"

"No, he heard something strange for a moment but nothing else. His job was to stick with Carter."

Kelly played a hunch. "Did he intervene when the killer tried to get Carter?"

"Not his role. He was surveillance only."

"And Carter wasn't worth keeping alive, because he was just a piece of radical trash?"

"You said it, Kevin, not me. Some people feel that way. Maybe because he's mouthy. He makes enemies both inside and outside the Church. The last time he preached here, his sermon was on the pope's supporting Solidarity but not worker movements in Latin America. He makes certain people mad."

"Why was a watcher on him?"

"Carter may be mixed up in some terrorist stuff. He has contacts with the Red Brigade, PLO, IRA, et cetera. He plays a dangerous game."

Once again, Kelly wondered if the Trinity hadn't gotten involved in some radical antiwar business, maybe dragged into it by Carter. "Did your guy make the killer?"

"No. It was too dark. Never got a good look at him."

"You sure?" Kelly said, finding that odd. Anybody on night work should have had infrared cameras and binoculars.

Martin shifted uncomfortably. "He was sloppy and was reprimanded. There was one thing. . . ."

"What?"

"The killer was dressed as a priest."

Kelly felt numb. What the hell was going on?

"He did get some night shots of Carter later," Martin continued. "Compromising positions. Carter and a girlfriend."

Kelly shook his head disgustedly, wondering if women had always been another common bond of the Trinity.

Again without waiting for Kelly to ask, Martin filled him in. "After Carter left the Colosseum, he went to a photographer's apartment. Like him, she's in with a lot of radicals. He spent the night with her. The pictures show he wasn't hearing her confession."

Kelly's stomach began stewing. Martin had brought back to him why he had wanted a new life, one where looking in bedroom windows was one of the least destructive things you did. Suddenly, he remembered Franny Cook and felt more disgusted. All he was doing was looking in bedroom windows too.

Abruptly, Martin swung the car into a narrow street. "Here we are. Villa Martin."

The three-story, nineteenth-century, beige brick villa was set back about fifty yards from the road. It had a red tile roof, a courtyard edged by pillars, and was surrounded by an expansive yard. There were several gardens, and the forsythia, yews, and other shrubberies were freshly pruned to prevent them from concealing intruders. Precautions abounded. Trees had been removed so that there was an unobstructed view from the windows. A high, wrought-iron fence surrounded the entire property. Yelps came from the rear of the house where the guard dogs were kept.

Martin beeped twice. A man wearing the rough work clothes of a gardener opened the large, ornate wrought-iron gate barring access to the compound and waved Martin through. The cobblestone driveway leading to a parking area behind the house was covered with a layer of gravel so that cars or footsteps could more easily be heard. The presence of three parked cars revealed that the Martins shared the dwelling.

The rain stopped just as quickly as it started. Kelly climbed out of the VW and stretched cramped muscles. When he turned to follow Martin inside, he started laughing. A woman knelt by the door, a black shawl draped over her head.

"Bless me, Father, for I have overcooked the meat loaf," she wailed as they came up the walkway.

Gloria bounded to her feet and raced toward him. Though in

194

her early forties, she was slim and still youthful. Her auburn hair in a pixie cut made her appear boyish. She dived into Kelly's arms, the shawl trailing behind her.

"Great to see you, Kevin," she said, quickly jumping back. "Is this against the rules?"

"For you there are no rules," he replied.

"There never are for Gloria," Martin said.

"Not now, David!" she said sharply to her husband.

Kelly ignored the exchange. He was in no mood to probe. The last thing he wanted to hear was that their marriage was troubled. Maybe it was selfish, he thought, but he had too damned much on his plate right now to have to worry about them as well. Besides, it was probably nothing. He knew enough about himself to realize that when anxious he tended to project his insecurities onto others.

The meal was pleasant, and Kelly's apprehension about having the evening turn into a hellish reminder of the past proved groundless. He caught himself thinking he should have known better. These people were trained to be tactful.

Once the dishes were cleared, Kelly and Martin went into the living room where Martin brought out the box of Cuban cigars. "Wonderful, isn't it?" he said, passing the box, which Kelly declined. "We get them everywhere but at home."

Martin fixed drinks, gave one to Kelly, and settled back into an old leather chair. When Kelly tasted his, he felt as if everyone had his number. It was Wild Turkey.

A minute later, Gloria poked her head in the door. She wore a raincoat and a scarf covered her hair. "I have to go out for a little while, but I'll be back in plenty of time to say good-night, Kevin."

"You had better be," he replied.

Kelly recognized the ploy. He had seen it used often enough. Martin wanted time alone with him, and the less Gloria knew about business the better. When he turned to Martin, though, the little man's face was screwed into a peevish look. Kelly glanced after Gloria, who disappeared through the front door.

"Mark Williams was in town a couple of months ago," Martin said, mentioning a colleague from long ago.

"What's he doing now?"

"An AID program in the Philippines."

Their conversation touched on other mutual friends and concerns, including the relationship between Langley and the Holy See.

195

"From our standpoint, things are pretty good now," Martin said. "As you know, there was a real strain between John XXIII and us. Things weren't much better under Paul VI. He was against us in Vietnam, but he did cooperate when Lyndon sent troops into the Dominican Republic. But this pope's agenda largely corresponds with ours."

"I assume that when he met with Yasir Arafat it was at your instigation."

"No, not the Agency. The White House . . . when they wanted to get tough with the Israelis. A signal that public opinion could be turned against them if they didn't shape up."

Kelly changed the topic. "Dave, what do you know about Milites Christi?"

Martin raised himself slightly in his seat, a sign of discomfort that Kelly suddenly remembered. The congenial look in Martin's eyes was replaced by a cool, professional gaze.

"Odd outfit to say the least. You know about its founder, the Spanish mystic Miguel Perez, who as a peasant boy was supposed to have the stigmata, bleeding from the same wounds Christ did and all that?"

"Not much, really."

"Well, he was taken up by some influential people who built a movement around him, although the stigmata were never verified. The movement is growing steadily as a rallying point for people who think Christianity has lost its purity."

"What's the attraction?"

"Part of it is mystical. Perez died in 1974. There are a few cases of people who claim that by praying to him they were miraculously cured. But the big draw is Milites Christi's militancy."

"What do you mean?"

"A lot of members see themselves as either saints or sort of Green Berets in a war against evil. Membership is secretive, but what's obvious is that Milites Christi has a lot of rich contributors. Take a look at the big center they opened here earlier this year. They sunk a fortune into restoring the place."

"Are they dangerous?"

Martin shrugged. "Fanatics are always potentially dangerous, Kevin. You know that. As for Milites Christi? I doubt if they do much more than march around in funny costumes at secret meetings and whisper passwords to one another in Latin."

"Do you use them for anything, Dave?"

Martin laughed. "No, a bit too wacky. Even for us."

Martin got up and took their glasses. While fixing them each another drink, he asked, "What's with all the Milites Christi business?"

"There's some speculation at the Vatican that Milites Christi might have had a hand in the Falconi murder."

"I didn't know anybody was actually afraid of them."

"It's all conjecture. But could you check into it? Get me a file?"

"I'll see what I can come up with. Who's so worried? Clarizio?"

"How did you know?" As soon as the words were out of his mouth, Kelly knew better. Hell, Gracey knew. Why wouldn't Martin?

"It's my job to find out things," Martin said in his mock Italian accent.

In his normal voice, he added, "To get specific, I know you've been working on the Hogan investigation for him, so I assumed he brought you over here."

"There's something else you should know. I was in St. Peter's with Archbishop Clarizio yesterday when a slab of marble just happened to fall from the scaffold behind us. It just happened to fall right where we were sitting. If I didn't see it at the last second, I wouldn't be here now. Neither would the archbishop."

Martin's brow furrowed. "So that's what that was all about. I read something in the paper about an unexplained accident, but I didn't think much about it."

"What's weird is that I saw a priest coming off the scaffold a moment before it went."

"I take it you don't know who he was?"

Kelly stood up and paced back and forth, his right hand clasped behind his neck in obvious frustration. "I'm not sure. I only got a glimpse of him. Didn't even see his face, but there was something familiar about him. Dark hair. A big, muscular guy. I've been racking my brains ever since, but it's no good."

"If you come up with anything, let me know. I'll check it from my end."

"I saw so little of him, I doubt it, but thanks."

"Just trying to help the public. That's what your tax dollars pay for."

"If I believed that," Kelly said, "I'd be a happy man."

197

Staring back, Martin wondered how much this priest business had really changed Kelly. How much wasn't he telling him? Remembering some of Kelly's activities and his occasional uncontrollable temper, Martin realized he was still a little afraid of him.

12

THE NEXT DAY, CONNIE ROBBINS DROVE HER SLEEK, RED JAGUAR CONvertible up the winding country road. She felt exhilarated. Rome was almost an hour behind her. The day was crisp and the sky a clear blue. She loved driving the Jag with the top down, especially the first day after so much rain.

Monsignor Vincenzo Ruggieri at least could be commended for being discreet. She had never heard of Trastevere, the out-of-the-way country inn where they were meeting for lunch. She had run into Ruggieri two evenings ago at a party hosted by the cousin of an Italian archbishop who was about to be made a cardinal. Once again, Ruggieri had proved charming and suggested this outing. Feeling adventurous, she had agreed.

Just as the monsignor's precise directions stated, a driveway appeared off to Connie's right. There were the stone pillars that he told her marked the entrance to Trastevere. Once through the pillars, she entered a parklike setting and was pleased again. There was a graciousness about the manicured lawns, well-tended gardens, and proud, restored palazzo that was now a restaurant-hotel.

As she approached the restaurant, she saw Ruggieri standing on a second-floor veranda. She waved. A smile lit up his face.

As a valet took the car, the monsignor rushed down the steps. His delight in seeing her was obvious. Both his hands were stretched out to her in welcome. He looked quite handsome in a blue herringbone sports jacket, dark blue shirt, beige twill slacks, and beige Bally loafers.

"*Buon giorno*, Connie. I am so pleased you could come." He seized her hands and kissed them.

"*Buon giorno*, Monsignor. Or would you prefer me to call you *signore* or mister?"

"Even a priest is entitled to wear mufti once in a while, Connie."

"But surely not too often."

He laughed as he took arm and escorted her up the wide marble steps. Yet, he gave her a curious look. Something in her tone caused him to rethink the afternoon a bit.

On the veranda, he took her shoulders and turned her so that she faced the beautiful valley yawning below them. The view was spectacular and extended for miles and miles, sweeping across vast green forests and carefully tilled farmland that gave the appearance of a patchwork quilt.

"Once the Church owned all of that and much much more," Ruggieri said, stretching his arm so that he took in as far as they could see. "Incredible, isn't it, how circumstances change? But don't be surprised if the Church one day again has the power and authority to challenge kings and presidents and rule over all that you see and . . . Who knows? Perhaps the world."

"Those farmers down there might have something to say about it," Connie said.

"History teaches us that the world is in a constant state of flux and that the pendulum swings back."

"I hope that doesn't mean we're going to have to give up high-speed dental drills."

Ruggieri laughed again. "I am afraid you don't take me seriously. Come, I have booked a private room so that I can babble more nonsense to amuse you without disturbing anyone else."

Connie smiled to herself upon his mentioning the room. The little monsignor was very smooth and must be very sure of himself.

Opening the French doors off the veranda, Ruggieri stepped aside to let her enter before him. They went up a flight of marble steps and on the landing turned left. As they passed a huge, gilt-framed mirror, Connie caught a glimpse of them together. She had expected to feel ridiculous, seeing herself towering over this man. Instead, she shivered. The carnal look on his face had taken a lifetime to bring to perfection.

Ruggieri opened a door to the right, and they entered a large, airy room with a fireplace and a table set for two. "I have taken the liberty of ordering. I hope you don't mind," he said, holding her chair.

"When in Rome . . ."

There was a knock. Ruggieri admitted a waiter, carrying a bottle of wine, who poured a bit into a glass. The monsignor tasted and gave his approval.

"I will be back in a moment," Ruggieri said after the waiter left. He entered another door.

Staring after him, Connie waited expectantly. A few minutes later, she caught her breath. Ruggieri came back, wearing a black cassock and clerical collar. Neither of them remarked on his change of clothes.

The waiter returned periodically, serving them course after course while they talked pleasantly about people they knew in common. Ruggieri seemed to know almost as many of her friends in New York as in Rome, especially those connected to the Church. He told her amusing stories about members of the hierarchy and the wealthy and influential who either dabbled in or immersed themselves in Church affairs. But he also mentioned certain concerns, charities and organizations with which he was involved, some of which she knew and others she did not.

"Your husband is very rich and very helpful to certain elements of the Church."

"He tries."

"There is a worthy cause that perhaps you could get him to see in a generous light."

She had expected the pitch. Usually, she felt sorry for churchmen; they had to spend so much of their time scrounging funds from the wealthy. Ruggieri went on at length until she interrupted him as she finished her roast duckling.

"Why, Monsignor, suppose I just put you together with Cal. That way you and I won't have to waste the afternoon on this one topic. Now, what do you propose for dessert?"

He smiled. "That we make love."

Rising from the table, he walked across the room and opened the door he had entered earlier. She could now see that it led to a large

201

bedroom. Indifferently, he leaned back against the wall and gave her an amused look that said the next move was hers.

Arching her left eyebrow, Connie smiled. She had wondered how he would get around to this. At least he was civilized enough to get the meal out of the way. And at least he wasn't into those vague flirtatious games, so that a woman was not sure whether a man was merely playing or was sincere in his lust. She appreciated the care he had taken. The little monsignor was charming.

"By all means."

A few minutes later, he smiled when she lifted her dress over her head, appreciating her sensuality and thinking she was quite well preserved. Money allowed women of her class to maintain themselves. Her incredibly long legs were delicious.

He had imagined from the start that she would not be coy and was grateful that was the case. Some American women drove him to distraction. They wanted to make going to bed with a priest an act of mercy, or else they had to convince themselves they were in the throes of some grand, uncontrollable passion for the unattainable. Connie needed no such delusions.

The monsignor found himself intrigued. What, other than boredom, had brought her to his bed? There was always a reason that heightened the titillation, that made the act of making love to one of St. Peter's disciples that much more exciting. With each woman, it was something a little different, but it always had to do with a variation of curiosity, power, and punishment stemming from the way they had been raised. Could it be any other way? Sometimes he wondered if the priesthood hadn't been invented simply to keep women thinking there was something godlike about men.

He smiled at her. "A sensuous woman," he said, reaching out and delicately stroking her thigh.

Quivering, she leaned over and kissed him, wondering whether he would be gentle or rough. Priests were such complex creatures. Gentle, she imagined. He seemed such a sexual connoisseur that he had no need to punish her for his own guilt. She wondered if he believed in God but was afraid to ask. He might give the wrong answer. She gasped with pleasure as he nuzzled her breasts.

Ruggieri gently glided his hands over her body from her face to her knees. He stretched her out on the bed, and his mouth found her right breast. Whimpering as his teeth gently nibbled, she felt his hand delicately exploring between her thighs and buttocks.

202

She wondered how he would react when she asked him. Most were shocked by her boldness, her wantonness. The idea further incited her passion as she pressed against him, approaching that level of arousal she never reached any other way. Gripping his hair, she moaned softly as she whispered, "Will I have to tell this in confession, Monsignor?"

Ruggieri's eyes glinted. The issue he had wondered about was suddenly clarified. Instinctively, he gave the appropriate response. "You can confess now, if you like."

As his mouth traced invisible paths on her body, her voice sounded incredibly young and came in startled gasps. "Bless me, Father . . . I have . . . have sinned . . ."

❋

Gracey's apartment was difficult enough to locate for anyone who knew Rome well. Lane Woods felt as if she were walking in circles. The journalist said it wasn't far from the Pantheon, but passing the same streets over again, she wondered if she had misunderstood because of his English accent and had inadvertently written down the wrong street. Before having to call him again, she looked at her map and decided to try streets that sounded similar to Via Caro. She was finally successful.

Little more than an alley, the street hooked off Via dell' Umilta. Gracey's building stood midway down the block and was sooty with age. She climbed to the third floor and knocked. A moment later, the door was opened by a small-boned man with long, gray hair and eyebrows. He wore a wrinkled, threadbare, black oriental robe adorned with bloodred herons.

"Thailand," he said, explaining away the robe without any other greeting. "I bought this when I was a correspondent in Indochina."

"Very beautiful."

He stepped aside and she entered an apartment that was remarkably like the man's appearance. The furnishings were old and dusty. Oriental art on the walls hung askew as if made lopsided by an earthquake tremor. Books, magazines, and newspapers seemed to cover everything. The only relatively uncluttered space in the room was at a wooden desk with a typewriter and a lamp.

Without saying anything, Gracey cleared a space on a bamboo chair for her. He nonchalantly removed newspapers, a moth-eaten navy sweater, a maroon towel, a guide book to the Vatican, and a pair of grungy rubbers. Without ceremony, he tossed everything on a nearby table.

Once Lane was seated, Gracey sat at his desk in a high-backed wicker chair equipped with a frayed seat pad of faded blue corduroy. "Now," he said, taking off his wire-rimmed glasses and wiping them with his robe, "what do you want?"

"Mr. Gracey," she began.

"Call me Gracey," he interrupted her, somewhat annoyed. "Everyone knows me by that. As a bit of getting over formalities, I will tell you that, like Churchill, my mother was American and my father was English. I was born on your side of the Atlantic but educated on this side."

Though he was apparently making an effort to be friendly, the wheeze and his cautious eyes, which never fully met hers, made Lane uneasy. Keeping a smile on her face, she groaned to herself and wondered if she would be subjected to his life's history. So be it. Anything to keep the rats at bay.

The phone rang and Gracey answered. "Yes," he said. "Yes. . . . Certainly, Your Excellency."

Hanging up, he turned to his guest. "That was a bishop who wants to know if I will have lunch with him. He never calls unless he wants to leak something. Very little is done here openly."

"Reporting on the Vatican must be fascinating," Lane said.

"Yes, yes, it is. I must say the Vatican intrigues me still, which is why I have remained here more than ten years, turning down assignments to Moscow and Washington in favor of staying on."

He laughed to himself. "The Vatican is the one place on earth where you might think the difference between good and evil would be readily apparent, but here, as in the rest of the world, most of life is dominated by shades of gray. The pomp and circumstance are the symbols of the glorious side of the institution. Most people never glimpse the shadowy world of compromise that is here too."

"Where did Bishop Falconi fit into this morality play?"

Gracey gave her a curious look. "A morality play. Yes, that is one way of putting it. As for Bishop Falconi, he had a very critical role," he said sadly. "I liked the man very much."

The journalist took off his glasses again and wiped his eyes. "A true churchman. His guiding principle was seeing that no harm came to the Church. What you must understand, Miss Woods, is that such men know the weaknesses and faults of those who govern the Church, but they view their character defects the way other men may view a few moles on an extraordinarily talented and beautiful woman. The woman is much greater than her imperfections. Magnify that attitude a million times and you begin to understand the outlook of churchmen such as Falconi."

"Gracey, I told you over the phone I want to do a story about the investiture."

"Yes, the making of cardinals," Gracey said. "The word *cardinal* is Latin for 'hinge' and is an appropriate title for the men who bear it. Cardinals are the Church's most powerful princes. Success of Vatican policies often hinges upon their actions. They are the major fundraisers, diplomats, political theoreticians, guardians of doctrine, overseers of finances, advisers of popes."

"Was Bishop Falconi going to be made a cardinal?" Lane asked.

"No, no, he was not!" he said sharply. "This is the second time you mentioned the bishop. May I ask why?"

"While I am here, I would also like to look into Bishop Falconi's murder."

Gracey stared at his fingernails. "Have you found out anything?"

"No. I've been to the police and they ruled out robbery as a motive since his watch and wallet were found on his body. But that leaves a million or so motives about which I know nothing. Do you have any idea why anyone might want to kill him?"

Gracey smiled indulgently. "Don't rule out robbery so readily. I'm afraid too many of us place our trust in the obvious. Perhaps there is something more valuable than worldly goods involved."

Lane looked at him curiously. "Such as?"

"There are rumors that the bishop had information about something or someone that was—how shall we say?—unflattering?"

"Do you know what it was?"

"No. Not yet. But Gracey will know eventually. You can be sure of that."

The old journalist laughed his disconcerting laugh and glanced shrewdly in Lane's direction, thinking that perhaps months or even years from now he would be able to determine what had happened by paying attention to bits of information that leaked out of the Vatican. "You must take everything I say with a grain of salt. Much of what I ramble on about is merely the conjecture of a decrepit reporter following his nose for news."

205

"From what I've been told, your news judgment is very, very good."

"Thank you for flattering an old man. But truly, all I can say is that I am as much at a loss about Bishop Falconi's murder as you are."

"Surely, you know more than I do. Is there anything you can tell me?"

He hesitated. There was the intriguing tales whispered at the Vatican, but he had been able to check out only a few of the least consequential. He decided to tell her what everyone knew and accepted as fact.

"There are rumors that the bishop met an American priest the night he was killed. Damian Carter."

"Yes, I know that," she said, recalling what Damian told her about that night. What Damian failed to mention, if he knew, was the possibility Gracey raised that what Falconi gave him may have had something that someone else desperately wanted. Damian was so frightened. What was he given? A chilling thought occurred. Had Damian taken it? If he had . . . No, she told herself, if Damian had murdered the bishop, he would never have wanted this investigation.

"Obviously, this is a very difficult story to get," Gracey said. "I have thought about pursuing it with great diligence, but I have concluded that I should not."

"Why not?"

"The Vatican is my beat, dear girl. The danger of covering any beat is that you wind up not wanting to offend sources. You may get one wonderful story, but sources will cut you dead after that. Good stories go by the wayside because we beat reporters don't want to irritate our sources. So much for the power of the press."

"Which is all the more reason to help me," Lane said. "It will give you the satisfaction of seeing a story told but without your fingerprints on it."

Gracey silently brooded about the bishop's death and felt remiss for not trying to get to the bottom of it. As much as he made light of missed stories, he hated the practice as a necessary evil. The story, whatever it was, should be told. Perhaps this woman was right. He could help her and see the story become a reality. Perhaps the bishop could even be avenged. Another thought suddenly amused him. How would the Vatican respond to a reporter's digging into an area the Church might not want excavated? That could be fascinating to watch.

206

"I will help you," he said firmly.

"Thank you," she said, feeling the easing of a great pressure. "Perhaps you can start by putting me onto who is handling the Vatican investigation. Certainly they aren't entrusting it just to the police."

"No, the Vatican has its own investigation."

"Whom should I talk to there?"

Gracey smiled ironically. "Vatican functionaries are the most discreet people on earth. You will learn little or nothing from them."

Suddenly, something made sense to Gracey that had bothered him lately. "They may have brought in an American to help them. A Father Kelly. I ran into him several days ago."

Lane looked at him curiously. "I met a Father Kelly in New York recently. A large man, who had been in the army and his wife and daughter were killed."

"He is the one," Gracey said. "I knew him years ago in a far different context."

"What do you mean?"

Gracey's face took on a troubled look as he searched his memory. "When Kelly came to Vietnam, he was one of those young Americans whom I called true believers. They implicitly believed in authority and the rightness of their cause. Many of the Catholic officers fell into this category, probably because they had been trained not to question authority. Many of them changed, of course, when the reality of that nasty war came into conflict with their preconceived ideas and moral rectitude.

"Kelly did many things that probably still haunt him. When he first arrived, he participated in the 'pacification' project known as Operation Phoenix. He led a group of specially trained Vietnamese who came to be known for their brutality."

"What was their assignment?" Lane asked.

Rubbing his eyes wearily, Gracey said, "That was very shadowy, but there were stories about frightful carnage that surrounded young Lieutenant Kelly and his group. Eventually, the controversy grew too intense. They were disbanded, and Kelly was given a new assignment."

"To do what?"

"Again, nothing was ever directly said about Lieutenant Kelly's activities. There were exceptionally grim stories that circulated about him. Kelly became known as the Destroyer, and the North Vietnamese placed a hefty bounty on his head. It was taken for granted that he was one of the military who were recruited by the CIA."

207

Lane sat in shock. She knew a lot of awful things had happened in Vietnam, but she had always thought of them as the acts of fearful kids or moral cowards. Kelly had struck her as a decent guy. Suddenly, she became conscious of how much she had thought about him and the business with Franny Cook. Now strangely enough he turned up here. Was there a connection to Hogan?

"There came a time, however, when Kelly came to regard the cause in which he was involved as wrong. You can imagine the stress that caused such a man. I felt quite sorry for him. The true believers tended to take such revelations quite hard."

Gracey sat back. "So that is a little of the past that few people today probably associate with the good father."

Funny, Lane thought. The man Gracey sketched didn't sound like the man who came to her apartment. People change. Maybe it was the sad business about his family. Maybe it was what he did now. She wondered if her own attitude was shaped by the fleeting look of yearning that had momentarily crossed his face when he visited her that night. She wondered if he was aware it had been there. The ache in his eyes made her think of what a tough life priests must lead being deprived of close human companionship, cut off from women, giving up their sexuality. The thought made her sad. It was to unnatural.

For the first time, she thought perhaps she had been too harsh on Pat Hogan. Maybe taking on the life of a priest was to try to come to terms with an impossibility. The life simply seemed too difficult. Maybe the desire to be with someone just popped out in inappropriate ways. God, being single as long as she was, she knew all about that.

Gracey looked at her directly for the first time, seeing how she thoughtfully absorbed what he had just told her. He wondered what would happen if this young woman did indeed get to the bottom of the Falconi business. There were those tantalizing rumors. That gossip combined with the snatches of conversations, the worried look on a certain ecclesiastic's face when the homicide was mentioned. His years of plying his craft told him his hunches were right. Very important people were implicated in the murder.

"Do you think Kelly will help me?" Lane asked.

"You must convince him to do so."

"Where's he staying?" she asked.

"Don't worry. I will get you together with him."

Lane wondered at the direction Gracey was pointing. "Do you think anyone at the Vatican had anything to do with the murder?"

208

"Perhaps. If there are, the Vatican will deal with them."

"How?"

"One will probably never know, but it will be subtle. Vatican retribution manifests itself in almost imperceptible shifts in power, in rewards that are kept just a fraction of an inch from the grasp of those who want them. An Italian archbishop, for example, will never be a cardinal because he was involved in the scandal enmeshing the Vatican Bank. A German bishop was denied the Munich archdiocese because he proved lax on the contraception issue. Another is denied access to the pope after an affair he had came to the pontiff's attention."

"But a murderer?" Lane said.

Gracey shrugged. "All I can say is that I would not like to be anyone connected with it, no matter how peripherally."

"What should I do now?" she asked.

"Start looking into what Falconi was working on right before his death. Therein may lie the key to this business, as least as far as I can tell."

"Do you know anything?"

"A bit," he replied. "Now listen carefully."

13

VIA CHRISTI WAS THE NAME MIGUEL PEREZ GAVE TO HIS FIRST RETREAT house outside Madrid, and now it was the name of all the Milites Christi centers around the world. The organization's international headquarters was on a vast estate atop Rome's Gianicolo Hill. The property was the gift of an Italian financier who, in his will, left the bulk of his estate to Milites Christi rather than to his three sons and daughter. The siblings contested it, but the will, having been executed by one of the most prominent law firms in Rome, proved to be airtight.

Kelly checked his watch. It was twelve forty-five P.M. when the cabdriver dropped him at the compound. The two hours during which the center was open to visitors was just about to start. Kelly joined the tourists who climbed off tour buses and walked down the footpath to the entrance to the estate. Other than deliveries and official vehicles, traffic was banned from the complex. Under the watchful eyes of a black-uniformed guard, the visitors streamed through a narrow gate in the massive wrought-iron fence surrounding the estate.

Via Christi resembled a medieval monastery. A grassy lawn swept up to a cluster of Romanesque buildings of beige stone, orange-tiled roofs, and leaded windows that were at the end of a quarter-mile-long driveway. Ruins of small temples, doubtless dating back to the days of Caesar, were scattered about the grounds, adding to the institution's aura of antiquity and solemnity.

"Beautiful," a woman muttered.

"So serene," added another.

Such hushed comments continued in at least a half dozen languages, and Kelly agreed. He couldn't help comparing the setting to Gethsemane. There was a similar sense of isolation from the world at large, a feeling of peace where one could contemplate God. Physically, at least, Via Christi appeared to be a haven from the harshness of life, the sickness, the anxieties, the day-to-day wear and tear on the spirit. But he wondered just how benign Milites Christi really was.

A bronze plaque was mounted on a large rock by the front door of the main building. Inscribed in Italian, French, German, and English, the plaque stated that the foundations of some of the buildings dated back to the sixth century but had undergone frequent renovations.

Staying with the tourists, Kelly entered one of the buildings, an example of a medieval villa. The huge front door led to a ninth-century courtyard. Once through the courtyard, they entered a chamber where they were to be met on the hour by a tour guide.

Kelly spent the little time remaining studying a life-size portrait of Miguel Perez that almost covered one wall. His body was frail, but even from beneath a monk's coarse robe, a tensile strength radiated from his spare limbs and cadaverous face. His hands were clasped in prayer and his feet were bare. There were what appeared to be round bruises on the backs of his hands and his feet, apparently the marks of his stigmata.

Perez's most arresting feature, however, was his eyes. Large, soft, and doelike, they were the eyes Kelly had seen on swamis in India who proclaimed to be God, certain schizophrenics seemingly brimming over with love, and haunted men in Vietnam who had seen too much death and sought salvation in too many drugs.

Exactly on the hour, four young men wearing robes similar to that of their founder entered. Each called out in a different language to have people gather around him. The one speaking English was a tall, slim, serious-looking youth in his early twenties. Kelly reminded himself that a lot of well-intentioned young men entered Milites Christi, apparently sharing sincere motivations similar to those of peo-

212

ple who became Hare Krishnas or pursued some other form of religious extremism. There would always be youths who sought redemption in the bizarre. Catching himself, he realized that was what people must have said when Christ gathered his disciples.

What he found more disturbing than youths seeking a haven in Milites Christi were reports that priests joined too. Often, they were said to be men suffering mental breakdowns or a severe crisis of faith. They apparently believed that by adopting the punitive austerity for which Milites Christi was known, they could punish themselves for their failures and possibly find salvation.

"My name is José Maria Urizor, and I am from the Basque country," the young man said. "I will be your guide today. I am a seminarian here, and I will try to answer your questions. Unfortunately, there are areas of Via Christi that are off-limits to visitors, but I am sure that you will be understanding."

The practiced speech rolled effortlessly off his tongue. "Now, if you will follow me . . ."

Kelly was part of a group of fifteen people. They walked through a large doorway into a hall lined with paintings, marble statues, and glass cases, all presenting a hagiography of the founder. Some of the paintings depicted Miguel Perez as a boy with blood streaming from his hands, feet, and side. Others portrayed him as a man, a tortured look on his face as he beheld Christ's crucifixion. The statues depicted Perez in various saintlike throes of agony and ecstasy.

Urizor stopped before a glass case containing a priest's vestments for saying Mass. "Milites Christi was founded in 1938 by Miguel Perez. Father Perez was wearing these vestments when he disclosed his vision of the crucifixion."

"Pardon me?" a woman asked.

"Yes?" the youth said.

"I didn't think you were a religious order. Are you?"

"We are not yet recognized as an order. We are much like the Benedictines, Franciscans, or the Dominicans in their early history before the Church officially made them orders. That will come in time, probably very soon."

"How could Miguel Perez say Mass?" an elderly man asked. "He was never ordained."

"Father Perez believed that the holiness and the suffering of the way of Milites Christi warranted his followers acting as an order and he as one of the order's priests."

213

Urizor's gaze swept the group. "Perhaps this sounds arrogant to some of you, but actually it is just the reverse. Father Perez meant this in humility."

Many faces looking back at him still appeared troubled. How difficult it was getting through to them, Urizor thought. They come here for an hour and expect to be touched by the hand of God.

"Pope Pius XII recognized the greatness of Father Perez's mission," he continued. "He is reputed to have remarked that he saw three great signs for hope in the Church: the turning to Mary, the mother of God; the resilience toward communism; and Milites Christi. They all reflect strength in this troubled, godless century."

Urizor moved along, talking as he went. "That our movement came from Spain is not surprising. Spain has always been a land of great spiritual intensity and orthodoxy. The Jesuits were founded on the Iberian Peninsula in the sixteenth century. They were once the shock troops of the Catholic Church and the right arm of the Holy Father. Unfortunately, the Jesuits have become an example of the erosion of a Christian community. Their ministry has deteriorated to the point where it includes a circus clown and a former member of the U.S. Congress."

"Is there a difference?" a burly, white-haired man asked in a Tennessee twang, and everyone laughed.

The young man's face remained solemn as he waited for the mirth to die down. "We expect the pope to turn to us as the new elite of the Church."

"Why should he?" asked a short, balding man who had maintained the same perplexed expression on his face ever since the guide started speaking.

"As the world gets darker and darker, he will *have* to turn to us," Urizor said. "Ours is a powerful organization, a secret society built on a great spiritual strength. It is well-known that many rich and powerful people in the world belong, men who can help the Church in many ways when the need arises."

"Why all this secrecy?"

"For now, we believe it is best that our members don't reveal themselves so that the enemies of the Church will not know where to strike. But we will know who the enemies are. We will be ready."

"What is your day like?" a woman asked.

"We rise at five A.M. and pray for a half hour. Then we take a cold shower to mortify the flesh and pray for another hour. We attend

214

Mass said by one of our priests. During our workday, we maintain periods of silence. In the afternoon, we have a half hour of meditation, and we have spiritual readings in the evening. We pray and retire by ten P.M."

"That's wonderful," a middle-aged woman said. "Imagine young people here living like that when all we hear at home is about our youths becoming drug addicts."

"What about flagellation?" a man asked. "I've heard it is still practiced here. Is that true?"

"We flagellate twice weekly," Urizor replied. "The flesh needs to be purified, and it helps focus our entire attention on God."

As Urizor led the group across the grounds to another building, he pointed out the temple ruins and gave abbreviated histories of them. At length, they entered a large chapel that glowed with the soft, golden light of hundreds of candles. Towering columns lined either side of the center aisle leading to the main altar. The walls and ceilings were covered with frescoes depicting scenes of horned and winged demons crushing sinners in hell and saints writhing in ecstasy as God claimed them. Two smaller altars set in alcoves on either side of the church contained similar visions of hell with the Archangel Michael forcing the demons back into fiery, fouled depths. The face of the archangel was unmistakably that of Miguel Perez.

"We have four chapels on our grounds. This one the public may enter. The three others are private and for our three memberships."

"What are the three?" someone asked.

"The most exclusive membership consists of the deacons. This is a select group of wealthy and powerful laymen who are drawn from around the world. They are not only generous with their time and money, but determine how Milites Christi's spiritual and financial resources should be used. Another membership consists of priests who have left other orders and dioceses to devote themselves to Milites Christi. The third is the acolytes. They are men who are friends of Milites Christi and are helpful in many ways."

"Are they all Catholics?" a man asked.

"No. Many deacons and the acolytes are non-Catholics who are disenchanted with the direction of all Christian religions and see Milites Christi as the hope of the future."

"What about women?" asked a woman in her twenties who was standing with her husband.

215

"Women, of course, are not allowed to join, and this is the only chapel women may enter."

"Why?" the woman asked indignantly.

"There are many reasons given in the Bible for Christ choosing men as apostles," Urizor replied. "Let us just say that the woman is temptress. Only a fool brings the temptress into the temple."

"I hope you think of your mama when you say that, boy," a thickset man with gray hair called out. Turning to his wife, he said, "Mary, let's get out of here and wait on the bus."

They left, followed by the young couple. The rest of the gathering struck Kelly as looking uncomfortable, but the guide maintained a stoic demeanor. So much for Milites Christi joining the twentieth century, Kelly thought.

Urizor led them outside and pointed out the residences, the infirmary, and the other chapels, all of which were off-limits.

"What is Milites Christi's goal?" Kelly asked.

"The mission of our society is to reach out to the ruling and powerful classes and instill in them Christian principles," Urizor said. "Father Perez envisioned that one day Milites Christi will be an elite corps that will protect the Church's traditional philosophy and practices." He turned to the gathering. "We will now go to the administration building."

As they began walking, Kelly was startled to see a tall, dark figure wearing a cassock duck into a chapel about fifty yards away. He suspected the priest was the same one by the scaffold at the Basilica. Again, he felt that nagging sensation that he knew the man from somewhere else.

Kelly grabbed Urizor's arm and pointed to the chapel. "Who was that?"

"Pardon me?"

"The priest who just went into that chapel. Who is he?"

Urizor flushed. "I . . . uh . . . I . . . am not certain."

Kelly stared at the youth. He must have seen him. He was looking in that direction when Kelly was. Hurriedly, Urizor turned away and beckoned the others to follow him as he continued up the path.

Slipping behind the crowd, Kelly was grateful that Urizor was in the front of the group and had his back to him. He trotted over to the chapel. Just as he was about to open the door, a hand fell on his shoulder and another grabbed his bicep. He turned and found himself firmly in the grip of a husky, dark-haired youth wearing a robe. An

216

older, stocky man, who was similarly attired, stood with him, looking expectantly at Kelly.

"You must be lost, Father," the older one said coldly. "Unfortunately, the chapel is only for our members."

"Right," Kelly said, smiling while he pried the young man's hand off his arm, all the while noticing the professional way the older one took his measure. He thought there must be a level of membership that Urizor forgot to mention. The Holy Bouncers.

Urizor and his group of visitors stood about seventy-five yards off, looking at the three of them. Even from this distance, Kelly knew they were wondering what the hell had ever gotten into him. Angry that he hadn't had a chance to see the priest closer up, he headed off to rejoin his little herd of tourists. Once Kelly caught up to them, Urizor gave him a curious, almost fearful, look and continued toward the administration building without saying anything else.

Unlike the calmness of the other areas the group had visited, the administration center pulsated with activity. Men clad in robes rushed in and out of offices, nodding politely to the visitors. Phones rang. The muffled clicks of word processors and Xerox machines filtered into the halls. The place reminded Kelly of the fund-raising boiler rooms that some TV evangelists ran. He was sure that a lot of hard-sell pitches for donations went out to the rich men the organization wanted to reach.

"We now number more than ten thousand members," the guide said. "But because of the power of our members, we exert more influence in many countries than mere numbers suggest. We will become the voice of the Church. Now we are finished with today's tour. Thank you very much for allowing me to tell you something about our community."

Urizor looked warily at Kelly and moved off to the side. "If you have any further questions," he called out, "I will be available for a little while."

Kelly waited until several others in the group spoke with the youth. When he approached, he couldn't help noticing that Urizor grew obviously nervous. "Who was that priest who entered the chapel I was barred from?" he repeated.

Urizor's composure faltered. "I . . . I don't know who you mean."

Kelly locked his eyes on the youth's. "Please, this may be very, very important. Not just to me, but to the Church. If you don't think you can talk here, call me at the Hotel Navarro. My name is Kelly."

217

The seminarian's eyes opened in alarm and he actually backed up. "Please excuse me," he muttered, and hurried away.

Watching his retreat, Kelly wondered what was wrong. Why was the kid so jumpy?

The tourists had dispersed. Some walked out to the temple ruins. Others returned to the chapel. Still others simply strolled across the grounds, while the rest headed back to their buses.

Kelly stood in the driveway and gazed toward the chapel he had been prevented from entering, hoping to see the big priest emerge. Realizing the futility of that, he walked back to the entrance, figuring he could get a cab or even take one of the tour buses back to the hotel. He had to be content with having learned a little. For one, Milites Christi was more sophisticated than he had thought. Perhaps of much greater importance, he now knew the strange priest from the Basilica was somehow connected to the movement and apparently lived here.

A horn honked and Kelly got off to the side of the driveway as a limousine slowly rolled past. The two passengers in the backseat, a priest and a layman, were locked in conversation. Neither looked up.

Kelly was surprised. He recognized the layman. Charles Edwards. He assumed the tycoon was in Rome for the investiture. Kelly took Edwards's presence as almost a confirmation of the rumors that the American was a member of Milites Christi. The other was one of the Italian clerics who were at the Robbinses' party in New York.

❁

Two hours later, a valet who introduced himself as Umberto led Kelly into a large, tastefully furnished parlor. The crackling logs in the fireplace gave off not only a warmth on this cool day but the pleasant scent of cedar. The apartment did not appear as large as Clarizio's, but it was still quite grand, having an aura of elegance that was probably a hallmark of all the living quarters at the Vatican.

"His Excellency will be with you momentarily," the valet said. "Is there anything I can get you?"

"No, *grazie*," Kelly answered.

The valet excused himself and disappeared to other duties. Kelly paced about the room, looking at the large number of photographs on the walls. A great many were of Creedy with various members of the hierarchy, most of whom Kelly didn't recognize. Some he did, such as the American archbishops Murray and Dinsmore as well as several

218

powerful Italians, including Cardinal Tici, who was responsible for the Office of Religious Works, as the Vatican Bank was known, and Cardinal Strickland, who was secretary of state. There were also several shots of Creedy with Bishop Falconi.

"Lookin' at my rogues' gallery, Kevin?"

Creedy still bellowed as if he were on a roundup. The Texas accent hadn't been diluted by his years abroad either. The bishop quickly crossed the room, his hand outstretched. The hirsute priest of the late 1960s who had been lean as a whippet had evolved into a clean-shaven, ruddy-complexioned, handsome member of the hierarchy. The once jet-black hair had silvered. The red cincture around his waist emphasized a substantial girth.

"As someone who knows me from the old days before all this," the bishop said, waving a cigar around the room, "I don't think it's fitting that you kiss my ring. In fact, I'd find it damned embarrassing."

Creedy gave Kelly a playful punch on the shoulder. "Good to see you, Kevin. Good to see you. You know, I hardly ever see anyone from Gethsemane anymore. Once in a while somebody from the old place comes through town, but I'm so damn busy most of the time I don't get any chance to visit with them. When I go home, it's the same damn thing."

He shook his head as if recalling too many lost opportunities for good times. "I've got to start making time. Life's getting too short not to see the people who matter. Can't be just work, work, work. Isn't that right?"

Without waiting for a reply, the bishop took Kelly's elbow and steered him across the room. "These'll stir up the old memory."

A large portion of the wall contained photos of Gethsemane. The pictures were mostly of Creedy with students or with certain faculty members, including several of him standing next to Frank Maguire, much the way he had in the photos Kelly saw of him with cardinals and archbishops. Kelly wondered if he was more highly regarded by those Vatican luminaries than he was by the Gethsemane rector. Probably. After all, he was a hot-shot bishop now.

"Someday I'd like to go back to Gethsemane and teach again, Kevin. That's truly a worthwhile endeavor. Best years of my life were spent there. People look and see a bishop's robes and a big job at the Vatican and think this is glamorous and important and exciting, but hell, what's really worthwhile is teaching those seminarians."

Kelly smiled, thinking about what Maguire had said about Creedy's bitching about the teaching job's slowing down his career. It was a shame the pope wasn't on hand to grant Creedy's wish immediately.

Creedy blew a smoke ring and tapped a photo of himself with a droopy mustache. "My God, the changes we go through. When I look at those pictures at Gethsemane, I wonder how they let me walk around there looking like some damn gunslinger."

The bishop moved a few feet farther along and tapped another picture. "Look, look at this one."

The photo was of a Creedy about thirty years old with shoulder-length hair and a full beard; he was scowling into the camera. Kelly was amazed at how different the man looked.

"That was my incarnation the year I was on a fellowship at the University of Pennsylvania. Hell, I looked like Ringo Starr or some other rock 'n' roll nitwit."

Creedy laughed and Kelly joined him, finding the former teacher easier to take than he had expected. He'd been unaware of Creedy's self-deprecating sense of humor. Yet, he couldn't shake the feeling that there was a staginess about the way the bishop presented himself, which was similar to the way he had found him at Gethsemane. He was like an actor who never realized the play was over. Perhaps he had just changed his role to fit his new stage over here. Or maybe every day launched a new play.

What surprised him even more was the man's effusive friendliness. Kelly had had little to do with Creedy at the seminary, never even having had a class with him, yet the bishop acted as if there were a special bond between them, as if Creedy really wanted him to like him. He compared Creedy's style with that of Pat Hogan and found a lot of similarities. They both had in their makeup more than a bit of the politician who was always working the crowd. Kelly hated to think that Creedy was what Pat Hogan was evolving into.

"Sit down, Kevin," the bishop said, motioning him toward a chair near the fireplace and settling himself into another next to it.

"Now, Kevin," he said, his expression solicitous, "I assume you're here because of that business Archbishop Clarizio has you working on about Pat Hogan."

"Right."

Creedy sat back in his chair and thoughtfully rolled his cigar in his mouth with his right thumb and index finger as though lost in thought. He looked up suddenly and called out, "Umberto."

220

"If we're going to talk about this kind of thing, I think we should have a drink."

The valet entered the room. "Yes, Your Excellency?"

"A scotch and a touch of soda, Umberto. What'll you have, Kevin? Anything you want, we get it over here."

"Wild Turkey on the rocks."

"I guess you've already talked to Frank Maguire."

"Yes, he's the one who suggested I talk with you."

"A good man, Maguire. Always liked him." He glanced at Kelly out of the corner of his eye. "He mention me and the Trinity on that trip to Washington?"

"He did," Kelly replied, wondering what the hell had happened. He had gone through clips on the antiwar protest from both the *Washington Post* and the *New York Times* several times, the first time being right after Clarizio gave him the date and then after Maguire refreshed his memory about sending the Trinity to the demonstration. Both exercises drew a blank. There was a lot of coverage of the demonstration, but no mention of the Trinity, Creedy, or Gethsemane.

"You might remember the students and faculty voting for me to go down to Washington. I was mighty pleased to be singled out that way, very flattered that the student body thought that highly of me. Hell, anytime a group like that honors you, you know you must be doing something right."

"Maguire was concerned about a marked change in their behavior when the Trinity came back and thought you might have an idea why."

Umberto materialized, handed them their drinks, and left. The bishop took a sip and leaned forward confidentially, his smile slipping. The look on his face became that of a man who had just made a resolution to unburden himself. "Kevin, I went down with them to the demonstration, but I did something maybe I shouldn't have done. . . ." He paused and took a thoughtful puff on his cigar. "I ran into some friends and went off with them, thinking the Trinity would be fine without me.

"You gotta understand, Kevin. I didn't think anything of it. Hell, they didn't need a baby-sitter, and I figured they'd resent my tagging along like some damned chaperon."

He looked over at Kelly, his eyes brightening. "The demonstration was something to see. It seemed as if everybody but Nixon and Kissinger

221

were with us. The police even gave us the peace sign when the buses were rolling into town. There were a million or so people there, and the demonstration was as blissed out as a cow right after the bull leaves. There were no signs it would get out of hand and turn violent, and it didn't. It was like a big state fair or a picnic. People playing guitars, running after Frisbees and girls, and everybody having a real good time.

"Oh, there were a lot of drugs there too. But you remember we're talking early seventies, Kev. Hell, pot was equated with peace, and LSD was a shortcut to a religious experience. I knew people who thought their mission in life was to put LSD in the nation's reservoirs so the whole country could see God on a given day. Nobody then thought about these awful drug cartels or cocaine crazies."

Creedy glanced over at Kelly but immediately hid behind a wreath of smoke. "I did try to keep half an eye on the Trinity and ran across them a couple of times during the day. They seemed perfectly fine, except . . ."

Sitting back, Creedy rolled his cigar again, staring at the fireplace. He seemed unwilling to go on and took a long pull on his drink.

"What's wrong?" Kelly asked.

"Maybe I shouldn't tell you this, or maybe I should have told Frank Maguire a long time ago. I don't know. All I do know is that it's been a burn under my saddle ever since the business of Pat's possibly being made a bishop cropped up."

Kelly found himself irritated by Creedy's country-shucking coyness. "Just say what's on your mind, Bishop."

Giving him a hurt look, Creedy stretched his legs out and crossed them at the ankles while he puffed on the cigar again. "I want to help you all I can, but I don't know whether this is of any help at all. You be the judge."

Creedy drained his drink and set it down on the table between himself and Kelly. "Late that night, I ran across the Trinity again. They were drunk or stoned or something, which a lot of people were. They also had a girl with them."

He shot Kelly an anxious look. "Hell, I didn't think too much about it. They were different times, Kevin. Wide-open times. Everybody was experimenting, including a lot of priests and nuns, and don't let anybody tell you different.

"Anyway, the four of them were hanging all over each other, so you knew they already were pretty friendly." Creedy sighed. "The boys

222

were going to be ordained soon, and I guess I figured they were off on a last fling. I must have figured, 'Who am I to tell them what to do?'"

The bishop gazed into the fire. "But I was wrong. If I wasn't going to tell them, who else would?"

Kelly found himself once again thinking of Franny Cook and Connie Robbins. Was it possible that Hogan's actions with them weren't out of character? That he had a sexual history that went back a long way? That the Trinity did?

"Kevin, you knew them. Probably nothing happened between them and the girl. I kind of felt remiss about not mentioning it to Maguire. At the time, I thought it might get them in a bit of trouble they didn't need. Especially with their ordinations on the horizon."

The bishop shrugged. "Maybe something did happen."

With the impatience of a busy man, Creedy stood abruptly. Kelly rose too. The interview was over. The bishop put his hand on the priest's shoulder as he led him from the room and down the long corridor to the front door.

"I liked those boys a lot. They had a hell of a lot going for them, and I hated seeing any of them take a tumble. But there's no way of predicting how any of us in this world will turn out, is there?"

At the door, they shook hands. "I'm sorry I'm not much help, Kevin, but don't hesitate to pick up the phone if you need to bounce something off me. I'm always here for anyone from Gethsemane."

14

KELLY DIDN'T HAVE MUCH TO TRADE WHEN HE MADE A DINNER DATE with Gracey for this evening, but he had asked him a favor over the phone anyway. Gracey suggested a restaurant off Piazza Navona, which was a stone's throw from the Hotel Navarro. Shortly before nine, Kelly walked along the narrow cobblestone lane that led from the hotel to the Piazza. This time of evening the plaza was crowded with people going to dinner as well as jugglers, mimes, musicians, acrobats, and poor gypsy children who were dancing, selling flowers, and begging.

Kelly saw the restaurant immediately. Large and gaily lighted, it was part of a row of restaurants and cafés. When he entered, the maître d' was busy on the other side of the noisy, smoky dining room. Searching through faces, he quickly spotted Gracey sitting at a table in the rear. As always, the journalist had his back to the rear wall so he had a clear view of who came and went.

"Welcome, Father, welcome," Gracey said, half getting to his feet and shaking hands when Kelly reached the table.

"Thanks for coming, Gracey."

"I've asked someone else to join us. I hope you don't mind?"

"No."

Momentarily Kelly wondered what the old fox was up to, but didn't bother asking who it was. He was more curious to find out whether Gracey was able to shed light on a matter that bothered him probably a lot than it should.

"Did you have any luck?" he asked.

Gracey exasperatedly jammed the fingers of his right hand through his bushy hair. "Most curious after all these years. Most curious. When I mentioned Monsignor Witten's name, I was met with the usual wall of official silence. So, of course, I had to go to my unofficial sources."

The journalist held up his nearly empty drink and motioned the waiter for a refill. "Your Monsignor Witten made a large impact in the time he was here. A most brilliant man apparently. There was grand talk of his becoming Vatican secretary of state one day . . . perhaps even more. But then his behavior seems to have become erratic. Long periods on his knees in the chapel weeping. That sort of thing. He also took to flagellating. The use of the whip is not uncommon among certain clergy, particularly Spanish, but for an American, it was very peculiar. He also became very distant. Very cold. People around him became somewhat frightened by his behavior. Obviously, he was suffering a breakdown."

The journalist gave a sardonic smile. "Here is where Monsignor Witten's story becomes baffling. He was ordered to take a holiday. He went to Lake Como and never came back. There are dark stories about suicide."

"Yes, I've heard that."

"But one of my informants claims to have seen Witten since this alleged suicide."

Kelly looked at him sharply. "Was he certain?"

"The man is not given to dissembling, but he does acknowledge the remote possibility that he was wrong."

"Where did he think he saw him?"

"In Spain, shortly after his disappearance. My friend was sitting in a café when he saw Witten across the room. He called out to him, but as soon as the monsignor saw him, he left. My man could not catch up to him and did not see him again."

Kelly exhaled slowly. Witten alive? How the hell could he track him down? Go to a café in Spain where he might have been fifteen years ago?

"Thanks, Gracey. If you hear any more about him, I'd like to

226

know. Now I've got another favor to ask, but unfortunately I have little to trade."

The journalist's eyes became calculating. "What do you want to know about?"

"Falconi's murder."

Gracey remained unperturbed. "I thought as much. Is Clarizio luring you into one of his webs of intrigue?"

"Why do you say that?"

"Vatican sources... Isn't that a wonderful term? It sounds so discreet, yet so authoritative. Not like 'Washington' or 'Moscow' sources, which always register a certain distrust in readers. Anyway, Vatican sources say the pope placed Clarizio in charge of investigating the bishop's murder. I assume that he is bent on utilizing your somewhat, ah, rusty talents?"

"It's that obvious?"

"Old Gracey is not just an observer but a synthesizer too, which is what good journalists are. Why else would Dagger Tom have called you to Rome? To be frank, what else can you offer them except the skills you learned long ago?"

Of course, it was logical, Kelly thought ruefully. Transparent. He wondered if he was fooling anybody who might be observing him. Suddenly, he felt naked and ashamed. Everyone took it for granted that he hadn't changed, that he'd been deluding himself for years. This business of a new life was a joke. His karma held him in a headlock.

"What's wrong?" Gracey asked, taking in the painful look on Kelly's face.

"Nothing," the American replied.

Through sheer willpower, he pulled back from the dark thoughts and forced himself to be rational. Falconi's death and the Basilica incident came to mind. Clarizio turned to him because he had an emergency, a crisis. It was logical that he was chosen for this kind of business. Whom should the archbishop go to? A scripture expert?

He realized Gracey was still looking at him oddly. "Sorry, I just thought of something unpleasant. The archbishop and I were almost killed in the Basilica. A big piece of marble somehow fell across the seats where we were sitting."

"When did this happen?"

"Only a few hours after you dropped me at my hotel."

"What a terrible accident."

227

"If it was."

Gracey's eyes almost met Kelly's. "What do you mean?"

"Clarizio thinks it might have something to do with Falconi's death."

"What do you think?"

"That he's probably right. One thing I do know was that I saw a priest where he shouldn't have been right before it happened."

"Do you know him?" Grace asked, his eyes glittering with excitement.

"No, but he may be part of Milites Christi."

The journalist's curiosity mounted. For years he was tantalized by stories about Milites Christi, but he was never able to get them printed for lack of proof. Perhaps the time had come to make use of the material.

"What makes you think he may have had something to do with the 'accident'?"

"The Swiss guards who examined the scene shortly after it happened said there were signs that somebody tampered with the rigging holding the marble onto the scaffolding. The priest was getting off the scaffold when I saw him."

"What ties him to Milites Christi?"

"I'm pretty sure I saw him at Via Christi when I was out there today."

"Did Clarizio ask you to go?"

Subtly, Kelly encouraged Gracey's interrogation, doling out enough information to whet the correspondent's appetite. Before deciding to horse-trade with Gracey, he carefully weighed the benefits for himself. Reporters had a lot of avenues to pursue that wouldn't be open to him. Besides, a story at some point might be useful to scare whoever was behind whatever the hell was going on. He kept what Martin said about a priest attacking Carter to himself.

"Yes, he wants me to check them out."

"What was your impression?"

"Rich and powerful? Definitely. A potential internal political problem for the Church because of the extreme conservatism? Of course. But murder? I just don't know. What do you think? Is Milites Christi crazy enough to do that?"

"Why condemn the whole society?"

Kelly looked at him curiously. "What do you mean?"

228

Gracey's lips curled in exasperation. "What makes you think Milites Christi is any more a monolith than the church Herself?"

"What are you driving at, Gracey?"

"There are different strains of voices in Milites Christi, representing different factions. Of course, they are all very conservative, but they are not harmonious. And some are not as ethically restrained as others."

Kelly listened intently, anxious for any information about the secret society. Even when he checked with the office of the Vatican secretary of state, which was supposed to keep tabs on groups such as Milites Christi, he learned little.

"How do you know?" he persisted.

Gracey's wheezy laugh was disconcerting. "Journalists learn a great many things that never reach the public. True stories that, for one reason or another, publishers are afraid to print, broadcasters are afraid to air. Sometimes they fear libel. Sometimes they fear offending someone of great importance. Sometimes journalists simply censor themselves. Sometimes you are convinced of the veracity of what you hear but simply can't get the documentation to prove it. Whatever, we in the business trade such stories among ourselves."

"What are some of these stories about Milites Christi?"

Gracey sat back and examined his fingernails. "Just how important is this to you?"

"Very."

"There should be some reciprocity in our arrangement," Gracey said slowly as he stared at his nails.

Kelly held open his hands. "Sorry, Gracey. I told you I don't have much to trade, and I just gave you all of it."

"Oh, but you do have something else of value."

"What?"

"Your investigation of Patrick Hogan. When the investigation is over, of course. But it would make a wonderful story either way it goes. 'The Making of a Bishop' or 'The Unmaking of a Bishop.'"

Kelly mulled over the proposal. Once he presented the findings of his investigation to Clarizio, the Vatican grapevine would inevitably pick it up. When that happened, Gracey would learn most of the story from his sources anyway. True, if the story leaked, Clarizio would get ticked off, and Kelly knew it would be traced back to him. But by then it would be old news.

"Okay."

"Good, Father Kelly. Very good. Our dinner guest will be able to assist you with the Falconi business as well. Providing you be of some help to her, of course."

"Of course," Kelly echoed sarcastically.

"She's an American journalist. A TV reporter from New York who came over for the investiture and wants to dig into the murder. You met her recently."

Kelly tried not to show any emotion. "Lane Woods?"

"Yes. As you understand, I can't do the story myself. I would lose too many of my sources if I probed a matter that may result in great embarrassment for the Church."

Lane Woods, Kelly thought, was more enterprising than he had realized. Gracey had a reputation for never working on a story for someone else. She must have been persuasive as hell or Gracey had his own ulterior motives.

"So what can you tell me now about Milites Christi?" Kelly asked.

Gracey carefully glanced around the dining room and lowered his voice. "There are those within the organization who have lost sight of right and wrong as they pursue their particular brand of godliness."

"What do you mean?"

"Some members, important members, for instance, were part of the Vatican Bank scandal back in the early 1980s. The Church investigated their roles and took appropriate steps with regard to those over whom it had any control."

"What else?"

"A group of them are believed to be involved in the assassination of Archbishop Romero in El Salvador. In Nicaragua, Guatemala, and El Salvador, the same group is said to be behind the thugs who destroyed medical clinics and social action programs run by religious orders and harassed and intimidated priests and nuns."

"Good God," Kelly said. "You mean Milites Christi is a front for death squads?"

"No, not Milites Christi. My informants say there is a tiny anonymous faction within the organization undertaking such activities. They are extraordinarily rich and powerful and apparently quite mad. They can easily hire others to do their dirty work, and no evidence links them to the deeds."

Kelly felt chilled. "Who are they?"

230

"That I don't know. Apparently few people do." Gracey laughed ruefully. "They are a secret society within a secret society."

"Surely, you've got something on them."

Gracey lowered his voice again. "Only that they call themselves the Apostles."

Kelly wondered if Clarizio knew of the group's existence. He wouldn't be surprised if that was one more thing the archbishop held back. "Why doesn't someone get the word to the rest of the membership about what some of the brethren are doing?" Kelly asked.

"Unfortunately, attempts at that meet with no success," Gracey replied. "The leadership of Milites Christi is extremely defensive. They are aware that this pope and certain others in the hierarchy are highly suspicious of them. They tend to view any such criticism as an assault on the organization itself."

Suddenly, Gracey half rose to his feet again and looked toward the door. "Father Kelly. Our guest has arrived."

Kelly half turned in his chair. All thoughts of murder momentarily evaporated as he spotted Lane Woods threading her way through the crowded tables. He couldn't help thinking how absolutely lovely she was. He flushed and stood, suddenly feeling very awkward.

From the corner of his eyes, Gracey caught the rapt look that passed quickly across Kelly's face. Well, well, well, he said to himself. He squirreled away the emotional flash in his mental file on Kelly. One could never tell what might come in handy.

Janet Simpson's amber eyes were alert and wary. Defiantly, she held one of her high heels by her ear, ready to strike. The stocking on her left leg was smooth to the knee but the top doubled down to her calf. A leather thong that was tied to her wrist dangled to the floor. Otherwise, she was naked.

"Just stay the 'ell back, mister, or I'll scream so loud it'll wake the bloody dead!"

Her shrill cockney accent grated on Charles Edwards's ears, but his eyes feasted on her young, supple flesh. Initially, he feared she might be too thin, but without clothing, her lithesomeness made her appear virginal: the upturned breasts, the curve of her stomach, the slight swell of her unblemished thighs and buttocks. He just wished she were more passive, but that was just a matter of time.

231

Edwards was in Rome for the cardinals' investiture and to see how Monsignor Ruggieri was progressing with the plans for the papacy on which they were working. There was also some mining and other business to which he could tend. But he saw his true mission whenever and wherever he traveled as placing young women such as this girl on the path to salvation.

"There is no need for alarm," he said soothingly. "This is just a game, a fantasy. Forgive me. I should have told you. I will pay you more."

The scowl on Janet's heart-shaped face became less intense, and the look in her bright eyes grew more calculating. She twisted a lock of her long, wavy auburn hair, the way she always did when she was indecisive. " 'Ow much?"

"Shall we say another hundred dollars."

She looked at him suspiciously, wondering if she could trust him. He was frail and old. What the hell could the scrawny bastard do to her? Besides, he was obviously loaded. The hotel was one of Rome's most expensive. His charcoal silk suit, white silk shirt, and shoes were all custom-made.

Damn, it was tempting. She was stranded. The Italian producer of what was supposed to be a high-class porno flick had flown her here from London and then abandoned her when his financial backing went bust. He wouldn't answer her calls, let alone give her the return airfare. Since yesterday, she had counted on pickups in hotel lobbies to amass the money to get back to London.

Hell, weird whims weren't that unusual. From the telltale glitter in his eyes, she knew she'd be able to get a better price out of him.

"You swear you won't hurt me?"

"Of course."

Damn it, Janet, she thought, you get yourself into some strangies. She tried to forget how frightened she'd become when he bound the leather thong around her wrist and started tying her hand to the bed post. She'd freaked. Jack the Ripper's come back to life and he's in Rome, she'd thought. But another hundred. That would make three hundred for this one job. She could go home.

"Two hundred extra. Right now!"

Edwards paused and smiled. Taking his wallet from his breast pocket, he removed four more fifty-dollar bills and handed them to her. "You drive a hard bargain."

Janet's emotions seesawed as she stuffed the money in her hand-

232

bag. She was pleased to have just stumbled on an extra two hundred dollars, but she never liked the freaky stuff. But what could he do?

"Untie me the minute I tell you to. Right?"

"Of course. I'm sorry to have upset you."

Gingerly, Janet climbed back on the bed, stretched out on her stomach, and held her breath. Edwards gently took her right hand and tied it to the bedpost. Securing another thong around her left wrist, he tied that to a bedpost as well and patted her shiny hair. She looked up at him, wondering at the weird ways some people got their jollies. But if they pay, they pay. Who was she to moralize?

Grabbing her right ankle, he tied another thong around it and bound her leg to the bottom of the bed. He did the same with her left leg.

"Hey, not so rough," Janet cried out.

Suddenly, she felt intensely vulnerable. Wriggling, she could barely move as he shoved something soft under her thighs and belly.

"Kneel up a bit. I want to put a pillow beneath you."

She arched her body as high as she could, but there was barely enough room for the pillow. She settled back, realizing how much higher her bottom was now than the rest of her. Her stomach fluttered.

"Hey, I don't do Greek."

When he didn't answer, she thought, damn! She did that once and was sore for a week. "I've had enough of this, pops. Let me go. Fun's over."

Pulling at the cords, she barely moved. The more she tugged, the deeper the leather bit into her wrists and ankles. "Come on!" she yelled. "Let me up, for Christ's sake."

Ignoring her pleading, Edwards went into the bathroom and returned with a washcloth. Pausing, he surveyed his handiwork. He breathed heavily. As the naked girl struggled, her smooth body stretched taught, her bottom rose a fraction of an inch higher. What was she? Eighteen? Nineteen? Still young enough to be saved.

As Janet writhed, sweat beaded her brow. She was panting. Her face was crimson from the exertion. Her wrists and ankles ached as the bindings cut deeper and deeper. She started to panic. God, he could do anything to her. Anything!

Her desperation excited him, but the thought of what she would soon be like aroused him even more. Reaching out, he ran his fingers up her leg, along the smoothness of her round buttocks, and down the long crevice between them. Her hips inadvertently twitched. Her

233

skin was silky and warm. His hand stroked her back and side, touching the hollow beneath her arm and slipping down to her breast. Digging under her, he felt her nipple and squeezed.

"Hey," she yelped more uncertainly as fear crowded in again. "Come on, you bastard. Untie me."

Edwards shoved the washcloth in her mouth. "You have a great deal to atone for, young woman. A great deal."

Taking a suitcase, he returned to the bathroom. He removed all his clothes and hung them on a hanger on the back of the door. Kneeling, he opened the suitcase on the floor. He extracted a coarse brown robe with a cowl. Standing, he lowered it over his head.

His movements were slow, deliberate, as he thought about cleansing the spirit of this woman. How fortunate she was to have met him. He was going to set her on the road to salvation. He would help her repent. She would be cleansed in the eyes of God.

He buckled a large leather belt around his waist. Removing a large cross on a chain from the suitcase, he hung it around his neck. Finally, he knelt by the bag and took out a whip with five short lashes and made the sign of the cross over it. Closing his eyes, he prayed to be strong, that he would not succumb to temptation.

When Janet saw Edward emerge from the bathroom, her heart jumped wildly. She screamed a silent, piercing shriek that went unheard as he walked toward her. His pace was slow, measured. The whip was held in front of him in two outstretched hands.

In horror, she craned her neck so she could see him as he paused by the side of the bed. His eyes gleaming, he raised the whip in his right hand and lashed across her buttocks.

"Whore!" he yelled.

Again, her shriek went unheard as pink welts spread across her thighs and buttocks. In anticipation of the next blow, she wrenched and pulled at her bindings, her body quivering. Again, the tendrils slashed her. Three. Four. Five. Tears flowed down her cheeks and she thrust and squirmed to avoid the lash. Eight. Nine. Finally, she lost count. The agony was excruciating.

Feverishly, Edwards stared at her bruised, swollen lips and her tear-filled eyes. Now, her body merely twitched as he continued flailing her. Gasping, he finally lowered the whip, resting it on her buttocks. He pried the cloth from her mouth. With the sleeve of his robe, he wiped the perspiration from her brow.

234

"Beg for forgiveness," he ordered.

"I'm sorry," she whimpered. "I'm so sorry. I'm so sorry."

"This has been most enjoyable," Gracey said. "Unfortunately, I have another appointment."

The journalist picked up the check, ignoring both Kelly's and Lane Woods's attempts to pay. "My treat for your being such delightful company," he said as he left.

Before Gracey was halfway across the room, Lane signaled the waiter for more coffee and turned back to Kelly. "So what about this priest you saw at Milites Christi?"

Despite his apprehension about Lane Woods's appearance, Kelly thought the dinner enjoyable. But he grew tense as she asked more and more questions. He found himself resenting that he couldn't simply act with her like any man with a woman he believed attractive. Without realizing it, he became prickly.

"You want to know everything right now, so I can throw a Pulitzer in your lap?"

"Are we being blunt again, Father Kelly?"

He caught himself and his reply was more subdued. "No, just a bit of a pain in the ass, I guess."

"So, are you willing to help me get the Falconi story?"

Kelly didn't reply immediately. As with Gracey, he didn't want to appear anxious.

"If you help me," he finally said.

"Fair enough. Look, I know there may be things you won't be able to tell me, but what I need most of all is the truth. If I ask you about some development and you can't discuss it, just say so. Otherwise, simply tell me what you can."

"Okay, okay," Kelly said, knowing he had to be more careful about what he said to her.

Once again, he had found her easy to be with. Too easy. He had talked a lot about his past and current lives, more than he had ever intended. He had even almost blurted out that Falconi's killer might be a priest, and he hadn't meant to bring that up right away. What Kelly found more worrisome was how damned appealing he found her. Chagrined, he thought of Pat Hogan and the young girl from the

TV station. Only days ago, he wondered how the hell Hogan could jeopardize his career like that. Now, here he was trying to drag out any extra minute he could to be with this woman. So much for getting lost in his work. Sublimation was always tougher than it sounded, but it wasn't this rough before.

"There's no need to look so pained," she said, misinterpreting his mood. "You make out better than me on this deal. I'll share whatever I get with you, no holds barred. You aren't exactly the competition."

"I said okay!"

She wondered why he was so edgy. After first talking like a human being, he now sat there monitoring everything he said as if the pope were standing over his shoulder. Increasingly, she found herself angry. He *did* stand to gain more than she. Maybe he didn't trust her. As a show of good faith, she decided to cut him in on an interview she was trying to line up for later this evening. Picking up her purse, she slid her chair back.

"I'll be back in a minute. I've been trying to make an appointment to see someone Damian mentioned. She said she would be in about now."

Kelly watched as she wove between the tables and thought again how gracefully she moved. The long legs, the wide, firm hips. Get a grip on yourself, he ordered.

Suddenly, he became conscious of a man who occasionally glanced over at the table. He was by himself and trying to pretend he had no more interest in the priest and the reporter than anyone else in the place, but he wasn't doing a terrific job of it. Kelly realized the guy had been watching them all evening. He was of medium height, lean, and had sallow, bland good looks. The kind of face that easily blended into a crowd. One of Martin's people? Maybe. It was like Martin to have him tailed if he thought Kelly would stumble onto something useful. If not, who was he? What was he after? And whom was he after? Himself or Lane?

Kelly kept his gaze trained in the direction in which Lane had disappeared. He avoided taking note of the tail again. She returned a few minutes later, smiling as she sat down.

"The woman's name is Carla Sarfina. Damian wants me to check in with her. Damian says she called a friend of his with something about the Falconi business. The friend wasn't able to get back to her. I'm going over there now. It's okay if you want to come along."

236

Kelly wondered if she was the woman Martin had mentioned. Now, he wished he had pumped Martin for more information about her other than the fact that she spent a night with Carter. "Thanks, but why take me?"

"To show I'm on the up-and-up," she said with exasperation. "One of us should be."

Kelly's face reddened. "Two of us can be blunt."

"Glad you got the message."

"Do you know anything about her?"

"She's a photographer who's linked to a lot of extreme left-wing causes. From the way he talks about her, Damian regards her very highly."

"He would," Kelly said.

"Do I detect a note of disapproval?"

"The whole business of political priests makes me uneasy."

"Why?" Lane asked.

"In 'Nam, I knew of priests who worked hand in glove with the Agency, including Diem's brother, Bishop Thuc, who led an army. Other priests worked clandestinely with the Viet Cong."

He shrugged. "What good did it do? In Latin America, you've got priests backing populist movements while others throw their weight behind the oligarchies and military dictatorships those movements oppose. It seems to me they're canceling each other out."

"What would you do?"

"Let priests lead by example and the world will be better off for it."

"You're an idealist."

"So I've been told. Now, let's see what Damian's radical princess knows."

They left the restaurant and walked across the plaza and back to the Navarro to get a cab. Kelly glanced around unobtrusively. The man from the restaurant was strolling leisurely behind them. Kelly considered confronting him, but figured that wouldn't be productive right now. The guy wouldn't tell him anything, and there was no sense worrying Lane.

Twenty minutes later, they climbed out of a cab in front of the dilapidated apartment building that Lane said was the woman's address. A car came to a halt about a block behind them and its headlights were turned off. Kelly was sure it was the same Fiat that had been following them since they left the Navarro.

The stairwell was dark, and at one point, Lane grabbed Kelly's arm to steady her as she almost lost her footing. "Thanks," she said.

"Navigating the catacombs had to be easier than this," he replied.

When they rapped on the top-floor door without a name, murmurs of conversation seeping through the door stopped. A moment later, a woman's voice called out, "Who is there?"

"Lane Woods and Father Kelly."

The door was unlocked and a woman's head cautiously peered out. "You didn't tell me he was a priest."

"I didn't think it mattered. Damian's a priest."

"But of a special kind," Carla replied testily. "Come in. Come in."

Kelly appreciated Carter's taste in women if not his politics. With her dark Mediterranean looks and beautiful chestnut hair, Carla radiated an earthy sensuality. She entered the living room and introduced the man and woman sitting there. The man was broad shouldered, heavily muscled, and in his late twenties with unruly dirty-blond hair. He wore an expensive sweater, slacks, and a leather jacket. His name was Lorenzo. Kelly assumed he was one of Rome's rich who was more interested in bodybuilding than radicalism.

He glanced at Kelly and Lane with ill-concealed disdain. "We will discuss that later, Carla," he said laconically.

The woman stared at Kelly with undisguised loathing. Freckle faced and snub nosed, she had black hair cut short and parted like a man's. Her jeans and flannel shirt were frayed and faded to a grayish blue from countless washings. "Christ, a priest," she said disgustedly in the harsh nasal accent of Northern Ireland.

"Shut up, Madeleine," Carla said.

Kelly wasn't fazed by the woman's outburst. He had run into too many embittered Irish over the years, rebels against the old fire-and-brimstone Catholicism that had dominated Ireland and much of the United States for too long. They were all working off old wounds, old emotional scars inflicted by a lot of priests and nuns who became teachers during an era when teachers took out their frustrations on their students.

"This is Lane Woods," Carla said. "She is an American asking about Falconi's murder. She is with a magazine . . ."

"A TV station in New York."

"I'm so impressed," Madeleine said.

238

"The priest is named Kelly. I don't know why he is here other than the fact that the woman brought him."

Kelly wasn't sure what to say to these people, so he laid his cards on the table. "I'm investigating Bishop Falconi's murder."

"Going to sweep everything under a Vatican rug and make the scandal nice and tidy the way they always do over there?" Lorenzo asked with a bored insolence.

"What makes you think there is a Church-related scandal?" Lane asked.

"We happen to know the last person to see Falconi alive and we know what was going down," Madeleine said.

"I assume we are talking about the same person," Lane said. "Damian Carter put me onto this story."

"What do you mean 'what was going down' that night?" Kelly asked.

"Why Falconi was giving away Vatican secrets," Madeleine said with a sneering laugh.

"What secrets?" Lane asked.

"You'll know soon enough," Lorenzo said.

"Everyone will know!" Madeleine said shrilly.

"Be quiet, both of you," Carla said wearily. "It is time you left."

"Don't let us hold you back," Lane said sarcastically.

"Cunt," Lorenzo said.

Suddenly, Kelly bent down, grabbed Lorenzo under his arms, and lifted him out of the chair. He held him suspended in the air so his feet didn't touch the floor. The youth tried to drive his knee into the American's groin. Anticipating the move, Kelly turned sideways, yanking the Italian down and butting him in the face. Kelly let go. The youth tumbled to the floor, moaning, his hands tentatively exploring his face.

"You broke my nose," Lorenzo said in disbelief. "You broke my nose. You can't do that! You are a priest!"

Kelly knelt over him. "There's nothing in the vows against it, Lorenzo. Now apologize to the lady or I'll break every bone in your body."

Panicked, the young man looked up. "Sorry," he muttered softly.

Thinking about what Gracey had told her about Kelly, Lane recoiled. "I can take care of myself," she said crossly.

Kelly looked at her as he slowly stood. "I know that. It was just a reflex reaction."

"Let's get out of here," Madeleine said, glaring at Kelly while helping Lorenzo to his feet.

Carla locked the door carefully once they left. Coming back to the living room, she sat down and rubbed her neck. "Lorenzo can be a pig, but you didn't have to do that."

"So I've been told," Kelly replied.

Lane flushed but wasn't going to apologize.

Carla wondered how much Damian had told them. "So how is Damian?"

"Fine but still frightened," Lane said, trying to see what kind of reaction that would get from the woman.

"Yes, he still would be."

"His friend told him about your call. Has he gotten back to you?"

"We have been missing one another," she said worriedly.

"Why is he so scared, Carla?" Lane probed. "Why are you?"

Suddenly, the photographer realized how little these two knew. If Carter hadn't told them, she certainly wouldn't. "Soon everyone will know," she replied in the same enigmatic way the other two had.

"An intriguing answer," Lane said. "Could you be a bit more specific?"

"No, if Damian wanted you to know, he would have told you. He may very well do that soon enough."

Kelly and Lane exchanged glances. The note of finality in her tone told them that she would say no more.

15

AS HE MADE HIS WAY TO THE BASILICA, KEVIN KELLY PUSHED HIS WAY through the thousands of people jamming St. Peter's Square. The throngs waited to get a glimpse of the College of Cardinals and the men who were about to be made cardinals. At one point there was a hole in the crowd, and he spotted Lane Woods surrounded by a TV crew as she interviewed an American archbishop. He started to make his way toward her but thought better of it and changed his course.

Finally, he reached the Bronze Door, showed his invitation to one of the monsignors collecting them, and was directed down the aisle. Kelly entered a pew and took his seat next to Perdomo, while nodding to Bisleti and the other members of Clarizio's staff as well as a few of Clarizio's relatives who had made the trip from Sicily for the ceremony.

"One day you'll probably be up there, Enrico," he said.

"Don't be absurd, Father Kelly," Perdomo replied irritably, and looked away.

Kelly wondered at the man's mood swings while he looked around the Basilica. Settling back, he was prepared to enjoy the pageantry. He missed some of the mystery and beauty of ritual that was stripped away from the Church by Vatican II. The investiture was a vestige of a bygone era. The seats reserved by Clarizio were excellent. The Basilica itself looked even more glorious than it had when he came here with the pronuncio. Everything appeared perfect. The scaffolding had disappeared. Vatican workers had replaced the damaged thrones.

Dignitaries from all over the world were present. The entire Vatican diplomatic corps, dressed in morning suits, sat near Italian nobility, the men elegant and the women glittering as their diamonds, emeralds, and rubies flashed in the golden light of the cathedral. More than a dozen U.S. congressmen and senators were present, honoring the four Americans who were being elevated, the most from any nation. A great many Americans were numbered among the legions of hierarchy in attendance.

At precisely nine-thirty A.M., the silvery peal of trumpets rose above the roar of the multitude gathered in St. Peter's Square. The trumpeting signaled the start of the solemn ceremony marking the investiture of seventeen new cardinals of the Holy Roman Catholic Church. The procession of the College of Cardinals, their crimson raiment making them appear to have stepped from a Renaissance painting, was led by the venerable Marcello Braggia, whose mind at age eighty-seven was razor-sharp even though his bent, frail body scarcely heeded his command to walk.

Cheers erupted from the crowd as the men about to be elevated joined the procession, the loudest cheers reserved for the crowd's favorites. They slowly passed the Palantine and Swiss guards, and the noble guards, who were drawn from the ranks of Italian aristocracy. Death had thinned the cardinals' ranks from the maximum of one hundred and fifty-two.

Suddenly, the sharp turning of heads in the front of the crowd had a ripple effect. All eyes focused on the center aisle. Thunderous applause filled the four-hundred-foot-high domed basilica as the pope appeared. Clad in scarlet and gold and carried aloft by twelve scarlet-uniformed pontifical guards, the pope imperiously bent his mitered head to either side and lifted his hand to bestow his blessing. Kelly had seen many pictures of the pontiff, but they failed to capture the authority and dynamism in the strong peasant face.

After the pope mounted his massive gold throne, the cardinals, one by one, came forward and bowed to the supreme pontiff, a sign of their submission to his will. Then they went to their own thrones to the left or the right.

During the ceremony, Clarizio's specialness was lost on no one. The pope's own pectoral cross, which he had received upon being made a bishop, was placed around the new cardinal's neck. In his regal robes, the imposing Clarizio was a model of decorum as only befit someone so steeped in the ways of Rome. Of all the men receiving the red hat, he looked the most as if he were born to nothing else. The intense look on Clarizio's face wasn't joy at receiving personal recognition but a willingness to assume even greater burdens for the sake of his Church.

Kelly was glad to see that the cardinal did not appear as haggard as he did the other day but radiated the inner strength he had first noticed in the man. At least Clarizio had a few hours of respite from the worries that haunted him.

Following the ceremony, Kelly had a difficult time locating Bishop Gibbons. They had arranged to meet at the Obelisk in St. Peter's Square. Kelly swiftly realized that was almost like telling someone you'll meet them at Times Square on New Year's Eve. The plaza was mobbed. As he circled around the Obelisk, Kelly constantly shook hands with priests and members of the hierarchy he knew.

"Have you seen John Gibbons?" he asked repeatedly.

"About twenty feet behind you," a New York priest finally told him.

Standing on his toes, Kelly turned and spotted Gibbons talking to Archbishop Carl Clement of Minneapolis and Boston's Bishop Harry Mooney.

"There you are, Kevin," Gibbons boomed above the din as Kelly came toward him. "I was just telling our friends that it's unfortunate we have to leave here immediately, but duty has a way of coming before pleasure, doesn't it?"

"Always," Kelly said.

He shook hands warmly with Clement, who had been a big help to him during the Carruthers investigation. "Good to see you again," the archbishop said, "and under more pleasant circumstances."

When he turned to Mooney, the Boston bishop gave him a cool smile. A friend of Cardinal Carruthers's, he had been one of the ecclesiastics who had complained about Kelly's being too dogged during the investigation.

"Well, we've got to be going," Gibbons said.

As they strolled to a café near Kelly's hotel, they spoke of how impressive the ceremony had been and commented on the ecclesiastics in attendance. Once they were seated at a table, Kelly stared at Gibbons. "Okay, John. Why did you ditch Clement and Mooney?"

"There's something I have to tell you."

"What?"

Gibbons exhaled slowly and gave Kelly a perplexed look. "Bill Witten may be alive."

Suddenly, Kelly felt icy. Another sighting. "Who told you?"

"Joe Devine. I was talking to him about your assignment. This will sound a bit mad, but he swears he saw Witten just two days ago. I told him you'd want to talk to him."

"How certain was he?"

"Very."

After leaving Gibbons, Kelly returned to his hotel. The bishop had other people he wanted to see in Rome. Kelly didn't feel like attending any of the festivities organized for the new cardinals. When he checked for messages with the concierge, he was handed an envelope bearing the corporate logo of Gruson, Dilling.

In his room, he took off his jacket and collar, propped up a pillow, and stretched out on the bed. He carefully tore open the envelope and extracted the memorandum that Dave Martin had sent over on *Milites Christi*.

Kevin:

This is an overview. If you want more, let me know, but it should be enough for now.

Dave

Very little is known of the early life of Miguel Perez, the founder of Milites Christi. He was born about 1910, but there is an information gap until he was left at a seminary near Madrid in 1919, apparently abandoned. In his writings, he never mentioned his childhood prior to the seminary.

When he was fourteen, he later claimed, he suffered

from spontaneous wounds in his hands and feet and side from which blood trickled. The apparent stigmata, he said, recurred into early adulthood. For the rest of his life, bruises appeared in the locations of the wounds, according to his memoirs. The seminary never revealed this condition while he was there. There is no indication anyone in authority knew of this condition.

At age twenty, he left the seminary and began preaching in villages across southern Spain. It was then his condition was first publicized as a stigmata. Several village doctors authenticated the stigmata, but he refused to be examined by physicians at major medical facilities.

Perez became a protégé of Raphael Marie D'Ortega, a wealthy textile-mill owner. With D'Ortega's backing, the first Via Christi retreat opened outside Madrid in 1938. Perez envisioned his mission as creating an elite army that would expunge the "corruption" from the Catholic Church and build a purer Catholicism. This army would consist of men who were wealthy and powerful and drawn from the military, politics, business, and finance. He said it was important that the membership be capable of influencing situations and events. Another cornerstone of his preaching was a vehement anticommunism. Over the years, Milites Christi's mission became more evangelical and advocated the use of "Holy Force" to achieve its objectives.

Milites Christi's modes of operation are little known because the organization is a secret society. The membership is little known for this reason as well. Documents and the testimony provided by former members reveal the organization to exist as a well-financed entity that is not dependent upon the Catholic Church.

For various reasons, the present pope, like his predecessors, has refused to elevate Milites Christi to the status of a consider Perez for beatification, although influential people from all around the world have asked to have Perez considered for sainthood.

There is a growing sentiment among influential ecclesiastic and lay circles to elevate Milites Christi's status and to consider Perez as a potential saint. The pressure comes from influential cardinals and archbishops who have been beneficiaries of the organization's financial largess as well as wealthy men who are believed to be members of the organization.

Another reason this pope has been reluctant to reward Milites Christi is some of the controversial activities in which the organization has been involved. The organization was linked to the scandal of the P-2 lodge that was uncovered in 1981. In this instance, the head of Milan's Ambrosiano Bank, Roberto Calvi, who was a central figure in P-2, was also believed to be a member of Milites Christi. The Vatican Bank suffered major financial losses and great embarrassment from its dealings with Calvi. Calvi's body was discovered hanging from Blackfriar's Bridge in London, and police did not determine whether he was murdered or committed suicide.

In most Latin nations and increasingly in the U.S., Milites Christi gives a great deal of support to right-wing political organizations. In addition to money, the organization can bring to bear the weight of newspapers, magazines, and TV stations that are owned by men who are believed to be Milites Christi members.

As he finished reading, Kelly's eyes returned to the fourth paragraph. Just what was "Holy Force"? What methods would members of Milites Christi resort to in its name?

He reached for the phone to call Lane Woods to read her the report, but pulled his hand back as if he had reached for a cigarette. He'd stopped smoking ten years ago. Was he sharing or just looking for an excuse? If he got her on the phone, he'd wind up asking her if she wanted to have dinner or meet for a drink. Remember what you are, he cautioned himself. Keep professional. If something important comes along, share. Don't go looking for trouble.

He was disgusted with himself. Why be bothered now by the strictures of celibacy? Kelly remembered the diaries and journals of medieval monks so plagued by Eros that they fled their cells at night with rashes and welts covering their bodies. He'd always been able to sublimate by throwing himself into whatever he was doing. A woman wasn't part of the agenda. He figured he must be setting himself up in some way. Maybe it was this assignment. Maybe he wanted to show himself that he was no better than the next man. No better than Pat Hogan.

He admitted that loneliness was a factor. Since first meeting Clarizio, he felt more isolated than he ever had since entering the seminary. Another possibility occurred to him. Suppose he'd run his

246

course with the Church, just as he had with another institution years ago? Suppose he wasn't cut out to be a priest anymore?

"Damn," he whispered. "No one ever said life was supposed to be easy."

As he leaned back again, the phone rang. He eagerly grabbed it, despising himself for hoping it was her. "Yes," he answered.

"*Buon giorno*, Father Kelly. This is Monsignor Ruggieri. You left a message that you wanted to see me."

"Thanks for calling," Kelly said, glad that business at hand turned him from his turmoil. "Charles Edwards said you may be able to help me with an assignment I'm working on."

"Mr. Edwards? Of course. In fact I saw him at the investiture this morning, and I barely had time to say hello to him. If he thinks I can help you, I will certainly try."

"When can we get together?"

"I am afraid that I must leave for Milano this evening. Suppose we arrange to meet after I return?"

"I don't have a lot of time myself." Kelly checked his watch. It was shortly before noon. "Could you squeeze some time in this afternoon?"

Ruggieri laughed. "You are persistent. Suppose we meet at four o'clock at the Sistine Chapel?"

As he hung up, Kelly wondered about Ruggieri. Edwards said he was "brilliant." The ever-diplomatic Clarizio had stepped out of character by all but calling the man a liar. Gibbons was even more damning. Kelly grunted as he thought again of Edwards's report. Monsignor Vincenzo Ruggieri sounded like a Borgia come back from the grave.

The Sistine Chapel is one of the most magnificent masterpieces of Italian genius and reflects the glory of the days when the Church was the world's greatest patron of the arts. The Chapel was named after Sixtus IV, the fifteenth-century pope for whom it was built by the architect Giovannino de'Dolci. In the ensuing centuries it has become a symbol of the majesty of the Church.

A few minutes before four, Kelly stood in front of the ornate metal grate that allowed tourists and ordinary visitors to see the chapel but not to get too close, almost as if it represented the Vatican itself. Staring

247

through the grating, he thought how beauty was so much a part of the fabric of life at the Vatican. The chapel was put to use only on rare occasions, such as the conclaves where a pope was chosen. Kelly understood why. Even with the scaffolds around the walls for the preservationists who were trying to clean and restore the paintings, there was a striking solemnity and weightiness about the place. The rich display of art was intoxicating.

"Most people think of the chapel as simply a showcase for Michelangelo's frescoes," said a voice behind him.

Kelly turned and faced a small, slight man whose cassock was edged with a monsignor's piping. He recognized him as the cleric in the back of the limo with Edwards at Via Christi and from the Robbinses' party. The rapt look on the monsignor's face made him appear to be inhaling the art on the walls. Suddenly, the monsignor laughed and extended his hand.

"Vincenzo Ruggieri, Father Kelly. It is a pleasure to meet you."

"The same here," Kelly said, finding himself surprised. He hadn't anticipated Ruggieri's gregariousness.

The monsignor put his arm on Kelly's shoulder and pointed at various masterpieces. "That is *Moses on the Way to Egypt* by Pinturicchio and Perugino." Pointing again, he said, "That is *Moses and the Daughter of Jethro* by Botticelli. While over there is *Scenes From the Life of Moses* by Rosselli."

He smiled and his gaze turned to the huge fresco on the front wall. "But yes, Michelangelo was the master of them all, wasn't he?"

Kelly too stared at the painting the *Last Judgment* on the great wall behind the altar, having only seen it before in his father's books. The majestic representation of the last day of the world was dominated by the figure of Christ the Judge, who, with His raised arm, seemed to give a whirling movement to the entire scene. All the figures in the huge fresco appeared immersed in an apocalyptic gloom, pervaded by the drama of life and death.

"A truly remarkable man," Ruggieri said. "He painted that after painting the entire vault of the chapel."

Remembering that it had taken Michelangelo four long years to complete the frescoes, Kelly craned his neck up at the ceiling and tried to imagine what torturous work that must have been. The artist lying on his back for hours at a time to paint them. "I'm not sure whether the pope was punishing or rewarding Michelangelo by putting him to work here."

Ruggieri laughed and gave Kelly a mischievous look. "Most people who take on work for a pope wind up wondering that."

Given what he had heard about the monsignor, Kelly wondered if Ruggieri was making a mocking reference to himself. It was impossible to tell judging by the man's playful expression. On the way over, Kelly had wondered how someone apparently so devious was still in the Church. What he had failed to take into account was how charming the monsignor was. He had seen such charm at work before. The more engaging someone was, the more likely other people were to deny, excuse, or minimize their faults. Pat Hogan inevitably came to mind.

Opening the ornate wooden door in the grating, Ruggieri beckoned for Kelly to follow him inside. He walked up to the altar and sat on the top step. Kelly sat next to him.

"Americans are an informal people and I like that," the monsignor said. "Europeans are too serious. We treat everything with an intense respect that drains the joy out of much of life. When I come in here, I like to think of Michelangelo and his assistants sitting around like this, joking, eating their lunches, and talking about their lovers."

He turned his playful eyes on Kelly. "So, Father, why did you wish to see me?"

"Edwards gave me your name because of a background check I am making on an American who is being considered for the office of bishop. His name is Patrick Hogan."

"Ah, yes. There has been a lot of speculation here about when he would be elevated. So it is very soon, is it?"

"Perhaps."

"You mean, depending upon what you learn about his character?"

"Yes."

Ruggieri's handsome face clouded with pity. "What a terrible thing for him and even more terrible for you." He sighed loudly. "I will help you in whatever way I can."

Kelly briefly recounted the essence of the Edwards's charges about Hogan's abusing his position by fronting for Damian Carter before Falconi. He watched Ruggieri's face closely to see his reaction. The look the monsignor wore was simply one of concern.

"And that is all?"

"That's it," Kelly said.

The monsignor stood and slowly paced back and forth before the altar. "I think perhaps Mr. Edwards is making too much out of this. Yes, Monsignor Hogan did bring these matters to Bishop Falconi's attention, and yes, the bishop did get angry with the monsignor. The bishop investigated the charges, and they could not be substantiated. The bishop felt foolish, and worse, he was afraid that he had incurred the resentment of certain of his people who felt that he no longer trusted them. That hurt him the most.

"His anger at Monsignor Hogan did not last long. They were friends and these things happen. He just believed that the monsignor was naive and lacked proper judgment for having made such charges. But as far as I know, the bishop eventually dismissed the matter. I remember him making a passing joke about it by saying how he would watch the monsignor on television but would not trust him with anything of consequence."

"Were you a confidant of Bishop Falconi?"

Ruggieri smiled. "In a way. You see, the bishop had me do work for the Propagation off and on. I guess I was there in what one might say was a 'consulting capacity.'"

❋

As Kelly left the Vatican twenty minutes later, he realized how smooth Ruggieri was. Almost admirable. How charmingly damning the monsignor was about Pat Hogan. Ruggieri himself had seemed to offer no views of his own. It was all what Falconi was supposed to have said and done. Nothing terrible. All sounding very plausible and all implying that Hogan wasn't qualified to be much of anything but a TV clown. Kelly laughed. The monsignor was good. Real good. But what was his game? Why did he want Hogan to get the boot? What was *his* hidden agenda?

❋

Two hours later, Monsignor Vincenzo Ruggieri sat at a café off Piazza della Repubblica, near the train station. He tapped his Scotch and soda irritably with a swizzle stick and checked his watch again. He had to catch a train in an hour. Perdomo should have been here fifteen minutes ago. For the hundredth time, he wondered if the man could be counted on. Perdomo was such a naive ass. The last time they were together, he told Clarizio's secretary what he wanted and Perdomo acted stunned. Yes, stunned!

Ruggieri found it preposterous that the man could be so simple-minded. What about his bloodline? He thought of Perdomo's grand-father, whom he met once when he was a teenager. Old Giovanni Perdomo could skin a fox while the fox grinned with pleasure. But this one. Too much money and a mind suited for idleness. Having grown up surrounded by the rich, Ruggieri believed he knew the type well. Spoiled, weak fools who were almost constitutionally incapable of doing anything on their own.

He himself had grown up with the facade of money, uneasily leading the lifestyle of the wealthy. In reality, his father had to scram-ble, beg, steal every penny and count on the naïveté and greed of the Enrico Perdomos of the world to get by. The vineyards his father inherited were bankrupt, the soil eroded, the quality of what little wine was produced was appalling. Yet, his father, Aldo, was always able to get rich men to invest in his vineyards and other financial schemes. Aldo was so charming and always so heartbroken at the failure of nature or inauspicious times that resulted in the disappearance of the investments that his sincerity was never doubted.

It was his father's idea that Ruggieri enter a seminary. The cassock was the perfect cloak for a clever man. Everything was within the grasp of a man who knew what he wanted. What sound advice! Ruggieri smiled as he thought how he had saved himself at various times of trouble by behavior similar to that of his father. Certain members of the hierarchy had such a blind side; they elevated gullibility to the status of a virtue. Perhaps Perdomo had a bright future after all.

"Sorry I'm late, Vincenzo, but Eminenza had me do something for him at the last minute," Perdomo said as he sank onto the seat across the small table from Ruggieri. He looked tired as he summoned the waiter and ordered a red wine and indicated another drink for Ruggieri.

"Well, Enrico? Have you thought over what we talked about?"

"Yes. Yes," Perdomo replied tentatively. "I'm sorry, Vincenzo. I still cannot help you in these matters."

The little monsignor decided to try appealing to Perdomo's ra-tional nature one last time. "All I asked you to do, Enrico, was to get me a copy of the itinerary of the pope's visit to the United States when it is ready. Is that such an overwhelming favor? Think about it. Soon even the newspapers will carry most of the schedule for everyone to see."

"I know, Vincenzo. But it simply isn't right. I told you from the beginning that it wasn't right."

251

Ruggieri nodded sympathetically. "Poor Enrico. So many things you should have done . . . or not done."

Perdomo looked at him sharply. "What do you mean?"

"Perhaps I should not have left you alone at dinner with Antonio."

Stricken, Perdomo was at a loss for words as he stared at Ruggieri. Suddenly, he saw a hint of menace in the monsignor's eyes that was never there before. He closed his own eyes. Dear God, what have I gotten myself into? The man is Satan. "What," he asked, his voice cracking, "what are you talking about?"

"I just happened to run into the boy again the next day. He said you two had a lovely time. He even has photographs revealing how close you two became."

Suddenly, Perdomo could not breathe. He put his hand to his throat as it constricted. His vision blurred. Sweat beaded his forehead. Despair welled up within him as he thought of that night. What happened had preyed on his mind ever since, so that he thought he was going crazy. The events of the evening rushed back over him.

He had picked an elegant, out-of-the-way Italian restaurant. Still buoyant from their previous evening of fun, he called Ruggieri to tell him the restaurant's name and its address.

"Do you mind if I bring a friend? Vincenzo asked.

At first, Perdomo was surprised to find himself a bit jealous at having to share his new companion with anyone, but he quickly graciously acceded. "No. Not at all."

When he arrived at the restaurant, Perdomo found Ruggieri already seated. Vincenzo rose and delightedly embraced Enrico.

"How are you? How are you? My friend will be along in a little while."

Perdomo was elated that they would have a little more time together. They drank wine and once again talked about friends and Vatican gossip. Before he realized it, almost an hour had passed. Perdomo once again had drunk more than he usually did and was laughing at Ruggieri's irreverent humor.

"Vincenzo!"

Perdomo and Ruggieri looked up simultaneously. Ruggieri rose and clasped someone's hand. "Antonio, welcome! Enrico, meet another countryman, Antonio Pirelli."

Perdomo stood and found himself gazing into the clearest blue eyes he believed he'd ever seen. A slender young man of medium height and

252

athletic build stared back at him. With his blond hair, high cheekbones, and finely chiseled mouth, he could have been a male model.

"Enrico Perdomo, Signore Pirelli."

"Please call me Tony. Vincenzo has told me a great deal about you, Monsignor. I hope that we can become good friends as well."

Perdomo was glad that the three quickly fell into the same kind of lighthearted camaraderie that he and Vincenzo enjoyed. However, several times during the dinner, he caught himself gazing at the young man rather than paying attention to the conversation. Rarely had he ever seen a young man of such remarkable beauty.

As the evening progressed, Perdomo found himself more and more locked in conversation with Tony, who, like Enrico, was an opera enthusiast while Vincenzo was not. Indeed, they had a great many interests in common. Old movies, the theater, riding, and sailing.

"Unfortunately, I must leave you two," Ruggieri said, "but I have taken the liberty of ordering another bottle of Barolo, which you Philistines prefer to Brunello di Montalcino."

"*Ciao*, Vincenzo," Tony said.

"*Ciao*," Enrico said. "I really should be leaving now too."

"After the next bottle of wine, Monsignor," Ruggieri said in his imitation of Archbishop Clarizio. "While the archbishop is away, the mice should play."

Both Perdomo and Tony erupted in laughter.

Forty-five minutes later, Perdomo was in the back of a cab with the young man. "You must come to my apartment and hear some of my opera collection," Tony said.

Enrico felt warm and mellow. He realized that once again he had drunk too much, but he was beyond caring. "When?" he asked.

Tony brought his mouth close to Enrico's ear and his thigh pressed against Perdomo's. "Why now," he replied.

Looking at Ruggieri's mocking eyes, Perdomo tried to push the rest of that shameful evening from his consciousness. Tony was so beautiful. He had never meant to touch him, let alone to return to his room. He had tried to leave, but . . . the rest was a blur.

Never before had he broken his vows. The next morning he confessed his extraordinary moment of weakness. But what he hoped had ended in the confessional now appeared to be just the beginning.

For a moment, he concentrated on the rain that suddenly came hammering down, splattering the street outside the café like machine gun bullets. His mother's face came to him, a mask of horror and shame. Tears welled up in his eyes. His shortness of breath began to ease, and he fought to maintain a shred of dignity before this, this *vipero*. "What do you want, Monsignor?" he asked coldly.

Ruggieri leaned forward solicitously. "There, there, Enrico."

"Stop!" Perdomo shrieked.

"Now, Enrico, don't be like that. Those silly photos will never see the light of day. All I want is something that I asked before any of this happened. This is not some terrible thing. It is merely providing a little information. No one gets harmed. There is nothing to it."

Once again, Perdomo squeezed his eyes shut. He felt as if he were trapped in a nightmare. Soon, he would hear the alarm go off and it would be over, but when he opened his eyes again, all he saw was this evil little man's leering face. He wanted to weep, but he would not give Ruggieri the satisfaction. The shame. The humiliation. The terrible, terrible humiliation. He had seen several times what happened at the Vatican when a diplomat's weakness was exposed. He was hurriedly shipped off to a psychiatric hospital and then bleak posts in Africa, Australia, the Philippines.

God, could he ever make such a choice? Such a life was no choice. He flushed as he realized what a coward he was. All along, Ruggieri had known his mark well. If he wants this now, what else will he want later? Perdomo did not delude himself. There would always be a next time.

"Tell me again exactly what you want," he said quietly, thinking to himself that he was damned.

❈

A short distance away, the shops and cafés near the Trevi Fountain filled to overflowing within a matter of minutes as people ducked indoors to escape the torrential rainstorm that arose without warning. Lane Woods felt fortunate to have come early and secured a table. Dozens of people, most of them tourists, sought refuge. With resigned expressions, they stood by the doorway and erupted in a babble of German, French, Swedish, Spanish, or English, while waiting for a place to sit.

One tour guide with a little group of British senior citizens kept warning, "Watch out for the gypsies! Even little gypsies steal. Even the littlest gypsy steals!"

Lane grimaced. Just before entering the restaurant, she had been accosted by a ragged gypsy boy of nine or ten who demanded money while giving her the kind of leer she would have resented from a man four times his age. He also tried to grab her purse, but she had knocked his hand away at the last second. Instead of running off, he made a lewd gesture and laughed before slipping into the crowd. She still wasn't sure whether to laugh or be angry.

Now, she wondered what Carla Sarfina wanted. After the encounter at the woman's apartment, she had never expected to hear from her again. Even so, Carla called less than an hour ago, saying she wanted to meet, and named this café, which was only a few blocks from Lane's hotel. The photographer had to have information to give. Lane just hoped it was more useful than what the Vatican public relations man gave her on Bishop Falconi.

The monsignor at the Vatican press office was most gracious and claimed to be most sympathetic with her efforts to get to the bottom of the bishop's death, but he was as forthcoming as a sphinx. He gave her a saccharin version of Falconi's job that made the man sound like another Mother Teresa. Gracey had told her there were rumors that the bishop was investigating the activities of Milites Christi, but the monsignor became so vague on that point that he was useless. As for what Falconi might possibly have told or given Carter, forget it.

Carla's call bothered her. The woman sounded so strained. There was an edge of panic in her voice. What was wrong?

Kevin Kelly entered and glanced around before seeing Lane. On an impulse, she had asked Carla if it would be okay if he came along. She had not even been sure she could locate him; she had left word at his hotel where she would be. Another act of good faith. Maybe he'd open up a little more. Something else gnawed at her and she did not want to dwell on it. She liked having him around. But there was that expression on his face when she caught him looking at her sometimes.

"What's up?" he asked, taking the seat opposite her.

"Carla Sarfina wanted to meet. She wouldn't go into why over the phone."

Before she could say anything else, she stared in dismay at the doorway. Kelly turned around. Carla was coming toward them. Kelly and Lane exchanged concerned looks. The woman was disheveled. She stumbled across the room, knocking into tables. Hatless and her coat open, she was soaked to the skin. When she sat down, her face was blotchy and her eyes raw.

Lane reached out and touched her arm. "Carla, what's wrong?"

"It's Damian," the woman whispered. "He's dead!"

"Oh, my God!" Lane said softly. "Oh, God."

"How?" Kelly asked.

Carla propped her elbows on the table and held her head. She began sobbing. A waiter came over with a concerned look on his face, but Kelly waved him away.

"The same way the bishop was murdered."

"You mean he was strangled?" Lane asked.

"Yes . . . with a priest's stole."

"Dear God," Lane said, her right hand inadvertently going to her throat.

The photographer tried to collect herself and motioned for the waiter. "Cognac," she ordered.

Noting how pale Lane was, Kelly called after the waiter, "Make that three." Turning back, he said, "Carla, do you know anything else?"

She shook her head affirmatively but held up her hand, a sign that she wanted a moment to collect herself. When the drinks came, she took a brandy snifter, drained the glass, and motioned for the waiter for another. Coughing, she looked from Lane to Kelly and cleared her throat.

"Damian's friends called from New York this afternoon. They found him in his room, strangled. Just before they called, they took his body and placed it in a church so they would not have to get mixed up with the police."

"What was Damian doing?" Kelly demanded.

"He was looking for someone to translate a document that appeared on the film."

"What film?" Kelly asked.

Realizing she probably wasn't making much sense, Carla breathed deeply and made another effort to pull herself together. She tried to explain the sequence of events. "The night Falconi was murdered, he gave Damian film. He told him that, if anything should happen to him, Damian could use the information on the film as he saw fit."

"What kind of information?" Kelly asked.

Carla sighed. "We didn't know. He brought the film to me to develop right after he left the bishop, but it was a document that turned

256

out to be written in Latin. He was supposed to have it translated in New York."

"Do your friends have the document now?" Lane asked.

"No, I asked them."

"Then where is it?" Kelly demanded.

"They don't know. It was missing."

"Who are they and how can I reach them?" Kelly asked.

"I cannot tell you," Carla replied.

"Carla, I give you my word as a priest that I will not reveal who they are."

"You have my word as well," Lane said.

Shuddering, Carla stood and pulled her coat around her shoulders. "I will call and ask. If they will talk to you, I will contact you."

Kelly clenched his fist in frustration. "Okay. I'm at the Navarro. You know where Lane is."

After Carla left, Lane was ashen. "My God, Kevin, what's so important that someone is killing for it?"

They sat staring at one another, both at a loss for words, the smashing rain driving out all other sound in the café. Finally, Kelly ordered another round of drinks and told her what he knew about Milites Christi and gave her a copy of Martin's report that he had been carrying, waiting for the right moment to hand it to her.

"There's something else you should know. Right after the killer got Falconi, he came after Carter."

"How do you know?"

"Damian was being followed from the moment he set foot in Rome."

"By whom?"

"The people I used to work for."

She remembered what Gracey said about Kelly's having been with the CIA. "Why, for God's sake?"

"He worried them. He knew too many people who were involved in political activities they oppose."

"But Damian would never have hurt a fly."

Kelly rubbed his eyes. "Sometimes even the gentlest people get too caught up in what they do. They see everything in terms of us and them. When that happens, they start making excuses for their side. Creating their own rules."

"Did this person watching Damian see the bishop being murdered?"

257

"No."

"But he must have seen who tried to kill Damian?"

"He didn't get a good look at him," Kelly said. "But from the way he was dressed, he may have been a priest."

Disgustedly, Kelly thought he should have withheld that piece of information and tried to backpedal. "I . . . uh . . . . I'd appreciate it if you don't use that last bit of information without checking with me."

"Why?"

"I don't want to tip anything to the killer just yet that we know anything about him."

"Okay, but only if I don't get it from another source too." Suddenly, Lane started shaking. Kelly pulled off his coat and put it around her. "There's more," he said. Briefly, he told her about Lawler's and Edwards's reports and his meeting with Ruggieri. "They're going after Pat hammer and tong, but I'm not sure why."

"How does Milites Christi figure into this?" she asked.

Kelly made a fist and tapped his thumb against his teeth in frustration. "I don't know yet. That's just one of the things about this mess that has me stumped."

"Can we get out of here?" she asked.

Kelly called for the check. They left the restaurant a few minutes later, both feeling drained by what was unfolding around them. There were no cabs in sight, and they swiftly became soaked as Kelly walked Lane back to her hotel. Neither knew what to say or do. Suddenly, Lane started crying.

"Poor Damian . . . poor, poor, lost Damian," she moaned.

The pain and sadness in her words articulated what Kelly himself thought about Carter's frenetic life since Gethsemane. When he looked at Lane, he found her tears made her appear frail and lonely. Without thinking, he put his arms around her and held her. The two of them stood on the dark street, clinging to one another. They seemed afraid to move, as if the earth would crack open and their next step would be into a void from which there was no return.

16

KELLY TOOK A DEEP BREATH AS HE LOOKED AT DAVE MARTIN, WONDERING how much the CIA man already knew and whether Martin would give him any information at all. He had to try.

"Okay, Dave. Here's what I have. Damian Carter is dead, apparently killed by the same person who murdered Falconi. Carter had received some kind of document on film from Falconi. Whatever it was seems to have resulted in their deaths."

"What does Clarizio think?" Martin asked.

"I haven't told him yet. His secretary said he'll be back soon. I'm going over there after I leave you."

"Who else knows?"

Kelly shrugged. "Carla, you, me, and Lane Woods, an American TV reporter who's over here. From what Carla said, the New York cops may not even have found Carter's body yet."

"How does the reporter know?"

"The Sarfina woman called her and she brought me into it."

"Why?"

"She wants to do a story on Falconi's death. We're sharing notes."

259

Sitting in the Gruson, Dilling headquarters, Kelly felt like the angel of death as he spread word about murder. Tugging at his collar, he wasn't sure whether it was the stiff cloth chafing his neck or if it was nerves. He wanted to yank if off and was sure Freud would've been able to write a book about why.

"Can you tell me anything?" he asked. "Anything that will point me in the right direction?"

With his elbows propped up on his desk and his chin in his hands, Martin stared back noncommittally. "The murders appear to be well orchestrated, or we have an international nut case on our hands."

"Dave, don't repeat the obvious."

Martin's mouth tightened at the sarcasm. Tact had never been one of Kelly's long suits. Besides, he was under a lot of pressure. Kelly had made it abundantly clear he wasn't crazy about this assignment, and to make matters worse, he was frustrated because it wasn't going well. Maybe it was more than that. Maybe he was edgy because of the woman. Kelly always took relationships seriously. The Agency. The Church. His wife and daughter. Perhaps this woman. That was the area of his life where Kelly lost perspective. He took relationships too seriously.

"I've checked our people and Rome's Red Squad," Martin said. "The killer doesn't appear to have anything to do with the Italian radicals. Our monitors don't see any PLO connection either. We're also checking on the Mafia. Nothing has come back yet."

"Dave, I asked you what do you make of this," Kelly said irritably. "Not what procedures you've followed."

Martin looked at him coolly. Kelly didn't seem to realize at times whom he was working for. Or whom he wasn't working for. Martin continued in the same noncommittal tone, "We can probably rule out a maniac since there is an indication the killings are related. Whoever is behind it has the funds to buy plane tickets to another country to execute the victims and had the skill to track them down. You may be right about the film, but until we know what it contains, it's idle speculation."

Frustrated, Kelly opened a new line of questioning. "Why didn't your report mention an ultracrazy faction of Milites Christi?"

"What do you mean?"

"I've heard rumors that a group of formidable Milites Christi members may be funding some of the death squad activities in Central America, especially those against priests and nuns."

260

Martin paused and picked up a pencil before resuming. "There has been some speculation about that, but so far we have no evidence that it is true."

"Uh-huh," Kelly said, staring at Martin.

Martin looked away. "Maybe you've been out of the business too long."

"No, I should never have gotten into it in the first place," Kelly muttered.

"I'll do a computer search on killers who have used religious objects in their murders and see if that turns up anything," Martin said. "Otherwise, all I can do is keep following 'procedures.'"

"Yeah, you do that, Dave."

An hour later, Cardinal Clarizio fought to maintain his composure as Kelly concluded his story. The totally unexpected had happened. Damian Carter was dead. Murdered! The cardinal closed his eyes and breathed deeply, trying to clear his head of the slight dizziness and to quell the nausea rising in his stomach.

"Thank you for telling me, Father Kelly. You are certain that he was strangled in the same manner as Bishop Falconi?"

"That's what I was told, Your Eminence."

"Have you uncovered any clues to the killer's identity?"

Kelly told him what he had learned about what had transpired between Bishop Falconi and Carter at the Colosseum. "All I know is that the document was in Latin. An extremist faction of Milites Christi may be involved, but nothing's certain."

"Yes, nothing is certain," the cardinal said, more to himself than to Kelly.

Kelly was concerned about how much Carter's murder had upset the cardinal. All the fatigue and anguish he had noticed in the churchman's face before the investiture was there again but worse. Clarizio was so ashen, Kelly thought, he might be physically ill as well as being under a great mental strain. He was glad Perdomo was living at the cardinal's apartment in case a doctor had to be called.

"I should go back to New York and try to find the people Damian Carter was staying with when he was killed," Kelly said.

As he spoke, he tried not to think that his decision had anything to do with Lane or the warmth of her body pressed against his tonight

261

or her returning to New York. Eventually, they had drawn back from one another, embarrassed. The rest of their walk was in silence. A block away from her hotel, Lane turned to him. "That won't happen again, will it, Kevin?" she half asked, half stated.

"No. No, it won't," he had replied.

"I'll go the rest of the way by myself. A long time ago I vowed never to come between any man and his wife. I'm not about to come between a man and his God. I think it best that I return to New York on the next flight I can get. Besides, I want to look into Damian's death."

As he watched her walk away, Kelly felt more confused than he had since he was a young man. Part of him suffered from the devastating pain of regret, as if he were watching his only connection with life disappear. Yet, another part of him was grateful they had resisted what should never have been. For a moment, he had wondered about the nature of sin and if, on occasion, not committing one might actually be worse than committing one. He decided to leave it to the philosophers.

"Yes, yes," the cardinal said, sounding even more distracted than Kelly. "You go to New York. I am leaving for Washington tomorrow. You may contact me there."

The cardinal took the American's arm and led him to the front door. "I do not trust very many people these days, Father Kelly, but I do trust you."

"Thank you, Your Eminence."

Clarizio looked up at Kelly and concern flickered in his eyes. "No, I thank you, Father Kelly. You have been burdened with too much already."

Fifteen minutes later, the cardinal hurriedly left his apartment. At this time of night, he did not pass anyone in the corridors. The chapel he entered was deserted. He went to the altar and knelt, his head bowed.

"What have I done?" he whispered. "What have I done?"

At the Navarro, Kelly managed to book a seat on an early-evening flight to New York. Finding the people Damian was staying with shouldn't be too difficult. Somebody who knew something about it would probably talk. If not, he could get a trace on calls to and from Pat Hogan. Carter was sure to have checked with his friend before his death and most likely, from his hideout. He'd have to check out the Witten sighting too.

262

His musings were interrupted by a soft knock on the hotel room door. "Be right there," he called out.

When he opened the door, Kelly tried not to show his surprise. "Thanks for coming, Mr. Urizor."

The Milites Christi seminarian was pale, and he looked anxiously up and down the corridor. "May I come in?"

"Sorry," Kelly muttered, and stepped aside as the young man quickly entered. Before closing the door, he too checked the corridor.

"I haven't much time," Urizor said, rubbing his hands anxiously. "Why do you wish to know about the monsignor?"

Kelly figured the youth came this far because he thought something was wrong. He decided to try to shock him into opening up. "He may have tried to commit murder."

Urizor's face grew whiter. He slumped on a corner of the bed. His left hand covered his mouth as he said, "Oh, my God!"

"What can you tell me?" Kelly demanded.

Urizor looked at him indecisively. "What is your involvement?"

"I was with Cardinal Clarizio in St. Peter's Basilica when someone tried to kill the cardinal. I saw that priest at the scene."

"Then I was not imagining things," Urizor said.

"What do you mean?"

"I was asked to pick up something at the monsignor's room several weeks ago. When I entered, I saw a Beret do you mean?"

"I was asked to pick up something at the monsignor's room several weeks ago. When I entered, I saw a Beretta pistol in a half-open drawer. I told one of the deacons, but he said that was impossible."

"How did you know the make of the gun?" Kelly asked.

"My father has one. But that is not all that is strange about that priest. Ours is a religious life that is based on cooperation. This priest is separate from the rest of us."

"How?"

"For some reason, he has no work assignments and comes and goes as he pleases. He spends a great amount of time in the White Chapel, weeping. Others say that the sounds of flagellation come from his room nightly. Yet . . ."

"What?"

"Yet, he doesn't have an air of sanctity. He is too troubled . . . too . . . cold . . . too unsaintly. I am not the only one who thinks this way. Frankly, there are many of us who are afraid of him, afraid of the look in his eyes."

"What's his name?"

"I don't know. I know he did not come to Milites Christi through ordinary channels. Our administrators have nothing to do with him. He is there as a favor to some very important people and primarily deals with them."

Nervously, Urizor rose to his feet. "I must be going."

"One more thing," Kelly said. "When you were in his room, did you see whether he had more than one stole?"

Urizor thought for a moment. "No."

As he drove the limousine along Via Veneto, Paolo Bisleti, as always, appreciated the feel of the Mercedes, a clone of the one he drove in Washington. He enjoyed driving. When he had pledged himself to serve the cardinal, he had volunteered for the job as chauffeur. Being behind the wheel of the finely crafted limo gave him a sense of control over an otherwise chaotic world.

The Mercedes came to a stop just past Harry's American Bar. An elegantly tailored man wearing a black silk suit and a pearl-gray fedora opened the rear door and climbed in. As soon as the door slammed shut, Bisleti maneuvered the limo into the heavy traffic again.

"Driver, take me to the Paris," Vittorio Zoppa ordered imperiously.

Raising his head, Bisleti disdainfully flicked his fingers beneath his chin while Zoppa laughed. A few blocks later, the priest turned right, parked, and shut off the engine. Abandoning the driver's seat, he climbed into the rear so that his friend could easily see his hands and face while he questioned him. The tinted windows ensured that no one would see them.

"Why did you call? What have you learned?" he quickly motioned.

"Your American priest, this Kelly, is being followed," Zoppa said. "I told my man to remain relatively open so that the follower would know there were two people watching the American in case he had any plans to harm him."

"Good. Was the priest followed back to New York?"

"Yes."

"Who is after him?" Bisleti queried.

"An American, but we don't know yet who he is working for."

"Have you looked into Milites Christi?"

"We are checking."

"How?"

"My cousin is a member."

Bisleti's eyebrows rose and he gave Zoppa a curious look. "Is he a believer?"

Zoppa laughed. "No. No. He complains all the time that he is not paid enough to put up with fanatics. Uncle Riccardo thought it would be a good idea. You never know when such an affiliation might be needed. In all likelihood, my cousin will become an extremely important man in the organization."

"Why?"

Zoppa shrugged. "He is very manipulative."

"Has he heard anything about Bishop Falconi or about what happened to Cardinal Clarizio and the American at the Basilica?"

"Certain people in Milites Christi seem to look on Falconi's death as God's work for some reason. My cousin was talking to a very powerful member who hinted that perhaps God needed some help in calling the bishop to heaven, but it was all very vague."

Bisleti listened impatiently. The cardinal needed facts, not more ambiguity. "What else did your cousin say?"

"A very private meeting of some of the most powerful members of Milites Christi from around the world will be held in two days. They remain in Rome after the investiture specifically for this meeting. The whole business is so secretive that he was lucky to be told that much."

"Where will they meet?"

"Via Christi."

"Your cousin won't be invited?"

"No. This is only for very, very big guys from Europe, Latin America, and the States."

Bisleti listened with excitement. The cardinal and Kelly had told him about a group of Milites Christi titans getting out of control. Could it be these men? "It would be nice to be a fly on the wall at one of those meetings," Bisleti motioned.

Zoppa gave him an amused look. "Perhaps that is possible."

"How?"

"We may have a fly there."

"Who?"

"Remember Ruggieri? Vincenzo Ruggieri?"

Bisleti scowled. "Of course. I still run into him occasionally. The man is a swine, but he deludes many people."

"My cousin says that Ruggieri has insinuated himself with this group of powerful Milites Christi members. He is so well thought of that he too will be in attendance. They actually trust him."

Zoppa laughed and Bisleti joined him. Both shared the same thought. Sound judgment rarely flows from wealth and power.

"So?" Bisleti motioned.

"He turned to us a while ago and was true to his nature. He never fulfilled his side of the bargain. It would not be hard for me to find out what transpires at the meeting . . . and whether he knows anything about Falconi or your cardinal."

Bisleti looked at Zoppa for a long moment. He knew the methods by which his friend extracted information. Could he condone such activity, even in a case such as this? He smiled slightly. When going through the seminary, he often thought the questions about moral ambiguity lacked a basis in reality. The world wasn't ideal. Saints never outnumbered sinners.

"Do what it takes," Bisleti motioned. He shrugged. He already had so much time to spend in purgatory that a little more probably wouldn't make that much difference.

While Bisleti made his rationalizations, Kevin Kelly walked across the campus of Fatima College, a beautiful little school in Westchester, about an hour's drive from St. Mary's Church in Harlem. The institution was one of the small Catholic women's schools that had managed somehow to survive relatively intact the social and financial turmoil of the 1960s, 1970s, and 1980s. The majority of the girls who walked the paths of the parklike campus and hallways of the Tudor buildings struck Kelly as well-scrubbed throwbacks to what their mothers must have been in the 1950s and early 1960s. Plaid skirts, pastel angora sweaters, and pearls were still de rigueur.

He'd done what he could for the time being about locating the people who'd found Carter's body. Rather than anxiously wait by the phone, he decided to kill part of the day by moving on another matter that bothered him.

A nun at the administration building directed him to Joe Devine's office on the third floor of the main hall. When he got there, the teacher's door was open, and as he approached the doorway, Kelly realized Devine was talking with a student. Kelly moved back a discreet distance. A few minutes later, Devine said loudly, "I hope everything turns out okay, Ginny." A young girl clutching books to her chest hurried out.

Kelly rapped on the door and entered. "Joe, how are you?"

"Good, Kevin," he said while he stood and shook hands. "Well, pretty good."

The tall, thin priest grimaced and took his seat again, motioning Kelly into one on the other side of his desk. He tipped his wooden chair back so it leaned against the wall. "It's tougher being young today. There are so many murky issues to deal with."

"What do you mean?"

"Girls stream through here asking about the morality of the pill, diaphragms, and condoms, and fearful they might have AIDS." Devine paused. "There are girls who want abortions or worry about drugs. Others are dating guys who are divorced. Others want to know what's so terrible about somebody's being gay."

Listening, Kelly wryly realized how wrong he'd been. These students weren't clones of their mothers. They were children of the sexual revolution. He didn't envy Devine's having to deal with a school full of bright young women asking questions that priests had a tough time answering among themselves.

"Like a lot of priests, I can't bring myself to spout the party line," Devine said with exasperation. "So, I leave a lot of issues up to their own consciences."

"I usually do the same thing," Kelly said. "It's a lot of years since answers were found in the Baltimore Catechism."

"But it's a cop-out, Kevin. People come looking for answers to the problems torturing them and we throw them back on themselves."

Kelly shrugged. "Sometimes telling people to accept responsibility for their actions isn't all that bad."

"And how many angels can dance on the head of a pin?" Devine said with a derisive laugh. "Don't mind me. I haven't seen you in ages, and what do I do but rant about issues that confound theologians."

Kelly remembered Devine as a tense man with a rueful sense of humor. In Vietnam, he was like a hummingbird the way he hovered around nervously as he tried to get something done. Kelly had never seen a man less patient with military red tape. Now he was impatient with the Church's trying to fit a messy world into ironclad doctrine.

"So you want to pump me about my seeing Bill Witten, huh?" Devine said.

"When did you see him?"

"Last Thursday."

Kelly felt uneasy. That was the day before Damian Carter was killed. Could there be a link? He brushed the preposterous notion from his mind. "Where did you run into him?"

"At JFK Airport. I was waiting for my sister to come in from London."

"You're sure it was Witten?"

"Certain."

"Why?"

"I had just arrived in Rome for a doctoral program at the North American College when Bill first came over. We both lived at Casa Santa Maria and spent a fair amount of time together playing tennis and going to restaurants. He helped me with a lot of my course work. We got to know each other pretty well."

Devine's brow furrowed. "I never did believe all those stories about suicide. He just wasn't the type."

"To play doubting Thomas for a minute, how are you so sure it was him you saw? It's been a lot of years. We all change."

"He looked pretty much the same. More mature and like the rest of us, getting gray, but in very good shape. Bill was quite an athlete and took care of himself."

"Did you talk to him?"

"I approached him, but when he saw me, he looked very uncomfortable and walked away very quickly. Obviously, he did not want to talk. My sister's flight arrived. I didn't see him again."

The two reminisced about Vietnam for a while before Kelly got up to leave. "Joe, if you happen to see him or hear anything else about him, please let me know. I'm at St. Mary's in Harlem."

As he walked out of Devine's office, Kelly wished the ex-chaplain had more to go on. He thought how the lives of the Trinity seemed weirder all the time. Weird and sad. One dead. One missing. One under investigation.

Hogan had managed to arrange for Damian Carter's funeral Mass to be celebrated at St. Pat's. He could imagine how much crow Pat must have swallowed for Cardinal Murray to have let him hold the Mass at the cathedral. Now here was this Witten business. He didn't know what to make of it. Hell, Devine hadn't even talked to the guy, yet he was positive he'd seen him. That held as much water as a UFO sighting.

Driving back, Kelly thought maybe Devine just wanted to believe he saw Witten because he had never accepted his friend's suicide. Then maybe not. The man was far from being a fool. Where did he get the audacity to make snap psychological judgments about Devine?

At St. Mary's, Tim Brady wasn't around, so Kelly checked the calls on the answering machine, a nerve-racking litany of suffering parishioners. A welfare mother with three sick kids had run out of money and had nowhere to turn. A family had been burned out and needed a place to stay. A woman wanted Brady to try to talk her son out of becoming a crack dealer. Kelly found himself thinking of the bingo games he ran in Brooklyn. At least bingo players were relatively happy.

Toward the end of the calls was one from Pat Hogan. Kelly had a moment of disgust when he thought of everything he had learned about the man, but he called back. Maybe Hogan knew by now what he had come across. "What's up, Pat?"

"Can we get together this evening? It's important."

Kelly agreed, while his stomach roiled.

On the way to the TV studio, Kelly decided not to mention the business about Witten. Nothing was certain, and Hogan would have a tough enough time dealing with Carter's death. For the same reason, he couldn't bring himself to mention his interview with Franny Cook or that it was her boyfriend who had jumped Hogan. Nor, he thought, could he bring up Connie Robbins.

Was it compassion for Hogan's suffering for his friend, he wondered, that made him want to hold back? Was it his own troubling relationship with Lane Woods? By the time he reached Hogan's dressing room, he found it difficult to meet Hogan's gaze when Hogan opened the door.

"Kevin, I won't insult you by asking how your investigation is going," Hogan said, closing the door behind Kelly.

"Drop it, Pat. Just let me say again how sorry I am about Damian's death."

Hogan rubbed his face wearily. "Thanks. I will miss him very, very much." Almost inaudibly, he added, "So very, very much." The

269

monsignor fixed his eyes on Kelly. "My asking to see you must have disturbed you, and I'm sorry. This has nothing to do with me or whatever the Church decides to do with me. Damian is the reason I asked you to come."

Kelly gave him a curious look as Hogan walked to his dressing table and picked up a white envelope.

"I want you to read this," Hogan said, handing over the envelope.

Kelly accepted it and extracted a letter to Hogan from Carter. It was dated the day before Carter was killed. He glanced over at Hogan, who sat down before a mirror, put a towel around his neck, and began applying makeup for his show. He remembered reading somewhere that Hogan never let the professional makeup people fuss over him.

"Go ahead, read it," Hogan said, returning his look in the mirror. "You won't disturb me."

"Okay," Kelly replied, feeling ghoulish. It was like reading a letter from the grave.

Dear Pat,

Our last meeting left me ashamed. I should have come back or called you. You know I would never do anything to hurt you.

In any event, I have enclosed a copy of the material I told you Falconi gave me. I told you it is in Latin. In another era, it would have been absurd for a priest not to know enough Latin to go through a document. So much for progress. I'm trying to reach our favorite Latin scholar to translate it. I will give this to him tomorrow. Other than you, he is the only one I trust with it.

How is Kevin Kelly's investigation going? Poor Kelly. He tried to reach me, but pardon the impertinence, I have a few more important matters on my agenda at the moment than extolling your virtues. Your biggest failing is your standing by a friend who sometimes is in need of common sense. That and your ability to recognize the Church's imperfections while seeing the strengths that have kept Her going these two thousand years. Sometimes I envy you that ability, but not always. It breeds complacency. It's still not too late to join those trying to make a better world and a better Church.

This may seem odd, but you may want to have Kelly help you determine what to do with the Falconi

*information. Kelly is more than meets the eye. Some of my
sources happen to know about his roots. You have no
amateur chasing your shadows. But enough said. From my
muddled reading, the Falconi material is explosive. I will
know just how volatile right after our friend translates it.*

*Let's hope this makes amends for some of the
embarrassment I have caused you over the years. A man
has never had a better friend than you.*

Keep the faith,

Damian

Hogan glanced over at Kelly, who caught his eye and stared back
with a perplexed look. "I'm not going to ask what Damian learned
about your background. That's not important. However, the material
he sent along may well be. Maybe I should give it to Murray or
someone else in authority, but I am entrusting it to you because
Damian thought I should."

Hogan stood and walked to his overcoat hanging on the back of
the door. Kelly's excitement mounted as the monsignor extracted a
sheaf of papers and an envelope from an inside pocket, turned, and
handed them to him.

"Thanks, Pat," Kelly said, aching to look at them.

"Damian told me about this the last time we met," Hogan said.
"I'm afraid I was very skeptical. Part of me still is. One of Damian's
missions in life seemed to be to involve me in certain misadventures.
Perhaps to keep me humble."

"This time it looks as if Damian was right, Pat. He did get whatever
it is from Falconi, and it may well be explosive."

Hogan's face relaxed a bit for the first time during the evening.
"Wouldn't it be wonderful if Damian was vindicated?" he said. "Perhaps all his atonement meant something after all."

Before Kelly could ask him what he meant, Hogan looked at his
watch. "Sorry, Kevin, I have to go. If you want to stay around, we
can get something to eat after the show."

"No thanks, Pat," Kelly said. "I've got to get back."

Leaving Hogan's dressing room, Kelly made his way toward the
exit, but changed his mind. He turned and walked in the direction of
the XTV news set. The evening news program was over. One of the
show's coanchors was reading copy from an AP wire machine. Other

271

newspeople were talking to one another about which shots were best for different stories. Kelly approached the anchor.

"Pardon me, is Lane Woods around?"

The man looked at Kelly and then at his collar. "She'll be back in a few minutes, Father. Why don't you wait."

"Maybe another time," Kelly said.

"Who shall I say dropped by?"

Kelly paused for a second before replying. "Don't," he said. "Maybe I'll come by again."

No, I won't, he ordered himself as he walked away, feeling more foolish than ever.

"Kevin!"

Kelly turned and saw Lane rushing up to him. She grabbed him by the arm. "Let me get my coat and I'll be right with you."

A few minutes later, they were on Sixth Avenue. "You hungry?" Kelly asked.

"Famished." She took his arm again and stepped into the street to hail a cab. "I know a little place on the West Side."

Once they were seated in the restaurant, Lane gazed across the table at Kelly. "Are we still working together, Father Kelly?"

"I am if you are." He started telling her about his visit from Urizor, and he told her about the document Hogan gave him.

Throughout dinner, they skirted anything personal and discussed the implications of a killer being at Via Christi, wondering if this priest had killed Damian as well as Bishop Falconi. Whenever he found himself staring at her, Kelly averted his eyes, reminding himself of their last conversation, trying to find an equilibrium when around her.

Suddenly, Lane leaned across the table, her brow furrowed. "It was stupid of me to have called out to you."

"It was dumb of me to drop by your news show."

"Kevin, when a woman reaches my age and she's unmarried, she's often had a lot of sexual involvements she'd rather not think about. I like you and I know you like me. We haven't even been to bed together, but I feel that I know you better than most men I've known."

She looked away. "I don't want to add one more disastrous relationship to my unlucky charm bracelet. It wouldn't be fair to either of us. I . . . I've got to know where you stand."

Listening to her with a sinking sensation, Kelly wished he had the guts to have stayed away from her. In her presence, he felt unsure

272

about everything, confronted with impossible choices. He wanted to cling to the priesthood and he wanted her.

"My God, Lane," he said. "I can't kid myself, and I'm not going to lie to you. You overwhelm me. I remember what I gave up when I'm around you, and I'm no longer certain it's worth it."

As she Looked down at the table and thought about what she'd last said to him in Rome, her eyes filled with sadness at her lack of resolve. Her words were barely audible. "I don't have a segment on the late news tonight. I'm going home now. You can come back if you want."

On the subway back to St. Mary's, Kelly was in turmoil. He was a lot later returning than he had expected. To divert his mind from Lane Woods, he anxiously took out the material Hogan had given him. He felt more frustrated as he skimmed the document. His Latin was too rusty to get the gist of the report. Slipping the envelope into his inside coat pocket, he thanked God again for John Gibbons. If the bishop was available, he'd get the document to him tomorrow.

Exiting the subway, he swiftly left behind the lighted stores along Broadway. Walking in the darkness, he was lost in thought. The document concerned the pope, but he didn't get much more out of it than that. Why did Falconi give it to Carter? What was so important that two men died?

He was jostled and looked up startled, balling his hands into fists. A large black wearing an old army field jacket stared back just as surprised.

"Sorry," the man muttered, just as Kelly said the same thing.

Watching the man's retreating back, Kelly realized how tense he was. He felt like an ass for having dropped his guard. Around here, that could make the difference between life and death. He quickly scanned the terrain. The streetlights were broken, making it difficult to see. The derelict houses and apartments appeared empty. A dozen or so people were lined up outside a boarded-over building across the street. A crack parade.

He moved on warily. The rectory was only another three blocks. Once again he wondered how Tim Brady did it, living in the midst of such desolation and hopelessness. Brady had been pastor of St. Mary's for the last eight years, a job with no grounds for optimism.

273

The neighborhood got worse and worse, and hopelessness took its toll. The old lived in terror. More and more mothers were junkies. The young died of AIDS or overdoses or were gunned down by drug dealers' outlaw justice. Where did Tim get the fortitude to go on?

As a priest, Kelly had never had to deal with the worst of the human condition. His first parish was a mostly blue-collar, Italian neighborhood in the Carroll Gardens section of Brooklyn. The people worked hard, their houses were well maintained, and the neighborhood, largely because some mafiosi were parishioners, was drug free. He was sorry when he left to earn a master's degree in business administration at Stanford. Ever since, he had had no parish assignment but lent his business background to pastors at a wide variety of churches. There were many times when he missed parish work. What he could do at St. Mary's made him feel more like a priest than his work as a financial consultant did.

A priest, he thought. A priest. How could he remain a priest when he felt the way he did about Lane? He felt guilty about rejecting her tonight, but what else could he do? How had his life suddenly become such a quagmire?

Kelly suddenly realized why Brady stayed on in this parish. Everything was clear-cut. The man truly followed Christ. He sacrificed his life in hopes of making other people's lives a little better.

Someone was hurrying along behind him. The desolate look on Lane's face when he'd left her came to mind as he moved to the inside of the pavement. How could he have let things get so out of hand? How could he have hurt her like that? Suddenly, pain exploded in his head and he staggered. Before he could turn, he was hit again. Losing consciousness, Kelly toppled to the ground.

A few minutes later, he heard voices that seemed to be very far away but suddenly grew very close. His head was pounding, and he couldn't make out right away what they were saying.

"Oh, Christ, it's that priest from St. Mary's," one voice said.

Kelly opened his eyes and stared into a beam of light. He knocked the flashlight so that the light moved out of his face. He sat up and felt his head, which was sticky with blood. "Who are you?" he rasped.

The flashlight moved and played on two men who stood over him. He caught their faces, blue uniforms, gun belts, and badges.

"Nick DiProspero, Father. We met when you were with that hit-and-run victim on Lenox Avenue. This here is Sergeant Dickson."

"What happened?" Kelly asked.

274

"We were driving by when we saw a guy mug you," Dickson said. "He got away."

DiProspero helped him to his feet. "You feel okay?" he asked. "Want to go to the hospital?"

"No. No thanks."

"What's missing, Father?" the sergeant asked.

Kelly checked his wallet, watch, and cash in his pants pocket. "Nothing."

"Strange," Dickson said. "He was going over you pretty good."

"Damn," Kelly muttered, reaching into his coat pocket. There was a rip in the lining. With relief, he felt the smoothness of the envelope far down inside. Inadvertently, the Falconi file had slipped through the tear in the lining. His only precaution was an accident, he thought ruefully while berating himself for being stupid and careless.

"Think you could identify him?" DiProspero asked.

"I never saw him."

"You want to file a complaint?" the sergeant asked.

"Would it do any good?"

Dickson held open the back door of their squad car. "Come on, Father," DiProspero said. "I know it's only a couple more blocks to St. Mary's. But around here, a few blocks might as well be a million miles."

"Strange nothing was taken," Dickson said again during the ride.

Kelly didn't answer. He thought he knew why. The guy didn't find what he wanted. It made sense. Kelly thought about having been followed in Rome. Why wouldn't he be tailed here? He gingerly felt his head again, and it dawned on him how much he'd forgotten. His timing, thought processes, and reactions were all off. He realized how long he'd been a priest.

When he entered the rectory, Kelly found himself alone. Brady was out sacrificing himself to the neighborhood. He went to the kitchen and poured a stiff drink before going into the pastor's office and dialing John Gibbons's number.

The bishop picked up on the third ring.

"John, it's Kevin," he said, briefly explaining what he had, trying it to the deaths in Rome and here. He didn't mention the attack on himself tonight.

"Do you have time to translate this thing?"

"Don't be preposterous," Gibbons said irately. "You don't have a fax machine there do you?"

"No."

"Then fax it down tomorrow morning," he said, giving Kelly a fax number at his university office.

"Thanks, John. Oh, I forgot to tell you that I talked to Joe Devine."

"Do you believe him?"

"I'm from Missouri."

Before turning in, Kelly hid the report under a floorboard in an unused room. If anyone broke in, they'd have to tear the house down before they found it.

Connie Robbins luxuriated in the oversize bathtub and wondered if Cal knew she was having an affair. And if so, with whom. She decided no on both counts. Vincenzo was very, very discreet, and for that she was most grateful. But even if Cal saw him in bed with her, he might put it down to some strange ecclesiastic ritual of which he was unaware, rather than believe she bedded a priest.

Still, she wondered why Cal was behaving so bizarrely. He was going out at odd times of the night and not breathing a word about it to her. Usually, he nattered on and on about things that she didn't understand and cared about even less, even going into detail with her about *his* liaisons, as though seeking her goddamn approval.

What Connie found most annoying was that she had expected him to go back to New York right after the investiture. He wasn't crazy about Rome and was usually itchy after being here a few days. She had looked forward to his departure, so she could spend more time with Ruggieri. What was exasperating was that he showed no sign of wanting to leave.

She wondered if she should break it off now with the little monsignor before there was any chance of things getting messy. They had only been together a few times, and she had no illusions about him. He was a taker. Pure and simple.

Climbing out of the tub, she realized that she had yet to gain precious little insight into his character. She wrinkled her nose. Lack of character was more like it. Their relationship was based on a simple bargain. She paid for everything. He worked his magic in bed. Despite the warmth of the room, she shivered.

While drying off, she examined her body in the full-length mirror on the back of the bathroom door. She thought of the monsignor's

276

muscular body and how willingly she submitted to whatever he asked of her. Nude, she entered the bedroom.

"What took you so long?"

Ruggieri's voice made her tremble. Her attention was riveted on his black cassock folded neatly on a chair and his clerical collar on the night table. Her hands covered her breasts as she knelt before him and bowed her head.

17

IN WASHINGTON, KELLY WAS STRUCK BY THE INTENSE LOOK ON JOHN
Gibbons's face as the bishop held open the door of his apartment. The
copy of the Falconi document Kelly had faxed to him this morning
was clutched in the bishop's right hand.

"Thanks for catching the last shuttle out," Gibbons said.

"How serious is it?"

"Very serious, Kevin. Very dangerous and damning."

"Don't keep me hanging, John."

Gibbons shook the papers in front of his face. "This is an unsigned
letter to what appears to be select and powerful members of Milites
Christi."

His eyes flashed angrily. "Kevin, they are plotting to have one of
their own men made pope."

Kelly's eyes opened in astonishment. "How the hell could they?"

The bishop started pacing anxiously. "I don't know." He shot
Kelly a puzzled look. "There are vague allusions to some action being
taken soon that will move this along. They go on and on about it in
general terms. That and a lot of the usual nonsense about corruption

279

and rottenness in the Church and the world at large, and them stuck with the job of saving both."

"Who's their papal candidate?" Kelly asked.

"It's not in here. But the document lists churchmen who are at least sympathetic to Milites Christi. A fair number of the American hierarchy fall into that category."

The bishop's indignation rekindled as he looked again at the names on the list. "I *knew* Milites Christi had gained the support of a some influential members of the clergy, even a few in the Curia. But this list shows they've made greater headway than I thought. Too many churchmen simply see Milites Christi as representing generosity, devoutness, and old-fashioned, law-and-order religion. They don't take the time to examine what the organization really stands for, and they'd be hard-pressed to get much information if they tried."

Gibbons threw the document on a table in front of him. "Damned secret societies shouldn't be permitted in the Church."

"How can they talk about a pope at this stage of the game?" Kelly asked.

Gibbons's voice lowered. "Not too many people know this, Kevin, but the pope is ill. Seriously ill. There is speculation that he might not pull through."

"So they've got it all figured out," Kelly said quietly. "They have their candidate in place, ready to spring him at the right moment."

Gibbons looked over at Kelly. "What kind of man do you think they chose?"

Kelly mulled over the question for a moment. "He would not be one of the few members of the hierarchy who are openly proselytizing for Milites Christi."

"Why not?"

"Such a man would be considered too fanatical by the rest of the hierarchy. No. My bet is that he's a bishop or a cardinal who was once greatly respected but now is out of favor."

"Like Lucifer," Gibbons muttered. "What's your reasoning?" he asked more clearly.

Kelly rubbed his hands across his eyes. "That's the kind of guy Milites Christi could flatter while he licks his wounds and resents the pope."

"What else?"

"He'd have to be well-known and acceptable to most of the hierarchy, especially the Americans since we have so much financial clout at the Vatican. The way he screwed up would have to be a matter of interpretation. The pope has trimmed the sails of many members of the hierarchy over the years. Many of them would sympathize with someone the pope is down on."

Gibbons appreciated how well Kelly crystallized his thinking. It made sense. "When are you seeing Clarizio?"

"Tomorrow morning. I faxed him a copy of Falconi's report when I sent you one. Is there anything else I should flag for him?"

"I've saved the most alarming news for last," Gibbons said grimly.

"What?"

"There are references to using 'Holy Force' to achieve their aims."

Kelly remembered the phrase from Martin's summary. "I've seen the term, but I'm not sure what it means."

"Perez meant it as legitimate pressure on the state to gain measures to proselytize Christianity. When he was alive, Milites Christi backed various politicians and received trade-offs in terms of educational funding, construction programs, what have you. Since his death, the term has taken on a more sinister connotation. For some members of Milites Christi, 'Holy Force' is a euphemism for illegitimate and, I believe, occasionally brutal methods of getting what they want. Of course, it's all done in the name of God."

"How do you know?" Kelly asked, thinking again how anemic Martin's analysis was.

Gibbons quit pacing about the living room, momentarily indecisive about how he should answer. He finally decided that Kelly had come this far. He had to take him further.

"Please don't mention this to anyone, Kevin," the bishop said. "For the past eight months, I have been part of a secret papal commission investigating Milites Christi's activities in this country. I have counterparts in other countries."

The bishop sat on the sofa and stared at Kelly. "Mostly, we interview past members to see how the organization operates. We want to determine Milites Christi's budget, recruiting policies, donations, the names of clergy and laymen who are sympathetic to the movement. Ultimately, we want to ascertain how much of a treat they pose to the Church. A major area of investigation is Holy Force. How it is used and why. When we finish, there will be a comprehensive report on the organization."

"One the pope can use when the time is right?"

"I assume so."

281

"What examples of Holy Force have you come across?"

Gibbons grimaced and paused again. He stared intently at Kelly. "You for one."

"What are you talking about, John?"

"That food poisoning during the early stage of your investigation of Carruthers."

"You mean it wasn't an accident?"

"No."

"Damn," Kelly whispered.

The bishop continued angrily, "The pope had questioned Carruthers about the rumors surrounding him, but the cardinal tried to outfox him. He publicly expressed sympathy for Milites Christi and then acted as if the pope were persecuting him for it. Suddenly, a lot of powerful people, who appear to be part of Milites Christi's most fanatical wing, spoke up in Rome on his behalf. He must have thought the pope wouldn't want to offend those people by going after one of their most important ecclesiastic supporters. Instead, the pope became furious and ordered the investigation you headed. When you started, boom, suddenly you were laid up with food poisoning. A faction of Milites Christi took credit for it."

While listening, Kelly began feeling more manipulated than ever. How big a role had Gibbons played in his being involved in all of this? Had the bishop involved him in the Carruthers investigation? How about the Hogan business? Who put Clarizio on to his background, if not Gibbons? Why had he been kept in the dark about so damn much?

His shock over the possibility of danger to the pope forced him to set aside his anger. Calm down, he ordered himself. Now isn't the time.

"Do you know the major figures behind this fanatical wing?" he asked.

"No. All we know is that they are the ones who received the material Falconi got his hands on. What we do know is that they call themselves the Apostles."

"Do you think they had Falconi and Carter killed?" Kelly asked.

"A strong possibility, but there's no proof."

Kelly tried to absorb everything he was just told. He reached in his pocket and popped a Tums in his mouth as his stomach started boiling. "Are they true believers or simply cynics using Milites Christi as a front?"

282

Gibbons shook his head disgustedly. "If they were just cynics, it would be easier to take. From what little we know, they are believers who each give millions to Milites Christi. They are fanatics, Kevin, who delude themselves into believing that evil somehow can beget good."

The bishop grew angrier as he continued. "They're like a bunch of bastardized Nietzscheans. As far as I can tell, they see themselves as 'supermen' who are above the common herd and capable of creating their own moral order. They elevate ruthlessness to a virtue. You can't tell where men like that will stop to get what they want."

The next morning Cardinal Clarizio sat at his desk in his office at the Vatican mission in Washington. Silver sunlight streamed through the window behind him and warmed his neck and back, taking away some of the ache his bones felt during winter and early-spring months. He wished Paolo had accompanied him back. Bisleti, the only one on his staff in whom he confided, had remained in Rome in anticipation of getting more information about Milites Christi. Paolo could make himself unobtrusive. As he slipped through corridors and lingered near doorways, he learned things that were not meant to be overheard.

Clarizio's thoughts were interrupted by his secretary. "Father Kelly is here, Eminenza."

"Show him in, Enrico," he said, and rose from his desk.

A moment later, Kelly entered and knelt to kiss the cardinal's ring. "Please, have a seat, Father, and tell me what you have learned."

For the next five minutes, Clarizio gave the appearance of listening, but in his mind he was mourning the deaths of two priests. He had known for weeks what was in the report. It was he who had Bishop Falconi take the document to Damian Carter. The plan was to use Carter to embarrass Milites Christi when the time was right. To stop this group who called themselves the Apostles. Murder had never crossed his mind!

"Thank you, Father," he said when Kelly concluded. "Once again, I appreciate all you have done."

Twenty minutes later, the cardinal put the finishing touches on the itinerary of the pope's impending trip to the U.S. The task was calming after Kelly's visit and momentarily let him forget the Falconi report, which was locked away in his office safe. When he inevitably thought of it, his guilt returned.

Staring at the pope's itinerary, he didn't feel the sense of satisfaction he usually experienced upon the completion of such a task. He had parceled out His Holiness's presence among the most powerful men in the American hierarchy with the kind of delicacy and skill on which he had built his reputation. The cities' political importance or their vitality as centers of Catholicism guided how much time the pope spent in each.

"Enrico?" Clarizio said in the direction of the open door connecting his secretary's office to his.

A moment later, Monsignor Perdomo appeared in the doorway. "Yes, Eminenza?"

"The pope's itinerary is complete at last. His Holiness has checked and double-checked what I proposed. I have included his alterations. You can now send it in code to each of the archdioceses involved."

Perdomo approached Clarizio's glistening chestnut desk and paused before taking the paper from the cardinal's outstretched hand. "I . . . uh," he stammered.

Clarizio looked up irritably. "What is it?"

Lately, he found Perdomo coming up short. He was mopey, distracted. Simple tasks seemed to be too much for him. When Clarizio asked him if there was anything wrong, his reply was always negative. This simply wasn't working out. The man left his mind somewhere. Perhaps he should start looking for someone else. Now, he resented the way Perdomo didn't reply but stood staring at him, tongue tied like a simpleton.

"Just do it, Enrico!" Clarizio said in exasperation.

The secretary flushed. "Yes, Eminenza."

Perdomo took the document and left so quickly he seemed to be fleeing. Clarizio's vexation changed to concern as he looked after him, wondering if he should insist that Perdomo see a doctor. When he accepted the itinerary, the young man's hand trembled.

When he returned to St. Mary's that evening, Kelly was barely in the door when the phone rang. Brady wasn't around, so he answered.

"Hello. St. Mary's."

"Father Kelly?"

"Yes."

"This is Franny Cook. I . . . I'm very sorry to disturb you."

"That's okay, Franny," he said, glad that videophones weren't part of life yet, so she couldn't see the dismay on his face. "What can I do for you?"

"I've been trying to reach you for the longest time, but you weren't available." Her words sounded like a reproach.

"I was out of town."

"Oh. . . . I wonder if you would mind coming down. There's . . . there's something I must tell you. I know it's kind of late and you must be very busy. But this is . . . it's important."

Kelly looked at his watch and out of earshot of the receiver muttered, "Damn it." It was after eight. He had hoped to settle in for the night. "About an hour?"

"Thank you," she said. "I knew you couldn't say no."

As he hung up, the whole conversation struck Kelly as strange. What information could she possibly have that she hadn't told him? "She probably has videotapes," he growled. He got his coat back on, climbed upstairs, and stuffed his small tape recorder into his coat pocket.

A little less than an hour later, he pressed the bell of her apartment and she buzzed him inside.

"I knew you would come to me," she said when he reached her landing. She wore black tights and a pale blue T-shirt. Her hair was undone and streaming over her shoulders.

When he looked at her expression, Kelly became uncomfortable. More a smirk than a smile. Besides her peculiar greeting, the look in her eyes was odder yet, as she tried to hold his gaze longer than necessary. Suddenly, she glanced down at her T-shirt and leotards. "I just came in from my aerobics class when I called you."

Without another word, she turned around and led the way to her studio apartment. Following, Kelly couldn't help noticing that, without the camouflage of baggy clothing, she was fuller figured than he had realized. Something else was apparent now that she was unswaddled. The little Catholic maiden moved with the sensuous grace of a Saigon hooker.

Alarm bells went off in his head. Watch your step, Kevin. Watch your step.

285

When she closed the door behind him, the apartment was as dim as before. Once again there was an open wine bottle on the floor and two goblets. Tensely, Kelly took the chair he'd sat in previously.

Franny sat on the floor and poured him a glass of wine. She remained kneeling as she held it out to him, one of her breasts touching Kelly's right knee. She was braless and he felt the hardness of her nipple through his pant leg. He shifted his leg.

She smiled and sat back on the floor. "Where have you been?"

"Rome."

"I'd love to go to Rome," she said dreamily. "I'd love to see the Vatican and the ruins. It must be wonderful."

"I didn't have much time to sightsee."

Franny held her wineglass in front of her eyes when she looked again at the priest. "Lane was there too, wasn't she?"

Kelly gazed at her steadily. "Yes, yes, she was. She was covering the investiture of the new cardinals."

"Did you see her while you were there, Kevin? Do you mind if I call you Kevin?"

Kelly was about to tell her, yes, he did mind, but he just wanted to hear what she had to say so he could get back to the rectory. "Okay, call me Kevin. And yes, I did run into Miss Woods several times over there."

"I know," Franny said, stretching out on the floor. "She told me. Then she started asking me all kinds of questions about priests."

Kelly put on a blank face and looked at his watch.

"Like how easy is it for them to leave the priesthood. That kind of thing." She raised the glass in front of her eyes again and added, "She especially wanted to know how serious it is if a priest goes to bed with a woman." She smiled mischievously. "I guess she was wondering about Pat, huh?"

"I wouldn't know. Look, Franny, it's getting late. Why did you ask me down here?"

She knelt in front of him again and suddenly raised her T-shirt over her head, exposing her breasts. "I can be better to you than Lane," she whispered.

Kelly took the flimsy shirt from her hand and covered her with it. "Please, put this back on, Franny."

Struggling to his feet, Kelly felt outraged as something suddenly became very clear. His anger turned to disgust at what she had done,

286

not to him, but to Hogan. Turning people against him. Damaging someone's reputation.

"You never slept with Pat, did you?"

Dropping the shirt again, she rose, slipping off her leotards so that she was nude when she stood in front of him. "Don't be afraid, Father. Pat was a coward. He wanted to. You want to. Don't be afraid."

Kelly suddenly became concerned. "You need help, Franny. Let me put you in touch with somebody."

She shook her head sadly. "That's what Pat said. But you are just afraid. Don't be afraid of what you want. What you need."

Kelly forced himself to be calm. "Why did you try to hurt Pat by telling people those stories?"

Suddenly, she appeared confused. "I . . . I didn't mean to hurt him. He liked me. I know he liked me. I want you to like me."

She stepped back, trembling. "Why are you so afraid of me?"

Not knowing what else to do, Kelly edged to the door. "I'll call you tomorrow after I find someone you can talk to."

"Where are you going?" she demanded.

He didn't answer.

"You leave and I'll tell on you," she said dully. "I'll tell them what you did to me. I'll tell, you'll see."

Kelly quietly shut the door, wondering who could help her and how? She was so locked up in some fantasy that she wasn't capable of comprehending what she was doing or all the harm she had caused.

As Kelly boarded a subway car, it was twenty after three in the morning in Rome. A weary Monsignor Ruggieri nosed his Porsche through the gates of Via Christi and waved to the guard. He shrugged to ease the tension knotting his shoulders.

"What a night," he said, and gave a strained laugh.

The meeting had gone better than he had anticipated. A major decision was made, and that was the important thing, he told himself. Yet, when he thought of the magnitude of the plan that was adopted, he shivered and swallowed nervously. There could be no turning back.

He had been amazed at how many of the Apostles readily embraced the plan. That had stunned him, and Ruggieri knew he wasn't squeamish. As expected, some of those in attendance were initially

287

shocked and frightened by the proposal, but after hours of intense debate, they had all acquiesced. Of course, no one preferred such a drastic solution, but extreme action had to be taken for the good of the Church. That was the determining argument. Still, Ruggieri was awed by what they had decided. He was astonished when he thought of what he stood to gain.

"Holy Mother Church, you will do well by your Vincenzo."

He felt so drained that it was all he could do to keep his eyes on the road. He decided to sleep late and cancel his noon rendezvous with the Robbins woman. That was a dying ember anyway. She had a certain charm, but she had served her purpose. Was there anything else he could get from her? Was there anything else he wanted? She had given him her body, a little money, and her husband. That was enough. He wasn't greedy. How would he break it off? He yawned and abandoned such thoughts. There was no rush.

Turning a curve in the road, a black limousine overtook his Porsche. Once in front of him, the limo slowed. He tried to get by, but every time he did, the limo veered to the left or right, blocking him. Finally, his car was forced over to the side of the road. The limo came to a stop diagonally in front of him, preventing Ruggieri from driving away.

For a moment, he was tempted to try to back up and turn around. Fatalistically, he realized that would be useless. If they had waited for him to leave Via Christi, they knew his movements. It might be worse if they had to chase him. He climbed out of his car and greeted the burly man approaching him.

"Good morning," he said.

"Come with me," the man replied. "Your car will be taken care of."

Ruggieri followed as the man walked back to the limousine and opened the back door for him. The monsignor stepped into the rear and he almost felt relieved. He had been expecting this meeting for months.

"How are you, Vittorio?"

"Good, Vincenzo. Better now that you are so near me."

The door closed and the limo glided into the night.

That afternoon, Connie Robbins checked her watch again and felt foolish. Rapidly, she paced up and down in the suite at Trastevere and paused only to take another glass of wine. The day was full of the unexpected. First Cal this morning, after staying out until some ungodly hour, had acted so strangely, saying he had to go home right away, almost as if he were afraid of something. Looking at her watch again, she realized Cal was already somewhere over the Atlantic.

Now Vincenzo was more than two hours late. He had gone to the same damn meeting that Cal attended and should have had the decency to call if he wanted to sleep late or if something came up. By the time she drove back to Rome, her whole day would be ruined.

"Damn it," she muttered, and arched her neck as she studied her face in the mirror, looking for signs of age.

Admitting to herself that the affair had run its course, she wished Ruggieri had the nerve to confront her and tell her how he felt. She had misjudged him. Usually, priests were so guilt ridden that they hid like children when they could no longer go on with a liaison. There had seemed to be none of that in the little monsignor. But obviously there was. She smiled wryly. He was more a priest than he realized.

As she prepared to leave, she took another sip of wine and glanced around the room. Suddenly, she felt hollow. Why was she even here? Why was so much missing from her life? Why did she feel so lonely lately, so utterly alone?

She realized, of course, that these were basic life issues that she should be dealing with in a better fashion. But how? Whom could she turn to? A priest? She laughed mirthlessly.

Settling into the driver's seat of the Jag ten minutes later, Connie wondered if her life with Cal would have turned out differently if they had been able to have children. Perhaps she should have married someone she loved. She sighed and the corners of her mouth curled down. No use crying over spilt milk, dearie, she told herself. Putting on her sunglasses, she started the engine and headed up the driveway.

Five minutes later, a gust of cold air bit her face as she concentrated on gunning the Jag into a hairpin curve. She stopped thinking of what might have been. If she complied all the qualifiers in her life, the list would go on forever.

❋

Enrico Perdomo stood at the front door of Royal Oaks when Father Bisleti arrived. With a hasty nod, he took the priest directly to the second-floor study where Cardinal Clarizio awaited him. Perdomo was burning with curiosity. The cardinal was so tense. Repeatedly during the past few hours, Clarizio had asked when Bisleti's plane was due to arrive. Anxiety wasn't like him.

This morning Bisleti had sent a message to Clarizio, using the secret code the two men used only with one another. Now, Bisleti was hurrying so much he almost tripped on Perdomo's heels. What was going on?

As soon as he led Bisleti into the study, Perdomo bowed slightly and murmured, "Eminenza, Paolo is here." Bisleti pushed by him. As he was about to leave, Perdomo was stopped at the doorway.

"Enrico, I would like you to stay. Perhaps you can be of some assistance to me."

The cardinal watched as his secretary came back into the room with an obvious expression of surprise and took a chair a discreet distance from both men. Clarizio wondered if Perdomo's recent lapses were at least in part his own fault. He knew he had been testy lately. He may not have devoted sufficient time to developing the monsignor. Perhaps he should give him more responsibility, make him privy to some of the weighty issues with which churchmen must deal, even the most dreaded.

"Enrico, an issue of vital importance has arisen, and I want you to understand what is happening," the cardinal said. "Later, I may seek your counsel on what we should be doing."

"Yes, Eminenza," the astonished secretary managed to say.

Perdomo riveted his attention on the cardinal. Clarizio turned to Bisleti, who pulled several sheets of paper from his pocket and handed them to the cardinal.

"Thank you, Paolo," Clarizio said.

The cardinal seized the pages and immediately began reading, grateful that his friend and loyal servant had told him earlier that he would write out what he had learned about this despicable business. Clarizio frowned and his hand trembled several times. Occasionally, he glanced uneasily at Bisleti. When finished, he carefully folded the pages and put them up his sleeve.

"Enrico, please get Paolo a pad and pen."

Perdomo hastily retrieved them from the desk and handed them to Bisleti. As he turned to go back to his seat, the cardinal beckoned him to take a chair next to him.

"Enrico, I am going to tell you what Paolo has learned before I ask him any questions. The matter, as you must have gathered, is of great urgency."

Perdomo's eyes never left Clarizio. He managed to keep his demeanor serious, but his heart soared with joy that the cardinal was finally willing to admit him to his confidence on a matter of significance. "Thank you for your trust, Eminenza," he said humbly.

The cardinal sighed and straightened one of the folds in his cassock as he determined where to begin. "The Church is in great danger and the pope is under immediate threat. You, of course, are aware of Milites Christi and some of what the organization does. The pope, as you also know, has not been sympathetic to the aspirations of Milites Christi. What you do not know is that a faction within Milites Christi is plotting to gain control of the papacy."

Clarizio saw the stunning effect his words had on the young man. Perdomo's eyes widened in amazement, but otherwise, he sat so still that he could have been a statue. The cardinal felt sorry for his secretary. No one should have to hear such things could happen within the Church, let alone the dreadful business that he was about to add.

"Yes, it does seem incredible," he went on. "We have known for some time that members of Milites Christi had plans to try to make pope someone in the hierarchy who is attuned to its goals. We assumed that they meant to do this at the next conclave after the pope dies. But that is not the case. Paolo has just learned that they intend to try to . . ."

Clarizio paused and closed his eyes as he spoke the next few words. "They intend to assassinate the pope."

"Oh, my God," Perdomo gasped. "Does the pope know?"

"After I received Paolo's message, I cleared the way for him to see His Holiness."

Clarizio turned back to Bisleti, wondering how he got his hands on this incredible information. "I assume you had no problem?"

Bisleti shook his head no and looked at both men. These past several days he had felt his affliction more acutely than he ever had, even from the first moment he awoke in a hospital bed and was told that he would never be able to speak again. But today he had managed. And he had basked in a glory that he had never thought was possible. He, Paolo Bisleti, who had done so much wrong in his life, was able to be the dutiful servant of the ruler of the Holy Roman Catholic Church. His Holiness himself had thanked him and blessed him.

He had left the Vatican in a state of joy, his heart never lighter, his vision never clearer. He imagined that was much the way the repentant thief who was crucified with Christ must have felt. He could never explain his sense of awe or joy to anyone.

Clarizio perceived what his confidant had no means to say. There was a glow in Paolo's eyes. He himself could imagine how gracious the pope had been. He could also imagine how angry the pope later became by what was told him, and how His Holiness would brave what must be confronted. He worried that the pope was too daring. The pontiff truly acted as if he counted solely upon Divine Providence to safeguard his welfare. Such an attitude simply made his own task that much more difficult.

"There is no timetable here," Clarizio continued. "Yet, we have indications that it will be soon."

Bisleti wrote out, "My sources will find out when and where the assassination attempt is to take place. You and I will immediately be alerted." He handed his note to the cardinal.

"How?"

The priest again wrote quickly. "I have given them our code. If something should happen to me, they will still be able to reach you."

"Very good, Paolo," Clarizio said.

The cardinal turned to Perdomo and handed him the responses Bisleti had written. "Will you please tell Father Kelly what we have learned. Also, be very careful when you do. These assassins are powerful. Don't underestimate them. I want you to call him from my private line. The others may not be safe."

Again Perdomo's eyes widened. "Of course, Eminenza. Of course. When?"

"This evening."

Bisleti hastily wrote something and handed it to Clarizio, who turned once more to his secretary. "When you call Father Kelly, relay a message for him from Paolo. Tell him he is still being followed."

"Of course. Of course," Perdomo replied, feeling vaguely foolish. He stood. "Is there anything else, Eminenza?"

The cardinal looked up at the eager young monsignor and could not help smiling. "Isn't that enough, Enrico?"

"Yes, Eminenza! Yes!" He turned to go and wheeled around. "Thank you for taking me into your confidence, Eminenza."

As he left the study, Perdomo was so overwhelmed that Clarizio had shared this terrible secret with him that he felt like weeping. He fully realized the import of what he had just learned. He was involved in one of those rare moments in history when tragedy looms like a tornado on the horizon and threatens to wreak havoc. The future of the papacy and perhaps the very Church were at stake.

Suddenly, the trepidation he felt was compounded by guilt as thoughts of Ruggieri seared his mind. He felt a sharp pain in his breast. How could he have been so weak? How could he have left himself so open to scandal? Now that he was edging into the inner circle, would his life, instead of bringing honor to the Church and his family, simply be a succession of compromises and betrayals?

"St. Mary's," Kelly answered the phone automatically.

"*Buona sera*, Father Kelly, this is Enrico Perdomo."

A minute later, Kelly pulled on his coat. He walked to a bar a block and a half from the rectory. The noise died when he entered. Nobody turned to look at him, but impassive black faces monitored him in the mirror behind the bar until the bartender smiled and said, "What can I get you, Father Kelly?"

Conversation erupted again like water bursting a dam.

"Nothing, George, thanks. I've got to use your phone. How's your boy?"

"Stayin' out of trouble for a change."

When he was at St. Mary's last year, Kelly had been asked by the bartender to get his son into a Catholic high school. He thought the boy could use a more disciplined environment than that found in public schools. Kelly met with the teenager, finding him bright and articulate and a bit of a wise ass. He saw why the father was concerned. He got the kid into a school.

At the pay phone in the back, he returned Perdomo's call. "Okay, Enrico. What's all the cloak and dagger about?"

Perdomo filled him in on what Bisleti had discovered. As he absorbed the information, Kelly became frightened, and fear always put him in a bad humor. He started taking it out on Perdomo. "Hurry up!" he almost shouted. The man was so damn literal minded that he repeated everything in the minutest detail.

Kelly drummed his fingers on the side of the phone. Toward the end of his briefing, Perdomo added, "There is one last thing. Father Bisleti has a message for you."

"For God's sake, just tell me," Kelly snapped.

The cardinal's secretary remained calm. "Paolo says you were followed from Rome, perhaps by one of the American intelligence agencies that followed you over there."

"Great!" Kelly muttered, wondering who it was and why. The killer? Martin? "Thanks, Enrico. Sorry I was testy."

"Under these circumstances, none of us is himself," Perdomo replied.

As he walked back to the rectory, Kelly thought again about how he been lured into this intrigue through the Hogan investigation and how something was off base from day one. Now, smack up against this assassination craziness, he reached the same conclusion. The Pat Hogan investigation didn't make sense. Lawler's report. Edwards's. None of it. But what about that note about the Trinity? Maguire confirmed that something weird had happened in Washington. Creedy implied as much. But what?

If Clarizio and the pope didn't take the issue directly to Hogan, maybe he should. How else could he find out what the three of them had done? But then he'd just have Hogan's word for it.

It struck him that Hogan was being set up. But why? And who was doing it? He couldn't help thinking that, in some way, it was tied to the plot against the pope.

18

AT SIX-THIRTY THE NEXT MORNING, LANE WOODS SHIVERED HALF IN response to the icy cold and half from being on unfamiliar terrain as she stood on a desolate corner of Third Street and Avenue B in lower Manhattan's Alphabet City. Wind-whipped trash fluttered around the intersection like sick, starving birds. A quarter of the way down the block a homeless man slept in a nest of cardboard, blankets, and plastic bags. Through the grimy window of an abandoned, wheelless school bus across the street, she made out the head of a junkie who was shooting up.

Suddenly, a tall, thin woman with short dark hair and wearing a gray coat and a short blue veil hurried around the corner. "Lane, I'm so sorry to keep you waiting," the woman said. "I worked at St. James's shelter in Brooklyn last night. The bus bringing the homeless back to Manhattan just dropped me off."

Listening to her, Lane felt guilty. Saints still roamed the earth. She herself did nothing for anyone, while this woman devoted twenty-four hours a day to helping the less fortunate. "Sister Mary Joseph, believe, me, you don't have to apologize for anything," she replied.

"I just wish one of the sisters had been there," the Sister of Charity said, taking Lane's arm and guiding her south on Avenue B. "We would never have let them take Damian's body to Corpus Christi. It looks like we have something to hide. The boys who did it were worried that the FBI would use his death against Sanctuary in some way."

Lane knew the fear was well-founded. She had done stories about the FBI's tapping phones, intimidating members of Sanctuary, and breaking into churches and offices of the movement that took in Central Americans who had fled political repression in their homelands but were denied asylum in the U.S. In the past decade, the interfaith Sanctuary members had helped thousands of refugees at great risk to themselves.

"I won't publicize anything until you say it's okay."

Lane had no problem giving her word to the nun. Sister Mary Joseph was only one of dozens of religious who gave her help on stories. Sometimes they were helpful to a fault. She often found such people so naive that she warned them about what *not* to say on the record.

A few minutes later, the nun shoved open a chipped and dented black metal door of what appeared to be an abandoned tenement. The windows were boarded up and graffiti covered the walls. Inside, however, was a beehive of activity. Several nuns, clad in plain dresses, short veils, and crosses around their necks similar to what Sister Mary Joseph wore, darted about. The rest was a sea of brown faces. Children raced around while voices in Spanish and English called after them. Men and women were cleaning up breakfast dished, filling out forms, or sitting in clusters drinking coffee and talking and laughing and listening to the radio.

"Good morning, Sister," a bearded, thickly built young man in his early twenties said. He looked at Lane suspiciously.

"Michael. This is Lane, my reported friend who wants talk to you about Damian. Lane, this is Michael Parker. He's one of our coordinators."

"Lane Woods," Lane said, extending her hand.

"I know who you are," Parker replied, tentatively taking her hand. "When Sister said she wanted to bring a reporter, I didn't know it was you."

"I hope you're not disappointed."

"That remains to be seen."

Lane was accustomed to the suspicion and reluctance to be forthcoming on the part of a lot of activists. "Michael, Sister Mary Joseph and I have a good relationship built on mutual trust. I just hope we can establish that kind of trust between us."

"We can talk in there," he said, pointing to an empty office. "Do you want coffee?"

"Love some. Black."

A minute later, they sat on opposite sides of a gray metal desk sipping coffee. Parker's eyes were fixed on his cup as he spoke. "I realize we shouldn't have taken Damian's body, but we got frightened. Newspapers might have a field day. 'Murder at Sanctuary' and all that. The FBI would use it as an excuse to try to shut us down. Anyway, that's what we thought."

"Who is 'we'?"

"I don't want to tell you that right now. He's another worker here, and I haven't been able to tell him I was meeting you. If he says it's okay, I'll give you his name later."

"Fair enough."

"I guess you have questions."

"How do you know the document Damian wanted translated was stolen?"

"He was going to give it to Father Malcolm, a former classics teacher at the seminary he went to. Father Malcolm helps out down here sometimes. I called him and asked him if Damian gave him the material. He hadn't."

"Why did you do that?"

"I knew how important it was to Damian. He said it contained very vital information. He was uptight about it. When I found him, his room had been ransacked. Come on, I'll show you."

Parker got up and opened the door. He crossed the large room Lane had first entered and took the stairway to the fourth floor. Long corridors with rooms on either side stretched off each landing. Sounds of voices, music, and the smell of cooking odors filled the hallways. Wide-eyed children paused and stared up at Lane as she went by. She smiled at them, but wondered at the dramatic dislocation of so many lives and marveled at these people's resiliency.

Halfway down the corridor on the fourth floor, Parker took a key out of his pocket, unlocked a door, and pushed it open. "I kept it the way it was. I guess, on one level, I've always known I'd have to tell the cops."

He stepped aside and Lane entered first. The narrow room con-

297

tained a cot and a small bureau. A perfectly centered crucifix on one wall was the only item that appeared undisturbed. Everything else was chaos. Clothing and paper were strewn about. The mattress was torn and half off the cot. The bureau drawers were emptied and lay on the floor where they were dropped or thrown and their contents scattered about.

"Do you have the stole that strangled him?" Lane asked.

Parker went to the bureau and removed a long, narrow strip of purple silk. "This was wrapped around his neck. Just the way Bishop Falconi got it right after talking to Damian."

"How do you know that?"

"Damian told me. He was a good friend, Miss Woods. We talked about a lot of things. He must have, uh . . ."

"What?"

Parker looked down at the floor, then he looked at Lane. "Damian must have known whoever did it."

"Why?"

"Damian was a little paranoid, Miss Woods. He would never have let in somebody he didn't know. Plus, there were a lot of people downstairs. They're so jumpy about immigration agents, FBI, or police, they don't let anybody in if they can help it."

What he said struck Lane as making sense. But that meant the killer might be someone on the left. Other than Pat Hogan, leftists were the only people Damian had trusted. "Was there anyone around acting suspiciously that day?"

"No, not anyone I saw. At least not that day."

"What do you mean?"

"The day before Damian was murdered, some priest came around asking questions, some of them about Damian. I didn't tell him anything. The chancery sometimes sends people around to check up on us. Cardinal Murray isn't exactly a big fan of ours, and he certainly had no use for Damian."

"What did the priest look like?"

"A big guy. Middle-aged. Good-looking. Tall, well built. Dark complexioned."

Lane wondered if she should tell Kevin Kelly and caught herself. Of course, she had to. He had said the murderer might be a priest! She was still embarrassed by the last time they were together and knew he was too. Another step further and they would have opened themselves to . . . to what? Most likely a lot of pain and humiliation. They

298

had decided to stay away from each other until the time came when they could be friends. She wondered if that was possible.

"Would the people downstairs have been suspicious of a priest walking in?" she asked.

Parker looked at her and bit his lip. Slowly he shook his head no. "The clergy are the only people they count on."

That evening at St. Mary's, Kelly entered the rectory sitting room and joined Tim Brady, who was watching the news on television.

"Settle in for an update on the mayhem at loose in the world," Brady said with an ironic chuckle.

There was a report about the problems of the Gorbachev regime's holding the Soviet Union together. Another news segment focused on the newly appointed bishop of Brooklyn and Queens condemning New York's governor for his not adopting a tough antiabortion stand despite his being a Catholic.

"Great time to be a politician, huh, Kev?"

"You've got it," Kelly said. "Life isn't tough enough for the governor with all the economic and social pressures on him. Now he's being sent to hell by a new bishop."

Suddenly, the image of Lane Woods outside a building on the Lower East Side appeared on the screen. "The New York radical priest Damian Carter was apparently murdered by the same killer who strangled Bishop Falconi in Rome several weeks ago. The killer may be a priest..."

"Good Lord," Brady said. "Did you hear that!"

When he turned and looked at Kelly, Brady was amazed to see the priest gripping the sides of his chair. Kelly's knuckles were white with anger as he listened to the rest of what she'd learned during the day. Her report didn't mention either Sister Mary Joseph or Parker.

An hour and a half later, Kelly sat rigidly in Lane's apartment. "Why did you do it?" he demanded accusingly. "I thought you weren't going to use the fact that the killer might be a priest unless you checked it with me."

"Unless I got it from another source."

"Why does that have a bearing on it?" he demanded.

Lane stared at him. "I don't feel like I have to apologize for the report. I said I would use the information if I got it from another source, which I did. Ii I got the story another reporter could too. Besides, you don't know who else he might be after and they should be forewarned."

She turned and walked over to the massive wall of windows and kept her back to him. "After our last meeting, I assumed that any working relationship we had was off."

Kelly rose wearily, suddenly feeling very much in the wrong. "Sorry, Lane. Look, this whole thing has been my fault. I've been going through a lot of turmoil since I started the investigation of Pat Hogan. Unfortunately, one of the people I've had a great deal to do with during this period is a beautiful, intelligent woman. I became very confused about who and what I am. I'd like you to forgive me."

Lane turned. "Oh, let's stop acting like kids. We both made a mistake." She crossed the room and held out her hand. "Can we start over . . . on a purely working relationship?"

He shook her hand and smiled ruefully. "Maybe we'll even be friends one day if we're lucky."

"By the way," she said, "thanks for that damning Franny Cook tape. I already apologized to Pat Hogan."

Kelly had dropped a copy of the tape he'd made of the Cook girl at the studio after he left one at the chancery for Bishop Lawler. Still another, he had sent to Jimmy Shields, even though he hadn't wanted to. The tape was rough, but the young man should know how troubled the girl was, so that he wouldn't blame Hogan for the rest of his life. He had put a note with it, saying that Franny was getting help.

"I got our psychiatric people to talk to her," Kelly said. "I hope they can do something for her."

When Kelly left her apartment, Lane felt relieved. For the most part, the tension was gone. Who knows? Maybe they would come out of this friends, if that wasn't asking too much.

❈

Kelly had just finished saying Mass and was in the rectory kitchen fixing breakfast when the phone rang. Brady was already out trying to find a place to live for a family that was burned out of their apartment two days ago. The mother had called hysterically again last night, saying the city had put them up in a hellhole crawling with rats and junkies.

"St. Mary's," he sang out, wondering what new disasters would open the day.

"Kevin?"

"Yes."

"It's Joe Devine. You're going to think I'm nuts after what I'm about to tell you."

"A fair warning."

"Okay. I saw Bill Witten again."

Kelly became more alert. "Where?"

"Same place. Kennedy Airport. I took my sister back last night. When I tell you the rest of this, you're going to call the men in the little white coats."

"Go ahead."

"He's still a priest."

"What!" Kelly exclaimed.

"He was wearing his cassock and collar. What bothers me is that the last time I saw him, he wasn't."

Kelly started wondering about Devine.

"Did you talk to him this time?"

"No. He looked right through me, but I got something better."

"What?"

"I had just dropped my sister off when I saw him. We were both exiting the terminal. I followed him to his car and he didn't see me. I got his license plate number."

Quickly, Kelly grabbed a pencil and paper. "Give it to me."

Devine sounded strained. "Kevin, after you check this out, would you please let me know what you find? I mean, I know it's him, but if it's not, I'll have to find out why I'm seeing a ghost."

The moment Kelly hung up, the phone rang again. "St. Mary's," he answered.

"Is Father Kelly there?" a vaguely familiar voice asked.

"Speaking."

"This is Connie Robbins. You called."

Kelly caught his breath. "Yes, I . . . I wonder if I could talk to you about something, something important."

301

A note of impatience entered her voice. "Father, are you unfortunate enough to be heading up a fund-raising drive? If so, just drop me a line and I'll send you a check."

"No, Mrs. Robbins, I'm not begging."

"Then what is it?"

"It has to do with Monsignor Hogan."

"Oh, my. You do sound very serious, don't you. Actually, I happen to be free this evening. Why don't you come down."

Shortly after eight o'clock, Connie Robbins ushered Kelly into the expansive living room of her apartment. She looked striking in gray slacks and a white cashmere sweater. "Please, sit down."

Kelly felt a little ill about being here and having to bring up what was on his mind. He sat dejectedly on a blue velvet sofa.

"What are you drinking, Father Kelly?"

"Wild Turkey on the rocks."

She fixed his drink and one for herself. She sat on the same couch he was on. "Now, you look like death, so I imagine your visit is serious. What do you want to know about Pat?"

Kelly stared awkwardly at his drink. "I don't like doing this, Mrs. Robbins . . ."

"For God's sake, Kevin, call me Connie or I'll start to feel like one of those dowagers who collar priests in the back of church on Sunday and complain about their arthritis. And just what is it that you don't like?"

"Okay. Tell me what's going on between you and Pat in an apartment down on Mercer Street and I'll be on my way."

"I . . . see," she said slowly. "What's going on between Pat and me. That is an interesting way of putting it, isn't it? Sounds juicily raunchy."

She stood with a bemused smile on her face. "I assume this is part of your investigation of Pat?"

Knowing that he was being toyed with, Kelly reddened. "Yes."

"Well, Kevin. You've nailed us. Our passion just became . . . what's the word? Uncontrollable?"

Kelly eyed her steadily. "Okay, Connie. So I've made an ass out of myself. It's not the first time. Now, will you tell me what's going on?"

302

"No." She marched to a closet, took out his coat and threw it to him, and put on a fur coat. "But I'll show you."

Ten minutes later, they were entering the building in Soho that Kelly had followed them to one night. She rang one of the doorbells and they were buzzed inside. An elevator took them to the fourth floor. When they got off, they entered a large loft that was sectioned off into a living room, a kitchen, and a large dormitory like bedroom with about a dozen cots.

A half dozen young women were in the living room watching TV. Several others were in the kitchen. They were all pregnant.

A girl came over to them. "Hi, Connie. We weren't expecting you." She turned to Kelly. "I'm Barbara King."

"Father Kelly," he replied, looking at Connie questioningly.

"Welcome to the love nest, Kevin."

"Love nest?" Barbara said, giving them both a perplexed look.

"A private joke between Father Kelly and me, Barb," Connie said.

The girl gave her another curious look and returned to the others. "If you need anything, let me know," Barbara said as she left.

"Okay, what is this?" Kelly asked.

"This, my dear Father Kelly, is one of Pat's good works that no one except you and me and the girls who go through here know about. The girls are all unwed mothers. Pat set this up about a year ago. He keeps it going on his salary. Even after he gives a big chunk of the salary to Catholic Charities and Uncle Sam. He came to me for help in finding a suitable apartment, and I managed to convince him to let me work here whenever I can."

A little chastened, she added, "Pat always wanted to do something for unwed mothers. Sometimes, I think he knocked up his high school sweetheart before running off to the seminary."

"Why do you do it?" Kelly asked.

She gave him a wistful smile. "Maybe to show myself I'm not quite as bad a person as I often think I've become."

Turning on the living room lights of his apartment, Pat Hogan reviewed this evening's "Life Has Meaning" about people who cared for infants with AIDS. The pacing had been a little slow. Most of the guests had been earnest but for the most part, inarticulate. Wryly, he thought how much more difficult it was to make goodness interesting than evil.

He had just settled into a chair with a book when the phone rang. "Hello."

"Howdy, Padre."

"Marty, how are you?"

Hogan suddenly felt very weary. The singer Coltrain had taken him up on his offer. He called routinely seeking advice or simply wanting to talk about life and death, topics he apparently found it difficult to discuss with anyone else. Coltrain's calls came after he had too much to drink, and Hogan had to spend a lot of time coaxing him off the phone.

"I've got some church news for you, Padre."

"What?" Hogan asked patiently.

"You know the visit the pope's making here?"

"Yes, I know. I'm part of the group meeting him when he comes to New York."

"Hell, I know you'll think I'm drunk again, but here goes. There are some good ol' boys who are talking about knocking him off."

"Okay, Marty. That's not very funny. Why don't you go to bed before you wind up doing or saying something you'll regret."

"I know it sounds weirder than owl shit. But I swear to God, they're talking about killing your pope. I'm telling you, Padre, it's real depressing."

"Right, Marty. Right. Everything will look better in the morning."

Hogan sighed. Until a moment ago, he had forgotten that it was an hour earlier in Texas, making it only nine-thirty there. Getting Coltrain in bed before midnight was a miracle. He himself yawned and looked at his watch. He wanted to turn in soon; he had promised a friend he would take his six-o'clock Mass in the morning.

"Okay, okay, Padre," Coltrain mumbled. "I gotta go."

"Take it easy, Marty," Hogan said.

A few minutes later, the phone rang again.

"Padre, it's me," Coltrain said. "I know it just sounds like I'm shitfaced again, but I'm telling you the truth. They're sitting around tonight like some kind of Mafia dons talking about rubbing out the pope. It's scary."

"There are always drunks sitting in a bar mouthing off about what they would like to do to important people," Hogan said. "If you're that worried, tell the police to warn them to watch their step."

Coltrain sounded both drunk and exasperated. "Padre, I didn't make myself clear. These ain't a couple of lowlife rednecks. We're talking about the Forrest brothers. They *own* the goddamn cops like they own every other damn thing in this part of the country."

Hogan sat up in his chair. The Forrest brothers were cattle barons who funded a variety of ultraconservative causes, some of them Church related and just about all of them highly questionable. Two things gave Coltrain's story some credence. First, the Forrests *were* friends of the singer. The second was the brothers' open disdain for the pope's progressive stances on economic issues and his strong defense of human rights.

"Me and the Forrests get drunk together once in a while," Coltrain rambled on. "When we do, they talk a lot, including telling me about some of the real loco stuff they get into. I know I drank maybe too much, but believe me, what I'm saying is on the level."

Hogan wondered if Coltrain just misunderstood the millionaires. From past phone calls, he knew the singer could get things pretty garbled when he drank. "Can you tell me anything else?"

"I figured you'd ask me that so I made some notes. . . ."

The phone dropped with a clatter and there was a rustle of papers.

"Sorry, the phone slipped. Okay, they're not in this alone. They mentioned something called 'Miles Christy' or something like that. I guess they're members of it along with a bunch of other rich guys."

"Could it be 'Milites Christi'?"

"I guess so. Anyway, they talked about a hit man already putting a few notches on his gun for them."

"Are you certain?" Hogan asked tensely.

"Sure as JFK was blown away. One was a bishop with an Italian name and the other was a New York priest they hated because he was a communist."

Hogan caught his breath and then asked slowly, "Were they Bishop Falconi and Father Damian Carter?"

"That sounds right."

Suddenly, Hogan remembered the document Damian had sent him. There had to be a link.

"Did . . . Did they say when or where they were going to have the pope killed?"

"No. . . . No, I'm pretty sure they didn't."

"Can you find out?"

There was a pause. "I guess I can try, Padre, but I don't want them getting suspicious of me. If they knew about this call, I'd be smoked meat."

Hogan spoke urgently. "Please, Marty. If you can think of anything else or learn anything at all, let me know."

As soon as he hung up, Hogan leafed through his Rolodex until he found Kelly's name and dialed his number. Brady answered. "Tim, this is Pat Hogan. Is Kevin there?"

A minute later, Kelly was on the line. "What is it, Pat?"

"I have to see you. Will you be around for a while?"

Within the hour, Hogan and Kelly sat huddled in the rectory office. They wore similar grim, intense expressions as Hogan finished narrating what Coltrain told him. "So there appears to be a cabal to kill the pope, Kevin. When you tell Clarizio, he can cancel the pope's visit."

Kelly frowned. "The pope won't back out."

"Why not?"

"He already knows about the threat."

"Damn it," Hogan said, shaking his head in dismay. He should have known. From making his documentary, he knew how stubborn the pope was. "I assume Lane's news report was right about the killer?"

"All too true," Hogan replied.

Briefly, Kelly repeated what he had told Lane. "It makes sense, Pat. Right before Cardinal Clarizio and I were almost turned into angels at St. Peter's, I saw a priest nearby acting suspiciously. I think I spotted the same guy out at Milites Christi's headquarters in Rome."

Hogan sat back chilled, not knowing what to say as the full implications of what Coltrain had told him sank in. "What can I do to help?"

"If Coltrain comes up with anything else, tell me immediately. Other than that, pray."

He looked at the monsignor. "There's something else you can clear up, but it's about yourself."

"What?"

"I'll be right back," Kelly said.

He hurried to his room and returned with Lawler's report. "Look at this and tell me who the anonymous woman is."

Hogan read and his face reddened with anger. "Using that poor girl and Connie against me. Thanks for telling Lane Woods what happened with Franny. Maybe I should have, but I didn't want to hurt the girl." He threw the report on the desk. "The 'other woman' is my cousin, Peggy Sullivan. She lives in L.A. and visits New York periodically. I see her when she's in town. I'll give you her number."

"Just so I can take the last of Lawler's ammunition away from him," Kelly said. "He already knows what Franny Cook's really like. And I told him the nature of your 'affair' with Mrs. Robbins."

Hogan turned to him, a little embarrassed. "I . . . I just want to thank you for what you've done. Someone less diligent would have believed everything and let me swing in the wind."

It was Kelly's turn to be embarrassed, not wanting to acknowledge how he had once thought Hogan guilty as sin.

Hoping to relieve the tension pain in his upper back, Cardinal Clarizio slowly rolled his neck from side to side while he sat at his desk. He was more tired than usual. Worry cut into the few hours of sleep he usually got at night, making the pain worse. He arose slowly and walked to the French doors that opened onto the flagstone veranda and the sweeping lawns and gardens of Royal Oaks. The pastoral sight was soothing. The world was so deceptive. So much beauty and so much evil coexisted.

"Are you all right, Eminenza?"

"As all right as possible under such circumstances, Enrico. The phone call from Father Kelly confirmed the plot against His Holiness. He also said that the assassination attempt would be made during the papal visit. We don't know where."

"In this country," Perdomo said fearfully. "But that means it is imminent!"

"Exactly, Enrico. I must alert the pope and then the Secret Service." Suddenly, he sounded exasperated. "How do they know the schedule?"

"What, Eminenza?"

"The assassins must already know the pope's itinerary. An attempt on the pope's life would have to be executed very precisely, leaving little to chance. Somehow, there must have been a breach in our security. Perhaps in one of the archdioceses."

"Perhaps," Perdomo said quietly.

The luster in the monsignor's eyes dimmed and he licked his lips nervously. Was it possible? Was Ruggieri somehow mixed up in this terrible business? Perdomo's heart sank. The man was a snake. A liar.

A blackmailer. An extortionist. Yes, he was capable of heinous betrayal of his Church and his leader. Was it possible that he, Monsignor Enrico Perdomo, had placed the pope's life in jeopardy by his cowardly behavior?

Suddenly, he felt like weeping as he saw his life with excruciating clarity. What a vain, self-centered creature he was! So childish. So self-absorbed that he only saw how the world reflected him. With a strange sense of freedom, he saw his hopes and ambitions evaporate like snatches of dreams. He had no future in Rome. No future in the Church. Remorse overwhelmed him. "Eminenza, there is something I must tell you," he said almost inaudibly.

Clarizio looked curiously at his secretary. The young man's face was drawn. Fear and despair haunted his eyes. Yet, he also saw unmistakable strength of purpose. Perdomo was going through great personal turbulence. The cardinal sat down next to him. "What is it, my son?" he asked gently.

Perdomo knelt at his feet. "Eminenza, I have sinned. It was I who revealed the pope's itinerary to outside sources," he said in anguish.

As he talked on about Ruggieri and what had happened, the monsignor realized that the rest of his life would be spent atoning for a few stolen moments of pleasure. One thought crystallized. He would try to be a good priest wherever he was sent. If he could be forgiven. If he were allowed to remain a priest.

Listening to his secretary with more pity than anger, Clarizio now understood why the young man was incredibly tense for so long. He had been like a corked bottle ready to explode. He hoped the confession brought him peace. In his years as a priest, Clarizio had heard the confessions of men great and small. Long ago, he realized that human nature was sinful. No one escaped.

"What shall I do, Eminenza?" Perdomo asked tearfully when he finished relating everything that had happened.

"Pray, Enrico. Go and seek God's forgiveness."

"Yes, Eminenza," Perdomo said.

His eyes downcast, the monsignor rose unsteadily. As if in a trance, he walked to the Chapel of the Madonna that was in the west wing of the great house and toward a very different life from what he had ever expected.

Clarizio watched the monsignor's retreat. So much harm and so much grief. He felt a flicker of admiration for his courage. How many men could have revealed what the monsignor had? Death often seems preferable to shame.

The cardinal returned to his desk and rolled his neck again. The pain was much worse than before. He rubbed his eyes and forced himself to concentrate on what Perdomo had told him. Ruggieri. Anger stole over him at the mere thought of the man. Of course. The man should have been defrocked years ago. Who knows how much evil he has wrought in the name of God. His presence on earth was a form of blasphemy.

Clarizio sat back and wondered how he could entrap Ruggieri. The man had powerful allies. Perdomo's word alone was not good enough. He needed something else. He needed to weave a silk noose for the man and his friends to step into, one that he could pull at the right moment and snare his prey.

The following Tuesday, Pat Hogan sat in his dressing room, trying not to show either his alarm or his anger. The pope was starting his tour here in two days, and since learning about the assassination plot, he had feared the worst. He knew he should be thankful for what he'd just heard, and he was. But all he could think of was how incredibly stupid and dangerous the rich could be.

He glanced at Connie Robbins sitting across the room. Despite what she had come to tell him, she had still taken the time to be beautifully made up. She was tensely smoking one cigarette after another. A shudder of revulsion swept through him as he thought of the man she'd married. He caught himself. Thank God she had come to him.

"I don't remember you smoking, Connie."

"I don't, but damn it, Pat. This has me a nervous wreck."

"I wish Cal had come himself."

"Oh, don't blame him. He's so damned ashamed at having gotten mixed up in this that he couldn't. You know a lot of his mouthing off about the Church is pure bluster. Unfortunately, other people don't. That's why this group of monsters welcomed him to the club."

Connie still felt wrung out. Late last night Cal came to her wearing his bad-boy face. She had hoped to God that he wasn't going to confess yet another affair with yet another bouncy little blonde. Instead, he told her he had become enmeshed in a plot by a bunch of the world's

309

richest and craziest men to assassinate the pope. He pleaded that he hadn't realized what he was getting into. How, at the meeting in Rome the night he was out so late, the grumbling of rich men about the state of the Church and the world had swiftly escalated to a horrendous plot.

Connie had listened in amazement. At first she was almost tempted to laugh. Then the full impact of the horror hit her. The idiot was being truthful!

"Cal, you've got to tell, Pat," she said. "He will know what to do."

"I can't. I can't," he replied. "I feel like such a damned fool."

"Well, I will then," she replied.

From his perceptibly relaxing, she realized that was what he wanted all along. Good old Connie would clean up after Cal. No wonder he addressed her as "Mother" half the time. Mommy who protected poor Cal. To date, the messiest of these undertakings had been confronting greedy Lucy or whatever the hell her name was and making certain she had an abortion. Until this. What an odd thing marriage was. For richer or richer, her mother always told her. Her mother never knew the price one paid to live on top of the world.

Connie stared levelly at Hogan. "So what are we going to do, Pat?"

"You're certain it will take place at St. Patrick's?"

"Yes, damn it!"

"Cal will have to be questioned."

"I know," she replied. Wearily, she stood and pulled her Russian sable around her shoulders. "Why don't you just lock him away in some monastery when you're done and throw away the key." She sighed and gave Hogan a tired smile. "Don't bother. He'd just condo the place and make another fortune."

19

TWO DAYS LATER, CARDINAL CLARIZIO STOOD ON THE APRON OF THE runway at Kennedy Airport. Father Kevin Kelly was at his side. They were in the midst of a multitude of churchmen from the East Coast who strained with excitement as the papal jet taxied to a halt at 8:14 A.M., one minute ahead of schedule.

The roaring engines had barely died when the pope, the cape of his stark white cassock fluttering in the brisk air, appeared in the plane's open doorway. The crowd cheered and pressed forward as the pope raised his hand and blessed the multitude. Off to one side of the runway, however, was a large, vociferous contingent of chanting demonstrators. Their causes ranged from advocating the use of condoms to help prevent the spread of AIDS to the right of women to become priests or to have abortions.

The first person the pope met was the U.S. secretary of state and the next was the secretary general of the United Nations, which he was scheduled to address later in the day. Before greeting anyone else personally, the pope wanted to address the massive crowd.

311

"Greetings to you in America," he said into a bank of microphones. "Thank you for welcoming me. I bless you with all my heart."

The cheers of the crowd drowned out the demonstrators' angry yells.

Clarizio caught the pope's eye and then turned to Kelly. "I will remain with him," Clarizio said. "I assume the Secret Service agent has taken the necessary precautions?"

Yesterday, Kelly met Robert Sands, who was heading the Secret Service operation, and found that he liked and trusted him. A sturdy man of medium height with brown hair, and a wide forehead, Sands projected low-key authority.

"Yes," Kelly replied. "I'll be in the car with Bob Sands, who is directing their operation. It's right behind the one that you and the pope and Cardinal Murray will be in. It meant pushing Bishop Von Kirkland into the police commissioner's car, and the bishop's none too happy about it."

"The bishop will survive," Clarizio said dryly, thinking how the pope's chief bodyguard not only became overly zealous but overly arrogant at times.

"Between the Secret Service, the FBI, and the New York police, all the precautions are taken at St. Patrick's that can be," Kelly said.

Clarizio's brow was etched with worry when he looked up. "That is all well and good, Father. But you are the only one who may be able to identify the assassin."

The words scared Kelly. The pope's life might be riding on circumstantial evidence about the killer. Suppose he was wrong? Suppose the priest he had seen was pure coincidence? Suppose the priest Lane told him was asking questions about Damian Carter was somebody else? Ever since glimpsing the man, he had racked his brains about how he knew him. Why wouldn't it come?

While thoughts of the killer whipped through his mind, Kelly watched as the pope stepped from the microphones and prepared to greet individually scores of churchmen and politicians.

"Welcome to New York," Cardinal Murray yelled above the din as he pushed through the crowd in order to be first. Bishop Lawler scrambled along by his side. Then came the archbishops of Philadelphia and Atlanta, whose cities were not on the itinerary. Kelly spotted Pat Hogan in the midst of the Church's royalty, already accepted as one of them, the way they deferred to him. Hogan was someone more special than any of them because of his celebrity status.

312

They were followed by the governor of New York and the mayor of New York City and a gaggle of lesser politicians. Suddenly, Cardinal Clarizio materialized by the pope's side. He whispered something and the pope looked directly at Kelly and gave a slight, gracious bow of acknowledgment.

Kelly smiled back gravely.

TV camera crews dutifully recorded the proceedings. Reporters with microphones made their preliminary commentaries. Secret Secret Service and state and local police hovered anxiously in the background. Taking in the scene, Kelly knew he wasn't cut out to be pope. Who would want to go through this?

"Hello, Kevin."

Kelly looked to his left and found himself staring into Lane Woods's eyes. She smiled at him and he smiled back, glad her gaze was straightforward and friendly.

"Hello, Lane."

"Something's wrong, isn't it?"

"What do you mean?"

"You wouldn't be here. I know what you've been working on. Remember? Is the pope in danger?"

Kelly glanced around nervously. She was too good a reporter to speak loudly enough for anyone else to hear, but he wanted to be sure anyway. He silently commended her ability to put two and two together. He owed her an answer, but how much did he owe her? The thought made him uneasy.

Fortunately, Bob Sands came up. "Father Kelly, we're getting ready to leave. Please come along."

"I'll tell you later, Lane. That's a promise."

"Everything? Like why you're with the Secret Service?"

She seemed determined to make his life difficult one way or another. He started following Sands and turned back to her. "Everything I can."

The pope entered a specially constructed bubble limousine to begin the twenty-five-mile procession through the streets of New York to St. Patrick's. He was in the middle of the backseat, between Cardinals Clarizio and Murray. The bubble was bulletproof and enabled the pope to stand in the back. As soon as he was inside, the pontiff began waving and blessing the throngs.

Kelly climbed into the black Secret Service car and kept his eyes on the pope. He prayed that the assassin didn't get different marching

313

orders. Robbins would talk only to Hogan, but he had told him that the attempt would be at relatively close range, but he didn't know how. Short range gave them a chance to stop the assassin. A slim chance, but a chance. Kelly was sick with worry. There were too many ways to kill. A bomb. A bullet. Poison. He didn't want to think about it, but he had to. His only certainty was that the killer wouldn't use a priest's stole this time around.

Kelly's biggest fear crashed over him again. Suppose he couldn't recognize him?

"The guy has guts," Sands said, staring at the pope. "Let's hope he leads a charmed life too."

"Right," Kelly replied, wishing that just for once the pope weren't so damned pigheaded.

The pontiff had insisted on going through with the itinerary that he and Clarizio had originally worked out. Any change of plans, he said, might alert the Apostles that their plot had been uncovered. They would just try again.

Robbins gave up the names of the plotters to Hogan on the condition that his name be kept out of the conspiracy. But even with the names, Kelly realized that he, the police, and the feds were hamstrung. What could they do about the Apostles? They only had Robbins's word and Robbins would talk only to Hogan. There was probably no way in the world the Apostles could be traced to the assassin. The pope was right. If they failed today, they'd probably just wait for another occasion.

For his part, Kelly worried that an assassin's plans could change too easily and for no apparent reason at all. Maybe he'd do it somewhere other than St. Pat's? Eighteen thousand policemen lined the route. A hundred thousand cops couldn't stop a sniper's bullet.

The entourage slowly crept through the city. Oblivious to the worry and fear, millions thronged the streets and cheered as the pope passed. Thousands of others waited at St. Patrick's while tens of thousands of others were on their way to the cathedral, hoping to get a glimpse of the pontiff. One of them had figured out how to kill him.

At a hotel on Eighth Avenue near Fiftieth Street, a tall, dark-complexioned man dressed carefully. His close-cropped hair was graying at the temples and his eyes were deep set. The muscles in his back rippled when he pulled on a T-shirt, covering the angry welts on his flesh. He forced the shirt into his black pants. Next he put on a cassock. Then a stiff, white clerical collar, which he fastened with a gold stud. The cassock, as well as the sash he put around his waist, were trimmed with the red piping of a monsignor. A white surplice went over the cassock.

He examined himself carefully in the mirror. Though not vain, he knew he was good-looking and was grateful. Attractive people were trusted.

From a suitcase on the bed, he extracted rubber-lined, leather gloves that fit his hands like a second skin. Next, he removed pieces of lightweight plastic and began assembling them by sliding each piece into a groove. He worked calmly, efficiently, as he had a thousand times until he had perfected the technique. Less than fifty seconds later, he held in his hands a miniature air gun. A narrow tube the length of a drinking straw but of a slightly larger gauge functioned as the barrel and was mounted on a ten-inch piece of flat plastic.

From the bag, he extracted a crucifix. He unscrewed one end and withdrew a miniature CO_2 cartridge. He fastened the cartridge to one end of the plastic gun.

He hefted the device, pleased with its weightlessness, and pulled up his right sleeve. With his left hand, he quickly used rubber straps to fasten the contraption beneath his right arm, between his elbow and wrist. He picked up a can of shaving cream, went to the vanity mirror and drew a circle the size of a man's head.

He unscrewed another arm of the crucifix and withdrew an insulated capsule, a sixth the size of a 35mm film cartridge. He twisted off the top. A puff of cold air escaped. Carefully, he removed a tiny, poisonous dart made of ice that was an eighth of an inch long. Deftly, he inserted it into the chamber.

He recrossed the room. Fifteen feet from the mirror, he stretched his arm toward his reflection and raised his hand. The CO_2-activated trip sprung. The ice dart spattered against the mirror in the center of the circle and immediately started to dissolve, leaving a trickle of harmless-looking water.

Three unobtrusive canisters each containing an ice dart remained in the crucifix. He foresaw the need for only one.

Each of his movements was deliberate, unhurried. Long ago, he had forced himself to do everything slowly, carefully. From another suitcase he removed and envelope and took one hundred dollars in

315

twenties from the roll of five thousand dollars and added it to the thirty-four dollars he already had. Priests never carried a great deal of cash. From another envelope, he removed a passport, a driver's license, two credit cards, and a celebret, the letter from a bishop granting a traveling priest the right to say Mass wherever he was. The identification said he was Monsignor Charles Bonzano, a native of Rome.

"God works in mysterious ways, my friend," he muttered, and smiled.

He checked his watch. Eight forty-five A.M.

Chilly wind whipped beneath the sunny skies as the pope's entourage wound through Harlem after having rolled through parts of Queens and the Bronx. The cars came to a halt in front of St. Timothy's, where His Holiness left his limousine to stand on the church steps where he spoke momentarily with William Cummins, a black bishop. At one point, the pontiff turned to the multitude of African Americans gathered before him and stretched open his arms as if to embrace them all.

"The One Universal Church is for everyman," the pope said fervently in English. "Black man, white man, yellow man, it does not matter. God does not see the color of skin, but the goodness of hearts."

Bishop Cummins knelt and kissed the pope's ring a second time as His Holiness made ready to depart. The symbolic bowing to authority was lost on no one. The potential for a serious schism over an African American Catholic Church was on everyone's mind. The crowd applauded when the pope blessed the people one last time.

From Harlem, the convoy slowly moved south into the silk stocking district of Manhattan's Upper East Side. As always along the itinerary, the sidewalks were jammed with onlookers. People waved and cheered and the pope waved back or gave his blessing. Wherever they went, however, demonstrators lined the route. Some held aloft hand-lettered cardboard signs proclaiming "Don't Bar Church Doors to Gays." Others declared "Not the Church—Not the State. Women Should Decide Their Fate."

Suddenly, at Eighty-sixth Street, someone darted through the police barricades and ran toward the pope's car. The limousine and the cars behind it screeched to a halt. Secret Servicemen leaped from the car, guns pointed. Kelly was right behind Sands. A sea of uniformed police converged.

"Don't shoot!" Kelly screamed.

A boy wearing a jeans jacket and a hooded sweatshirt, khakis, and sneakers froze before the pope's limousine when he saw the guns. He was about fifteen years old. His mouth opened but nothing came out. Trembling, he slowly raised his hands over his head as police grabbed him and threw him to the ground.

"I just wanted a closer look at the pope," the boy finally said as police cuffed his hands behind his back and dragged him to a squad car. "That's all! That's all! I swear it!"

"Jeezus," Sands muttered as he put his gun away. He patted Kelly on the shoulder. "Nice call, Kelly."

Kelly caught Clarizio's eye and shook his head in exasperation. The cardinal wore a stricken look, but he gave him an appreciative glance. The pope stared at him intently.

"Let's roll," Sands said, and everyone returned to their cars.

As the pope's limo continued on, the tall, dark monsignor stood on Fifth Avenue at Fiftieth Street by the southwest corner of St. Patrick's. Walking toward Madison Avenue, he passed demonstrators being ordered by police into a pen made of blue wooden sawhorses a block from the Gothic cathedral. Their placards were directed at both the pope and Cardinal Murray. One sign berating the Church's stand against the use of contraceptives bore a picture of Cardinal Murray emblazoned with the words "Public Health Menace No. 1." Another declared "The Pope Won't Preach Safe Sex."

As he moved through the tide of faithful, he removed his raincoat and placed it along the wall running by the cathedral. All the while, he carefully scanned the ever-growing body of clergymen who were gathering on the sidewalk. Police had asked the diocese to see that the clergy came early so that they were seated in advance of the pope's arrival.

The morning was raw, and the older priests, monsignors and bishops wore topcoats over their robes to keep out the chill. Within another ten minutes, more than six hundred clerics lined up behind three altar boys, the center one carrying a large gold cross.

The procession of priests was colorful. Most of the influential churchmen from the East Coast who were not at the airport to greet the pope were here, dressed in the royal red robes of bishops. Following Jesuits in their barristerlike black gowns were Paulists in plain black cassocks and starched white collars, Dominicans in white tunics and black capes with hoods. Bearded Franciscans and Capuchins wore coarse brown habits; Carmelites, their white wool mantles with brown hoods; Augustinians, white-sleeved tunics with capes, hoods, and black leather belts; Redemptorists, black cassocks, cloaks, and birettas. The Passionists stood out in their rough-mantled tunics with a heart embroidered on the chest. Trappists wore stark white wool habits; the Josephites wore deathly black. There were other orders as well, but most were diocesan priests who wore simple white surplices over their cassocks.

The monsignor took note of the white envelopes most of the priests carried in their hands. Another petty obstacle. Yesterday, a helpful woman at the chancery explained the admission procedures. Invitations were necessary. St. Patrick's was too small to accommodate all the clergy who wished to attend.

Moving slowly along the sidewalk, he examined faces as though looking for a friend. Finally, he edged into line next to an aged, dottering priest who was struggling to his feet after sitting on the steps of cardinal's residence. The corner of the old monsignor's invitation stuck out of his coat pocket.

"Let me help you, Father," the monsignor said, taking the man's arm.

The old priest's hands trembled and his eyes were milky. "That is most kind of you, my son. Most kind."

After placing the priest in line, the monsignor bowed slightly and left him. A few moments later, he slipped into line again, only toward the front, an invitation in his hand. As he walked among the priests, he felt comfortable. He wore the anonymity of the group like a cloak. He wondered if most men became priests as a way of losing themselves, of seeking oblivion. He sighed as he remembered an expression from his youth: "The priest will be understood only in heaven."

The line slowly moved along Madison, snaking around the block and along Fifty-first Street before turning onto Fifth Avenue and into the cathedral's great bronze doors. They walked beneath the figures of Our Lord, the Twelve Apostles, the Blessed Virgin, and St. John

318

the Baptist. In the vestibule, the priests surrendered their invitations and waited to proceed one by one through a metal detector. As the monsignor waited his turn, the priest next to him remarked about the tedious procedure as well as the presence of so many police.

"It is a sad era when the pope himself is no longer safe."

"Yes," the monsignor replied, wondering at how little so many priests knew of their religion. Starting with Peter, few popes ever took safety for granted.

He evaluated the security. The FBI, Secret Service, and of course, New York City police were everywhere. Since the news reports that a killer might be a priest, he had expected as much.

Before stepping through the metal detector, he removed the crucifix from around his neck and turned to the priest checking everyone through. "Will you please hold this?"

A priest smiled. "Of course."

After stepping through the detector, he took back the crucifix. "Thank you."

He followed the clergy up the marble-floored nave or center aisle, past the pews filled with city and state officials, the representatives of the stock exchanges, the media moguls and one influential Catholic bankers, the department store owners, the industrialists and the financiers as well as family members of prominent churchmen. The front pews on either side of the altar contained the Knights of Malta, who were the elite of Catholic businessmen and dressed in their dark uniforms replete with sabers and plumage.

Several minutes later, an elderly priest in the vestibule frantically searched his pockets over and over, assuring the doormen that he had an invitation. Eventually, he was forced to leave. There could be no exceptions on such an occasion.

Archbishops and bishops proceeded to their seats in the sanctuary, to the right and left of the altar. The first sixteen rows of pews stretching the breadth of the cathedral were reserved for the clergy. The monsignor with the crucifix entered one off the center aisle that was nearly full.

Glancing around, he assumed the men positioned intermittently along the side aisles with sophisticated walkie-talkies were from the Secret Service. Carefully, he looked up at the graceful, vaulted ceiling, enjoying the smell of incense in the air. He had studied architectural plans of the cathedral and was glad to be here again after so many years. Everything looked much as he remembered: the bronze detail, the stained-glass windows telling the history of Christianity and the mysteries of the faith.

Turning, he smiled as he savored the great roseate window soaring like a giant kaleidoscope above the magnificent organ. Suddenly in the choir loft below the organ pipes, he noted two men carrying rifles dissolve into the shadows. Even from this distance he recognized their weapons as high-powered 223 rifles. The rifles used a high-velocity shell only the size of a .22, but were known for their deadly accuracy. Snipers.

He had anticipated heavy precautions. For days he had thought of little else, the kind of challenge he relished. He believed his solution to be foolproof. He would go undetected. The spring mechanism was easy enough to discard. His identification was in order. Besides, it would be assumed until there was an autopsy that the pope had succumbed to a heart attack.

Still, as he unobtrusively unscrewed an arm of the cross to slip out the CO_2 cartridge, he wondered if the moment he hoped for would present itself. The moment of doubt evaporated. Why not?

The rest of the ride to St. Patrick's was uneventful. As the entourage approached the cathedral, the throngs jamming the sidewalks grew ever larger until they were enormous. Police had difficulty keeping onlookers away from the street. They shoved people behind sawhorses and at times locked arms to keep swarms from breaking through.

The greater the multitude, the more the pope seemed energized. No one watching him would ever have thought he was seriously ill, let alone that he knew a killer might be waiting for him somewhere in the crowd. He beamed and waved to everyone. At one point, the pope clasped his hands together over his head like a prize fighter. The crowd roared like crashing waves.

The papal convoy came to a halt before the cathedral. Sands jumped out of the Chrysler as the door of the pope's bubble limo opened. Kelly was at his heels. A phalanx of Secret Service agents surrounded the pope.

Looking over the crowd, Kelly was struck by the vastness of the sea of humanity. The pushing, shoving swarm tried to close in on the pontiff. Most of them had waited more than ten hours to get a glimpse of the pope. Relief, frustration, and fervor was etched in their faces. From a block away, the chants of hundreds of gay rights and pro-choice activists sounded like a dirge from a Greek chorus warning of impending tragedy.

Kelly tried seeking out the tallest men in the crowd because of the size of the priest he'd seen, but in the commotion that was impossible. The roaring crowd undulated and swayed chaotically against police lines. At any given moment, hundreds of people verged on crashing through the barricades, but the blue line of police held time and again.

"If the killer's in that mob," Sands shouted in Kelly's left ear, "maybe God can save the pope, but we sure as hell can't."

Kelly didn't need to hear it. He was very frightened. His mouth was dry as his eyes darted about frantically. His stomach was on fire. How could he ever spot the killer? How could the pope be protected? It was impossible.

Yanking Kelly's arm, Sands motioned for him to follow. The agent ran up the steps and entered the cathedral just before the pope turned from the crowd and into St. Patrick's.

Moments later, the pontiff entered the center aisle, which was slightly longer than a football field. As he took his first step toward the alter, the choir erupted into strains of *"Ecce Sacerdos Magnus."* "Behold the high priest, whose life has pleased God. . . ."

"Unbelievable," the elderly priest to the monsignor's right exclaimed. "Security wasn't this heavy even when President Johnson attended Cardinal Spellman's funeral."

The monsignor smiled back pleasantly. "So sorry, so sorry," he grunted in heavily accented English to keep the man from chattering and possibly from remembering him later. He motioned with his hands that he could not understand most of what the man said.

In their colorful plumage, Cardinals Murray and Clarizio preceded the pontiff, who was surrounded by a cluster of bishops and monsignors as they made their way up the aisle. Everyone in the cathedral was standing as the voices of the choir resounded. "Before the Lord hath promised that he shall become great among his people."

The monsignor breathed deeply. The preparation, the waiting, were over. He measured the deliberate pace of the churchmen coming up the aisle. Slowly, almost leisurely. As the pope drew nearer, he stretched his arm toward him and raised his hand.

Abruptly, as though sensing danger, the pope leaned over a pew and embraced an elderly monsignor he recognized. The pellet struck the breviary of a priest across the aisle. The perplexed priest felt the tap and looked at his book and then up at the ceiling. Annoyed, he wiped beads of water from his breviary with his sleeve.

There was no time to insert another dart. The pope had already moved out of striking distance. To maintain his composure, the monsignor closed his eyes and told himself to be patient. He would have another chance. The pope would leave the same way he entered. He must.

✧

Kelly ruefully remembered how small he once thought St. Pat's seemed compared to the surrounding skyscrapers. Today it was enormous. The basement, altar, pews, confessionals, choir loft—everywhere anyone could conceivably place a bomb had been carefully searched. Nothing was found. The assassin would have to turn up somehow. Kelly watched the papal party enter the sanctuary behind the altar rail. Would he dare it here? Sometimes the boldest method was the best. But how?

Sands grabbed his elbow. "Come with me, Father," the agent said, pulling Kelly to the right.

Sands spoke through his walkie-talkie, but Kelly couldn't hear what he said. They pushed through the crowded rear to the right-hand aisle. Sands hurried up the aisle until he entered the ambulatory behind the main altar. Another agent rushed over carrying a bundle. Sands grabbed it and shook out a bishop's robe.

"Put this on, Father," he said. "We've arranged for you to sit with the members of the hierarchy on the altar."

As Kelly took off his coat and pulled the robe over his head, he felt Sands shove something in his hand. He looked down and saw what looked like strange glasses. "What are these?"

"Binoculars," Sands said, holding out a walkie-talkie. "You'll need this too, and here's a map of the cathedral. Priests are in the first sixteen rows of pews. There are ten sections of pews across the width of the cathedral. If you spot the guy, tell us his seat by telling us how far off an aisle he is. Use the code on the map."

322

As Kelly started walking away, Sands grabbed his arm and pulled him around. "Father, don't screw around. If anybody looks even remotely like he might be the killer, sing out. I'd rather pick up a hundred people if we get the right one. Okay?"

"Okay," Kelly said.

Moments later, he entered the altar and unobtrusively took one of the seats closest to the altar rail and almost directly across from the cardinal's scarlet cushioned throne. His view of one side of the cathedral was clear enough. He'd have to switch to the seats next to the cardinal's throne to see the priests on this side of the cathedral.

Taking up the binoculars, he started with the first pew of clergy and began examining faces. Hurry, he ordered himself. Hurry, for God's sake. The pope was scheduled to spend only fifteen minutes here before going to the UN. Trying to remain calm, Kelly pored over the faces of clergymen, praying he'd see the killer before it was too late.

Seven minutes later, Kelly spoke softly into the walkie-talkie. "Check out the priest who is in the eighth row, second pew from aisle three. The fourth man in from the aisle."

Seconds later, Kelly watched as two men tapped the priest in question on the shoulder and led him away.

Another six minutes and Kelly repeated similar instructions. He had just switched to sit on the opposite side of the altar. "Row twelve. Far left aisle. Fourth pew from the right. The priest on the left end of the pew."

Watching again as that man was led away, he was disgusted. He knew he'd made a mistake. "Forget him," he said into the walkie-talkie. "Now that I see him a little better, he's not the one."

"Keep going," Sands's voice came back. "Keep going!"

Beads of sweat trickled down Kelly's face as he saw the pope rise to prepare to leave. He forced himself to move more quickly, but not too quickly. He had to study certain priests momentarily before dismissing them, undecided whether to call them out to Sands. Damn it! The entire clergy stood as the pope came through the altar rail.

Suddenly, Kelly froze the binoculars on a large, dark figure. "I see him," Kelly said quietly. "Row thirteen. Just left of the main aisle. The second man in . . ."

The pope edged into his field of vision. "God! He's raising his arm toward the pope! He may have a gun!"

"A positive ID?" Sands asked, his voice deadly calm.

"Yes! Yes!" He wasn't mistaken. He had finally recognized the man. The identity horrified him.

As he spoke, two shots came from the choir. They were so close together they exploded like one, roaring like an avalanche through the cathedral. The monsignor pitched into the aisle as if he were thrown by a giant. The back of his head was blown away. Simultaneously, the pope crashed to the floor.

Kelly's scream blended with the thousands of others that ricocheted throughout the cathedral as everything happened at once. Secret Servicemen threw themselves on the pope's body. Hundreds of police converged on the center aisle as if leaping from the walls. Pandemonium erupted as thousands of stunned people broke out off their shock and pushed forward with dread. A single question formed on everyone's lips: "Is the pope dead?"

Ten minutes later, the cathedral was cleared. Only law enforcement officers and Kelly stood in the aisle near the assassin's body. The pope was safe but shaken. At the moment the snipers fired, a Secret Service agent had thrown the pontiff to the floor and fallen across him. As soon as he was allowed to stand, the pontiff was rushed to his limousine.

"What did you want?" Sands asked Kelly when he finally had time to come over to him.

"Come with me," Kelly said grimly.

He led the agent to the relative privacy of the Altar of the Holy Vail on the Fifty-first Street side of the cathedral. When they were out of earshot of anyone, he turned, furious. "What the hell's going on?"

"What do you mean?" Sands stared intently at Kelly.

"The killer, damn it."

"What do you mean?" Sands demanded.

"The killer's name is Donner," Kelly said heatedly. I think it's Carl Donner. He's an assassin, for Christ's sake. For our government!"

Kelly threw up his hands in disgust. Sands probably didn't know any more about this than he did. The left hand never knew what the right was doing.

Suddenly it dawned on him who probably knew who was behind this all along. Who had gotten Kelly neck deep in this trouble? Who had known his record and manipulated him from day one like some goddamn puppet on a string? Who didn't seem surprised by what was in the Falconi report?

Kelly wheeled around and stormed down the aisle. All the original resentments he'd felt rushed over him. The seminary, the priesthood, the years of trying to forget, didn't mean anything. He felt haunted. He'd never escape the past. Not with Clarizio calling the shots.

Late that evening, Kelly was on his third Wild Turkey. He sat across from Tim Brady, listening to the pastor's "bitch list," as Brady called it, when he rattled on about what he needed to make St. Mary's a proper parish.

"Then I've got to get money of fix up the gym, so we can get the teenagers around here off the streets. Then . . ."

Usually the bitching frustrated and depressed Kelly. They both knew he'd never get what he wanted. Tonight Brady's complaining was white noise. It kept Kelly from thinking too much about what had happened. And what Clarizio would want from him next. Striking back at the Apostles. Never for a minute did he think Clarizio was above revenge. He'd want the Apostles cut down and he'd want Kelly to do it.

Clarizio had had enough use of his hide. Let him exploit somebody else.

"There are so many old people in the parish who are afraid even to go out for a walk that I'd like to get a bus service to take them shopping, maybe over in Riverdale or even someplace in Queens so they wouldn't have to be afraid. Then . . ."

A knock on the rectory door cut off Brady. "If it's for you, what shall I say?" Tim Brady asked Kelly as he got up to answer.

"The same," Kelly muttered.

"Come on, Kev. The damned phone's been ringing off the hook all day, and I'm tired of telling the callers and the people who come by that you can't be disturbed."

Kelly shot him a withering look.

"All right. All right," Brady said, holding out the palm of his right hands as if to ward off the evil eye.

A minute later, Kelly heard Lane Woods asking for him. He came out and stood behind Brady.

325

"It's okay, Tim. Let her in."

Brady stepped aside and Lane crossed the vestibule, involuntarily shuddering as she entered the metal grate.

"Hello, Lane. I'm sorry. I forgot that I said I'd talk to you. But as you know, a few things happened."

"Uh-huh. Like the pope almost being killed."

"Look, Kev," Brady said. "Why don't you take my office. I want to go to bed and read for a bit."

"Sorry, Tim. This is Lane Woods. Lane, Father Brady."

"Call me Tim," Brady said as they shook hands. "I'm grateful he's finally willing to talk to somebody other than me. Good night."

"Good night," they both echoed.

Kelly led the way into the office. "This humble abode is what's left of a once-flourishing parish, but it does come with bourbon. Can I interest you in one?"

"Why not," Lane said, taking the chair in front of the desk that Kelly had been sitting behind.

A moment later, he came back with a clean glass and poured her a generous amount of Wild Turkey and added to his own. "Like I said, I'm sorry I didn't get back to you."

"We've been through that. Now tell me what happened."

"I don't know how much of this you can use. What I'm telling you is strictly on a background basis. You can't quote me and you probably won't be able to be verify very much."

"I'll be the judge of that."

He shrugged. "For some reason, I knew you'd say that."

Briefly, he filled her in on the assassination plot. He gave her the names of the Forrest brothers, but omitted the roles Cal Robbins and Marty Coltrain had played. He also gave her other vital information that hadn't been carried yet by the media, if it ever would be. "Now, here's the kicker. Twenty years ago, this guy Carl Donner was a CIA assassin. For all I know, he was today."

"What!" she exclaimed.

"You heard me."

"I'm telling you, I met the man when I was in the military. I only met him once, but I knew what he did for us."

"How did you know?"

"Damn it, Lane. I was doing the same thing!"

20

THE NEXT AFTERNOON, KELLY DROVE THROUGH THE MOUNT AIRY SEC-
tion of Philadelphia. He'd been looking for any chance to get out of
New York to avoid the expected call from Clarizio. He wanted to put
as much distance between the cardinal and himself as he could. The
chance came when a friend in Washington called, saying he had traced
the license plate number Joe Devine had given him.

Turning off Emlen Street onto Wellesley Road, a small street of
neatly kept two-story row homes, he scanned the house numbers and
parked in the middle of the block. The trip from New York took nearly
three hours and he checked his watch, realizing how close he'd cut
it. It was five to three. The girl on the phone had said that Mr. Witten
was due in at three. Kelly's trace didn't have a first name on the owner.
Just the initial W. Maybe Witten had a brother Walter who looked
like him? If this was the right Bill Witten, how the hell did he wind
up here? Priests don't live like this. And who the hell was the girl?

He went up to the porch, heaved a bewildered sigh, and knocked.
A moment later a young woman in her early twenties opened the door.
Judging by her jeans and old sweater, he took her for a college student.

She was pretty, with dark hair and a creamy complexion. Her gray eyes appeared serious and intelligent.

"Yes?" she asked.

"You must be the person I spoke with on the phone. You said that Mr. Witten would be in this afternoon."

"I . . . I didn't know that you would come by. I thought you would call again."

She looked at his collar and black suit. "I'm Susan Witten. You want my dad. Come in, Father."

Kelly felt a surge of dismay. There was no way in hell Witten could have a daughter as old as this girl. He would have had to have sired her when he was in the seminary. Exhaling a stream of stale air, he wondered if he'd just tumbled on to another sordid little secret. About to beg off, he decided to get to the bottom of whatever the hell it was and followed her inside. Maybe it's the wrong guy? In his heart, he knew that was wishful thinking.

"Please sit down," she said.

Kelly sank down on a sofa covered in a blue floral print and looked around. The house was neat and modestly furnished. A loose-leaf binder was open and books were face down on the floor by an oversize stuffed chair.

"Sorry to interrupt you, Susan. It looks as if you're getting ready for a test."

"No, they were for a final exam." She waved a hand at the mess on the floor. "I'm graduating from Temple University."

She was about to say something else but the phone rang. She went to a nearby table and answered it. "Hello, Dad."

Kelly made a motion to her. She cupped the receiver. "Hold on, Dad." She looked at Kelly curiously.

"I'd appreciate it if you didn't tell him I was here. I'd like this to be a surprise."

Shrugging, she talked into the receiver again. "How late? . . . Okay. See you then."

After she hung up, she turned to Kelly. "He's running a little behind schedule and didn't want me to worry." Her brow furrowed. "Why didn't you want him to know that you were here?"

Kelly looked at her sheepishly. "I'm not certain that your father is the William Witten I am trying to locate. Judging by you, I doubt if he is. He couldn't have had a daughter your age."

328

Susan laughed a little as she sat in the chair she had vacated when Kelly knocked on the door. "Poor Dad. A lot of people think he must have gotten married when he was nineteen when they meet me. He isn't my real father. I'm adopted, but he's the only father I've ever known. I was only a little girl when the Wittens adopted me."

"Where's Mrs. Witten?"

"My mother died five years ago of cancer. Now it's just Dad and me."

Susan got up. "Let me get my photo album. Then you can tell if Dad is the man you want."

Two minutes later, she sat on the sofa next to Kelly and opened up a large album. She flipped past several pages and opened to a photo of a handsome, dark-complexioned, serious-looking man wearing a bathing suit at what was obviously a beach resort. He was tall and muscular, and the years had made the features craggier, more interesting. Examining the face, Kelly knew there was no doubt in his mind. Staring back was Gethsemane's chess master.

"Well?" she asked expectantly.

"That's him."

"It's funny, Dad has never mentioned any priest friends. He's pretty religious, but he's not the kind of guy who stops and chats with the priest after Mass."

Susan turned the page and there were other photos of Witten. For a moment, Kelly was stunned. Several shots were of Witten in a policeman's uniform.

"Your dad's a cop?"

"Like cassocks, they don't give those uniforms to everyone," Susan said with a trace of exasperation.

"Sorry," Kelly said. "Sometimes I'm a little slow on the uptake."

"Actually, he's been a detective for the past two years." Again her brow furrowed and she stared at him. "How do you know Dad?"

Her expression reminded Kelly of Witten's intense gaze. Funny how children picked up parents' mannerisms. Instinctively, he became cautious. Kelly didn't want to create any more problems for Witten than his presence would anyway.

"Oh, we knew one another a long time ago. I just want to ask him about a mutual friend."

Susan was still leafing through the album. A series of pictures were of Witten and a striking blonde.

"That's Mom," she said. "These photos were taken before she was diagnosed. After she was sick, she wouldn't let anyone take her picture."

Several pages later, she pointed to a picture of a couple smiling into the camera. "These were my real parents," Susan said, and smiled. "A couple of hippies. My mother's name was Martha Crawford, but I don't even know my father's name. My mother wasn't married when she had me."

Kelly glanced cursorily at the picture as Susan turned the page, then caught his breath. "Could I see the photo of your parents again?"

"Sure," she said, and returned to the page.

Stunned, Kelly stared at the couple. He recognized the man immediately even through the excess hair. The woman was familiar too. He knew that he had seen her picture before, but he couldn't remember where.

Suddenly, he had a hunch that the girl's parents were a very big factor about why he had been sucked into this whole business. He wondered if Witten realized who the guy was. Or who both of them were.

"What's wrong?" Susan asked, staring at Kelly strangely.

"Nothing. Your mother was very pretty. You resemble her very strongly."

"Thank you. My mother died when she was very young, but I'm not sure how. I guess my father died too."

A moment later, the front door opened. Kelly stood and looked at Bill Witten for the first time in nearly twenty years. As Witten stared back, both recognition and resignation flashed across his face. Painfully, he looked at his daughter and back to Kelly.

An interminable silence engulfed the room. Finally, Witten seemed to exert great willpower and his face became impassive. "How are you, Kevin?" he said, stepping forward with his hand outstretched.

"Good, Bill," Kelly said, shaking hands.

"I saw the 'Clergy' sign on your dashboard." The tone of Witten's voice was forced neutrality. The look in his eyes was that of a man who accepted his death as he stepped in front of a firing squad. "I wondered if someone from the Church was here."

Susan looked at her father strangely, with a trace of alarm. She went over and touched his arm. "Are you okay, Dad?"

"Thanks, Suzy. I'm fine," he said, patting her hand, but never taking his eyes off Kelly. "You've met?"

330

"Yes," Kelly replied. "I told her we were friends from a long time ago."

Suddenly, Susan felt awkward. Something was very wrong. Her father, who was always so self-assured, was ill at ease. Who was this priest? What did he want? Why was her father upset that he was here? She and her father were always close, and they got closer after her mother's death. From the way her father looked at her and his tone of voice, she instinctively knew that whatever it was had to do with her.

Realizing how reluctant they were to talk in front of her, she decided to leave them alone even though she didn't want to. She went to a closet by the door, took out a pea jacket, and put it on. "I have to go out for a little while, Daddy. There are some things we need from the store. Do you want anything?"

"No thank you, Suzy."

"How about you, Father?"

"No thanks."

The moment the door closed behind his daughter, Witten sat down in a large chair and wearily rubbed his face. Before today, this moment had only occurred in his nightmares. "I knew this day would come. I just never knew when or who it would be. . . ."

He looked up. "What brings you here, Kevin?"

"Damian and Pat."

"Ahhh." The sound came like a soft cry. "Why don't you just drop it, Kevin?"

Kelly stared at Witten. This wasn't the reaction he'd expected. What did the man mean? Had he thought he was here because of Witten's vanishing act? "Drop what?"

"This investigation of Pat. Damian's dead. What other pound of flesh does the Church want?"

Kelly stared at him. "How do you know about my investigation?"

"Pat told me."

Kelly started to feel as if he were in the midst of a clever riddle and he were the only one who didn't know the answer. "You mean you're in touch with him?"

"I always have been. Both him and Damian."

"Why didn't you have them clear up all those stories about suicide?"

"Why? They worked to my advantage. I wanted out of the Church, and I didn't want a lot of prying about why I left."

"Why did you leave?"

Witten looked down at his strong hands and flexed them. He gave a brief, ironic laugh. How could he ever get anyone to truly understand? He wasn't sure he understood himself. Too many pressures. Too much guilt. Too much hypocrisy. How many years could a man deceive himself as well as everyone else? "Put it down to a crisis of faith, Kevin. Most of us get them. Some of us find them more severe than others do. One day I woke up and realized I was living a lie. That I simply didn't belong there."

Kelly had heard similar sentiments echoed often enough by priests over the years, a good many of them men who had left. Sometimes they stopped believing in God. Usually, they stopped believing in themselves. But in this case, he couldn't shake the feeling that there was some other reason. He also had the feeling that it tied into the strange linkage he'd found between Susan and her real parents and Witten.

"Susan is a beautiful girl," Kelly said.

Witten tensed. Guarded, he stared back. What does he know? Is he fishing or does he really know something? "Yes, yes, she is."

"She said she doesn't know who her father is. Did you ever find out?"

Witten became tenser. Is he toying with me? "No. No. We . . . I married several years after I came back here. I guess Suzy told you that Mary died of cancer. Anyway, we adopted Suzy shortly after we were married."

Kelly monitored Witten's expression carefully as he answered. Witten was as taut as a stretched wire. Obviously, he was holding back, but he believed the man was telling the truth. What he found strange was that anyone would adopt so shortly after getting married rather than wait to have children of one's own.

As if reading Kelly's mind, Witten continued, "I knew Suzy's maternal grandmother, who was raising her." He pointed out the living room window. "The old lady was a widow and lived right across the street. She was sick and we helped her with the child. There were no close relatives, and finally we offered to adopt Suzy and the grandmother agreed. She died several years later."

Kelly stared hard at Witten, trying to figure out what had happened to the Trinity. If someone had told him at the seminary that one day he would be sitting in a row house in Philadelphia talking to Bill Witten the cop, the friend of the murdered radical Damian Carter, because of his investigation of Pat Hogan the TV celeb, he'd have had guys with the net come for him. Yet that was exactly what he was doing. Life is as neat and orderly as an oil spill.

"Bill, you know I'm here about Pat. I wanted to talk to Damian before he died but never managed to. I want you to clear up something for me."

Witten stared suspiciously at Kelly. His tone was guarded again. "What?"

"Frank Maguire says the three of you changed after you came back from that Washington antiwar demonstration where you represented Gethsemane."

"What did he mean?"

"He said all three of you were moody and not focused on your studies, among other things."

Leaning back, Witten tried to appear more relaxed and sound offhanded. "Oh, I wouldn't put much stock in that. I think it was probably just preordination jitters."

What a lousy liar, Kelly thought. The man's smile was more a grimace and he averted his eyes. His sounded as much at ease as if he'd swallowed a razor blade.

"There's more to it than just Maguire's concern."

"What?"

"I talked to Dirk Creedy over in Rome."

Suddenly, Witten's eyes narrowed as he dropped all pretense of casualness. Kelly had sniffed out something. He was like a good cop who gets his teeth into a corner of a case and won't let go until he has the rest of it. After what Damian told him about Kelly's background, he should have realized Kelly would scuff up dirt from the past. But how much did he know? Apparently not too much or his questioning would be more direct. He stared at Kelly intently, challenging him to go on. "And?"

"And Creedy says he went off with some of his radical friends and only ran into you a couple of times during the day and night."

"So?"

"So, he said he saw the three of you wandering around and you seemed to be high on dope or something."

Witten's expression grew more troubled. Cold sweat trickled beneath his shirt. Unconsciously, he wiped the perspiration that appeared on his brow. Dear God. After all these years. His next question wasn't so much hostile as inquisitive. "Did he say anything else?"

333

"Yes. There was a girl with you, and you all seemed to be pretty chummy. Maybe chummier than seminarians should have been with a woman."

"I see." Suddenly, Witten stared at his hands again and suddenly appeared very haggard. Did Creedy know? If so, why hadn't he said anything?

"What can you tell me, Bill?"

Witten looked up. His eyes were sorrowful, tortured. Kelly remembered seeing the agonized gaze whenever the seminarian Witten contemplated a great injustice. "The look of the martyrs" was the way it had struck him. It was the expression Christ must have worn in the Garden of Gethsemane.

"Nothing," Witten replied in a low voice. "I think you had better go, Kevin."

Kelly realized he was now staring at a piece of granite, at least on that issue. "Why did you cold-shoulder Joe Devine? I only found you because he got your license plate number."

Witten laughed hollowly. "I was on a stakeout at JFK, looking for a big-time drug dealer from Philadelphia."

"Is that why you were dressed as a priest?"

"Cover," Witten said. "It wasn't my choice but my captain's." He laughed ironically. "The captain thought I could pass for a priest."

Kelly thought of the indelible mark that was put on a man's soul at ordination. Once a priest, always a priest. Was it only a myth? He stood and headed toward the door, debating whether he should tell Witten who Suzy's father was. Maybe that would open him up? Maybe it would simply make him even more resolute about not talking. Besides, Kelly believed he now knew a way to start unlocking the puzzle of the Trinity.

"Okay, Bill." He took out a notepad and wrote out his phone number in New York. "In case you change your mind, here's where you can reach me."

Witten stood and opened the door for him. "I'm sorry, Kevin." He seemed genuinely regretful when he said it.

"So am I."

Witten followed Kelly out to his car, thinking how life can change in a flash. Less than an hour ago, he had looked forward to getting home and being with his daughter. Now he wished he had never arrived. "Unless it's absolutely necessary, I would appreciate your not telling anyone that you found me."

334

"I'll only tell Devine so he doesn't think he's seen a ghost, and I'll ask him to keep it to himself. Say good-bye to Suzy for me. And good luck."

Kelly climbed into his car and started the engine. He felt like a heel for tearing apart a man's life, laying Witten open to so much uncertainty. What right had he? As he drove away, he looked in the rearview mirror. Oblivious of the cold, Witten still stood coatless on the sidewalk. That anguished look still on his face. A living martyr.

Forty minutes later, Kelly sat before a microfiche machine at the main Philadelphia public library in the center city. Again, he had checked out clippings on the Washington demonstrations following the bombing of Cambodia. The first time around, he was looking for something directly connected to the demonstrations. This time, he knew better.

Carefully, he combed through the Washington Post clips for March 20, 1972. The first time he checked them, he had wondered why whoever wrote the note had not put the actual date of the demonstration, March 19. But he now knew the note was a guide. Finally, on page 37, he stared, his heart pounding. He closed his eyes for a moment and exhaled sadly before looking again. The picture of a young woman gazed out at him. The resemblance was uncanny. She could have been a clone of Suzy Witten, but it was the other way around. The story beneath the picture was brief.

The rest of story related how the police had no suspects. They asked anyone to come forward who might have knowledge of the girl's movements prior to her death or who might know the identities of her companions.

Kelly made a copy of the story and picture and turned off the viewer. Recalling Creedy's statement about seeing the Trinity with the girl, he sighed deeply. He also thought about Maguire being so troubled over the disturbed Hogan, Carter, and Witten. The riddle of the Trinity. The crime of the Trinity. Was it guilt that had taken its toll over all these years?

When he thought of Suzy's photos, he grew angry. To what depths would a man sink? Was there no shame? How in God's name could that man be the girl's father?

On his way out of the library, Kelly's outrage mounted. The

335

DEMONSTRATOR FOUND DEAD IN CATHEDRAL

A 22-year-old antiwar demonstrator was found raped and strangled at St. James Cathedral early this morning.

She was identified as Martha Crawford of Philadelphia. Police said she was last seen in the company of several young men.

Her body was found by Archbishop Paul Pizzaro, the pronuncio or Vatican ambassador to the United States.

The archbishop said that his secretary received an urgent call, asking that he come to the cathedral. The caller said it was a matter of life and death.

"When I arrived, we found the girl lying in a pew in the rear of the basilica," the archbishop said in a statement. "She was dead. I had never met her nor have I any idea who called. Her death is a terrible tragedy."

horror of what he had learned chilled him, stoking his anger. By the time he called Witten, he was in an icy fury.

"Bill, I'm coming back. I'll be there in a half hour."

"Kevin, we've already talked. I'm sorry. There's nothing left to say," Witten said.

"Don't bullshit me, Bill! I'm coming back. And buddy boy, you'd better be there!"

He slammed down the phone. There was only one thing he was certain of right now. Somebody was going to get burnt very badly.

Witten stood in his front door as Kelly drove up.

"I asked Suzy to go to a friend's house," he said as Kelly came up the walk. He turned and led the way inside and motioned for Kelly to take a seat. Kelly's fury was obvious. What had happened? What had he found out in this brief time?

"Why are you back here, Kevin?"

Kelly glared at Witten, glad Suzy wasn't around because of what he had to say. The shock and pain could be devastating. "You could have saved me a hell of a lot of trouble if you'd just told me what

336

happened in Washington when the glorious Trinity screwed up," he said angrily.

"What do you mean?" Witten asked warily.

"You know better than me. But I do know Suzy's mother's name was Martha Crawford, and I know what happened to her. And I'll lay ten-to-one odds that you and Carter and Hogan were with her at the demonstration. And I'll bet you three had something to do with her rape and murder."

Witten slumped down in his chair and put his hand to his forehead. His eyes closed and the blood drained from his face. "Please, for God's sake, don't tell Susan."

"Don't tell her what? What you and your buddies did to her mother?"

Witten wearily rubbed his face, the way he had after Kelly reappeared in his life the first time. "I spoke to Pat after you left. He said that if you came back, I should tell you what happened to the three of us in Washington."

"Even though he's not going to come out of this looking good?"

Witten opened his eyes. "None of us do, Kevin." He exhaled loudly.

"Well?" Kelly asked impatiently.

Looking at a loss for a moment, Witten began, "We were thrilled when we were picked to go to the demonstration. It represented a lot at the time. What we had achieved and the way everyone viewed us. You were never terribly involved in seminary life for reasons of your own. We were. A lot of people seemed to think that life at Gethsemane revolved around us. We were aware of that and tried to live up to the honor.

"In any event, each of us was very committed to ending the war and wanted to do whatever we could. We took a train to Philadelphia and then one of the demonstration buses to Washington. Our first stop was at St. James Cathedral where we prayed for cessation of the fighting. Then we went to Dirk Creedy's hotel, but we didn't spend much time with him. We spent the rest of the day much the way everyone else did. We listened to speakers, joined in some of the singing, and helped people make placards with slogans denouncing the war. We also spent a good deal of time with the Vietnam Vets Against the War to find out how they felt about what they had been through.

337

"At nightfall something happened. All three of us started acting crazy. We each had a couple of beers, but it wasn't that. We alternately felt giddy and afraid and just extraordinary and confused. We had hallucinations."

Witten's voice sounded perplexed as he remembered what had happened twenty years ago. From the rote way the story was repeated, Kelly could tell it was a worn-out record. But one with unaccounted-for gaps. Obviously, he still couldn't comprehend what he had felt and seen.

"In retrospect I believe someone gave us LSD. I've read about acid trips, and the descriptions are similar to what we went through. Yes, we did somehow pick up with Susan's mother at some point. Someone introduced us to her, but none of us could ever remember who did. She was very distressed and wanted to stay with us. The rest of the night is a series of disconnected, crazily distorted events. For some reason we went back to the cathedral. Martha must have been with us. Later, we just didn't remember. None of us really remembered much of anything after that until we woke up at the motel where we were staying."

Closing his eyes, Witten shuddered. "The next day, we were all frightened. Most of our conversation on the bus and train rides to Gethsemane consisted of trying to piece together what had happened. There was a lot of disagreement.

"I had bought a newspaper in Washington and started reading it. I saw Martha's picture, but because of the insanity of the night I didn't even recognize her. We were almost back at the seminary when Pat started reading the paper and asked if she was the girl who was with us the night before. We all agreed she was. We came to the realization that we must have killed her. The story said that there had been one rapist and apparently one murderer. It could have been any one of us. We each believed we were the one responsible.

"To protect one another, we never told the police that it was one of us. It wasn't simply to protect ourselves. I was willing to turn myself in and so were Damian and Pat. We talked ourselves out of it on the chance that it actually was one of the other two. So we all escaped being punished for the crime."

"But not the guilt," Kelly said.

"Ah, the guilt. The guilt. No, no one escaped the guilt. Guilt destroyed the Trinity. Damian lost faith in himself and turned his anger against the Church in a hope of finding punishment to fit his crime. I lost faith in God when I was in Rome. But of the three of us, I think it has probably been the hardest on Pat."

"Why?"

"He created an incredibly busy life for himself so that he has no time for contemplation. He told me once that he's afraid to spend time with himself. He's afraid of driving himself crazy."

Kelly was uneasy. What Witten said made a weird kind of sense. He recalled what Creedy said about drugs during that period. Anyone could have slipped LSD to the Trinity. Would that stand up in a court of law? Suddenly, he felt an odd sympathy for them. What a terrible thing to have to live with. How it affected their lives. Suddenly, he was curious about the strange odyssey Witten's life became.

"What about you, Bill? How did you wind up here?"

"After Gethsemane I went to Rome and did pretty well at the educational opportunities I was given."

Kelly nodded at the understatement.

"What happened to Martha kept preying on my mind. I concluded that my faith in God was destroyed. Over and over, I asked myself the same question. 'What kind of a God would allow that to happen?'

"The tension got to be too much. I guess I had a breakdown of sorts. I took a vacation, hoping I could see things more clearly if I put some distance between myself and Rome. I went hiking and spent the time contemplating my life. Eventually, my faith in God was restored, but I had to distance myself from the Church. I would be living a lie if I remained a priest. So, I simply walked away. I kicked around Europe for a few months and then came back here.

"By the time I returned, I had made up my mind what I should do with my life. I read in the follow-up stories about Martha that she had a baby daughter. I decided to see what I could do for her daughter as a slight attempt to atone for what I had done to her mother.

"In a way it was easy. Martha was from Philadelphia and I was too. It wasn't difficult to learn where her family lived. I befriended Suzy's grandmother. Through the grandmother, I learned about Martha's life. What kind of a girl and young woman she was. Her likes, her dislikes. That she wanted to be an artist. She went to Little Flower High School and the University of Pennsylvania and she spent a year in Rome studying art.

"I came to know and love her child. Also, during that period, I met a wonderful woman and married her."

Witten looked at Kelly and smiled ruefully. "No, I did not get a dispensation from Rome. After what I had done, none of that mattered anymore. What is one more sin when your soul is already mortally wounded? Suzy filled you in about her adoption and the death of my wife."

Groaning as though he had just passed through a brutal ordeal, Witten opened his hands palms outward in supplication. "Suzy is my life, Kevin. You are now in a position of taking the rest of my life away from me and destroying Pat as well."

"I'm sorry, Lane, but there's no way we can run that story," Edmund Murphy said.

Lane Woods had half-expected as much, but she was still infuriated. "Ed, you're a Catholic. These men tried to kill the Pope. The religious leader of your church. And you want to sit on the story. There's no guarantee they won't try again. Doesn't that mean *anything* to you?"

Murphy cringed. Christ, didn't she think he felt terrible? He had often wondered what he would do if he was confronted by having to choose between acting courageously or not. Deep inside himself, he knew he always lacked the guts to do what was truly right. Practicality dictated every step he had ever taken in his life. He couldn't change now. The station was his life. How could he risk losing it?

"You don't have to remind me," he said grimly. "I've gone over it and over it with our lawyers, and this is the way it must be. These men are very, very powerful. They'd sue, and with their kind of money they'd be able to break me financially before we even stepped into court."

He still had trouble accepting the fact that such a group had tried to kill the pope. God, they passed themselves off as pillars of the Church. The donations they gave. The public piety. But when he read Lane's report, he knew it was true and the truth horrified him. Charles Edwards! My God, the son of a bitch spent more time on his knees at St. Patrick's than Cardinal Murray.

Looking at Murphy, Lane thought of her father and how so many people had caved in to their fears of what would happen to them if they didn't go along with the McCarthy witch-hunts. She found herself feeling sorry for Murphy. Fear does terrible things to people. Terrible things they often have to live with for the rest of their lives.

340

Murphy couldn't meet her gaze. His eyes were hollow and his face was drawn. He looked as if he'd been up all night and he had. She knew how conscientious he was. Backing down like this must be tearing him apart. Still, it terrified her that people could literally get away with anything because they were rich and influential. Over the years, she had seen other rich people get themselves and their children out of jams because of who and what they were. How a wall of money insulated them from scrapes with the law and from people they hurt.

She thought of Damian Carter and Bishop Falconi. Until now, a part of her never accepted before that such people could get away with murder and something as outlandish as trying to kill the pope. My God, she wondered, how much evil goes on in the world and we never find out who is really responsible?

By the time he got back to St. Mary's, Kelly felt pulverized. Witten was right. It *was* his call. What should he do? He could never right the horrible wrong. What good would it do to wreck Witten's life and his daughter's to boot? Not only could he blow Hogan's bishop boat out of the water, but he could have him thrown out of the priesthood and maybe into jail. All he had to do was tell the FBI about a twenty-year-old murder. That's all. Kelly the Destroyer.

In the rectory, he threw his coat over the back of a chair, went to the kitchen, and grabbed the bottle of Wild Turkey. He looked at the bourbon with disgust and shoved it back. What would that solve? He'd been looking for too much solace in the bottle lately. Besides, he needed to figure out what had happened, and he needed to have his wits about him. In Brady's office, he put his feet up, glad the pastor wasn't around. He didn't want to talk to anyone. He needed time to think.

He believed Witten. The guy told a hell of a story and none of it self-serving. But it didn't make sense. Hogan, Carter, and Witten weren't the kind of guys to rape and murder, at least unless they were temporarily insane. The acid business didn't hold water on that score. Somebody probably gave it to them, but he'd never heard of a case where acid created a murderer.

There was another factor in the equation, one Kelly couldn't quite figure, but he had his suspicions. Mr. Charm. The once-upon-a-time hippie. Suzy's father. His thoughts, however, were clouded by

341

the anger he felt at the way he'd been used. Why hadn't he been left alone? Why the hell didn't Clarizio give somebody else the lousy job of investigating Hogan's background?

Suddenly, the phone rang. Kelly answered and heard Bishop Gibbons on the line asking how he was. "John," he started, "I'm so goddamn mad at the way Clarizio manipulated me and maybe you too that . . ."

When he finished, he almost felt the iciness of Gibbons's voice when the bishop replied. Kelly's face started burning as Gibbons began reading him the riot act.

21

TWO DAYS LATER, KELLY SAT IN CLARIZIO'S OFFICE AT ROYAL OAKS. After Gibbons's call, he had cooled off, accepting that the cardinal's use of him had been honorable. the pope was alive because of it. Gibbons had told him to get a grip on himself, that he wasn't doing himself or anyone else any good by feeling sorry for himself.

The fate of the Trinity was still an open question. Realizing that he alone had to come to a decision, he hadn't mentioned to Gibbons or anyone what he'd found out. When he tried to weigh out justice, he always reached a stalemate. Serving justice would inflict terrible pain. What good would it do? Kelly leaned toward doing nothing. He'd screwed around with too many lives already.

While waiting for Clarizio, he talked with the cardinal's new secretary, a plump, pleasant, prematurely bald monsignor who introduced himself as Aldo Manzini.

"Enrico's in Botswana?" Kelly said. "I never would have called that."

"Yes. He decided to devote his life to the missions."

Kelly gave Manzini credit for discretion. He wondered what poor

343

Perdomo had done to be shunted off to never-never land. Missionary work was a test of fire for such a man's vocation, if not his soul.

"Ah, there you are, Kevin," Clarizio said as he entered the room.

Kelly rose and started to kneel to kiss the cardinal's ring, wondering at the newfound familiarity. Clarizio had never called him by his first name before. The cardinal further surprised him by motioning him for him to stay where he was.

"That will not be necessary," Clarizio said, taking the chair next to Kelly. He looked at Manzini. "Monsignor, you are excused," the cardinal said curtly.

"Yes, Eminenza," the secretary said, looking a little startled by the abrupt dismissal.

Kelly smiled to himself. The cardinal's breaking in a new pony.

Once again, Clarizio focused his attention on Kelly, taking in how worn the priest looked. None of this had been easy. "The pope wants me to convey to you how grateful he is. He was only sorry that he did not get a chance to thank you personally, but you can be assured, one day he will."

"There's no need," Kelly protested, thinking how childishly he'd reacted recently. "Besides, if Pat Hogan hadn't been able to find out where the assassination was to take place, the whole issue would have been moot."

"Yes, we are grateful to Monsignor Hogan as well," Clarizio conceded.

The cardinal rose slowly. "So much has happened, Kevin. The assassin is dead, but who is to say they will not send another?"

Here it comes, Kelly thought resignedly. "We know who they are."

"Yes, but it is the problem we have always had. What proof do we have?" Clarizio replied. "No one will dare call for the arrest of such rich and powerful men without a great deal of evidence."

"I know," Kelly said. "Coltrain is scared to death. Robbins and his wife would never talk. I'm sure Ruggieri won't open his mouth."

"I'm sure you are right," the cardinal said dryly.

"Then what can we do?"

Clarizio spread his long, thin fingers. "I have a plan. The man they intended to make pope is Paul Pizzaro—"

"Pizzaro!" Kelly interrupted. That fit. One of the Vatican's fallen angels. Suddenly, another piece of the jigsaw puzzle about the Trinity started falling into place as well.

"Yes. His Holiness has already dealt with him. But that still leaves the others—"

"I'm sorry for interrupting you, Cardinal. Who was Pizzaro's secretary when he was in Washington?"

"Manuel Garcia. He is now the—"

"No, no. I'm sorry, your Eminence. I meant his secretary early in 1972."

Clarizio frowned as he thought back and glanced swiftly at Kelly. "You mean around March twentieth?"

"Yes."

"Vincenzo Ruggieri," Clarizio replied coolly. "Perhaps the major reason Monsignor Ruggieri was never defrocked was because Archbishop Pizzaro in his main protector. Archbishop Pizzaro has many influential friends in Rome and around the world."

"Most of them in Milites Christi?"

"Many of them, apparently. Some within the Curia as well."

"Would Pizzaro have any reason to try to block Pat Hogan's being made a bishop?"

"None that I know. Why are you pursuing this line of questioning?"

"If you don't mind, Your Eminence, I'd rather fill you in if my hunch proves to be right."

"As you *always* wish," Clarizio said with a trace of exasperation. "Now, as I was saying, this is what I would like you to do. Father Bisleti is already in Rome . . ."

Three days later, more than the usual number of tourists roved through the Colosseum. The day was unseasonably warm and the sky a deep blue. Kelly took off his topcoat, thinking he'd have to get the lining of the pocket mended. He stood behind a fence, staring down into the arena, and glanced at his watch. He had asked Ruggieri to meet him here for no other reason than the irony that this was where it had all started. He arrived early so he could go over again what he intended to say to the monsignor. He had Dagger Tom's agenda. He also had his own.

Ever since learning of Ruggieri's involvement, Kelly wondered how the hell a priest could behave the way Ruggieri did, participating in murder and assassination attempts and God knows what else. The man *was* a throwback to the Borgias. Surprisingly, Kelly found he harbored little animosity toward him. What was the point? Hating Ruggieri would be like hating part of himself, and he had once done that for longer than he liked to remember.

He had a sense of detachment. Sitting here reminded him of the rare occasions when he waited for enemy agents when he met them for business reasons. The business was no less brutal than the one in which Ruggieri engaged. Maybe he understood Ruggieri better than he wanted to admit.

"*Buon giorno*, Father Kelly."

Kelly turned as Ruggieri came the last few steps toward him. The lightness of the monsignor's tone belied the tension he was obviously under. His face was drawn, his complexion sallow, and circles hollowed his eyes. Yet he moved quickly, a trace of jauntiness still in his walk as it was in the elegant cut of his cassock.

"Thanks for coming, Ruggieri," Kelly said, although he knew the monsignor had little choice. Kelly didn't like to think of the monsignor as a double agent, but that, in effect, was what he was. Bisleti's friends said Ruggieri would take back to the Milites Christi conspirators whatever communication Kelly gave him from Clarizio. If he didn't the consequences wouldn't be pleasant. Kelly didn't want to know what they might be.

"It is best to bend to the strongest wind," Ruggieri said. "A bit of wisdom from my father." A corner of his mouth twisted.

"Cardinal Clarizio has a message for your pals," Kelly said. "No more assassins. If the pope is killed, their names will be publicized immediately as the assassination conspirators. Their names have already been turned over to Interpol as well as trusted law enforcement officials in each of their native countries."

"What else?"

"They are excommunicated, effective immediately. They must make a full confession and beg the pope's forgiveness."

"What else?"

"They are going to pay for their sins, Ruggieri. Pay through the nose. As partial penance, each must contribute one hundred and fifty million dollars during the next three years to a special relief fund that will be used for the poor in their own countries and for the needy in Africa."

Ruggieri raised his eyebrows at the last dictate. "Many men have bought their way into heaven for less."

346

"Lastly, Milites Christi is being disbanded."

"Is that fair to the thousands of devout members who had nothing at all to do with this matter?"

"Maybe not, Ruggieri. But the pope is meeting with the heads of Milites Christi this week and ordering them to dismantle the society. Milites Christi created an atmosphere that gave rise to these creeps, so it must take the fall."

"I will tell them."

"When?"

"They are meeting at Via Christi tomorrow night. I shall inform them before then."

"Why are they meeting?"

Ruggieri smiled for the first time. "Why, to address this very issue. The rich and powerful often get frightened too, Father Kelly. More so than people who lack their vast resources can realize."

The monsignor leaned over as he brushed off his cassock, making clear his intention to leave.

"Not so fast, Ruggieri. There's something else I want to ask you about."

"What?"

"It was you who wanted Hogan out of the way, wasn't it?"

Ruggieri's eyes moved furtively from side to side, and he bit his lips. "Why should I want that?"

"The way I figure it, you were worried that if Hogan became a bishop, he'd have a lot of power. Power to check personally into some of the charges Damian Carter was always bringing to his attention. I kind of figured you had your hand in some of the funny-money deals."

"Interesting," Ruggieri said noncommittally.

"I figure too that maybe someday he'd remember something about Martha Crawford's rape and murder."

Ruggieri's face went white. Slowly, he grasped the fence and sighed wearily. "Poor Martha."

For a moment, the monsignor buried his face in his hands. His voice was hoarse when he spoke again. "There are many tragedies in my life, Father Kelly. She is the greatest of them."

He smiled bitterly. "You see, I loved her. She was studying in Rome when we met. So fresh. So beautiful. But it could not last. You know the priesthood, Father Kelly. Nothing of that nature can last. It ended when I was sent to Washington as Archbishop Pizzaro's secretary."

347

"Why did you kill her?"

Suddenly, Ruggieri knelt and said, "Father, I want you to hear my confession."

Kelly was startled, "Come on, Ruggieri, stop clowning."

"I am very serious. You cannot deny my request."

Feeling trapped, Kelly realized instantly what the man was doing. If Ruggieri confessed to him under such circumstances, he would never be able to divulge what he heard. He paused. What difference did it make? The odds against Ruggieri's ever being brought to justice were enormous. If he got to the bottom of what happened, he could probably still help Witten and Hogan in some way. Otherwise, no one would ever know. Slowly, he raised his hand and made the sign of the cross.

Ruggieri looked carefully at Kelly and being his story. "Bless me, Father. I have sinned. A year after she came home, Martha found out where I was. She came to the pronuncio's mission in Washington late in the day, demanding that I talk with her. She told me about the child. She wanted me to leave the priesthood and marry her."

Ruggieri was sweating. His eyes were bright, glistening with tears as he rushed his story.

"I tried talking to her, but she was completely unreasonable. Completely! I became frightened. We walked to the demonstration and ran into the three seminarians. I needed to get away from her and think. I managed to leave her with them, telling her I would meet her again at the cathedral later that night."

"What was wrong with the seminarians?" Kelly asked.

Ruggieri made a dismissive notion with his hand. "They were high on drugs."

"How do you know?"

"I met Dirk Creedy, whom I knew from his visits to the pronuncio. He taught at their seminary. He told me one of his friends had given them a drug as a joke when I asked why they acted so strangely."

"So what happened next?" Kelly asked. So much for Creedy's reluctance with Maguire.

"I . . . I . . . spent hours trying to think. I went to a bar and got very drunk, and while getting very drunk, I got very angry. Being the pronuncio's secretary meant I was in an excellent position to become a person of influence in the Church. The girl was threatening to destroy

348

my career. She . . . she had no right! By the time I reached the Cathedral, I was not in my right mind.

"I persuaded her to make love. It was not rape, as the newspapers said. I thought if she could see that I loved her, she would love me and not want to harm me. Then we argued. She began yelling and crying, saying that she would go to Archbishop Pizzaro. I had to stop her! I did not mean to kill her. I swear it."

"What did you do then?"

"I panicked and told Pizzaro. He made me come to my senses. We made up a story."

"Why did Pizzaro help you?"

Ruggieri laughed ironically. "How would it look for the secretary of the ambassador from the Vatican to have killed a woman with whom he had an affair? Pizzaro's own career would have been jeopardized. After all, if he could not control his secretary, what would he be fit for?"

Suddenly, he looked curiously at Kelly. "How did you know?"

"Through your daughter. She showed me a picture of you and her mother, the only picture she had of her parents."

"Ah," the monsignor said simply. "Now will you please grant me absolution."

Kelly thought of the poor dead girl and the horror the Trinity went through for years and years as a result of what this man had just told him. One day, God would weigh Ruggieri's actions, but until then he would have gotten away with murder. The way the monsignor related the story made him sick. So disgustingly self-centered. He had no more remorse than if he had killed a fly.

"No," he replied. "No absolution."

Suddenly, Ruggieri felt a profound fear. "But you must! You must!"

Panicked, he grabbed Kelly's arm. "You must. Please, for God's sake!"

"There are several conditions then."

"What are they?"

"First, you write to Hogan and tell him what happened in Washington. You don't have to identify yourself as the murderer, but you must make it clear that he and his friends had nothing to do with it. When you have done that, I will give you the other conditions."

Ruggieri became icy. "I know why you are doing this," he hissed. "It's because I have done what you have done, isn't it?"

349

Kelly suddenly felt sick. "What do you mean?"

"The blood on your hands, Father Kelly. All the blood on your hands."

Kelly recoiled. For a second, he thought that Ruggieri was right. He was condemning himself. No, he told himself.

"No!" he said, yanking Ruggieri's arm away. Guilt was as good a defense as an offense. "What I did was different, Ruggieri. I never killed anyone I loved."

✦

The White Chapel was off-limits for the night. Via Christi's staff and seminarians had been warned not to intrude upon the guests who would be meeting there. Shortly after ten o'clock, the tires of a limousine crunched the gravel driveway in front of the church doors. The back door opened. The first of the Apostles emerged.

"Check out the chapel to see that it is empty and that no listening devices are there," the man told his chauffeur in Italian.

The chauffeur took a briefcase with a bug scanner and entered the church. Five minutes later, he emerged. "The place is secure," he said, and climbed behind the wheel.

Standing with his back to the chapel, Nikos Spartakos watched his car disappear down the driveway as it headed for the parking area behind the administration building on the far side of the compound.

In the shadows of a stand of trees fifty yards away, Madeleine Ryan peered through infrared field glasses at the ghostly figure. "Fucking unbelievable," she whispered.

"What's wrong!" Lorenzo whispered.

"Look," she said, handing him the field glasses. Her hand trembled as she passed them. After all their talk, she couldn't still quite believe that they were here, about to do what they had always said they would if given the chance.

Putting the glasses to his eyes, Lorenzo adjusted the lenses as the man mounted the chapel steps. The figure wore a coarse hooded habit like that of a medieval monk. He pulled the binoculars away. He didn't want to see the men, to put human faces on them.

Quickly, Lorenzo handed the glasses back to Madeleine, angry that she had made him see the man's ordinary round face with glasses, like some high school teacher. "Just write down their names," he said, trying to sound normal. "The way he's dressed is just another manifestation of capitalistic degeneracy."

Finding courage by sneering at the absurdity of the sight, Madeleine began her list. One by one, the Apostles arrived. Every time another figure emerged from a limousine, she identified him from the photo file the movement had amassed and put his name on the list. At length, she turned to Lorenzo. "All ten," she whispered.

His heart pounding, he read the names.

—Nikos Spartakos, the Greek shipping magnate.

—Luigi Gramaldi, the Milanese investment banker.

—Albert Durer, the German electronics tycoon.

—Julio Lorca, the Venezuelan oil magnate.

—Francis and Karl Forrest, American cattle barons.

—Martin Chesterfield, the British racehorse breeder.

—Charles Edwards, the American mining magnate.

—Constantine Beauchamp, the French industrialist.

—Manuel Callera, the Spanish investment banker.

Suddenly, there was a rustling of leaves about twenty feet away. They froze. Shaking, Madeleine put her hand on Lorenzo's arm. Forgetting she had the field glasses, she stared into the darkness with dread.

"Damian!" she whispered as loudly as she dared.

"Damian," a whisper responded, returning the code word derived from the cause's newest martyr.

A figure crept silently toward them. It wasn't until she was less than ten feet away that Madeleine recognized Carla Sarfina. "Pace e fraternità."

"Pace e fraternità," Carla replied. "Are we ready?"

"Be patient," Lorenzo replied. "A few more minutes." Taking back the field glasses, he raised them and stared intently at the chapel, wishing he could witness what was taking place and wondering if he had the nerve to do what must be done.

While the radicals waited in the shadows, Kelly sat in Cardinal Clarizio's Washington office, wrapping up his findings.

"So that's the story, Your Eminence. At least as much of it as I can tell you."

"Thank you, Kevin," Clarizio said as he sat back at his desk. "So there appear to be no obstacles to Monsignor Hogan's being made a bishop."

"None that I found."

"You have done excellent work," Clarizio said, "but I am a bit perturbed that you gave the results of your investigation of Monsignor Hogan to that Vatican newspaper correspondent Gracey."

"Your Eminence, you told me to do whatever I felt I must to uncover the truth."

"So I did. Why did your TV reporter friend tell you the story about the plot against the pope would not be picked up by the media?"

"She confirmed what we thought. No one will ever be able to prove that those powerful men were behind the assassination attempt."

Clarizio was tense, hoping that Paolo was all right. He hadn't liked what the priest proposed, but he could see no alternative. They must know what was happening. "Just thank God," the cardinal said, "that we have passed unharmed through a very dangerous moment. The Apostles have already agreed to the pope's conditions."

A shadow fleetingly crossed the cardinal's face. "Just a few more questions."

Kelly rubbed his eyes wearily. "Of course."

"Why was the Agency following you?"

"According to Dave Martin, they got wind that Bishop Falconi was somehow abetting radicals. That led to speculation that maybe the pope was going to pull off something that would upset the U.S. or at least the heads of the Agency. By following me, they hoped to learn about what was going on."

"What about the assassin's links to them?"

Kelly himself wondered about that. Donner had been a strange duck. The morning after the assassination attempt, Sands called him secretly and gave him background that he had learned. Donner was a native New Yorker and had been an altar boy at Cardinal Hayes High School and even served Mass at St. Patrick's on several occasions. What Kelly remembered when Sands mentioned it was that Donner was known as the Chameleon; he always took on the coloration of the people who were his intended victims. Diplomats, government officials, military officers. Donner had killed the Buddhist monk Kelly had refused to assassinate. What Kelly remembered too was that Donner was Dave Martin's man.

"After Vietnam, Carl Donner turned free-lance. He was hired by several Central American dictators; apparently that's how the Apostles got on to him. Martin claims they haven't used him for years, and that they had no hint of the plot against the pope."

"Why do you say 'claims'?"

Kelly stared back seriously. "Because we will probably never know the truth."

"Thank you for being so frank, Monsignor."

Smiling wryly, Kelly let the cardinal's slip of the tongue go by. He wasn't about to correct him over something so inconsequential.

"Unfortunately, my lack of trust comes from experience where they are concerned."

"God often works in unique ways, Monsignor. If you had not had such experience, the Church might be in grave danger today."

Kelly cocked an eyebrow as he stared at the man known for not making mistakes. Clarizio smiled back.

"Yes, it is 'monsignor,'" the cardinal continued. "Congratulations. The pope wishes to show his appreciation. This is one way."

Kelly flushed with embarrassment. What had he gotten himself into? He could already hear John Gibbons's laughter. Yet, he couldn't help feeling pleased. Damn. A battlefield promotion. "Thank you, Your Eminence."

While Kelly received his honor with mixed emotion, the last guest entered the White Chapel, his head bowed. As he made his way up the center aisle, his footsteps echoed eerily. Shuddering shadows, formed by the light of hundreds of flickering candles, gave an eerie sense of movement to the life-size statues of saints and the huge murals of tortured souls writhing in the flames of hell.

Manuel Callera prostrated himself before the altar. *"Pax vobiscum,"* he intoned before rising, entering the altar rail and mounting one of the ten intricately carved thrones that were placed in a circle before the altar. As Callera took his seat, the men looked at one another.

"Where is Monsignor Ruggieri?" Beauchamp asked.

"He will not be here," Edwards said. "I spoke with him this afternoon."

"About the pope's demands?" Gramaldi asked.

"That and other matters," Edwards replied. Disgustedly, he

looked around the room, calculating rapidly. Men of power, prestige, and great wealth. A collective net worth of more than $7 billion and they looked frightened, humbled.

"We have said we will do as the pope asks," Lorca said gloomily. "What choice do we have?"

Heads began nodding in assent.

"*Perhaps* we should accede to the pope's demands," Edwards said.

"What do you mean?" Durer asked sharply.

"He means, my dear Durer," Spartakos said, and he paused and nodded graciously to Edwards, "and you correct me if I am wrong, Charles—he means that we stop acting as if we are beaten. That we bide our time until the moment is right and strike again."

"That is exactly what I mean," Edwards said.

"And strike so that it can never be traced back to us," Karl Forrest said.

"That's right," his brother added. "If we start acting as smart as all of us are supposed to be, we can exercise our will and there are no trails to our doors."

"What about Cal Robbins?" Durer asked.

"I'm afraid he was our weak link," Edwards said. "One day, he must be tended to."

"Never again can we trust anyone outside this room," Edwards said.

"What about Monsignor Ruggieri?" Beauchamp asked.

The men looked from one to another. Edwards spoke again. "The monsignor still has his uses. After that . . ."

The others nodded without his having to say more.

Outside, Lorenzo nervously checked his watch and turned to Carla and Madeleine. Himself and two women, he thought. Is it possible that we are about to do what we planned? What odd messengers of death we are. He felt sick and frightened. "It is time to leave," he said thickly.

Fifteen minutes later, the three of them sat in a car a quarter mile from Via Christi. Lorenzo turned to pick up a radio transmitter from the backseat. His vision was blurry and he felt icy. He licked his lips and swallowed. All he had to do was twist the dial and it would be over. When he tried to place his fingers on the dial, his hand trembled violently. He was unable to move.

"Well?" Madeleine said.

"I . . . I can't," Lorenzo whispered.

Suddenly, Carla thought of the man she had loved and the screaming woman she had seen tortured in Santiago. She leaned over the front seat and seized the transmitter. Angrily, she turned the dial to the proper frequency. Despite their distance from the White Chapel, the tremors of the explosion shuddered through the car.

"Damian," Madeleine said in awe.

"Damian," Lorenzo said.

Carla remained silent, tears filling her eyes.

Lorenzo tried not to panic. He forced himself to start the car and drive away carefully. It would not do to be stopped in this area tonight for any reason. In the backseat, Madeleine, with a look of unabashed admiration, took the transmitter from Carla's hands and began dismantling it with a screwdriver, throwing pieces out the window every few minutes. She wore gloves on the remote possibility that someone would come across a piece of the device and identify what it was.

"Who do you think called to tell us that those dogs would be there tonight?" she asked once again.

"A friend," Carla replied. "We will probably never know his name."

The next morning, Monsignor Vincenzo Ruggieri sat at a café off the Piazza della Repubblica sipping an espresso as he reread the story about the bombing at Via Christi. Because the chapel was made of stone and the windows were few and narrow, the bomb had created an implosion. The Apostles who were still inside had died instantaneously. So had the priest.

He folded the paper and placed it on the table. What should he do now? Where could he turn?

Archbishop Pizzaro could no longer help him. Despite his worry, Ruggieri smiled when he thought of Shivers's new posting and admired the pope's imagination. Helsinki. He almost laughed out loud.

He realized there was not the slightest chance that he could escape being defrocked this time. It would be better if he disappeared for a while. Perhaps fortune would turn his way again in Rome when there was a new pope. His telegram to the Argentine woman should have arrived. He'd met her earlier in the year. An immensely rich widow, she repeatedly asked him to come to Buenos Aires for an extended stay. His Spanish was excellent. He wondered how he would like Latin America. It could be very interesting.

The sadness of lost possibilities suddenly engulfed him. Ah, the glory that might have been, he thought. With Milites Christi's man at the helm, the Church could have forced Her way onto the political world stage. With armies of well-armed, fervid youth, the papacy could have burst out of the restrictions of the Vatican and become a power with which to be reckoned on all fronts. He could have been one of the leaders, the favored few of the new ecclesiastical order.

Looking again at the photographs of the dead Apostles arrayed across the front page of the paper, he felt sad. Luigi Gramaldi. Karl Forrest. Charles Edwards. He smiled wanly. They resembled mug shots of criminals. Three dead. Three who decided to remain a few more minutes talking to one another after their fellow plotters left. Life is very strange. Perhaps he should let the fortunate ones know his whereabouts. There was always the chance they would need one another again.

He glanced also at the photo of Paolo Bisleti. From what the bomb experts determined, the priest was in a crawl space above the altar. There was no explanation as to why he was there. Ruggieri wondered how Clarizio felt about his spy's death.

Scanning the pictures one last time, Ruggieri asked himself a final question. Did he regret having placed the call? No. For all their religious fervor, he had never deluded himself about what kind of men the Apostles were. He felt no remorse or even anger at what he supposed they might have come around to doing to him. Their self-preservation would have come well before their personal consideration of him. As for Bisleti, he was unlucky. He was in the wrong place at the wrong time. It was the way of the world. But sometimes life did strike him as being most unfair.

He went back to the letter he had been writing before becoming engrossed in the newspaper story. Bishop Hogan would receive it within the week. He would also write to Monsignor Kelly saying that he had fulfilled his demand and expected absolution. One never knows, he thought. A man should try to insure his future in as many ways as possible.

356

22

PAT HOGAN INADVERTENTLY CHECKED HIS WATCH AS HE READ THE LAST
of Ruggieri's letter over the phone to Bill Witten. Hogan felt as if he
were on a treadmill. In a few minutes, he was to officiate at the wedding
of a prominent politician who was a widower. Then he had to head
over to the studio. After the show tonight, he and Kevin Kelly were
going to dinner, a sort of celebration that everything had turned out
well for both of them. Then he had to catch a late flight to Austin to
be the principal speaker at a fund-raiser.

"Incredible!" Witten said when the letter ended.

Listening to the choking emotion in Witten's voice, Hogan realized the exoneration of the Trinity in Martha Crawford's death still
hadn't hit him. What would he do when it did?

"The letter came this morning, Bill. I wouldn't have disturbed
you at work but I knew you would want to know this right away. It is
amazing, isn't it?"

There was silence on the line as both men were lost in thought.
Witten finally spoke. "Though the letter doesn't mention him, I detect

357

Kevin Kelly's hand in this. You said he went to Rome during the investigation. How else could this have come about?"

"I thought the same thing. I'm seeing him right after the show. I'll thank him then."

"Thank him for me too," Witten said. He paused and softly added, "I just wish that Damian had known before he died."

"So do I. I . . . I guess the only good to come out of this is that we didn't all go to our graves with it on our consciences."

"Something good did come out of it, Pat," Witten said.

"What?" Hogan asked skeptically.

"Suzy."

Hogan smiled, glad Witten could see that and wishing that he had been able to do so as well. He envied Witten's ability to understand instinctively what matters. "Yes. Yes, she is. She's a wonderful girl."

"We're sorry you couldn't make her graduation."

Hogan flushed. "Oh, my God, Bill. It completely skipped my mind. Please tell her how awfully sorry I am."

"She knows how busy you are." Witten's voice drifted off as his thoughts returned to the startling letter. "Now I guess I'll always wonder how we would have turned out if we had known the truth all along. Good night, Pat."

After hanging up, Hogan stared in the dressing room mirror, deeply ashamed for having forgotten the graduation. How could he have hurt Susan and Bill that way? How did his life get so filled with the unnecessary that he could treat cavalierly two of the few relationships in this world that really meant a great deal to him. What had he become? He didn't like the answer that came to mind.

Right before the show started that evening, Pat Hogan walked over to the producer. "Jack, I want to hurry the show a bit so I have about two minutes at the end."

"Why?" the producer asked.

"You'll see," Hogan said, smiling mysteriously.

The show was about nuns who want to enter the priesthood. The Immaculate Conception sisters who argued the case were articulate and controversial, as was the Jesuit from Washington who rebutted them. From the audience's cheers and howls, Hogan knew it was a

358

good show, but he was so preoccupied he barely heard the arguments. He hoped he was doing the right thing.

"Thank you very much for presenting your respective sides of this intriguing issue," Hogan told the nuns and the priest as he escorted them off the set.

Coming back, Hogan turned back to the cameras. "For the past three years, you have been very good to me. You have shared your lives with me, and I feel that it is only right that I share with you a decision I have reached."

He took a deep breath and continued, "The fact that the Church has honored me by intending to promote me to bishop has been in the news the last few days. My investiture is scheduled to be held a month from now in Rome."

As he smiled his gaze swept over the people in the audience, who smiled back without realizing they were. "I . . . I am not going to accept the office of bishop, and I am going to leave this show. When I was a young man and entered the seminary, I had many ideas of how I could best serve God. Since then, I have detoured time and again from those ideals. Now is the time for me to attempt to return to the duties of a priest. . . ."

Ten minutes later, Monsignors Kevin Kelly and Patrick Hogan slipped out of a back door of the studio and down a stairwell. "So, you honestly think I'm doing the right thing, Kevin?"

Kelly looked back at him seriously. "Yes . . . Yes. I do. I also think it's a very gutsy move, and I hope you like missionary work. Congratulations."

"Thanks, Kevin. And both Bill and I want to thank you for whatever you did to have that letter sent from Rome."

Kelly brushed the gratitude aside. "Where would you like to eat?"

"Not the Four Seasons."

Kelly laughed. "How about a little soul-food place I know in Harlem. The food's good, it's dirt cheap, and there's a good chance you won't be recognized."

"Not recognized? Sounds too good to be true."

"Tell me that a year from now, when you complain because nobody remembers you," Kelly said with a laugh.

Hogan joined his laughter. Stepping into the cool night air, Monsignor Hogan felt free. As the burden of shame lifted from his shoulders, he felt freer than he ever had in his life.

Acknowledgments

Thanks to Joe Michenfelder, George Winslow, and George Lynch for reading the manuscript and for their suggestions. I also want to thank Arlene Friedman for the idea for the book, Jane Meara for her editing and enthusiasm, and Joan Stewart for her agenting. As always, a special thanks to Lenore.

fore encountered. You walk past prostitutes and beggars who ask for your spare change, and you give it to them because you believe that generosity is a virtue, no matter how the money is spent. Starry-eyed, you wander into a dark section of the park, when you realize that a man is following you. You look over your shoulder, and he is gaining, and you walk faster. You sense danger. You pray, which, you realize, you had been doing constantly as you rode, not out of obligation or hope or fear but out of a natural communion that had become as second nature as the spinning of your pedals. The man is still there now, but you do not fear him. You turn instead to face him. He stops. You do not avert your eyes from his. You smile, a dare. And then he moves silently into the trees. You are not surprised by this. You believe you are protected, that no one can hurt you.

"This world, and life itself," writes Rick Bass, "is nothing but an amazing receptacle for spirit." It is no wonder that *spirit* is linguistically related to the word *respiration*. Cardiovascular fitness is the body's way of efficiently circulating air.

To be filled with spirit.

Now I moved to the spot where my bicycle had been. My ground pad, which I'd not needed on the bleachers, was lying on the ground. About ten yards farther I found my gloves. I stood, numbly trying to consider alternate explanations. A custodian or groundskeeper had moved it maybe. But no, not on a Sunday. My heart sank. I dropped my helmet. No. I raised my hands to my head.

No, no, no.

I walked around the track that surrounded the field. It was lighter now, streams of sunlight causing the dew on the grass to sparkle. And in that dew I saw a thin line stretching across the field, the unmistakable prints of bicycle tires.

Gone.

"The serial number should help," said the policeman, as he wrote it down on his report. We were standing outside the convenience store, beside the phone, the same phone where I'd left my wallet the night before.

"What are the odds?" I asked.

"Not bad, really," he said. "But it could be a while—sometimes up to a year. You might just stick around a day or two, see if it turns up."

Stick around. Where else was I going to go?

I watched the police car drive away. Just a day on the job for him, I thought. Another stolen bicycle.

I returned to the high school, where a man now jogged on the track. I asked him if he'd seen anything unusual, and then I told him about my bike.

He shook his head with sympathy. "It's a big problem here," he said. "Burglary. About a month ago my house was broken into. There's a big meth problem here."

"It's everywhere," I said. In the previous five years every place I'd lived was struggling with methamphetamine production and abuse.

"It's worse here," said the man and sighed. He wished me luck, waving as he continued with his run. I started moving in concentric circles around the outside of the stadium and then along the neighborhood streets. It seemed hopeless. I felt numb, not sure what to feel. On the street corner there was a café, and I went inside. The café was crowded. I felt claustrophobic. The customers were mostly elderly or middle-aged parents with children. I was seated at a table in the corner by a window. I watched the street outside carefully, everyone who passed a potential suspect.

I wandered aimlessly, no conscious destination in mind. I headed back up that hill from the night before, past the soccer field, where two teams of Hispanic men competed, their families and friends lining the sidelines. Past the field, to the edge of the parking lot, which was now full of cars, there was a sign: DIVINE REDEEMER. I walked toward the chapel. I scarcely noticed the people milling around, men in suits and ties, women in their Sunday dresses. Near the church entrance people stood on the sidewalk, and I caught the eye of a man, who smiled at me in greeting.

"What time is mass?" I asked him.

"Eight-thirty," he said.

"What time is it now?"

"Eight-twenty."

I was still numb, somewhere between denial and heartbreak. I walked through the open church doors and sat in a pew in the back, self-consciously hoping that I would go unnoticed.

The church filled quickly, and mass began. I rose with the congregation and silently mouthed the words to hymns I didn't know. I hadn't showered, was wearing the clothes I'd slept in, the clothes I'd worn on my ride the day before. Now they were the only clothes I had. During the middle of the service the priest, Father Schray, asked the ushers to open the doors in back, to let in some fresh air. Even though the church chapel was large, I couldn't help but think that I was the inspiration for the sudden request for fresh air. And yet during the sign of peace, the people nearest me shook my hand warmly, saying, "Peace be with you," and with the welcoming touch of those human hands, despite all my efforts to stop them, tears formed, and I was relieved to be seated again, hoping no one had noticed.

Father Schray began his sermon. He spoke about overcoming adversity, about forgiveness.

After the service I walked outside and stood lingering on the sidewalk, trying not to be conspicuous. Congregation members gathered in small groups, talking easily to one another. It was sunny, and cheers could be heard from the soccer game across the parking lot. When Father Schray came out, he saw me.

"Are you waiting to talk to me?" he asked.

I said yes, but it was only when I said it that I realized it was true.

"I'll be right with you," he said.

An usher and a woman sitting at a table set up outside the church introduced themselves. I told them I was embarrassed about my appearance.

The usher dismissed my concern with a flick of his hand. "I used to fight fires," he said. "We would show up to a church in a strange town wearing a jump suit, covered in mud. And you know what I discovered? God doesn't care."

Slowly, people started leaving, the cars moving quietly out of the parking lot. Father Schray walked over to me. "Now, how can I help you?" he asked. He was tall, had white hair and glasses. I told him my story.

223

"Oh my," he said. "Follow me." We walked back inside, and he led me down the aisle to the altar and instructed me to kneel. I had never prayed before an altar in this way. In the church where I grew up, we had prayed from where we stood in our pews, and we didn't kneel. For most of my adult life I had scarcely attended church at all. I felt slightly self-conscious, kneeling there before the statue of Christ.

There were larger problems in the world—natural disasters, poverty, brutality, war, terrorism. Every kind of heartbreak imaginable can be seen on any given week on CNN. A forty-year-old man losing a bicycle was not a tragedy. And yet that bicycle had been with me for over twenty years, had gained for me a certain identity, a definition I had often relied upon. My original trip was an accomplishment often worn on my sleeve. No matter how unhealthy and sedentary my lifestyle became, I could always recall that summer. The bike, though, could be replaced. What I mourned more than anything was the loss of my journal.

I thought of that man in Stanley Park. Had it been faith that had saved me? Somewhere there was a line between that kind of trust and naïveté, and with age, such faith had slowly diminished from my life. I had not dismissed it so much as set it aside. But now, I realized, it was faith, too, that I'd been seeking to reconnect with on this trip.

Father Schray was in a time crunch. He was leaving that afternoon for a retreat. He needed to pack, to prepare the materials he'd need. It must have been a frantic morning, preparing for mass, getting ready to leave, greeting the parishioners after the service. Human goodness can be measured in part by the way one makes time for a dirty unshaven stranger.

Calmly, with no sense of concern for his own schedule, Father Schray knelt beside me and prayed for a safe return of all I had lost. Then he walked me to his office and let me sit down in a comfortable chair. He gave me suggestions about where I might stay. He called in to his office two women, leaders of the Divine Redeemer prayer group, and explained my plight. Then he led me to a large room with cafeteria-style tables and introduced me to a couple, who gave me coffee and doughnuts and then drove me to Wal-Mart, stopping first at a grocery store. The man and I waited in the van, while his wife